商 務 英 語 菁 英 ❸
商海博弈・知性表達

商務英語
職場王

【美】Amanda Crandell Ju 著　巨小衛 譯

A Guide to the Way People
Actually Talk, Write, and Do Business

前 言一

　　您手上拿的這本書有別於以往任何一本商務英語書。之所以説它獨一無二，是因為這裡面全都是真實商務世界的英語口語。書中列舉的表達技巧，能夠幫助時下廣大華人的職場人和西方世界的同行們自如地溝通交流。這本書著重實用技能，透過這本書您會發現，您所提高的不僅僅是英語表達能力，還有商務技巧，從而讓您的生意做得更好。

　　50個商務主題中每個都包括常用短語、文化、商業理念以及主題詞彙，最後以實境對話的形式將所學的都應用於實踐。最重要的是，所有內容都能現學現用，簡明扼要兼具實用於一體。So，商務技巧和英語能力齊頭並進就這麼簡單！

　　除了實務部分，「商務詞彙」部分囊括了商務場合最基礎、最常用的詞彙。您也可以透過「商務禮儀十大要訣」來了解一些和西方人做生意的學問。此外對於初學者來説，最有價值的要屬「商務口語300句」了，這部分是不同一般商務場合英語短語的全面集合。您再也不需要對無法用英語自如表達而感到鬱悶了。

　　您既可以提高口語，又能在生意上取得成功，一舉兩得，何樂而不為呢？如果您正好在尋找一本能夠給您這種力量並使英語實力進步的書，那就不用再找了……您手上的這本就是。

　　祝您好運！

Amanda Crandell Ju

巨小衛

筆者想藉此機會感謝為本書提供特別幫助的人：Linda Crandell Mansfield,巨小兵,Alvin Crandell,Dorina Tamblyn和Charity Yulan Ju。

目錄
Contents

職場英文短句300 Business Spoken English—300 Sentences

掌握電話技巧 Telephone Skills

⊕項全能之五
熟悉辦公事務 In the Office

⊕項全能之六
高效組織會議 Meetings and Interviews

⊕項全能之七

拉進客戶關係 Client Reception

⊕項全能之八

介紹自己和公司 You and Your Company

十項全能之九

成為談判高手 Negotiation

十項全能之十

瀟灑做簡報 Presentations

十項全能之一

商務詞彙

Business Vocabulary

公司部門名稱 Company Department Designations

accounting department 會計部

administration department 行政部

budget department 預算部

communications department 通訊部

consumer affairs department 顧客服務部

contract department 合約部

distribution department 經銷部/物流部

engineering department 工程部

environmental department 環境部

finance department 財務部

franchise services department 特許經營服務部

government relations department 政府關係部

human resources department 人力資源部

information technology (IT) department 資訊部

legal and compliance department 法律遵循部

logistics and supply chain department 物流和供應鏈部

management department 管理部

marketing department 行銷部

operations department 運營部

packaging engineering department 包裝工程部

procurement department 採購部

public relations department 公共關係部

purchasing department 採購部

quality department 品管部

research and development department 研發部

retail department 零售部

sales department 業務部

transportation department 交通/運輸部

wholesale department 批發部

職稱 Addressing a Supervisor

CEO (Chief Executive Officer) 首席執行長/行政總裁

CAO (Chief Administrative Officer) 首席行政長

CFO (Chief Financial Officer) 首席財務長/財務總監

COO (Chief Operations Officer) 首席運營長

CTO (Chief Technology Officer) 首席技術長

President 董事長

vice-president 副董事長

director 主任/主管

assistant director 助理導演/局長

co-director 助理主任/聯合主任

財務類詞彙 Financial Terms

A.T.M. 自動提款機/自動櫃員機

currency 流通；貨幣

banknote 鈔票；紙幣

debt 債務

borrow 借貸

deposit 存款

budget 預算

donate 捐贈

cash dispenser 自動取款機

exchange rate 匯率

cashier 出納

fee 費；酬金

cash 現金

interest 利息

check 支票

invest 投資

coin 硬幣

辦公用品名稱 Office Equipment

armchair 手扶椅

laser printer 雷射印表機

cabinet 櫃子

monitor 顯示器

computer screen 電腦螢幕

office equipment 辦公設備

computer 電腦

office furniture 辦公傢俱

copy 複印

operating system 作業系統

correctional tape 修正帶

overhead projector 投影機；高架投

cubical 辦公隔間

影機

desk 桌子

paper cutter 切紙機

desktop 桌面；桌上型電腦

paper shredder 碎紙機

drawer 抽屜

paperclip 迴紋針

fax 傳真

printer 印表機

highlighter 螢光筆

scanner 掃描器

ink jet printer 噴墨印表機

staple remover 拔釘器

laptop 手提電腦

stapler 釘書機

swivel chair 轉椅

telephone 電話

typewriter 打字機

whiteout 修正液

windows 視窗

word processor 文字處理器

電腦常用詞彙 Common Computer Terms

boot up 開機

browse 瀏覽

cable modem 纜線數據機

cable 電纜

CD (compact disc) 光碟

connect 連結

copy 複製

cut 切斷；剪切

disconnect 斷開

DVD player DVD播放機

Ethernet 以太網

hard drive 硬碟驅動器

HD DVD (high definition DVD) 高清晰DVD

home theater system 家庭電影院

hook up 連結

install 安裝

jack 插座

headphones 耳機

volume 音量

keyboard 鍵盤

memory reader 內存讀卡器

monitor 顯示器

mouse 滑鼠

paste 黏貼

pixel 像素

plug in memory reader 插件；插入

SD card 安全數位卡

Speaker 音箱；揚聲器

Mp3 player Mp3播放機

surf 上網

switch off / on 關閉/打開

turn off / on 關掉/打開

unplug 拔去

update 更新

網路常用詞彙Common Internet Terms

blog 部落格

browser 瀏覽器

chat rooms 聊天室

build a webpage / website 建立網

頁/網站

chat with clients 和客戶聊天

check E-mail 查看郵件

cookie 庫存記號

dot com 網路公司
download files 下載檔案
E-mail 電子郵件
follow a link 用戶點選連結
go on the internet 上網
go online 上網
hyperlink 超連結
install software 安裝軟體
instant messaging (IM) 即時訊息
Internet connection 網路連接
ISP (internet service provider) 網際網路服務提供者
laptop computer 手提電腦
link 連結
meet people online 線上遇見（人）

modem 數據機
MSN 微軟聊天工具
post a comment 張貼評論
post a video 發布影片
scan for viruses 病毒掃描
search engine 搜尋引擎
send E-mail 寄郵件
shut down 停機；關閉
start up 啟動
surf the internet 上網
the Internet 網路
URL (webpage address) 網頁地址
web browser 網路瀏覽器
webpage 網頁

行業名稱 Industries and Career Fields

agricultural sciences 農業科學
architectural design 建築設計
art and design 藝術與設計
biology 生物；生物學
biomedical sciences 生物醫學科學
broadcasting 廣播
business administration 工商管理
chemical engineering 化學工程
communication technology 通訊技術
computer programming 電腦程式設計
computer sciences 電腦科學
construction management 建築管理；施工管理
construction trades 建築行業

consumer science 消費學；消費科學
cosmetology 美容學
culinary arts 烹飪藝術
engineering technology 工程技術
engineering 工程；工程學
human resources 人力資源
journalism 新聞業
law enforcement 法律實施；執法
law 法律
marketing 行銷
medical professions 醫療
psychology 心理學
public safety 公共安全

religious studies and philosophy 宗教學和哲學
sales 銷售

social sciences 社會科學
teaching 教學

政治詞彙 Political Terms

transportation 運輸
bipartisan 兩黨的；兩黨聯立
bleeding heart 老好人（假惺惺）
campaign 運動
caucus 領導班底；決策委員會
checks and balances 權力制衡
convention 公約
dark horse 黑馬；冷門
delegate 代表；委員
demagogue 煽動者
fence mending 復交的
filibuster 阻擾議案通過
front burner 緊急事件；當務之急
GOP(grand old party) 共和黨（大老黨）
grass roots 基層的；民眾的
ideology 意識形態
incumbent 現任
lame duck 即將卸任官員
left-wing 左翼

lobby 遊說團體
machine politics 機械政治
McCarthyism 麥卡錫主義
muckraker 醜聞揭露者
photo-op 拍照
platform 政綱；黨綱；宣言
political party 政黨；黨派
poll 民意調查
pork barrel 議員為選民爭取到的地方建設經費（政治分贓）
primary 初級的
pundit 評論員
reactionary 反動的
red tape 繁文縟節
security 安全
silent majority 沈默的大多數
slate 板岩；候選人名單
smoke-filled room 幕後政治妥協
spin 翻轉；塑造公眾的方式看問題
swing vote 關鍵投票

餐飲詞彙 Food and Beverages

fresh 新鮮的
off 變味的

expired 過期的
raw 生的；生肉

ripe 熟的

rotten 腐爛的

tough 硬的

undercooked 未煮熟的

unripe 未熟的

hot 燙的；熱的

mild 軟的

salty 鹹的

savory 美味

sickly 令人作嘔的

sour 酸的

spicy 辣的

stodgy 油膩的

sweet 甜的

tasteless 淡的；沒有味道的

barbecue 烤肉；燒烤

buffet 自助餐

four-course meal 四道菜餐

picnic 野餐

snack 零食；速食；小吃

TV dinner 冷凍快餐；冷凍食品

bite 咬

chew 咀嚼

swallow 吞咽

heat 加熱

poach 水煮

roast 烤

steam 蒸

stew 燉

bitter 苦的

bland 淡的

creamy 含奶油的；奶油色的

crisp 脆的

crunchy 酥

旅行詞彙 Travel

accommodations 住宿

airplane 飛機

airport 機場

arrival 抵達

automobile 汽車

baggage 行李

bicycle 自行車

boarding pass 登機牌

book a hotel 訂旅館

car rental 汽車租賃

carry-on luggage 隨身行李

cart / wagon 旅行車

crash 撞車

drive 駕車；開

east 東方

have an accident 出車禍

journey 旅行；旅程

map 地圖

north 北方

port 港

ride 乘；騎

road / way / path 路

ship 船

south 南

traffic 交通

train 火車

transportation 運輸

traveler 旅行者

trip 旅行；旅程

walk 步行

west 西方

十項全能之二

商務禮儀十大要訣
Ten Keys to
Good Business Etiquette

　　無論你身在世界的哪個角落，總有一些被普遍公認的商務禮儀規則存在。商務禮儀從本質上講的是關於如何與人打交道或建立關係。在商業世界裡，決定你成敗的是人；而禮儀，是實現你商業潛力最大化的一個途徑。

　　商務禮儀總是圍繞著兩件事，且兩者都取決於自身行為。首先，一個彬彬有禮的人，總是能周到考慮別人的利益和感受。其次，成功的人際關係主要在減少誤解。這兩件事將保證人們在你的身邊感到舒服，因此，在你的人際交往中，彼此間能有更好的溝通和更多的信任也就不再是什麼難事了。

　　商務禮儀涵蓋的行為有：在辦公室裡、與客戶之間、打電話過程中、寫電子郵件的時候，還包括別的商業往來：在商業旅行中、商務飲食中或別的情況之下。

　　這裡列舉十個商務禮儀要訣供您參考：

會議 Meetings

　　如果事情非常重要，必須召開會議，那一定要考慮到與會者的時間並保證有充分的準備工作。

　　事前通知：

　　⊙目的

　　⊙預計持續時間（必須掌握會議截止時間，並不是每個人都願意超時繼續進行）

　　⊙議題內容

　　通常被（人們）忽略的是：對於與會者的出席和時間表示感謝，並（至少以文字的形式）對與會者為實現（上次）會議的目標所作出的貢獻表示肯定。與會者常在離開時留下疑問：我們的建議是否被採納，我們的關注和貢獻是否被認可？將會議的（無論多麼簡單的會議）大綱或者紀錄發給出席的人員和缺席的人員，內容言簡意賅，但是對於所作的決定，包括措施項目都應詳述。

永遠不可以在當事人不在場的情況下就指派他專案任務，除非你別無選擇。在會議大綱中註明沒有當面通知當事人，對於每項工作的最後安排要有專人負責通知到未出席者。

電話 The Phone

無論如何都得回電話。即便你並沒有來電者希望得到的答案，打電話告訴他為了他所需的資訊，你現在都為此在做著什麼或者請對方指導在哪裡才能得到最確切的答案。

如果你打算出門，就委託某人幫你接聽電話，或者至少讓語音回答系統告訴來電者，你什麼時候回到辦公室並且什麼時候能夠回電。

當你致電並遇到接待員或者秘書接聽時，說明自己的身分並告知對方打電話的目的。這樣，你才能肯定你的電話會被轉接到你最需要的部門或最合適的人，你就能獲得恰當的資訊並且能夠得到更有效的幫助。

當你接聽電話時，說明身分或是自己所在的部門，即便是你被打擾了，接電話時也要滿懷熱誠，至少要熱情，因為來電者並不知道打擾到你了。

確保你的語音留言系統正常，不會告知來電者信箱已滿、無處可以轉接電話或沒有應答。無論是設備系統的故障還是人的無禮，都要排除。

對話要人性化。許多人使用電子通訊設施（包括電話、語音信箱或電子郵件）聯絡，就像是在操弄自己的車一樣隨意。他們覺得既然不是和當事人面對面，就可以堂而皇之的粗魯、生硬或無禮。我們要保證，要充分利用這些媒體的長處，但要避免落入其弊端糾纏之中。

電子郵件 E-mail

主題明確。回想你曾收過多少封標題意義籠統、語意不明的電子郵件，簡單地以「你好」或者「給你」命名。

勿將郵件中出現在主旨內容之前的三大篇附帶資訊統統轉發。在你轉寄的郵件中，無關的資訊都應當刪除，如：「致某人備忘錄」的標題、地址或時間等。

在回答問題時，只需要複製原郵件中的問題部分即可，然後作出回應。你無需貼上所有過往的問題，但也別給出一個簡單到只有一個「是」字的回答。太直接籠統會讓讀者疑惑不解。

儘管在「寄件者」、「收件人」一欄中已有相關內容，但在郵件中還應包含地址和簽名。請牢記，你是在和人交流而不是冷冰冰的機器。

切忌全部內容都用大寫字母，因為這樣讀起來過於「沉重」。這會讓人覺得你太懶，不願意以正確的方式打字。郵件是一個書寫的媒體，因此書寫格式要遵守禮節標準。

打斷 Interruptions

除非遇到萬不得已的情況，否則應當盡量避免插嘴打擾（無論是在個人或團體的工作中，還是會議、電話，即便是在討論中也要避免）。大部分主管都覺得打斷屬下的非正式工作會議是無關緊要的，但是他們打斷的可能是一個將給企業帶來成功或效益的腦力激盪會議。

在不得不打斷對話、會議或者某人正專注的工作時，都應當道歉，然後儘快地表明你的需求，並且說明你已經考慮過將會打斷這個重要的工作和過程。

客戶、顧問和新員工
Guests, Consultants and New Employees

如果你請了一位新顧問，不管他在你的公司工作一天、一周還是更長時間，一定要確保他們有完成工作所需的所有資訊和資源。這不僅僅是出於禮貌，更是為公司的利益著想。把時間花在來來回回找東西上，對員工來說有些難堪，對公司來說就是損失。

給顧問或客戶與公司員工相同的工作空間。對於在公司程式設計的顧問，儘可能給他和別的程式設計員工相同的辦公隔間、相同類型的電腦設備等。這樣會避免你的員工感覺被輕視，或顧問感覺被隔離或被給予次等待遇等感受。

讚賞和認同 Appreciation & Credit

對於每個人作出的努力和貢獻都不要忘記表達你的讚賞和表揚。對於同事在任何方面表現出的成就，都不要忘記稱謝。

服裝和形象 Dress & Appearance

如果說同事或者客戶不在意你形象的話，那簡直就是對他們的指責。

衣服皺皺巴巴、滿口鬍渣、體味難聞或者蓬頭垢面（無論是有意還是無意），都暗示著你對人和事以及公司形象的不在意。

猶豫之中總是容易失之保守。如果你覺得穿牛仔褲參加某社交活動應該可行，但又不是很肯定，那最好穿熨燙好的卡其褲和短袖衫；如果你認為某場合需要著裝相對正式，那最好還是穿襯衫、打領帶；如果你對著裝的要求略知一二，那最好還是穿正式一點的服裝。

女士的服裝相對複雜。但是還是那句話，謹慎考慮、著裝講究。

經常練習最得體的裝扮（即便是在穿牛仔褲的休閒環境）。

社交 Social Settings

許多在聚會、晚宴或者在玩高爾夫過程中形成的印象，即使當時你們談的不是生意，也有可能會在以後促成某個商業活動。所以，盡量隨身攜帶名片。

引薦介紹 Introductions

在活動前，透過通訊錄或者「人物資料庫」，先了解一下在活動中可能遇到的人。

如果你忘記了某人的名字，你可以先介紹你熟知的人來「掩蓋」，「你認識約瑟・史密斯嗎？我們的財務代表。」通常在這個時候，你所不熟知的另一方會主動介紹自己。

如果這個方法行不通，承認想不起來總比不知所措要好一點。

西餐禮儀 Western Table Manners

叉子習慣放在左手邊，湯匙和刀通常放在右手邊。盤子在左邊，所以你的麵包盤應當在你的左手邊。杯子，包括咖啡杯，都應當在右邊。在宴會桌上，當你左右兩邊的人都有食物的時候，再開始用餐。如果你的菜還沒有來，但桌上的大部分人的菜都齊了，這時你應當鼓勵別人先開始用餐。取餐時，先拿你面前餐盤中的食物，別的菜可以請臨近的人傳遞。

總結 Conclusion

人無完人，總會有馬失前蹄的時候。忘記VIP客戶的名字、說出強烈的措辭評論或用錯了叉子，誰都會發生這種情況。這是一個真實的生活，沒有劇本，是我們自己行為構成的生活。

需要牢記的是，如果你希望身邊的人都感到舒服和尊重，那你就應該自問，是否已經做到了上述建議或商務禮儀。

十項全能之三

商務口語300句
Business Spoken English
–300 Sentences

好消息與壞消息
Sharing Good News and Bad News

I'm afraid there is some bad news... 恐怕有些壞消息……

I hate to tell you this, but... 我實在不願意告訴你，但是……

There's nothing left. 沒有什麼可以再失去的了。

I'm so sorry. 我真的很抱歉。

There's nothing that can be done. 沒轍了/沒辦法了。

It doesn't look so good. 看起來不太妙。

There are some developments that I need to talk to you about. 我需要和你談談關於一些發展。

I wish I could tell you differently. 我希望我能告訴你不同的結果發現。

What has happened has already happened. 事已至此。

We will have to find a way to move on. 我們總得想個辦法。

I am sorry to inform you that... 我很抱歉地通知您……

This will not happen again. 下不為例/不會再發生這樣的事了。

We are sorry for any inconvenience this has caused you. 我們為給您帶來的不便深表歉意。

I am truly sorry to inform you about... 我十分抱歉地通知您……

Due to circumstances beyond our control... 由於一些我們無法控制的情況……

There has been a problem with... 出現了一個問題……

We deeply regret... 我們深表遺憾……

It is our pleasure to announce... 我們很高興地宣布……

Let us be the first to congratulate you. 我們首先向您表示祝賀。

We are happy to announce... 我們很高興地通知……

It's with great joy that we... 我們很興奮……

Congratulations! 恭喜！

Let's all give (person) a hand!　讓我們一起為（某人）鼓掌！

I've got some great news for you.　我有好消息要告訴您。

Guess what! You won't believe the good news!　猜猜看！您不會相信這個好消息的！

You'll never guess!　你絕對猜不到！

Listen, I've got some great news about...　聽著，我有一些關於……的好消息。

表達需求與應答
Expressing and Responding to Demands

Please send us...　請寄給我們……

Could you tell me where...　您能否告訴我……在哪裡？

Would it be possible to have a...　有可能有一個……嗎？

I was wondering if it would be possible to...　我想知道是否可能……

I would appreciate it if you could have...　如果您可以……，我將感激不盡。

Would you mind...　您介意……

Can you tell me where I can...　您能告訴我，在哪裡能夠……

Do you know where I can get...　您知道在哪裡我能夠找到……

Can you help me with...　您能否幫我……

I would love to help you with that, but...　我很樂意幫助您，但是……

I can do that for you.　我可以為您做。

Don't worry, we can take care of it.　別擔心，我們可以應付。

Can you please...　您可以……

If you don't mind waiting a moment, I can...　如果您不介意稍等一會兒，我可以……

Would this be alright?　這樣行嗎？

I don't know the answer to you question, but let me help you find someone who does.　我不知道您問題的答案，但我能幫你找個能回答的人。

025

I can help you find someone who will take care of it for you. 我可以幫您找個可以協助您的人。

Can you tell me more about what you had in mind? 您能告訴我更多的想法嗎？

What you're asking for is impossible. 您的要求是不可能實現的。

It might be difficult to meet your requirements. 滿足您的需求對我來說有些困難。

It would be better if we... 如果我們……那會更好些。

發表意見與應答
Expressing and Responding to Opinions

I agree with you. 我同意你的看法。

You're right about that. 您是對的。

I think you've got it all wrong. 我想你完全搞錯了。

I think... 我想……

I'm convinced that... 我相信……

Wouldn't it be better if... 如果……不是更好嗎？

In my opinion... 依我看……

Generally speaking, I think... 一般來説，我覺得……

Personally, I think... 我個人認為……

The way I look at it... 我的看法……

I'd just like to say... 我只想説……

I'm quite convinced that... 我深信……

To be quite honest / frank... 老實説……

If you ask me... 如果你問我……

What's your view? 您有什麼想法？

How do you see the situation? 您怎麼看這個情況？

What's your take on it? 對此您怎麼想？

I think you've got something there. 我想你一定有了什麼新想法。

You've got to be kidding? 您肯定是在開玩笑？

Are you serious? 您是當真的嗎？

That's a great idea. 那是個好主意。

贊成與反對 Agreeing and Disagreeing

I agree with you 100 percent. That's so true. 我百分之百同意。真的。

I couldn't agree with you more. 我完全同意。

Tell me about it! 跟我說說是怎麼回事！

No doubt about it. You're absolutely right. 毋庸置疑，您完全正確。

Absolutely. You have a point there. 完全正確，您說的有道理。

That's for sure. That's exactly how I feel. 那是肯定的。跟我感覺完全一樣。

Exactly, I was just going to say that. 和我想說的完全一樣。

I'm afraid I agree with James. 恐怕我與James的意見一致。

I have to side with Daniel on this one. 在這點上，我站在Daniel這邊。

No way. I totally disagree. 不行，我完全不同意。

I'm not so sure about that. That's not always the case. 我不那麼肯定，事情並非總是如此。

I'm afraid I disagree. That's not always true. 我不同意。那並不總是如此。

I totally disagree. 我完全反對。

I'd say the exact opposite. 我要說的正好相反。

I beg to differ. 恕我不同意/我不敢認同。

Not necessarily. 未必。

You're totally wrong about that. 你完全錯了。

滿意與不滿
Expressing Satisfaction and Dissatisfaction

I am very happy with... 我很高興……

I really appreciate... 我真的很感激……

It's great that... ……真的太好了！

I wish they would have... 我希望他們會……

It would have been better if... 本來可以更好些，如果……

Too bad they didn't... 他們沒有……真是太糟糕了。

It was perfect that they... 他們……真是太棒了。

They should have... 他們應該已經……

It was not what I expected. 這不是我所期望的。

I was hoping for more... 我本期待更多的……

If they would have..., then... 要是他們能夠……，那……

It was just right. 恰到好處。

What a great job! 做得漂亮！

I wish I could have... 我希望我能夠……

The... was just perfect. ……非常合適/棒。

If it were up to me, I would have... 如果讓我決定，我就會……

They might want to consider changing... 他們可能要考慮改變……

In the future, they ought to... 未來他們會……

It was better than I imagined. 比我想像得要好。

It was out of this world! 太不可思議了！

I think I like... 我想我喜歡……

I can deal with... 我能處理……

I couldn't handle... 我不能應付……

...is just great! ……真是太棒了！

028

邀請與接受、拒絕
Making, Accepting and Declining Invitations

Would you like to... 您是否願意……

A bunch of us are going to...Would you like to come along? 我們一行人要去……您要一起去嗎？

We'd love to have you join us. 我們很希望您能加入我們。

Are you free? 您有空嗎？

Please join us. 請和我們一起吧。

Do you have plans? 你們有計畫嗎？

Would you like to attend... 您想不想參加……

Can you come? 你能來嗎？

Is your schedule free on Tuesday? We are going to... 週二你有什麼安排嗎？我們要去……

Can you pencil me in for Monday afternoon? 您能幫我暫定到週一下午？

It would be great if you can make it to... 如果您能夠得到……那就太好了。

I'd love to come. What time does it start? 我很願意來。幾點鐘開始？

Where should I meet you? 我在哪裡和您見面？

Sure, I'd be happy to... 當然，我很高興……

Can I bring... 我能夠帶……

Let me check my schedule and let you know. 我確認一下時間表，然後告訴您。

I'd love to come, but... 我很樂意來，但是……

It's too bad, I have something that day. 太不巧了，那天我正好有事。

I hope you have fun. 我希望你們過得開心。

I can't make it because... 由於……，所以不能出席。

If I can get out of this meeting, I can make it. 如果我能推掉這個會議，我一定能去。

I have a prior engagement. 我已經有約了。

Unfortunately, I can't come. I have something that night. 真不巧，我不能去。我那天晚上有事。

I have a meeting for that day. 那天我有個會。

Can we reschedule? 我們能改約時間嗎？

Can I take a rain check? 你能改天請我嗎？

Maybe if I had more notice... 如果我早點知道的話……

推薦與建議
Giving Suggestions and Recommendations

We could... 我們可以……

Let's go... 讓我們一起去……

What about (v. + ing)...? （做某事）怎麼樣？

How about (v. + ing)...? （做某事）如何？

I suggest we... 我建議我們……

I think it would be a good idea if we... 我想如果我們……那會是個很好的主意。

Shouldn't we...? 我們是否應該……

Don't you think we should... 您不覺得我們應該……？

I think we ought to... 我想我們應該……

It would be better if... 如果……那會更好。

I don't think you should... 我覺得你不應該……

You ought to... 你應該……

You ought not to... 你不應該……

If I were you, I'd... 如果我是您，我會……

If I were in your position, I'd... 如果我在您的位置上，我會……

If I were in your shoes, I'd... 如果換作是我，我會……

You had better... 您最好……

You shouldn't... 你不應該……

Whatever you do, don't... 無論你做什麼，都別……

埋怨與指責 Complaining and Criticizing

I'm sorry to have to say this but... 我很抱歉不得不這樣講，但是……

I'm sorry to bother you, but... 不好意思麻煩你，但是……

Maybe you forgot to... 也許你忘了……

I think you might have forgotten to... 我想你可能忘記了……

Excuse me if I'm out of line, but... 如果我失態了還請您原諒，但是……

There may have been a misunderstanding about... 關於……可能是個誤解。

Don't get me wrong, but I think we should... 不要誤會我的意思，但是我覺得我們應該……

I wouldn't do that. I would... 我不會那樣做，我會……

But if we... 萬一我們……

I'm afraid I have to disagree with you. 恐怕我不能同意你。

Don't get me wrong, ... 別誤解我的意思……

Even so, if... 即便是這樣，但如果……

Don't forget that... 別忘了……

Very true, but... 不錯，但是……

道歉與回應 Making and Accepting Apologies

I'm sorry to hear that... 我很抱歉聽到……

I am truly sorry that... 我真的很抱歉……

I wish things had happened differently. 我真希望情況不是這樣的。

It's my fault. I'm so sorry. 是我的錯，我很抱歉。

I regret deeply... 我深刻反省……

I am very sorry to inform you... 我很抱歉地通知您……

It was my mistake. 那是我的過失。

Whoops, my bad. 哎呀，壞了。

Please excuse me. 請原諒我。

I'm so sorry. 我很抱歉。

What can I do to make it up to you? 我該如何補償您呢？

Is there anything I can do? 有什麼是我可以做的？

It's Ok, don't worry about it. 好的，不必為此擔心。

Forget it. 沒關係的。

It's no big deal. 沒什麼大不了的。

No biggie. 根本不算什麼。

You're okay. 不用操心。

Don't stress. 別有什麼壓力。

It doesn't matter. 沒關係的。

Please be careful next time. 請下次注意。

I guess I can forgive you this time. 這次我會原諒你。

You're forgiven. 你已經得到諒解了。

感謝與回應 Giving and Receiving Thanks

Thank you so much! 太感謝您了！

I really appreciate... 我很感激……

You've really helped me a lot. 您真的幫了我大忙。

You've made a difference in my life by... 由於您……，使我的生活發生了翻天覆地的變化。

I can't thank you enough for... 我不知道該怎樣感謝您……才好。

I'm so grateful for your... 對於您的……我深表感謝。

Thanks a million! 非常感謝！

You are a lifesaver! 你真是個大救星！

You are my hero! 你真是我的大英雄！

You're the man! 你真是太棒了！

I am so thankful because... ……讓我感激不盡。

I greatly appreciate... 我非常感激……

I couldn't have done it without you. 沒有你，我是做不成的。

I owe you one! 我欠你個人情！

You're welcome. 不客氣。

It's been my pleasure. 這是我的榮幸。

I am happy to help. 我很樂意幫忙。

It's my pleasure. 我很榮幸。

No problem, anytime! 沒問題，隨叫隨到！

Don't worry about it! 沒事的！

Small kine! 小事一樁！

It was nothing. 沒什麼的。

稱讚與祝福 Giving Praise and Blessings

You're one of a kind! 你是獨一無二的！

Couldn't have done it better! 完美至極了！

Great job! 做得漂亮！

I can't believe how amazing you are! 我真不敢相信你如此之棒！

Thank you for your great solution. 感謝你提供了這麼好的辦法。

You've helped to raise the standard. 你做得比標準的還要好。

You've exceeded my expectations. 你超出了我的預期。

I wish the best for you and your family. 祝您及您的家人萬事如意。

I hope everything all works out. 我希望一切順利。

Best of luck in all you do. 好運連連。

Best wishes for success in all aspects. 萬事如意。

Hope you get everything you desire. 萬事順心如意。

You deserve the best. 你應該得到最好的。

Good luck in the future. 好運常伴。

I wish you the best of everything in your life. 我祝您萬事稱心如意。

Please send my love to your family. 請代我向您的家人問好。

If it wasn't for you, we'd be out of luck. 要是沒有你，我們可能就沒這麼幸運了。

You're the best! 你是最棒的！

May all your dreams come true. 祝你夢想成真。

May you reach all your goals. 祝您萬事如意。

May happiness be yours. 祝你幸福快樂。

誤會與解釋 Dealing with Miscommunications

I'm sorry, I must have misunderstood. 對不起，一定是我誤會了。

Did you mean...? 您的意思是……？

I think I caught the wrong meaning. 我想我會錯意了。

So what you're saying is... 那麼您的意思是……

I thought you meant... 我以為您的意思是……

I was under the impression that... 我本來覺得……

I was under the understanding that... 我本來以為……

It was my understanding that... 我原以為……

Don't you mean...? 難道您的意思是……

Can you explain that again for me? 您能否再為我解釋一遍？

I don't think I've got your meaning. 我想我沒有了解您的意思。

What was it that you meant? 您原本的意思是什麼？

Let me clarify... 讓我澄清一下……

We aren't on the same page. 我們理解有落差。

Let me explain it to you again. 讓我再為您解釋一遍。

You've got the wrong idea. 您理解錯了。

I must not have communicated clearly. 我肯定沒說清楚。

Let's try that one more time. 讓我們再確認一下。

What I meant was... 我本來的意思是……

What did you understand? 您的理解是什麼？

不同程度的肯定
Expressing Varying Degrees of Certainty

I'd say... 我要說……

It might... 也許……

It could be... 可能是……

It looks like... 看起來像……

Perhaps... 或許……

Maybe... 也許……

It's difficult to say, but I'd guess that... 很難說，但是我猜……

I'm not really sure, but I think that... 我不太確定，但我覺得……

There are about 500 words on the list. 單子上有大約500個字。

There are approximately 50 people in my class. 班上最多有50個人。

Research indicates up to 50% increase in sales. 研究顯示銷售成長超過了50%。

It's kind of a... 是一種類似於……

It's the type of... 是種……

To me it seems as if... 對我來說好像……

I think we'd better... 我想我們最好……

It might be better if... 如果……可能會更好。

Do you think...? 你覺得……?

I'm not certain, but... 我不肯定，但是……

It is definitely... 那絕對是……

You'd better believe that... 你最好相信……

I bet that... 我敢打賭……

I'm sure that... 我肯定……

Beyond a doubt... 毫無疑問……

I have no doubt that... 我深信……

There's no question that... 毋庸置疑……

表達可能性 Expressing Possibility

There's no way that... 沒辦法……

It can't be true. 那不可能是真的。

I don't believe that... 我不相信……

It's not going to happen that way. 不會發生這種情況的。

I don't think it's possible. 我覺得不可能。

It's a long shot. 這是一種猜測。

It doesn't work like that. 像那樣是行不通的。

I don't think so. 我不這樣認為。

That's impossible. 那不可能。

It could work. 應該可以的。

It should work. 應該能行的。

It might happen. 可能會。

I can see it happening. 我敢肯定會發生的。

It could happen that way. 那樣的話可能會發生。

Perhaps we will see... 也許我們會看到……

Maybe we'll get to see... 也許我們能看到……

Do you think it would work if... 你覺得如果……有用嗎？

Give it a chance, it could work. 試試看，有用的。

十 項 全 能 之 四

掌握電話技巧
Telephone Skills

接聽電話 Answering the Phone

個人的職業修養（individual professionalism）和公司的專業水準都可以從打電話時的問答間充分展現（reflects on）。成功接聽電話的表現在於能充分凸顯來電者的重要性，而不是自己。

熱情有禮，樂於助人（courteous and helpful），無論是誰打電話來，都會感到愉快。

⊙Hello, thank you for calling McKay Insurance. This is Barbara Michaelson.
　您好，感謝來電McKay 保險。我是Barbara Michaelson。

⊙Mediacom Entertainment, how may I help you?
　通訊娛樂，有什麼可以為您效勞的嗎？

⊙You've reached Electronics. This is Tad speaking.
　您撥的是Electronics，我是Tad。

⊙Hello, Samantha Smith.
　您好，我是Samantha Smith。

⊙How may I direct your call?
　您需要我幫您將電話轉接到哪裡？

⊙Would you please hold?
　您請稍候，別掛斷。

⊙May I transfer you?
　需要幫您轉接嗎？

⊙How may I help you today?
　今天有什麼可以幫助您的嗎？

自我介紹

以友善的語氣（friendly tone）報上你的姓名（identify yourself），無需過多說明和修飾，告訴來電者你很願意幫忙。確保自己的語氣友善、聲調柔和。

⊙Hello, Margaret Jameson. How may I help you?

您好，我是Margaret Jameson。有什麼可以為您效勞的嗎？

⊙Hello, you've reached human resources, Mark Adams speaking.

您好，這裡是人力資源部，我是Mark Adams。

⊙Good morning, thank you for calling. This is Noelle Jacobs.

早上好，感謝來電。我是Noelle Jacobs。

⊙Zhang Hongmei here. How may I help you?

我是張紅梅。有什麼可以幫助您的嗎？

稱呼恰當

在確認對方身分時，冠上稱呼（give a title），此後盡量使用「辦公室、辦公桌、線上」等詞彙。如果是接同事或者主管（supervisor）的電話，就無需說自己的頭銜。

⊙Hello, Mr. Saunder's office. This is Harold Lee. How may I help you?

您好，Saunder先生辦公室。我是Harold Lee。有什麼可以幫忙的？

⊙Hello. Mr. Fisher's office, Jordan Fraiser speaking.

您好，Fisher先生辦公室。我是Jordan Fraiser。

⊙Thank you for calling Gershon Labs. You've reached the desk of Ms. Stevens. This is George Mason.

感謝來電Gershon實驗室。這裡是Stevens女士的辦公室。我是George Mason。

所在部門單位名稱

如果接到像「是預約處嗎？」、「是人力資源部嗎？」的電話時，有必要說明部門單位的名稱和自己的名字。

⊙Bookkeeping. This is Jill Martin. How may I help you?

　訂票處，我是Jill Martin。有什麼可以幫您的？

⊙This is Customer Relations. John Fielding here. What can I do for you?

　這裡是客戶關係部的John Fielding，有什麼可以為您效勞的？

⊙You've reached the Marketing department. Liv Thomas.

　這裡是行銷部，我是Liv Thomas。

結束通話

結束時最好說「Thank you.」、「Good bye.」最好別說bye-bye或者ok，並且讓對方先掛電話（hang up first）。

A: Thanks for your help.

B: It's my pleasure. Please don't hesitate to call again if I can be of any assistance. Thank you. Good bye.

Ａ：非常感謝您的幫助。

Ｂ：不客氣，這是我的榮幸。如果還需要別的協助，歡迎您再次來電。謝謝，再見。

總結

問與答的對話間，個人修養、公司形象、服務態度都展現無遺。接電話很簡單，但很多細節都要深思，從禮貌用語到稱謂稱呼，從結束方式到語氣語調，都有許多講究，需要多多注意。

單字表

agent 代理;代理商	available 有空的;方便的
claim 主張;要求;索賠	couple 夫婦;一對
extension 擴展;延期	hold 保持;握住
lab 實驗室;研究室	line 線
office 辦公室;辦事處	particular 特別的;詳細的
probably 很可能;大概	receive 接受;得到
reception 酒會;招待會	unfortunately 不幸的是

片語表

at his / her desk 在他/她座位上	call back number 回電號碼
call back 回電話	calling for sb. 呼喚/找（某人）
check to see 檢查	file a claim 提出索賠;提出申訴
How may I help you? 我該怎麼幫助您?	I have sb. on the line for you.
I'd like to speak to... 我想和……	（有人）線上找您。
講話	I'm calling about... 我打來是關
let sb. know 告知（某人）;讓（某人	於……
知道）	No problem. 沒有問題。
Please hold. 請別掛斷。	put sb on hold 使（某人）處於候聽
reach (a person or a place) 接通	speak so sb. about it 和（某人）講
（某人/某處）	某事
speak with sb. 和（某人）通話	step away from her / his desk 從他/
sure 當然;確信的	她的位子上走開
take a message 留言	Thank you for calling. 感謝來電。

實境對話 1

A: Hello, thank you for calling McKay Insurance. This is Barbara Michaelson. How may I help you?

B: Hi Barbara. This is Debbie Vanders from Stateside Insurance. I'm calling about a claim we received from your office.

A: Is there a particular agent you'd like to speak to?

B: The claim was filed by Jordan Miller. It'd probably be best to speak to him about it. Is he available now?

A: I will check to see if Mr. Miller is at his desk. Would you mind holding on for a minute?

B: No problem.

A: Okay, please hold while I see if Jordan is available. It shouldn't be more than a couple minutes. (puts on hold).

C: Claim department, Jordan Miller speaking.

A: Hi Jordan, this is Barbara from reception. I have Debbie Vanders from Stateside Insurance on the line for you. Are you available to speak with her?

C: Sure. Please transfer her on over for me.

A: No problem. (To other line), Hello, Ms. Vanders, Mr. Miller is available. I can transfer you to his line now.

A：感謝您來電McKay保險。我是Barbabara Michaelson，有什麼可以為您效勞的嗎？

B：您好，Barbara。我是Stateside 保險公司的Debbie Vanders，我打電話來是有關我們收到貴辦公室的一份投訴。

A：您希望和哪位窗口通話呢？

B：這份投訴書是Jordan Miller負責的那個部門的，最好能和他談此事。他現在方便嗎？

A：我去看一下Miller先生在不在座位上，請稍等，別掛斷電話，好嗎？

B：沒問題。

A：好的，請稍等，我看看Jordan現在是否方便。就幾分鐘。（置於候聽狀態）。

C：我是投訴部的Jordan Miller。

A：您好，Jordan，我是櫃臺的Barbara。我這裡有一通來自Stateside保險公司的Debbie Vanders的電話找您。您現在方便和她講電話嗎？

C：當然，請轉接給我。

A：沒問題。（到另一條線上），您好，Vanders女士，Miller先生現在有空。我現在就給您把電話轉接過去。

實境對話 2

A: Thank you for calling Gershon Labs. You've reached the desk of Ms. Stevens. This is George Mason.

B: Hi. I'm calling for Katerina Stevens. This is her extension, right? Is she available now?

A: Yes, sir. You've got the right extension, this is Katerina's desk. Unfortunately, she is away from her desk right now. Is there something that I can help you with?

B: Umm... Actually I need to speak with Katerina about something...

A: I can take a message for you and make sure she gets it. She just stepped away from her desk, she should be back soon.

B: Well, I can call her back in a few minutes...

A: Why don't I take a message and she can get back to you soon?

B: That would be fine, except that I don't have a convenient call back number.

A: I could take a message for you, and you can try ringing her back in about twenty minutes. If I let her know you called and will be calling back at a specific time, then she will be prepared to receive your call.

B: Okay. Will you let her know her husband will call her back at 2:30?

A: Certainly.

A：感謝您來電Gershon實驗室。這裡是Stevens女士的辦公室，我是George Mason。

B：你好，我找一下Katerina Stevens，這是她的分機號嗎？她現在方便嗎？

A：是的，先生。您撥的分機是對的，這正是Katerina的座位。不巧的是，她剛從座位上離開。有什麼我可以幫忙的嗎？

B：嗯……事實上我需要和Katerina講些事情。

A：我可以幫您留言，她一定會看到的。她剛離開座位，應該很快就回來了。

B：好的，我過幾分鐘再打給她吧……

A：為什麼不留言給她，她很快就會回覆您。

B：那很好，問題是我這邊不方便提供號碼。

A：我留言給她，您可以20分鐘後打給她。如果我告訴她您打過電話並且還會打過來，她會等您電話的。

B：好的，請告訴她，她丈夫將在2：30打電話給她。

A：好的。

讓對方等候 Placing the Caller on Hold

讓來電者等候為其轉接電話，是商務電話中習以為常（second nature）的情形。彬彬有禮並提供快速有效地轉接，讓對方體會公司的優良服務。

先要說明一個讓對方等候的理由，然後以詢問的方式讓對方稍等。

⊙Thank you for calling Medford Insurance, this is Marcie Stevens. Would you please hold?

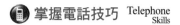

感謝來電Medford保險，我是Marcie Stevens。您能否稍等片刻？

⊙I'm sorry, I need to answer the other line. Would you mind holding momentarily?
對不起，我需要接聽別的電話。您是否介意稍等片刻？

⊙Let me check the information in our computer database. Could you hold for a moment, please?
讓我查一下電腦裡的資料庫。您可不可以稍等片刻？

⊙I'll take a look and see if Mr. Johnson is available to take your call. Would you like to hold for a moment, please?
我要看一下Johnson先生是否方便接聽您的電話，您可否稍等一下？

⊙We're experiencing heavier than usual call volumes. I need to place you on hold for a few minutes.
我們現在線路比往常繁忙。我得把您的電話保留幾分鐘。

尊重來電者的意見

一定要問來電者（caller）是否願意電話被保留，或者是否願意稍後回電話（be called back）。避免使用突兀的話語（abrupt phrase），要讓來電者知道可能要等多長時間。

⊙Mr. Samuels is meeting with a client at the moment. Would you prefer to leave a message on his voice mail? Or I can put you on hold?
Samuels先生目前正在見一位客戶。您方便留言到他的語音信箱？或者我可以將您的電話保留？

⊙I need to find the information you are requesting in my file cabinet. It may take a few minutes. Can you hold, or would you like me to call you back?
我需要在我的文件櫃裡找一下您要的資料。那可能要等一會兒。您能等嗎？或者我晚一點給您回電？

⊙I will transfer you over to Mr. Griggs' line. Please hold for just a moment.
　我將把您（的電話）轉接到Griggs先生的線上。請您稍等。

⊙We are experiencing a high call volume at the moment. I need to place you on hold for several minutes. Would you rather leave your name and number and I can call you back?
　現在是電話線路的尖峰時段，我需要把您的電話保留幾分鐘。您是否願意留下您的姓名和號碼，我晚一點給您回電？

繼續等待

如果來電者同意電話暫被保留，在過了你所說的時間後，一定要重新接通（return to the line）並詢問是否願意再等。

⊙Hello? Mr. O'Brian has still not returned to the office. Would you like to continue to hold for him?
　您好？O'Brian先生還沒有回到辦公室，您是否願意繼續等他？

⊙Ms. Lewis is still with a client. Did you want to keep holding for her? Or I can ransfer you to her voice mail.
　Lewis女士還在會見客戶，您是否願意繼續等待？或者我可以幫您轉接到她的語音信箱。

⊙Mr. Kline is still on the other line. Did you want to continue holding?
　Kline先生還在電話中。您要繼續等嗎？

確認回覆

在來電被保留後，應及時回覆確認進展，別長時間保留（hang there）。大約每隔30秒鐘應該告知對方接通近況。

⊙I am still looking through the information. Can you please hold for a few more minutes?

我還在找資料。您能否再等幾分鐘？

⊙I will be with you shortly, please continue to hold.

我會儘快，但要請您再稍等一下。

⊙I need to check on a few more items. Can you please continue holding for a moment?

我需要查看更多的項目，您是否可以再等一會兒？

總結

現代都市生活節奏飛快的標誌之一就是應接不暇的電話，或者電話被保留許久都得不到答覆確認。掌握禮貌用語或技巧，可以平息等待的焦急、舒緩忙碌的壓力。

單字表

agent 代理；經紀人

database 資料庫

figure 數據；數字

insurance 保險

matter 事情

originally 本來；原來

prefer 更喜歡；寧願

specific 具體的；明確的

voice mail 語音信箱

budget report 預算報告

experience 體驗；感受

file cabinet 文件櫃；文件箱

item 項目

momentarily 即刻；瞬間

policy 政策；方針

Sir 先生

transfer 轉移；轉送

片語表

at the moment 此刻
call volume 通話量
check on (sth.) 檢查（某事）
direct (a call) 直撥（電話）
for a moment 片刻；一會兒
give me a holler 喊我一聲/叫我一聲
have (figures / numbers) in 已有/存有
（數據/數字）
leave a message (on voice mail) 留言
（透過語音信箱）
speak to sb. about... 和某人談有關……
take your time 慢慢來；不必著急
Would you mind (doing sth.)？您是否
介意？

call sb. back 回電話（某人）
Can I help you? 我能幫您嗎？
didn't think so 本來就不這樣認為
final numbers 最後數據
give sb. a run over (of sth.) 允許某人充
分使用（某物）；獲准充分使用（某物）
I think I'll. 我想我會。
I was wondering if... 我想知道如果……
put sb. on hold 讓某人候聽
Sorry about that. 對此深表歉意。
take a look 看一下
with a client 和客戶在一起
You mean... 您的意思是……

實境對話 1

A: Thank you for calling Medford Insurance, this is Marcie Stevens. Would you please hold?

B: Uh, Okay.

A: Thank you. (Puts caller on hold)

A: Sorry about that Sir. We are experiencing a high volume of calls at the moment. What can I do for you today?

B: Yes. My name is Bill Smith and I'm calling about a specific insurance policy package. I have a few questions, and...

A: I'm sorry, I need to answer the other line. Would you mind holding momentarily?

B: Uh. I suppose...

A: Thank you. (Puts caller on hold)

A: Yes Sir. Thank you for holding. So you have some questions about a policy? I can transfer you to one of our agents...

B: Actually, I would like to talk to Mr. Samuels. He's the agent I originally spoke to about the matter.

A: I'll take a look and see if Mr. Samuels is available to take your call. Would you like to hold for a moment, please?

B: Okay.

A: (Puts caller on hold) Hello, is Mr. Samuels at his desk?

C: He's with a client now. He should be a few minutes more.

A: Okay, thank you. (Takes caller off hold) Mr. Samuels is meeting with a client at the moment. Would you prefer to leave a message on his voice mail? Or I can put you on hold?

B: Well... I think I'll just leave a message.

A: Very well. Please hold for a moment while I transfer you to Mr. Samuel's voicemail.

A：感謝來電Medford保險，我是Marcie Stevens。您能否稍等片刻？

B：嗯，好的。

A：謝謝。（暫時保留對方電話）

A：不好意思，先生。現在是電話線路使用的高峰。有什麼可以為您效勞的？

B：是的，我叫Bill Smith。我打電話要了解關於相關的保險政策。我有幾個問題⋯⋯

A：對不起，我需要接聽另外一個電話，您是否介意稍等片刻？

B：嗯，可以吧⋯⋯

A：謝謝您。（暫時保留對方電話）

A：你好，先生。感謝您的等候。您是説對政策有些問題，對嗎？我可以把電話轉給我們的經紀人⋯⋯

B：事實上，我是想和Samuels先生通話的。我最初就是和他談這個事情的。

A：我來看看Samuels先生是否方便接聽您的電話。您能否稍等一下？

B：好的。

A：（暫時保留對方電話）您好，Samuels先生在座位上嗎？

C：他正在見一位客人。可能還需要幾分鐘。

A：好的，謝謝您。（轉回線上來電）Samuels先生此刻正在與客戶見面。您方便在他的語言信箱中留言嗎？或者我將您的電話保留？

B：那……我想我留言吧。

A：好的，請稍等，我幫你轉接到Samuels先生的語音信箱。

實境對話 2

A: Good afternoon, Diamond International Group, Sunny Hong speaking. How may I direct your call?

B: Hello. Is Mr. Griggs available?

A: I will transfer you over to Mr. Griggs' line. Please hold just for a moment.

B: Okay. Thank you.

C: Hello. Bob Griggs. Accounting. Can I help you?

B: Hi Bob, this is Larry. I was wondering if you could give me a run over of the final umbers on the last budget report?

C: You mean for August?

B: Yes. You don't have the September figures in yet, do you?

C: No, not yet.

B: Didn't think so. Yeah. Then could you take a look at August for me?

C: No problem. Let me check the information in our computer database. Could you hold for a moment please? (Put's caller on hold). (One minute later) I am still looking through the information. Can you please hold for a few more minutes?

B: Sure, take your time.

C: Thanks (Puts caller on hold). (Two minutes later) I need to check on a few more items, can you please continue holding for a moment.

B: Okay.

C: I will be with you shortly, please continue to hold. (Puts caller on hold). (One minute later) I haven't been able to find the budget report for August in the computer database. I need to find the information you are requesting in my file cabinet. It may take a few minutes. Can you hold, or would you like me to call you back?

B: Don't worry, it's all good. Why don't you take a look around for the numbers and give me a holler when you find them. There's no hurry.

A：午安，鑽石國際集團，我是Sunny洪。您要找哪一位？

B：您好，Griggs先生有空嗎？

A：我給您轉給Griggs先生，請您稍等。

B：好的，謝謝。

C：您好，我是財務的Bob Griggs。有什麼可以幫您的？

B：嗨，Bob，我是Larry。我想知道我能用一下預算報告的最後數據嗎？

C：您是說八月份的嗎？

B：是的，您還沒有九月份的數據，對吧？

C：是的，還沒有。

B：我想也是（沒有）。那能幫我看一下八月份的嗎？

C：沒問題。讓我查一下電腦裡的資料庫。請稍等。（保留對方電話）。
　　（一分鐘後）我還在看資料，你能再等幾分鐘嗎？

B：當然，不急。

C：謝謝。（保留電話）。（兩分鐘以後）我需要查看更多的項目，你能否再等一會兒？

B：好的。

C：我會儘快的，請你稍等。（保留對方電話）。（一分鐘後）在電腦資料庫

　　中，我沒有找到八月份的預算報告。我要從我的文件櫃裡找一下您要的資
　　料。可能得等一會兒。你能等一等或者等一下我回電話給您？

B：別著急，都行。你再看看，找到的時候喊我一聲。不用急。

篩選來電 Screening Calls

有時候，篩選電話是迫不得已的，因為電話要找的人並不是任何時間都方便接
聽電話，尤其是一些不方便接聽的來電，同事可以幫忙先回話。

篩選來電的重點是：無論如何都不能讓對方感覺被輕視（putting down）。

⊙Mr. Melvin is not available at the moment. Is there something I can help
　you with?
　Melvin先生現在不方便（接聽您的電話）。有什麼我可以幫您的嗎？

⊙Can I let him know who's calling?
　我能否讓他知道是誰打的電話？

⊙May I ask who is calling?
　請問您是哪位？

⊙Mr. Zhang is meeting with a client. Can I tell him who called?
　張先生正在會見一位客人。能否告訴我您是哪位，我好轉告他？

⊙Ms. Kline is not available. May I take a message?
　Kline女士現在正忙，您要留言嗎？

「不方便接聽」的含義
電話要找的人雖然在辦公室但是很忙，或者有重要的事情不容打斷，或是他不
想接這個電話，都意味著他此時「不方便接聽電話（not available）」。

⊙I'm sorry Mr. Griggs is not available at the moment. Can I tell him who called?

不好意思，Griggs先生此刻不方便（接聽電話）。我能告訴他是誰打的電話嗎？

⊙Mr. Liu is currently unavailable. Do you have a number he can reach you back at?

劉先生正在忙。您能留個他可以回電的號碼嗎？

⊙Ms. Chen is unavailable right now. Can I take a message for you?

陳女士現在不太方便（接電話）。我能幫您留言嗎？

⊙Ms. Clancy is not available to take your call just now. Is there something I can help you with?

Clancy女士目前不方便接聽您的電話。我能為您做點什麼嗎？

語序

首先告知對方他要找的人現在正忙或者不方便接聽電話，然後再問對方的姓名和電話號碼（name and telephone number）。否則，對方會對「某人正在忙」有所懷疑。總之，在幫助同事節省時間的同時，不要讓來電者有不被重視的感覺。

A: Mr. Castro's office. Marshall Miller speaking.

B: Hello, may I speak to Mr. Castro please?

A: I'm sorry, Mr. Castro is not available. May I help you?

B: No, you can't. I have to speak to Mr. Castro.

A: I'll be glad to ask him to return your call if you will leave your name and number.

A：Castro先生辦公室。我是Marshall Miller。

B：您好，我能否和Castro先生講話？

A：不好意思，他現在不方便（接電話）。有什麼我可以幫您的？

B：不，您幫不了。我必須和Castro先生講。

A：請您留下您的姓名和電話，我會請他回電話給您的。

重要的電話

如果來電者說他是一個重要人物，該怎麼辦呢？或者他真有急事？那你可以這樣說來彌補：「他吩咐我說，如果是您的電話就可以打斷他。」這樣還能讓對方感到自己的重要性。

A: I'm sorry, Mr. Castro is not available. May I help you?

B: No, I have to talk to Castro. This is Paul Shin. Tell him I called and ask him to call me back.

A: Mr. Shin, Mr. Castro asked me to interrupt him if you call. I'll get him for you.

A：對不起，Castro先生現在不方便（接聽）。有什麼我可以幫助您的嗎？

B：不，我必須和Castro先生講。我是Paul Shin。告訴他我打過電話並請他回電話給我。

A：Shin先生，Castro先生吩咐過我，如果是您的電話，我就可以打斷他。我馬上為您接通。

必須要接通的電話

有些重要電話是不能錯過的。記住要把這些人的姓名記下來。

⊙I'm heading off to my meeting now. Please let me know if Margaret Hall or John Stevens calls.

我現在要去開會。如果是Margaret Hall或Johnson Stevens來電的話，請告訴我。

⊙Please hold all my calls. Don't interrupt me unless you receive a call from...
　幫我接聽所有的來電，除非是來自……的電話，否則不要打擾我。

總結

不管是方便還是不方便接聽的電話，都應當避免讓對方有「吃了閉門羹」的感覺。請來電者留言並保證會回覆，即便是沒能接通電話，對方也不會有被輕視的感覺。

單字表 ·······

certainly 當然
customer service 客戶服務
finish 完成
interrupt 打斷
unavailable 不方便；沒有空

currently 目前；現在
direct line 專線
hold 拿起；保持
should 應該

片語表 ·······

as soon as... 一……就……
check on 檢查
go ahead and (do sth.) 繼續做某事
hold all my calls 接聽所有我的來電
I'll be glad to (do sth.). 我很願意
（做某事）。
let sb. know 讓（某人）知道
receive a message 收到訊息
ship (an order) 貨運

as soon as possible 儘快
should be able to 應該可以
head off (somewhere) 離開/前往
I have to (do sth.) 我不得不（做某事）
leave (name and number) 留下
（姓名和電話號碼）
May I help you? 我能幫你嗎？
return a call 回電話

實境對話 1

A: Marshall, I'm heading off to my meeting now. Please hold all my calls. Please let me know if Margaret Hall or Paul Shin calls. I am expecting their call. My meeting should finish around four o'clock.

B: Yes, Sir. (Phone rings)

B: Mr. Castro's office. Marshall Miller speaking.

C: Hello, may I speak to Mr. Castro please?

B: I'm sorry, Mr. Castro is not available. May I help you?

C: No, you can't. I have to speak to Mr. Castro.

B: I'll be glad to ask him to return your call if you will leave your name and number.

C: This is John Taylor from *Interview Magazine*. Can you have him call me back as soon as possible? My number is 890-555-7875.

B: Certainly, Mr. Taylor. I will be sure he receives you message.

C: Thanks.

B: You're welcome. Goodbye. (Phone rings again) Hello. Mr. Castro's office. Marshall Miller speaking.

D: Hello. Is Mr. Castro there?

B: I'm sorry, Mr. Castro is not available. May I help you?

D: No, I have to talk to Oscar. This is Paul Shin. Tell him I called and ask him to call me back.

B: Mr. Shin, Mr. Castro asked me to interrupt him if you call. I'll get him for you.

A：Marshall，我現在要去開會，幫我接聽所有來電，但如果是Margaret Hall或Paul Shin來電的話，請告訴我。我正在等他們的電話。我的會議大概4點鐘左右結束。

B：好的，先生。（電話鈴聲響）

B：Castro先生辦公室。我是Marshall Miller。

C：您好，我能否和Castro先生通話？

B：不好意思，Castro先生現在不方便（接電話）。有什麼我可以幫您的嗎？

C：不，您幫不了。我必須和Castro先生講。

B：如果您能留下您的姓名和電話號碼，我會請他給您回電話的。

C：我是《面對面雜誌》的John Taylor。您能否請他儘快回電話給我？我的號碼是890-555-7875。

B：當然，Taylor先生。我保證他會收到您的留言。

C：謝謝。

B：不客氣，再見。（電話再次響起）您好，Castro先生辦公室。我是Marshall Miller。

D：您好，Castro先生在嗎？

B：對不起，Castro先生現在在忙。有什麼我可以幫您的嗎？

D：不，我必須和Castro先生講。我是Paul Shin。告訴他我打過電話並請他回電話給我。

B：Shin先生，Castro先生吩咐過我，如果是您的電話，我可以打斷他。我馬上幫您轉接。

實境對話 2

A: Hello, Jiangsu Tools. This is Mei Yuan. How may I help you?

B: May I please speak to Mr. Liu?

A: I'm sorry, Mr. Liu is currently unavailable. Is there something I can help you with?

B: I wanted to speak to Mr. Liu about our order. I don't know if you can help me or not. I wanted to see if our order has been shipped or not.

A: I can connect you with someone in the customer service department. Nick Jin should be able to check on your order for you. Would you please hold while I transfer your call?

B: Okay.

A: (Phone rings) Hello, Jiangsu Tools. Mei Yuan speaking.

C: Hello. I would like to speak to Emily Chen.

A: Ms. Chen is unavailable now. Can I take a message for you?

C: This is Linda Li. Please let Emily know I called and have her call me back as soon as she can.

A: Ms. Li, I know Ms. Chen would want to talk to you. I will go ahead and put you through to her direct line.

C: Thank you.

A：您好，這裡是江蘇工具。我是袁枚。有什麼需要我幫忙的嗎？

B：我能和劉先生通話嗎？

A：對不起，劉先生目前不方便（接電話）。有什麼我可以幫您的嗎？

B：我想和劉先生談談有關訂單的事情。我不知道您能否幫我。我想知道我們的訂單是否已經發貨？

A：我可以幫您接客戶服務部的相關人員。Nick金應該可以幫您查閱您的訂單。您能否稍等一下，我把您的電話轉過去？

B：好的。

A：（電話鈴響）您好，我是江蘇工具的袁枚。

C：您好，我想和Emily陳通話。

A：陳女士現在不太方便（接電話）。要我幫您留言給她嗎？

C：我是Linda李。請告訴Emily我給她打過電話，讓她儘快回覆我。

A：李女士，我知道陳女士期待和您通話的。我馬上幫您轉到她的專線。

C：謝謝。

留言 Taking Messages

沒有人能保證24小時不關手機、8個小時都守在電話機旁。而人工留言或語音信箱都能保證你在「第二時間」能有效收到這些信息。時間就是金錢！（Time is money!）商務溝通中，丟掉的可能不只是一個簡單的訊息，可能是大筆的利潤。以下的注意事項和步驟，將幫助你獲取準確且及時的電話留言。

電話留言要素

● 致電人的姓名
● 公司名稱
● 致電人的電話號碼和分機
● 打電話的日期和時間
● 希望在收到留言後的回應（回電話、等候第二次來電等）

⊙ I'm sorry, Mr. Erickson isn't here at the moment. May I take a message?
對不起，Erickson先生現在不在，需要我留言給他嗎？

⊙ I can take a message and make sure she gets back to you when she returns to the office.
我會留言並且保證等她回到辦公室就請她回覆您。

⊙ Would you mind spelling your name?
您介意拼一下您的名字嗎？

⊙ You're calling about the statistical report, is that correct?
您來電是為了統計報告的事情，對嗎？

⊙ Is there a number that Ms. Lawson can reach you back at?
有沒有Lawson女士可以聯絡您的號碼？

⊙ When would be a good time for Mr. Jenkins to return your call?
Jenkins先生什麼時間回您電話比較合適？

⊙Who can I tell her called?

　我該如何跟她說來電者呢？

⊙Mr. Lester, would you please spell your name?

　Lester先生，您方便拼一下您的名字嗎？

⊙And what company did you say you were calling from?

　還有您剛才說您是哪個公司的？

⊙Your phone number is 808-760-2394, extension 394. Is that correct?

　您的號碼是808-760-2394，分機號碼是394，對嗎？

作註明

如果需要越快越好的（ASAP）回覆，就應當在留言中註明。別只是把留言扔在他人的辦公桌上（just dump it on their desk），要放在醒目的地方。

⊙Mary Smith from In *Touch Magazine* called. She said it was urgent and to call her back as soon as possible.

　來自《感動》雜誌的Mary Smith打過電話。她說事情緊急要您儘快回電。

⊙Mark in Accounting needs you to return his call ASAP. He says its very important that you talk to him before 3pm today.

　會計部的Mark要您儘快回電。他說您一定要在今天下午3點前和他聯繫。

掛斷前再確認

用一分鐘的時間和來電者確認記錄的資料是否準確，拼寫是否正確。

⊙Just to confirm. You're calling about the auditing report, your number is 898-987-6768. You're calling from McKay Inc. and your name is J-U-D-Y, Judy M-I-L-L-E-R, Miller. Is that correct?

確認一下。您打電話是關於審計報告的事情。您的號碼是898-987-6768。來自McKay股份有限公司,您的名字是J-U-D-Y, Judy; M-I-L-L-E-R, Miller。對嗎?

⊙Let me make sure I have this correct. You're calling from Weifeng Machinery Manufacturing for Ms. Tracy. She can reach you back at 0086-1348287791. Is that correct?

我確認一下我所記下的是否都正確。您來自偉峰機械製造,要找Tracy女士,她可以回電0086-1348287791聯繫到您。對嗎?

簽名

如果你是留言記錄者,不妨在紙的下方簽上你的名字。如果留言對象有什麼疑問,可以來問你。

A: Marcy, did you take this message for me this morning?

B: Nope. It was Tony who took the message for you. Look, his name is right there at the bottom of the message. If you have any questions about it, don't ask me. Ask him!

A:Marcy,是你早上幫我記的留言嗎?

B:不是。是Tony幫你留的。你看,在留言的最後有他的名字。如果你有什麼問題,別問我,問他!

總結

留言資料的準確性直接決定訊息的有效性,尤其是關鍵訊息,如回電號碼和來電人的姓名。訊息有誤會直接導致聯絡失效,延誤生意。所以要相當的重視。

單字表 ....

cell number 手機號碼　　　　　　confirm 確認

contact 聯繫　　　　　　　　　　contract 合約

correct 正確的　　　　　　　　　coworker 同事

either 或者；也（否定句）　　　fine 好的

office number 辦公室號碼；公司電話　urgent 著急的；緊急的

片語表 ....

get back to sb. 給（某人）回電話　　good time 快樂時光

I'm calling from (place) 我自/從　　May I please speak to sb.? 我可否和

（某處）打電話　　　　　　　　　（某人）通話？

May I take a message? 我可以留言　No big deal. 沒什麼大不了的。

嗎？　　　　　　　　　　　　　　one more time... 再一次……

reach (someone) at 找到某人/聯繫到　return a call 回電話

某人　　　　　　　　　　　　　　return to the office 回到辦公室

What did you say you were...? 您剛才　This is (person) speaking 我是……

說您是……？　　　　　　　　　　speak with sb. 和……通話

實境對話 1

A: Hello. Thank you for calling McKay Publishing. This is Paula Abernathy
   speaking. How may I help you?

B: May I speak to Mr. Erickson?

A: I'm sorry, Mr. Erickson isn't here at the moment. I can take a message
   and make sure he gets back to you when he returns to the office.

B: Okay. Please tell him that Bernie Mackey called.

A: Mr. Mackey, would you mind spelling your name for me?

B: B-E-R-N-I-E M-A-C-K-E-Y.

A: Good. Thank you. And what company did you say you were calling from?

B: I'm calling from Benson Books. I wanted to speak with Mr. Erickson about the contract he sent to me last week.

A: When would be a good time for Mr. Erickson to return your call?

B: He can call me back before 5pm today, or call me tomorrow if he doesn't get back before then.

A: What number can Mr. Erickson reach you at?

B: My office number is 880-989-8976. He can call me there. Or my cell phone number is 880-987-8787. Either one is fine. It's not that urgent, though, if he doesn't get back to me today, no big deal.

A: Let me confirm this with you one more time. Your name is Bernie B-E-R-N-I-E, Mackey M-A-C-K-E-Y, calling from Benson Books. You would like to speak to Mr. Erickson about the contract he sent you last week. You can be reached at 880-989-8976, or you cell phone at 880-987-8787. He can call you before 5pm today or tomorrow. Is that correct?

A：您好，感謝來電McKay出版社。我是Paula Abernathy。有什麼我可以幫您的嗎？

B：我可以和Erickson先生通話嗎？

A：對不起，Erickson先生現在不在。我可以幫你留言並保證他回到辦公室就回覆您。

B：好的。請告訴他Bernie Mackey找他。

A：Mackey先生，您介意拼一下您的名字嗎？

B：B-E-R-N-I-E M-A-C-K-E-Y。

A：好的，謝謝您。還有您剛才說您是哪個公司的？

B：我是Benson圖書公司的。我想和Erickson先生談談關於上周他寄給我的

合約。

A：Erickson先生什麼時間給您回電話比較合適呢？

B：今天下午5點前都可以，如果他5點之前回不來的話，就明天再打給我。

A： Erickson先生打哪個電話號碼可以聯絡您？

B：我辦公室的電話號碼是880-989-8976。他可以打這個，或打我的手機，號碼是880-987-8787，哪個都行。不是那麼急，如果他今天沒辦法回覆我，沒關係的。

A：我跟您再確認一下。您的名字是Bernie：B-E-R-N-I-E；Mackey：M-AC-K-E-Y。您來自Benson圖書公司，您想和Erickson先生談有關他上周寄的合約的事情。他可以撥打880-989-8976或您的手機880-987-8787聯絡您。他可以在今天下午5點鐘之前或明天打給您。對嗎？

實境對話 2

A: Ms. Tracy's office. This is Tony Martin. Can I help you?

B: Hello. May I please speak to Ms. Tracy?

A: I'm sorry, Ms. Tracy is unavailable at the moment. May I take a message?

B: Yes, I'm calling from Weifeng Machinery Manufacturing. I need to speak with Ms. Tracy about the order she made two weeks ago.

A: Who can I tell her to contact?

B: My name is Danny Lin. She can call me back, or she can also talk to my coworker Jean Zhao.

A: Is there a number that Ms. Tracy can reach you back at?

B: My number is 0086-1348287791. She can also call me at the office, which is 0086-10876342.

A: Let me make sure I have this correct. You're calling from Weifeng Machinery Manufacturing for Ms. Tracy. She can reach you back at 0086-1348287791 or 0086-10876342. She can contact you, Danny Lin or

Jean Zhao. And you're calling about her order of two weeks ago. Is that correct?

B: Yes.

A: I will see that Ms. Tracy gets the message.

B: Thank you very much.

A：Tracy女士辦公室。我是Tony Martin。有什麼可以幫您的？

B：您好，我能和Tracy女士通話嗎？

A：對不起，Tracy女士目前不方便接聽電話。需要幫你留言給她？

B：可以，我是偉峰機械製造。我要和Tracy女士談談兩周前她下的訂單。

A：我該告訴她和誰聯繫呢？

B：我叫Danny林。她可以回電給我，也可以和我的同事Jean趙談。

A：有沒有Tracy女士可以聯絡您的電話號碼？

B：我的電話號碼是0086-1348287791。她也可以打我辦公室的電話，號碼是0086-10876342。

B：我來確認一下我記錄的是否正確。您來自偉峰機械製造，要找Tracy女士。她可以回電到0086-1348287791或者0086-10876342聯絡您。她可以找您Danny林也可以找Jean趙。您打電話是想問她兩周前的訂單。對嗎？

B：是的。

A：我會讓Tracy女士看到留言的。

B：非常感謝您。

打電話 Placing a Call

如果你想就公事打電話聯絡某人，或要和某人在電話上討論生意（business matters），那就得學會打商務電話。打商務電話無論何時都應當彬彬有禮（good manners）、和睦愉快（be pleasant）。你的態度可能直接影響到電話那一端的人對你的部門或公司的印象（impression），所以一定要專業。

自我介紹

自我介紹不僅僅是出於禮貌（courteous），更是節省時間的方式。如果是熟人之間的電話，只要告知姓名就可以了。

⊙Hello. This is Susan Smith calling for Mr. O'Hara. Is he available?

您好，我是Susan Smith，我想和O'Hara先生通話，他現在方便嗎？

⊙May I please speak to Mr. Xiao?

我可否和蕭先生通話？

⊙I'm calling in regards to the Gilbert account.

我打電話的來意是有關Gibert帳目的事情。

⊙Could I please speak to someone in the Marketing department?

我能否和行銷部的人通話？

⊙I'm Kelly Carter calling from Charleston Computers.

我是來自的Charleston電腦的Kelly Carter。

⊙Hi, this is Kelly from Accounting.

我是會計部的Kelly。

⊙It's Mark Mason from Edison Electronics.

我是愛迪生電子的Mark Manson .

⊙Hi, I'm Debbie Dickenson. I'm calling from Marblewood Estates.

你好，我是來自的Marblewood房地產的Debbie Dickenson。

確認

確認你的致電對象是否方便接聽電話，如果不方便，就試著和他約另一個時間再去電。

⊙This is Nancy from reception. Is Mr. Martin available to take a call right now?

我是櫃臺的Nancy，Martin先生現在方便接聽電話嗎？

⊙May I please speak to Mr. Ortega? If he's not available, when would be a good time to reach him?

我可以和Ortega先生通話嗎？如果他不方便的話，那什麼時候可以找他？

⊙I'm calling for Ms. Lopez. Is she available to take my call?

我找一下Lopez女士，她現在方便接我的電話嗎？

留言

可以透過留言把你的致電目的和聯絡方式留給你的致電對象。有必要讓記錄人用他的話（in their own words）重複留言內容，確保資料無誤。你也可以留言到對方的語音信箱（voice mail）。

⊙Can you please repeat back to me the message?

您可否把我的留言重複一遍？

⊙Can I please leave a message for him?

我能否留言給他？

⊙I can just leave a message. Can you connect me to his voice mail, please?

我只留個言，可否請您幫我接到他的語音信箱？

個別情況

作為秘書或助理，在你未完全掌握來電者的目的或事情的緊迫性之前，最好不要直接轉給老闆。

⊙Could you please connect me to extension 530?

請幫我轉接分機號530.

⊙May I please speak to Mr. Garcia? I'm returning his phone call.

我能否和Garcia先生通話？我是回電給他。

⊙I have Mr. Lopez on the line for Mr. Stevens. Is Mr. Stevens available to take this call? It's rather urgent.

Lopez女士要找Stevens先生，Stevens先生現在方便接聽電話嗎？事情有些緊急。

結束通話

在融洽的氣氛中（pleasant note）結束通話。感謝另一方給予的時間，（如果必要）預約另外的通話時間，並祝他有美好的一天。

⊙Thank you very much for your help.

感謝您的幫助。

⊙Thank you, have a nice day.

謝謝您，祝您有美好的一天。

⊙Please have Mr. Lopez return my call. Thank you.

請Lopez先生回電話給我。謝謝您。

總結

通話過程能反映個人修養或所在公司的形象。彬彬有禮地表達要求或提供資訊，可以請求別人轉接電話或轉達留言。掛電話之前不要忘記祝福對方。

單字表

accounting 會計；會計學　　　　billing 帳單；開票

certainly 當然；一定地　　　　　client 客戶

handle 處理

hold 持有；保持

important 重要

interrupt 打斷；中斷

matter 無論；不管

payment 支付

reception 接待；櫃臺

repeat 重複；反覆

片語表

at a later time 以後；後來

call sb. back 回電（某人）

dial an extension 撥打分機

discuss (a / the) matter 討論（這個/某個）問題

hard to say 很難說

have a chance 有機會

hear so much about sb. 久仰（某人）；聽說了很多關於（某人）

hold all calls 不接所有的電話；應對所有的來電

How can I help you? 我怎樣才能幫您？

in regards to 關於；有關

on a contract basis 以合約的形式

receive payment 收到付款

repeat back to sb. 向（某人）重複

return a call 回電話

right at the moment 正在此刻

take (sb's) call 接（某人的）電話

talk about 談及

Thank you for calling. 感謝來電。

under contract 依據合約

實境對話 1

A: Good Morning. Thank you for calling O'Hara International. This is Lisa Cooper. May I help you?

B: Hello. This is Susan Smith calling for Mr. O'Hara. Is he available?

A: I'm sorry, Mr. O'Hara is currently unavailable. Is there something I can do for you?

B: Well, if Mr. O'Hara can't take my call, could I please speak so someone in the Accounting department?

A: Certainly, I can transfer you now. Please hold. (transfers the call)

C: Accounting, this is Val speaking, how can I help you?

B: Hi Val, this is Susan Smith calling from Charleston Computers. I'm calling in regards to the Gilbert account. We did some work for O'Hara on a contract basis, and we have yet to receive payment.

C: Oh. Lincoln Lopez handles all the billing and payment for work done under contract. You'll need to discuss the matter with him. Unfortunately, he is not available to take your call right at the moment.

B: Can I please leave a message for Mr. Lopez then? Please let him know that I called and have him call me back at 8765-8788.

C: Certainly.

B: Would you mind repeating back the message to me?

C: Okay. Susan Smith calling about the Gilbert account. Please return her call at 8765-8788.

B: Please have Mr. Lopez return my call. Thank you.

A：早安，感謝來電O'Hara國際。我是Lisa Cooper。有什麼需要幫忙的嗎？

B：您好，我是Susan Smith，我想和O'Hara先生通話。他現在方便嗎？

A：對不起，O'Hara 先生目前不方便接聽電話。有什麼我可以幫忙的嗎？

B：如果O'Hara先生不方便接電話的話，我能否和會計部的人通話嗎？

A：當然，我現在就為您轉接。請稍等。（轉接電話）

C：會計部，我是Val。有什麼可以幫您的？

B：您好，Val。我是Charleston電腦的Susan Smith。我打電話是關於Gibert帳目的事情。依據合約，我們為O'Hara做了一些工作，但是還沒有收到款項。

C：哦，Lincoln Lopez負責所有依據合約的帳單支付。您得和他談這個問題。不巧的是，他目前不方便接聽您的電話。

B：我能留言給Lopez先生嗎？請您告訴他我打過電話找他，請他回電到8765-8788這個號碼。

C：當然。

B：您能否重複一下我剛才的留言內容？

C：好的。Susan Smith就Gilbert帳單的事情打過電話。回電號碼是8765-8788。

B：請Lopez先生回電話給我，謝謝您。

實境對話 2

A: Hello. Mr. Martin's Desk. This is Judy.

B: Hi Judy. This is Nancy from reception. Is Mr. Martin available to take a call right now?

A: He's in a meeting with a client. Is it important?

B: I have Mr. Stevens on the line for Mr. Martin. Can Mr. Martin take this call? It's rather urgent.

A: I was told hold all of Mr. Martin's calls and not interrupt this meeting. I'm sorry. Can you take a message? I can have Mr. Martin call Mr. Stevens back as soon as his client leaves.

B: Okay. (To caller on hold) I'm sorry, Mr. Stevens, Mr. Martin is meeting with a client at the moment. Would you like to leave a message? Mr. Martin can return your call as soon as he is available.

C: Hmm... If he's not available now, when would be a good time to reach him?

B: It's difficult to say how long his meeting will last. Let me take down your number and have him get back to you...

C: I can just leave a message on his voice mail. Could you connect me, please?

B: No problem. If you wish to call back at a later time, you can dial extension 530.

C: Thanks for your help.

B: You're welcome, have a nice day.

A：您好，Martin先生辦公室，我是Judy。

B：您好，Judy。我是櫃臺的Nancy。Martin先生現在方便接聽電話嗎？

A：他正在會見一個客戶。有很重要的事情嗎？

B：Stevens先生打電話找Martin先生。他方便接電話嗎？非常緊急的事情。

A：他指派我接聽所有的來電，就是為了不打擾會議。對不起。您能留個言嗎？我可以請Martin先生在送走客戶後立刻回電給Stevens先生。

B：好的。（轉至來電者）對不起，Stevens先生，Martin先生此刻正在會見一位客戶。您能否留言？Martin先生一有空馬上會給您回電。

C：嗯……如果他現在不方便的話，那什麼時間方便找他？

B：現在很難說會議會開多久。我記下您的電話，我會請他給您回電話……

C：我只需要留個語音。請您幫我轉接到他的語音信箱。

B：沒問題。如果您想過一會兒再打電話，您可以撥打分機號530。

C：謝謝您的幫助。

B：不客氣，祝您有美好的一天。

轉接電話 Transferring Calls

沒有人能保證每通電話都能接到要找的對象，也很難保證不錯過接聽電話。如果有人轉接，這兩種情況都可以避免。電話可能轉接到要找的人，也可能接到相關同事或者語音信箱。

禮貌

無論轉接電話或者將來電臨時保留，都要（courtesy）以禮相待。在轉接電話之前先要問「您願意我幫您轉到（like to be transferred）……？」

⊙I'm sorry, Mr. Garcia is not in at the moment. Can I transfer you to his voice mail?

對不起，Garcia先生現在不在，我能否將您的電話轉到他的語音信箱？

⊙Please hold while I transfer you to the Customer Service department.

我把您的電話轉給客戶服務部，請稍候。

⊙Ms. Kerry is available to take your call. I can transfer you to her private line.

Kerry女士現在方便接聽您的電話，我可以把您的電話轉到她的專線。

⊙Let me transfer you now.

我現在就幫您轉接。

⊙If you like, I can transfer you to a technician.

如果您願意，我可以幫您轉接給一位技術人員。

⊙Mr. Samuels is currently on the other line. Would you like to hold? Or I can transfer you to his voice mail.

Samuels先生正在接聽別的電話。您是否願意等一下，或者我幫您轉接到他的語音信箱？

⊙Would you like me to transfer you to the Billing department?

您願意把您的電話轉到帳單部嗎？

⊙Can I transfer you?

我能轉接您的電話嗎？

提供號碼

如果來電者同意轉接電話，作為接電話者的你，要給他那個電話號碼，以防（in case）電話被轉接後沒有接通，也可以為來電者的下次來電提供直撥號碼。

⊙I can transfer you to Ms. Staple's desk now. Her extension is 880.

我現在可以把你的電話轉接到Staple女士的辦公桌那裡，她的分機號碼是880。

⊙I will transfer you to Mr. Jeffrey's number now. His direct number is 8876-8766.

我現在把您的電話轉接到Jeffrey先生那裡。他的專線號碼是8876-8766.

要等線路轉接成功後再掛斷。

A: I will transfer you to Mr. Jeffery's number now.
B: Thank you!
C: Hello, Jim Jeffery. (A hangs up the line)

A：我馬上把您的電話轉接到Jeffery先生那裡。
B：謝謝你。
C：您好，（我是）Jim Jeffery。（A掛斷電話）

再轉電話

如果一個電話被轉遍整個公司還沒有找到合適的人，你不妨記下來電者的姓名和號碼，在找到合適人選（appropriate person）後再回電話給他。

A: I can transfer you to the Billing department.
B: I called Billing first! They transferred me to the Accounting department, who transferred me to Finance, who then transferred me to you. Isn't there anyone who can help me?
A: I'm sorry for your frustration, sir. Let me take your contact information and understand your situation better. I will find out who the best person to help you is and have that person call you back.

A：我可以把您的電話轉給帳單部。
B：我最開始打給了帳單部，他們把我的電話轉給了會計部，會計部又轉給了

財務部，財務部又轉給了你。你們就沒有什麼人可以幫我嗎？

A：對於您的煩惱，我深表歉意。讓我記下您的聯絡方法，更多了解一下您的情況。我會找到幫助您的最佳人選，並請他回電話給您。

總結

在現代社會，資訊就是商機，錯過一個電話導致錯失一個賺錢機會的例子屢見不鮮。轉接電話能避免這種情況。在轉接電話的過程中要有耐心且保持禮貌，充分理解來電者的意願，做到轉接準確。因為沒有人願意像皮球一樣被踢來踢去。

單字表

accounting 會計；財務	already 已經
amount 數量；數額	billing 帳單
customer service 客戶服務	department 部門
extension 擴展；延期	pay 支付
product 產品	service 服務
situation 情況；狀況	specification 規格；規範
still 仍然	technician 技術人員；技師

片語表

be interested in 對……有興趣	best person to help 最佳協助者
call sb. back 給（某人）回電話	contact information 聯繫訊息
direct a call 直接通話	hang up 掛斷
have (sb do sth.) 讓（某人做某事）	have a problem with (sth.) 在（某事上）有問題
have a question about (sth.) 對於（某事）有疑問/問題	if you like 如果你願意；如果你喜歡

in particular 特別是;尤其是
private line 專線
receive a bill 收到帳單
some kind of 某種
you guys 各位;你們

Is that alright? 還好嗎?
reach sb. 聯繫到;找到(某人)
should be able to 應該能夠/應該可以
take (sb's) contact information 得到
(某人)的聯繫訊息

實境對話 1

A: Hello, Pratt Broadcasting. This is Macy Gordan. How may I direct your call?

B: Well, I had a question about a bill I received from your company...

A: Would you like me to transfer you to the Billing department?

B: I suppose so...

A: Please hold while I transfer you.

C: Billing, this is Maggie. (A hangs up the line)

B: Hi, I have a question about a bill I received. I already paid the amount, but I still have a bill from you guys.

C: We can't answer any questions about bills that have already been paid. I will need to transfer you to the Accounting department. Is that alright? They should be able to help you.

B: Okay.

D: Hello, this is Accounting. Patty speaking. (C hangs up the line)

B: I want to ask about a bill I received after I'd already paid the amount. There's some kind of problem with my service...

D: If you have a problem with your service, you should talk to Customer Service. Please hold while I transfer you to the Customer Service department.

B: But...

E: Customer Service. This is Mary. How can I help you?

B: Yes. I have a problem with my bill...

E: I can transfer you to the Billing department.

B: I called Billing first! They transferred me to the Accounting department, who then transferred me to you. Isn't there anyone who can help me?

E: I'm sorry for your frustration, sir. Let me take your contact information and understand your situation better. I will find out who is the best person to help you and have that person call you back.

A：您好，Pratt廣播公司。我是Macy Gordan。您要接哪裡？

B：啊，我從貴公司收到的一份帳單……

A：您要我把您的電話轉接到帳單部嗎？

B：我想可以……

A：請稍等，我幫您轉接。

C：結算部，我是Maggie。（A掛斷電話）

B：您好，是關於我收到的一份帳單。我已經付過帳款了，可你們又給我寄了一份帳單。

C：我們無法回答任何已支付的帳單問題。我把您的電話轉給會計部，可以嗎？他們應該可以幫到您。

B：好的。

D：您好，我是會計部的Patty。（C掛斷電話）

B：我想問一份帳單，這份帳單，我已經付過了，可你們又發了一份給我。你們的服務是不是有什麼問題……

D：關於您的服務的問題，您應該和客戶服務部談。請稍等，我把您的電話轉接到客戶服務部。

B：但是……

E：客戶服務部。我是Mary。有什麼可以幫助您的嗎？

B：是的。我有一個問題是關於我的帳單……

E：我可以把您的電話轉給帳單部。

B：我最開始打給了帳單部，他們把我的電話轉接給會計部，會計部又把我的電話轉接給了你，你們就沒有人可以幫我嗎？

E：先生，對於您的煩惱，我深表歉意。讓我記下您的聯絡方法，更多地了解一下您的情況。我會找到幫助您的最佳人選，並請他回電話給您。

實境對話 2

A: Megatron Electronics. This is Ya Ping speaking. How may I help you?

B: Is Mr. Zhang available?

A: Are you calling for Mr. Xiaoping Zhang? I'm sorry. Mr. Zhang is not in at the moment. Can I transfer you to his voice mail?

B: I was hoping to talk to Mr. Zhang, but maybe there is someone else who could help me. I wanted to ask about the specifications on some of your products...

A: If you like, I can transfer you to a technician.

B: That would be great! Thank you.

A: Ms. Han, one of our technicians, is available to take your call. I can transfer you to her private line.

B: Can you tell me her number so I can reach her again next time?

A: Yes. Ms. Han's extension is 880. Let me transfer you now.

C: Technical department, this is Linda Han. (A hangs up)

B: Hi Linda, my name is Jeffery Wu. I wanted to ask about the specifications of some of your products. I was told you could help me.

C: Certainly. Which particular products are you interested in?

A：Megatron 電子，我是亞萍。有什麼可以幫您的嗎？

B：張先生方便接電話嗎？

A：您是想找張小平先生嗎？對不起，張先生現在不在。要我把您的電話轉接到他的語音信箱嗎？

B：我本來想和張先生談的，但是，也許你們別的什麼人也可以幫助我。我是想問些有關你們產品規格的一些情況……

A：如果您願意，我可以把電話轉接給技術人員。

B：那太好了！謝謝您。

A：韓小姐是我們的技術人員之一，她現在方便接聽您的電話。我可以把您的電話轉接到她的專線。

B：您能否告訴我她的分機號碼，這樣我下次可以直接聯絡她？

A：好的。她的分機號是880。我現在就幫您轉接。

C：技術部，我是Linda韓。（A掛斷電話）

B：您好，Linda。我是Jeffery吳。我想諮詢一下有關你們產品的規格。他們說您可以幫助我。

C：是的。您對哪些產品感興趣呢？

十項全能之五

熟悉辦公事務
In the Office

通知 Making Announcements

日常工作中，通知屢見不鮮（common occurrence）。通知的種類繁多，包括會議通知、會議更改通知、假日和聚會（holidays and parties）通知、主管階層（leadership）變動通知等。

無論是哪種通知，都應該做到資訊準確。在發放通知前都應該和相關人士反覆核對通知內容。

⊙As of November 25, 2008, working hours for employees will be changed to begin at 9am.
自2008年11月25日起，員工的工作時間改為從早上9點開始。

⊙We are pleased to announce an extended vacation schedule.
我們很高興地宣布延長假期表。

⊙Our holiday party will be held December 22.
我們的假日聚會將安排在12月22日。

⊙Please RSVP by November 22.
請在11月22日前答覆確認。

⊙New overtime pay policies will begin Saturday, July 25th. For more details, please contact Human Resources.
新的加班費政策將從7月25日，週六起開始執行。想了解更多內容，請和人力資源部聯絡。

⊙We'd like to announce some changes to management.
我們想通知一些有關管理階層變動的情況。

⊙Our office will be relocated to a new building, beginning June 17th.
我們的辦公室將於6月17日起遷至新的辦公大樓。

會議通知（Announcing meetings）

⊙The next staff meeting will be held on Wednesday, October 5, at 10:00 am.
下一次的員工大會將於10月5日，週三上午10點召開。

⊙The meeting will feature three guest speakers.
有3位嘉賓將出席會議。

⊙Refreshments will be offered at the meeting.
會議將提供茶點。

⊙Attendance is mandatory for all staff.
所有員工都必須出席。

⊙Please see the bulletin board in the employee lounge for a complete list of upcoming meetings.
請參閱張貼在員工休息室布告欄中預訂會議的完整清單。

⊙If you have any questions about the meeting agenda, please see me.
對於會議的議程如果還有什麼問題，請來找我。

會議更改通知（Announcing changes to meetings）

⊙Please note that the upcoming staff meeting has been rescheduled.
請注意，即將召開的員工大會時間更改了。

⊙The meeting will now be held on Monday, January 10th, at 2:00pm.
現在決定會議將於1月10日，週一下午2點召開。

⊙Please note that the May 14th marketing meeting has been moved to May 18th.
請注意，原定於5月14號的行銷會議已改至5月18日舉行。

⊙Due to a scheduling conflict, Tuesday's meeting has been postponed until next week.
由於時間安排有衝突，週二的會議延到下周召開了。

⊙The new date and time for the meeting will be announced next Monday.
會議的召開日期和時間將於下週一公布。

通知假日和聚會（Announcing holidays and parties）

⊙We are pleased to announce that all employees will be given an extra two days of vacation.
我們很高興地通知大家，所有員工將額外放假兩天。

⊙We've decided to award holiday paid leave for all full-time employees.
我們決定給所有全職員工有薪休假的獎勵。

⊙Our holiday party will be held on December 20th from 5:00 to 8:00pm at the Renata Hotel.
我們的假日派對將在12月20日下午5點到8點在雷納塔酒店舉行。

主管階層變動通知（Announcing changes in leadership）

⊙We are pleased to announce the appointment of Guo LingMei as our new director of Finance.
我們很高興地通知，郭靈梅被任命為我們的新財務主管。

⊙Effective immediately, our new technology consultant is Brenda Lin.
即日起，Brenda林為我們的新技術顧問。

⊙As of June 24, 2009 Wesley Williams will be in charge of all Human Resource department issues.

自2009年6月24日起，Wesley Williams將負責所有人力資源部的事宜。

⊙We appreciate all the work that Sophia has done for us, and send her off with a great vote of thanks!

我們很感激Sophia為我們所做的一切，讓我們一起用誠摯的感謝來歡送她！

總結

通知應做到簡明扼要，資訊點到為止。主管階層變動通知，要標明生效時間。

單字表

begin 開始
consultant 顧問；諮詢人員
detail 細節
especially 特別；尤其
issues 問題
mandatory 強制的；強制性的
overtime pay 加班費；超時費
policy 政策；方針
relocate 遷移
technology 技術

bulletin board 公告欄
contact 聯繫
directly 直接
human resources 人力資源
management 管理
memo 備忘錄；備註
pessimistic 悲觀
postpone 延遲
reschedule 重新安排

片語表

a bit 一點
effective immediately 立即生效
good news 好消息
hear about 得悉；聽說

as of 從……起；在……時
for a minute 一下；一會兒；片刻
have (sb's) attention 請（某人）主意
heard of 聽說過

in charge of 負責
make policy 發表/擬定方針政策
or else 否則；要不然
sleeping in late 睡得很晚
speak up 大聲説
what's what 什麼是什麼

keep track of (sth.) 保持對……的聯繫
new guy 新伙伴
good thing I (did sth.) 好在/幸虧我
（做了某事）
supposed to (do sth.) 應該（做某事）
working hours 工作時間；執行時間

實境對話 1

A: There are so many changes going on around here, it's hard to keep track of what's what!

B: What do you mean? I haven't heard of that many changes. The only thing I heard about was that there was a change about the time we are supposed to come to work. I saw the memo this morning. "As of November 25, 2008, working hours for employees will be changed to begin at 9am." So much for sleeping in late!

A: Haven't you also heard about the new overtime pay polices, scheduled to begin November 25th? They say to contact Human Resources for more details. So it can't be good, or else they would have told us directly.

B: Why be so pessimistic. It might be good.

A: You're right. Change is good, sometimes. Especially the changes to management.

B: What changes to management?

A: You didn't see that memo? Here, let me read it to you. "Effective immediately, our new technology consultant is Brenda Lin. As of November 24, Wesley Williams will replace Martin Ma in charge of all Human Resource department issues."

B: Wow... maybe that's why there are so many changes—a new guy's making the policies.

A: And one more important one you should know about... Our office will be relocated to a new building, beginning November 15th.

B: November 15th? That's tomorrow!

A: Good thing I told you about it!

A：這裡竟然有這麼多的變動，很難讓人了解什麼是什麼？

B：你是什麼意思？我沒有聽說有很多更動。我唯一聽說的調整是我們的工作時間。我今天早上看備忘錄上寫「從2008年11月25日起，員工的工作時間從早9點開始。」再也不能睡懶覺了！

A：你沒有聽說有關新加班費政策，將從11月25起執行的消息嗎？他們說詳情要和人力資源部聯絡。所以大概好不了，要不然他們就直接告訴我們了。

B：為什麼那麼悲觀？也許是好的呢。

A：你是對的，改變有時候也是好的。尤其是管理階層的改變。

B：管理階層有什麼變動嗎？

A：你沒有看那個備忘錄嗎？在這兒，我讀給你聽聽。「從即日起，新的技術顧問是Brenda Lin。從11月24日起，Wesley Williams將取代Martin Ma來負責人力資源部。」

B：哇……也許正因為如此才有這麼多的調整──新官上任三把火。

A：還有一件你應該知道的非常重要的事是關於……從11月15日起，我們的辦公室將遷到新大樓。

B：11月15日？那就是明天啊！

A：幸虧我告訴你了。

實境對話 2

A: Can I have everyone's attention for a minute? I have some announcements to make.

B: I don't think they heard you, you need to speak up a bit more.

A: Hello! Everyone! Can I have your attention please? I have something to announce. The next staff meeting will be held on Wednesday December 15th, at 10:00am.

C: Wasn't it supposed to be held tomorrow afternoon?

A: Due to a scheduling conflict, the meeting was postponed and rescheduled. The meeting will feature three guest speakers. The meeting is mandatory for all staff.

(Collective groan)

A: Now, now. Please see the bulletin board in the employee lounge for a complete list of upcoming meetings. If you have any questions about the meeting agenda, please see me.

B: Anything else, boss?

A: Yes, one more thing. Here's some better news. We are pleased to announce that all employees will be given an extra two days of vacation. We've decided to award holiday paid leave for all full-time employees.

(Collective cheering)

A: And one more thing. Our holiday party will be held on December 20th from 5:00 to 8:00pm at the Renata Hotel.

A：請各位注意一下，我有些事情要通知。

B：我想他們沒有聽見您説的話，您聲音再大點。

A：嗨！各位！請聽我説。我有些事情要宣布。下一次的員工大會將於12月15日，週三上午10點召開。

C：不是説明天下午召開嗎？

A：由於時間安排有衝突，延後了這次會議，並重做安排了。該會議將有3位嘉賓出席，所有員工都必須出席。

（埋怨聲）

A：現在，請參閱張貼在員工休息室公告欄中預訂會議的完整清單。對於會議的議程有什麼問題，請來找我。

B：還有別的事情嗎，老闆？

A：是的，還有一件事，是個比較好的消息。我們很高興地通知大家，所有員工將額外放假兩天。我們決定給所有全職員工有薪休假的獎勵。

（集體歡呼）

A：還有件事，我們的假日派對將於12月20日下午5點到8點在雷納塔酒店舉行。

轉達訊息 Conveying Information

不論在工作中還是在日常生活中，有效轉述訊息的技巧（skill）都有著重要的意義。清晰無誤地轉達訊息並且渴望共享是正確轉達的前提。

轉達訊息時，首先要向對方說明資訊的來源。

⊙Let me share the message I received from headquarters.
　我告訴你一條從總部那裡得到的訊息。

⊙According to what I was told...
　據我所知……

⊙I received notice from our department head that...
　我從部門主管那裡得到消息……

⊙The engineering staff reported to me that...
　工程人員向我報告說……

⊙That's not what I heard from Mr. Pratt. He told me...
　我從Pratt先生那裡聽到的可不是這樣。他告訴我說……

⊙I was told that...
　我知道……

方式

根據溝通的目的（purpose）、訊息的緊迫性（urgency）和聽眾的傾向來決定轉達訊息的方式。

⊙I know this might be a difficult message to receive, but I have to let you know what I was told by...

我知道這個訊息對你來說有些難以接受，但是我必須讓你知道，……告知我……

⊙I'm sure everyone will be happy to hear the news I received from the boss that...

我從老闆那裡知道了這個消息，我肯定大家聽了都會非常高興……

⊙I am pleased to pass along the information that...

我很高興地告訴大家……的訊息。

⊙Let me make an announcement that everyone will be surprised to hear—this comes straight from the top, people.

我通知大家一個直接來自主管階層的驚人消息。

⊙I need to let you all know what the people on top have been saying.

我要讓大家都知道當時主管是怎麼說的。

⊙Let me convey the concern and appreciation for you from the folks back home.

我來轉達一下大家回去以後對您的關心和感激。

語言

減少聽眾的理解障礙（minimize barriers），儘量使用簡單（simple language）準確的語言。

⊙Mr. Harris told me specifically, the deadline on the project is two weeks from today.

Harris先生明確地告訴我，專案截止日是從今天開始算的兩周時間。

⊙Headquarters said they need the reports by this afternoon.

主管們說下午他們要拿到報告。

⊙The department head told me to tell you that he wants to see you in his office.

部門主管讓我告訴你，他想在他辦公室見你。

⊙Mr. Young said he was pleased with our efforts.

Young先生說他對我們的努力非常滿意。

⊙Mr. Jackson said, and I quote, "You are the best!"

引述Jackson 先生的話就是：「你們是最好的！」

回饋

從聽眾那裡尋求回饋（feedback），以確認他們收到的訊息無誤。

A: Word from the stockholders is that we are not approved to go forward on this project. Understand?

B: So that means we can't do anything?

A: No, we can still work on some other projects, but the marketing project is on hold for now.

A：股東們說我們這個專案沒有通過。明白了嗎？

B：那意思是說我們什麼都做不了了？

A：不，我們仍然可以做別的專案，只是行銷規劃暫時被擱置了。

A: The department head told me that he wants to see you in his office right away. Got it?

B: So he's upset, then?

A: No, he's not upset. He's just running late and wants to meet with you before he goes off to his afternoon meeting.

A：部門主管告訴我說，現在就想在他的辦公室見到你。明白嗎？

B：他有些心煩意亂，是嗎？。

A：不，他沒有。他快遲到了，他想在下午開會前見你一面。

總結

「轉述」就是在兩者間傳話，以便了解對方的想法。轉述就要做到訊息準確完整、目的表達到位、語言清晰易懂。同時，還要透過對方的回饋來確認訊息是否傳達正確。

單字表

appreciation 賞析；感激	board (of directors) 董事會（主管級的）
bonus 獎金；紅利；補貼	deny 否認；拒絕
disappointed 失望的	engineering 工程；工程學
excitement 興奮；激動	executive assistant 行政助理
feasible 切實可行的	funding 資助
generous 慷慨的；大方的	headquarters 總部的；總公司的
implement 實施；完成	marketing 行銷
quote 引用；引述	review 複審；檢查
staff 職員；全體職工	upset 使煩惱；使心煩意亂

片語表

Are you serious? 你是認真的嗎？

by the way 順便

be impressed by (sth.) 對（某事）
印象深刻

from a (particular) viewpoint 從（特
別）觀點

let (sb.) know 讓某人知道

project plans 專案計畫

report to (sb.) 向（某人）報告

run late 後期運行

at this time... 在這個時候……

have to 不得不；必須

from a (particular) standpoint 從（特
別）角度

have funding (for sth.) （對於某事）的
資金

people on top 主管階層

receive (a message) 接受（某資訊）

right away 馬上；立即

share (a message) 共用（資訊）

實境對話 1

A: Let me share the message I received from headquarters. I know this might be a difficult message to receive, but I have to let you know what I was told by the board that they have reviewed our marketing project plans and the plans have been denied.

B: Denied? What does that mean? Why did they deny it? We worked so hard on those!

A: I knew you'd be disappointed. According to what I was told, the board was impressed by the project plans, but felt that it wouldn't be feasible to implement at this time.

C: That's not what I heard from Mr. Pratt, the executive assistant to the CEO. He told me that the plans were denied because they don't have funding for it.

A: Well, I think that may be true as well. The engineering staff reported to me that the project was feasible from an engineering viewpoint. But I was told that from a financial standpoint, the money is not available.

C: By the way, the department head told me that he wants to see you in his office right away. Got it?

A: So he's upset, then?

C: No, he's not upset. He's just running late and wants to meet with you before he goes off to his afternoon meeting.

A：讓我來分享一條從總部那裡得到的消息。我知道這個消息對你來說有些難以接受，但是我必須讓你知道，董事會告知我，我們的行銷專案計畫已經審閱了，但是被否決了。

B：否決了？什麼意思？為什麼他們要否決？我們付出了那麼多心力的工作！

A：我就知道你會很失望的。據我所知，董事會對這個專案印象很好，但是覺得現在執行是不可行的。

C：我從總裁行政助理Pratt先生那裡聽到的可不是這樣。他告訴我說，專案被否決是因為他們沒有投入的資金。

A：那，我想那可能是真的。工程人員向我報告說，這個專案從工程學的角度來說是可行的。但從財務角度來說，現在沒錢。

C：順便說一句，部門主管請你馬上去他的辦公室見他，明白嗎？

A：他有些心煩意亂，是嗎？

C：不，他沒有。他只是快遲到了，想在下午去開會之前見你一面。

實境對話 2

A: Can I get everyone's attention for a moment, please? Let me make an announcement that everyone will be surprised to hear—this comes straight from the top, people.

B: What's going on? What's all the excitement about?

A: I'm sure everyone will be happy to hear the news I received from the boss that we will all be receiving a special bonus at the end of the month.

C: A bonus? What kind of bonus?

A: I am pleased to pass along the information that our sales numbers have been record high, as have been our customer service scores. So as a special thank you, the company will be giving you each a $500 bonus this month.

B: Are you serious? That's great!

A: I need to let you all know what the people on top have been saying. Mr. Young said that he was pleased with our efforts. Mr. Kellogg wanted to convey his concern and appreciation for you. Mr. Jackson said, and I quote, "You are the best!"

B: That's the first time they've been so generous. Let's hope they start a new trend.

A: Well, that's about it. But just let me convey the appreciation the folks in the corporate offices have for all of you.

A：大家請注意。我通知大家一個來自主管階層的驚人消息。

B：怎麼了？有什麼值得興奮的消息？

A：我肯定大家都會很樂意聽到我剛從老闆那裡聽來的消息，我們會在這個月底得到一筆特別的獎金。

C：獎金？什麼獎金？

A：我很高興地告訴大家：客戶肯定我們的服務，且我們的銷售業績突破新高。因此公司決定在本月給每人發500美元的獎金，作為特別的感謝。

B：你說的是真的嗎？那太好了！

A：我要讓大家都知道當時主管是怎麼說的。Young先生說他對我們的努力非常滿意。Kellogg希望轉達他對大家的關心和讚賞。引述Jackson先生的話就是：「你們是最棒的！」

B：他們第一次這麼慷慨。真希望就此開始一個新局面。

A：就是這樣。我就是轉達一下公司層峰人士對大家的讚賞。

確認 Making Confirmations

在日常生活中，「確認」不僅有提示雙方、避免遺忘疏忽的作用，還可以利用這個程序對資訊進行更新、補充和完善。

確認資訊

可以確認的不僅僅是「預約」或者計畫會議，還可以確認航班、飯店等旅行資訊（travel information）。

⊙I'm calling to confirm our appointment tomorrow afternoon at 4pm. Is this time still convenient for you?

我打電話是想確認我們在明天下午4點的會面。這個時間您還方便嗎？

⊙Could you please confirm your address for me?

請您幫我確認一下您的地址，可以嗎？

⊙If you don't mind, let me confirm one more time. Your telephone number is 901-555-9853, correct?

如果您不介意的話，讓我再確認一次。您的電話號碼是901-555-9853，對嗎？

⊙So that's next Monday at 8pm for our meeting, right?

所以我們的會議定在下週一下午8點，對嗎？

⊙The flight is scheduled to leave at 4:55 pm, correct?

航班下午4：55起飛，對嗎？

⊙Just to be clear, our order is to be delivered by July 23, am I right?

再確認一下，我們的訂單是在7月23日送貨，對嗎？

⊙The discount you are offering us is 4%, right?

您給我們的折扣是4%，對嗎？

禮儀規則

確認要在前一天（a day in advance）進行。如果有變動，這個時候就應該明確提出。別提前三天就打電話（有些變化不可預知），或者當天才打，這會讓人覺得你的能力不足。確認電話要禮貌、簡短，要感激對方能抽出時間來幫你確認訊息。

⊙I'm calling to confirm my meeting tomorrow with Ms. Goldberg.
我打電話是想確認一下明天我和Goldberg女士會面的事。

⊙Is Mr. Thomas still available to meet with me tomorrow afternoon at 2pm?
Thomas先生還方便明天下午兩點和我見面嗎？

⊙I have a job interview scheduled for tomorrow morning at 10am. I'm just calling to confirm the time.
我有一個工作面試安排在明天上午的10點，我想確認一下。

⊙Will you still be able to make your appointment with us tomorrow at 4:30?
您是否依然能夠如期出席明天4：30和我們的會面？

電話確認

如果你對自己的聽力缺乏信心，那麼就不要嫌麻煩，核對一下相關的名稱拼寫、電話、地址等資訊。

⊙Would you mind spelling your name for me, Mr. Lewis? Thank you.
您是否介意為我拼一下您的名字，Lewis先生？謝謝您。

⊙So that's Jerome Lewis, J-E-R-O-M-E L-E-W-I-S, correct?
所以是Jerome Lewis先生，J-E-R-O-M-E L-E-W-I-S，對嗎？

⊙Let me confirm quickly, your number is 703-746-3432?

讓我簡短地確認一下，您的號碼是703-746-3432？

⊙Can you confirm your address for me? Is it 109 Jefferson Avenue? Do you have apartment number?

您能否確認一下您的地址？是傑弗遜大街109號嗎？有家裡電話嗎？

行前確認

出發前應該提前一個禮拜確認機票。在確認的過程中，你要確保航班資訊（flight information）無誤，說明你要求的特殊服務、特別的位置、特殊的醫療照顧等。你可以打電話到航空公司、官網站或者親自（in person）前往航空公司確認。

⊙I'd like to confirm my flight.

我想確認一下我的航班。

⊙My flight number is NH109, leaving from New York to Beijing.

我的航班號碼是NH109，從紐約飛往北京的。

⊙I would like to request an aisle seat, if possible.

如果有可能，我想要一個靠近走道的位置。

總結

繁雜的工作讓人頭暈目眩，在這種情況下，很容易把某個約定拋在腦後。確認預約不僅可以避免遺忘、節省時間，還可以幫你贏得專業聲譽。「確認資訊」同時也是補充、更新資訊的過程，能使您的活動更加有成效。

單字表

address 地址　　　　　　　apartment 部門

appreciate 欣賞　　　　　　confirm 確認

correct 正確的　　　　　　current 當前的

interview 面試　　　　　　move 感動；移動

quickly 迅速地　　　　　　schedule 時間表

spell 拼寫　　　　　　　　still 仍然

update 更新

片語表

client information 客戶資料　　have (sb's) name 知道（某人）的名字

if that's alright 如果沒問題的話　if you like 如果您願意

in the office 在辦公室裡　　　　make an appointment 預約

no problem 沒問題　　　　　　on file 存檔；有案可查

zip code 郵遞區號　　　　　　take a look 看一下

(time) sharp 準時　　　　　　with a client 見客戶；和客戶會面

yep 是的（口）

實境對話 1

A: Hello, Truman Consulting. How may I help you?

B: Good afternoon. I'm calling to confirm my meeting tomorrow with Ms. Goldberg. Is she in the office now?

A: I'm sorry. Ms. Goldberg is with a client now. I can take a look at her schedule and confirm your appointment for you, if you like.

B: Thank you, I would appreciate it.

A: May I have your name?

B: Oh, yes. My name is Jerome Lewis.

A: Would you mind spelling your name for me, Mr. Lewis?

B: No problem. J-E-R-O-M-E L-E-W-I-S.

A: So that's Jerome Lewis, J-E-R-O-M-E L-E-W-I-S, correct? And what time was your appointment with Ms. Goldberg tomorrow?

B: Yes, that's correct. I have a job interview scheduled for tomorrow morning at 10am.

A: Mr. Lewis, I see your interview is scheduled for tomorrow morning at 10am sharp. Is there anything else I can help you with?

B: No, thank you very much for your help. I appreciate it!

A：您好，Truman諮詢公司。有什麼可以幫您的嗎？

B：午安。我打電話是想確認一下明天我和Goldberg女士會面的事。她現在在辦公室嗎？

A：對不起，她正在見客戶。如果您願意，我可以看一下她的日程並確認您的預約。

B：謝謝。我很感激。

A：您怎麼稱呼？

B：哦，我叫Jerome Lewis.

B：您是否方便拼一下您的名字，Lewis先生？

B：沒問題。J-E-R-O-M-E L-E-W-I-S。

A：是Jerome Lewis先生，J-E-R-O-M-E L-E-W-I-S，對嗎？您和Goldberg女士約在明天什麼時間？

B：沒錯。我的求職面試約在明天上午的10點。

A：Lewis先生，我已經看到您的面試被安排在明天上午的10點整。還有別的什麼需要幫忙的嗎？

B：沒有，謝謝您的幫助。我很感激。

實境對話 2

A: Hello...

B: Hello, may I please speak to Simon Zhang? This is Sandra Hughes calling from BeiHai Electronics. I am calling to confirm an appointment. Will you still be able to make your appointment with us tomorrow at 4:30.

A: This is Mr. Zhang. Yes, I will be able to make the appointment.

B: Before the appointment, I would like to update the client information we have listed for you in our files, if that's alright.

A: Sure, no problem.

B: Let me confirm quickly, your number is 703-746-3432? That's the number we have on file.

A: Yes.

B: Can you confirm your address for me? Is it 109 Jefferson Avenue? Do you have an apartment number?

A: No, actually, that address is not current. Our offices have moved to 433 South Washington Boulevard.

B: That's 430 South Washington Boulevard?

A: No, not 430, it's 433.

B: Yes, 433 South Washington Boulevard, correct?

A: Yep.

B: And is that still in Buena Vista? What is the zip code there?

A: Yes, it's Buena Vista. Our zip code is 99805.

A：您好！

B：您好，我能和Simon張通話嗎？我是北海電子的Sandra Hughes。我打電話是想確認一下預約。您是否能如期出席明天下午4：30與我們的會面？

A：我是張先生。是的，我可以赴約。

B：在會面之前，如果方便，我想更新您在我們檔案中的客戶資訊。

A：當然，沒問題。

B：讓我簡短地確認一下，您的號碼是703-746-3432？那是我們登記的號碼。

A：是的。

B：能否為我確認一下您的地址？是傑佛遜大街109號嗎？您是否有室內電話？

A：沒有，事實上，那個地址不是現在的了。我們的辦公室搬到了南華盛頓林蔭大道433號。

B：是南華盛頓林蔭大道430號嗎？

A：不對，不是430號，是433號。

B：好的，南華盛頓林蔭大道433號，對嗎？

A：是的。

B：那還是在Buena Vista區嗎？那裡的郵遞區號是多少？

A：是的，還是在Buena Vista區。我們的郵遞區號是99805。

彙報工作 Reporting on Work

向老闆彙報工作是向他證明你很重要的大好機會。在介紹你完成的工作時要簡明扼要（clearly and succinctly）。

⋯⋯⋯⋯⋯⋯⋯⋯⋯⋯⋯⋯⋯⋯⋯⋯⋯⋯⋯⋯⋯⋯⋯⋯⋯⋯⋯⋯⋯⋯⋯⋯⋯

首先要開門見山，以一句話簡要概括你的彙報主題。

⊙Here are the reports you asked for.
這是您要的報告。

⊙Let me show you the results of our meeting.
我來介紹一下我們會談的成果。

⊙I've finished the analysis you wanted done. Would you like me to E-mail it to you?
我已經完成了您要的分析。要我寄電子郵件給您嗎？

⊙Let me give you a brief summary of what we've been up to this week.
我來簡單總結一下這個禮拜我們的進展。

⊙Here's the sales figures from our department.
這是我們部門的銷售數字。

⊙I've already completed the financial review. Please let me know if you have any questions about it.
我已經完成了財務審核。如果您有什麼疑問，儘管問我。

謙虛（be modest）

沒有人喜歡傲慢自大（arrogant）的員工，但這並不意味著你在完成一份很棒的工作後不該炫耀一下自己（toot your own horn）。因為出色的工作而得到讚賞（take credit）是合情合理的。

⊙While you were away certain things got accomplished and I'd like to bring you up to date on...
在你離開期間，一些事情都完成了，我依次向您介紹……

⊙If I could draw your attention to...
我能否請您注意……

⊙Here's an update...
這是一份最近更新的……

⊙I'd like to explain what's happening with...
我可以解釋一下在……發生的情況。

⊙If you have time, I'd like you to take a look at...
如果您有時間，我想請您看一下……

積極主動

老闆們都希望自己的員工積極上進（taking initiative），但身為員工的你，底線是不能越權（overstep your authority）。老闆不在期間，如果你能做一些聰明的決策，那就意味著他回來後能輕鬆些。這是他們樂意看到的。

⊙I hope you don't mind, but I've already taken care of that.
　我希望您不介意，我已經考慮到那個（方面）了。

⊙Don't worry about the appointment schedule. I made arrangements already.
　不必為預約時間安排而擔心，我都安排好了。

⊙I took the liberty of arranging your meeting with Mr. Gilbert.
　在您和Gilbert先生會面的安排上，我有充分的自由。

⊙The supplier called about the problem, but we've got everything under control.
　供應商曾呼籲過此問題，但是一切已在我們的掌控之中了。

建立信任

如果你能想老闆之所想，那一定會贏得讚譽（earn brownie points）。當你以詳細的報告來一個個打消他們的顧慮時，那就是他們對你建立信任（build their confidence）的開始。

A: I'm going to have to change my meeting schedule this afternoon. Please call Mr. Gilbert's secretary. I need to meet with him about the budget projections as soon as possible.

B: Don't worry about the appointment schedule. I made arrangements already. I took the liberty of arranging your meeting with Mr. Gilbert. Will 3pm be okay for you? If not, I can call to postpone the meeting.

A：我下午會議的時間必須要改了。請打電話給Gilbert先生的秘書，說我針對預算規劃專案需要與他儘快碰面。

B：不必擔心會面時間，我都已經安排好了。在您與Gilbert先生會面的安排上，我爭取到安排自由。下午3點，您可以嗎？如果不行，我可以打電話延期。

總結

只會埋頭苦幹，不懂彙報成果，收穫與付出就會不成正比。彙報時要做到積極主動、直接了當、不驕不躁、天衣無縫。總之，「只要您想到的，我都做好了。」那就一定能夠換來老闆滿意的笑容。

單字表 ....

analysis 分析	audit 審計；審核；查帳
certain 一定的；確定的	complete 完成
distribute 分發；分布	financial 財務的；金融的
internal 內部的；內在的	minutes 會議記錄
necessary 必要的	negotiate 談判
PPT presentation 投影片簡報	projection 預測；估計
result 結果；結論	successful 成功的
summarize 總結	vender 銷售（員）

片語表 ....

as soon as possible 盡可能快的	bring (someone) up to date 幫（某人）趕上
toot your own horn 自吹自擂	

by the way 順便；另外

earn brownie points 賺取印象分數

for your approval 期待認可

get accomplished 取得成就；完成

hammer out (details) 敲定（詳情）

I'd be happy to 我很樂意……

make sure that (something happens)
確保（某事發生）

draw up (a contract) 草擬合約

favorable terms 優惠條件

get a hold of (sth.) 掌控（某事）

give (sb.) enough time 給某人足夠時間

hand out 分發；散發

make arrangements 安排

postpone (a meeting) 延遲（某會議）

sales figures 銷售資料

實境對話 1

A: Larry, I hope everything went well in the office during the time I was in Shanghai this week.

B: While you were away certain things got accomplished and I'd like to bring you up to date. First, let me show you the results of our meeting with the venders. Here's a copy of the meeting's minutes. To summarize, we were able to negotiate favorable terms and draw up a contract. It took a lot of hammering out the details, but I feel we were successful. I've E-mailed the contract to your E-mail account for your approval.

A: Wonderful!

B: And here are the reports you asked for. I've also finished the analysis you wanted done. Would you like me to E-mail it to you?

A: No, that won't be necessary. Just make sure that a copy of your analysis gets distributed to the department. What about the sales figures? As soon as you get a hold of them, I would like you to make a financial review for me.

B: Here are the sales figures from our department. I've already completed the financial review. Please let me know if you have any questions about it.

A: Oh, well, that's great!

A：Larry，我希望我在上海的這個星期裡，辦公室的工作都進展順利。

B：在您離開期間，一些事情都如期完成了，我依次跟您報告。首先，我來介紹一下和供應商會談的成果。這裡有會議的紀錄。總而言之，我們與其談判獲得了很優厚的條件，並草擬了合約。雖然敲定的一些細節費了點周折，但我們仍有成就感。我把合約已經寄到您的電子信箱，請您核准。

A：好極了！

B：這裡還有些您要的報告。我也完成了您想要做的分析。要我寄電子郵件給您嗎？

A：不，沒有必要。只是確認你的分析結果發到部門。銷售指數怎麼樣？我希望一旦你掌握後，就能做給我一個財務審核。

B：這是來自我們部門的銷售數據。我已經完成了財務審核。如果您有什麼疑問，儘管問我。

A：哦，好！太棒了！

實境對話 2

A: I'm going to have to change my meeting schedule this afternoon. Please call Mr. Gilbert's secretary. I need to meet with him about the budget projections ASAP.

B: Don't worry about the appointment schedule. I made arrangements already. I took the liberty of arranging your meeting with Mr. Gilbert. Will 3pm be okay for you? If not, I can call to postpone the meeting.

A: Oh, great! Thanks! 3pm is fine. That will give me enough time to review our financial information.

B: I'd be happy to give you a summary of our financial department's situation. Let me give you a brief summary of what we've been up to this week.

A: Go ahead...

B: Here's an update of our budget projections. And we've also completed the internal audits.

A: Do you have a hard copy of that I can take with me to my meeting?

B: I've already thought of that. I've made a PPT presentation you can take with you and show them, and I've made several copies you can hand out.

A: I knew there was a reason I hired you!

A：我下午會議的時間必須要改了。請打電話給Gilbert先生的秘書。說我需要就預算規劃專案與他儘快碰面。

B：不必擔心會面時間，我都已經安排好了。在您與Gilbert先生會面的安排上，我爭取到安排自由。下午三點，您可以嗎？如果不行，我可以打電話延後。

A：哦，太好了。三點鐘就行。這樣我就有充分的時間來審閱我們的財務資料。

B：我很樂意給您一份我們財務部門情況總結。讓我簡單總結一下我們這個星期取得的進展。

A：請吧……

B：這是一份修正後的預算規劃。而且我們也完成了內部審核。

A: 你有沒有我可以帶到會議上的影本？

B：我已經想到了。我做了一個投影片簡報，您可以帶上秀給他們看，而且我複印了好幾份，您可以發給大家。

A：我就知道雇你肯定沒錯！

安排會面 Booking Appointments

很多的生意都是依靠（rely on）預約後的會面來發展的。透過線上工具預約也很常見。無論是服務業還是銷售業（sales or services），預約都已經成為辦公管理的必要部分。很多人透過日誌（log books）或者日程軟體來整理和記錄所有的預約資訊。

預約會面時間。

⊙When will you be available for your next appointment?
　您什麼時間方便下次會面？

⊙How is Wednesday, September 27th at 3pm?
　週三，9月27日下午3點怎麼樣？

⊙I would like to make an appointment to meet with Mr. Zimmer.
　我希望能夠和Zimmer先生安排會面。

⊙Can I help you schedule an appointment?
　我能幫您預約嗎？

⊙I'd like to set an appointment sometime this week. Tuesday is preferable.
　我希望能夠約到本週的某個時間。週二就比較合適。

⊙Do you have anything available for Saturday?
　週六您方便嗎？

⊙I'd rather have an earlier appointment, if possible.
　如果可能的話，我願意約得更早一些。

預約客戶

檢查自己的日程，並找到與客戶需求相吻合（suits）的時間。將該客戶的名字寫在日程表上，並註明要洽談的內容。

⊙Is it possible to get something sooner?
　有沒有可能提前些？

⊙Do you have anything else available in the afternoon?
　您下午有沒有合適的時間？

⊙Mr. Johnson is available to meet with you this week on Monday afternoon at 2pm or on Thursday morning at 9am. Will either of these times work for you?

Johnson先生在週一下午2點或週四早上9點方便與您會面。您哪個時間合適呢？

⊙I'm sorry, it seems this week is booked.

對不起，這個星期已經排滿了。

⊙This week we have an available opening on Friday morning. Would you prefer 9am or 10:30am?

這個星期五有一個比較合適的空檔。您願意約在早上9點還是10：30？

⊙How long do you expect your meeting to last?

您估計您的會議大致多長時間？

確認的形式

透過電子郵件或電話預約，電子郵件上可註明「座位有限，請速回執確認（an RSVP）」，並指明名額或座位只為其保留到某個時刻。將已經確認的出席者姓名和聯繫方式（contact information）登記造冊。

⊙To guarantee your placement, please respond to this invitation by January 15th.

為了保證您的位置，請在1月15日前回覆本邀請函。

⊙The meeting will be held on Monday, January 10th, at 2:00pm.

會議安排在1月10日，週一下午2點。

⊙As seating is limited, please RSVP by November 20th.

座位有限，請於11月20前回覆確認。

企業之間的預約

企業之間提供的服務（business-to-business service）透過電話預定。首先要查看公司網址（company websites）或者企業名錄（business directories），確認你所感興趣的部門主管姓名。上班時間（business hours）打電話並且指名要和某人講話。在推銷（sales pitches）服務和諮詢的預約過程中，要考慮到對雙方都適宜的時間。所有的預約時間都要詳細整理並記錄。

⊙Hello, may I please speak to Ted Johnson? This is Emily Brown calling from Stevens Consulting. I'd like to speak to Mr. Johnson in regards to an upcoming consultation.

　您好，我可以和Ted Johnson先生通話嗎？我是史蒂文斯諮詢公司的Emily Brown。我想向Johnson先生了解一些事情。

⊙We'd like to offer you a free consultation next week.

　我們希望能夠在下週為您提供一個免費的諮詢。

⊙Please let us know when you are available.

　請告知我們您什麼時間比較方便。

總結

無論是發展潛在客戶、列席會議或宴會，還是尋求服務，都應考慮到別人的日程，照顧到自己的時間。一旦確認，就應當登記在案，整理說明。在「時間就是金錢」的現代社會，在有著「一諾千金」的文化傳統國度裡，「爽約」實在是令人不齒的事情。

單字表

anticipate 預期；預料	consultation 諮詢
either 或者；也	engagement 約會；約定

111

however 然而；但是

opening 空隙；缺口

prefer 更喜歡；傾向

schedule 時間表；日程

upcoming 即將

last 持續

possible 可能的

preferable 更好的；更傾向的

sooner 更早；更快

weekend 週末

片語表

arrange an appointment 安排會見

fit (sb.) in 適合（某人）

get something 獲得某物；得到某物

I'd hate to have you (do sth.) 我不願意看到你（做某事）

in regards to 問候

meet with 會見；遇見

schedule an appointment 安排預約

set an appointment 安排約會

work (sb.) in 想方設法安排

work (for sb.) （為某人）工作

double-booked 重複預定

for nothing 徒勞地；白白地

I'd be happy to help you. 我很樂意幫助你。

I'd rather... 我寧願……

make it 達到目的；獲得成功

offer (someone) an hour 提供（給某人）一個小時

take a call 接電話

under an hour 一個小時內

實境對話 1

A: Can I help you schedule an appointment? When will you be available? How is Wednesday, September 27th at 3pm?

B: Is it possible to get something sooner? I'd rather have an earlier appointment if possible. I'd like to set an appointment sometime this week. Tuesday is preferable.

A: For this week? Let me see... Mr. Johnson is available to meet with you this week on Monday afternoon at 2pm or on Thursday morning at 9 am. Will either of these times work for you?

B: Well, I can't make it Monday. Do you have anything else available in the afternoon? I am not able to come in the mornings.

A: I'm sorry. It seems this week is booked!

B: Is there no way to work me in?

A: If it were possible, I would be happy to help you. However, Mr. Johnson is already double-booked, and even on some afternoons, triple-booked. I'd hate to have you come to the office for nothing if he is unavailable to meet with you.

B: How about the weekend? Do you have anything available for Saturday?

A: Well. How long do you anticipate your meeting will last? I can offer you an hour on Saturday, but if you need longer, I won't be able to fit you in until next week.

B: Well, I suppose it will have to be Saturday then.

A：我能幫您安排一個會面嗎？您什麼時間比較方便？週三，9月27日下午3點怎麼樣？

B：可能更早些嗎？我覺得越早越好。我希望能夠安排到本週的某個時間。週二就比較合適。

A：這個星期？讓我看一下……Johnson先生本週在週一下午2點或週四早上9點方便與您會面。您哪個時間合適呢？

B：週一，我不行。下午有沒有合適的時間啊？早上的時間我來不了。

A：對不起，這個星期都已經排滿了。

B：就沒有合適我的時間嗎？

A：如果有可能，我一定樂意幫助您。但是，Johnson先生（的時間）很多都被重複預定，有些下午甚至是三重預約。我實在不願意讓您白跑一趟我們辦公室。

B：那週末怎麼樣？週六是否有合適的時間呢？

A：那您的會面預計要多長時間？週六我能安排一個小時，但如果您需要更多的時間，我就只能安排到下週了。

B：那，我想就只能安排到週六了。

實境對話 2

A: Hello, Johnson and Sons, Can I help you?

B: Hello, may I please speak to Ted Johnson? This is Emily Brown calling from Stevens Consulting. I'd like to speak to Mr. Johnson in regards to an upcoming consultation.

A: I'm sorry. Mr. Johnson is not available to take your call. I can help you arrange an appointment with him, however.

B: That would be wonderful. I would like to make an appointment with Mr. Johnson. We'd like to offer a free consultation next week. Please let us know when he is available.

A: This week we have an available opening on Friday morning. Would you prefer 9am or 10:30am?

B: 10:30 would be fine, thank you.

A: You're welcome. How long do you expect your meeting to last? Mr. Johnson has another engagement at 11:30.

B: Our presentation should be under an hour.

A: Very well. I will schedule you for 10:30-11:30 on Friday morning.

B: Thank you very much.

A：您好，詹森父子公司。有什麼可以幫您的？

B：您好，我可以和Ted Johnson先生通話嗎？我是史蒂文斯諮詢公司的Emily Brown。我想向Johnson先生了解一些諮詢的事情。

A：對不起，Johnson先生現在不方便接聽您的電話，但是我能幫您安排一個和他的會面。

B：那太好了。我非常願意和Johnson先生預約，我們很樂意下週為他提供一個免費的諮詢。請告知我們他什麼時間比較方便。

A：這個週五的早晨有一個合適的空檔。您願意約在早上9點還是10：30？

B：10：30可能會好些，謝謝您。

A：沒問題。您估計您的會面大致要多長時間？Johnson先生在11：30另外有約。

B：我們的介紹應該在一個小時之內。

A：好的。那我就為您安排在週五的早上10：30至11：30。

B：非常感謝您。

安排上司行程 Creating an Itinerary for the Boss

對於老闆來說，沒有任何一種情景比秘書或行政助理（administrative assistant）把他的出差行程弄得混亂不清更頭痛的了。「我這次又得去哪裡？」、「我需要幾點鐘到那裡？」、「我要見誰？」、「幾點車來接我？」透過一兩頁紙（取決於行程的長短）就可以囊括所有出差者必備的資訊（need to know）。

詳盡合理的行程安排，能讓上司安心出門而無後顧之憂。

⊙Here's your itinerary for tomorrow. Please let me know if you have any questions.

這是您明天的行程安排。如果有什麼疑問，儘管問我。

⊙Don't worry about the details, I have you covered.

不用擔心細節問題，我都為您安排好了。

⊙Your flight information is here, I've already called to confirm, the plane is on schedule.

您的航班資訊在這兒，我已經打電話確認過了，飛行計畫正常。

⊙Don't forget your itinerary. It will keep you on track.

別忘了您的行程安排，它會保證您的一切都井然有序。

⊙Mr. Larson, if you would please review these travel documents and make sure the information is correct.

Larson先生，如果您願意，可以確認一下您的旅行相關文件。

⊙Let me know if I can help you with anything.

如果有什麼可以幫助您的，請告訴我。

和老闆討論出行計畫

去哪裡？什麼時候去？是否需要住宿（overnight stays）？和誰舉行會談？會議安排在什麼時間（scheduled）？掌握了上述重點之後，就可以親自（by hand）或者透過旅行社來預定機票和飯店（book the flights and the hotel），並記錄下相關的聯絡號碼。

⊙When would you like to leave? What return dates are you looking at?

您希望什麼時間出發？回程時間您看哪天合適？

⊙How many days should I book your hotel for? Will you require any additional accommodation?

我該為您預定幾天的飯店？您是否要多待幾天？

⊙How long do you anticipate your Monday meeting with the stockholders will be?

您估計週一和股東的會議要多長時間？

⊙Is there anything else you would like me to put on your schedule for Tuesday?

還有什麼別的事情要我安排在您週二的日程上嗎？

行程安排包含什麼？

一份行程應當包含航班班次、機場、航站大廈、起飛時間（departure time）、抵達的機場、抵達時間（arrival time）、到達後的地面交通（ground transportation）、接機時間地點（pickup time and place）和聯絡人、聯繫方式。如果有什麼可能的滯留（layover），也應當將資訊包含在你的行程安排之中，即便是遇到延誤（delay），老闆也不會不知所措。

⊙I'd like to order an airline ticket with the departure city of Dallas, arrival city of New York.

我想幫為您訂從達拉斯起飛，紐約降落的航班。

⊙On the first leg of your trip, from Beijing to Tokyo, expect a three hour layover in the Narita airport.

您飛行的第一段是從北京到東京，預計在成田機場停留3個小時。

⊙Charles Heaton from Builtmore Inc. will pick you up at the JFK airport in New York. His cell phone number is 907-555-1294.

Builtmore公司的Charles Heaton將在紐約的甘迺迪機場接您，他的手機號碼是907-555-1294。

⊙You should arrive in Munich by 4pm.

您將於下午4點抵達慕尼黑。

飯店的細節

確認你預定的飯店是老闆比較喜歡的（prefers）。包含飯店的名字、地址和電話號碼，還有預定確認號碼（confirmation number），還可以註明房型（type of room）。

⊙I've booked a standard non-smoking room at the Marriot hotel. Will that arrangement be acceptable?

我為你訂的是在萬豪飯店的一間禁菸的標準房，這樣的安排行嗎？

⊙Would you prefer a queen sized bed? I could even try to upgrade to a king sized, if you require.

您希望大床嗎？如果您要求的話，我甚至可以升級成特大床。

⊙The Hilton is a five minute drive from the airport. After Mr. Heaton picks you up, you should arrive at the hotel in plenty of time for your first meeting.

希爾頓飯店距離機場有5分鐘的車程。在Heaton先生接到你以後，您有足夠的時間抵達飯店參加您的首場會議。

總結

為老闆安排行程是件需要很細心的工作，要設身處地考慮他將遇到的情況，哪怕是些細節。準確估算時間和距離，同時也要考慮到老闆辛苦勞累的程度，這樣不僅能表現你的責任心，還能展現你的細心周到。

單字表 ....

acceptable 可接受的	accommodation 住宿
additional 額外的；附加的	anticipate 預期；預料
conference 會議；會談	flight information 航班訊息
full 慢的；完整的	non-smoking 無煙的；禁止吸菸的
overnight 隔夜的	prefer 傾向；更喜歡
require 要求；需要	standard 標準
stockholders 股東	transfer 轉移；轉讓

Phrases
片語表

book a flight 預定航班
worry about... 擔心……
king sized 特大號（床）；豪華（間）
make arrangements 安排
on schedule 如期；按時
plenty of (sth.) 大量的（東西）
put together 放在一起
return flight 回程航班
standard room 標準房
why don't you (do sth.) 你為什麼不（做某事）

book a hotel room 預定飯店
keep (sb.) on track 與（某人）保持聯繫
look at 看；瞅
make your way 安排您去
be packed with... 擠滿/裝滿……
put (sth.) on the schedule 將（某事）列在行程表上
red-eye flight 紅眼航班；隔夜飛行
that will be all 就是這些；到此為止
travel arrangements 出差/旅行安排

實境對話 1

A: Sarah, did you make my travel arrangements for the conference?

B: Yes, Mr. Jacobs. Here's your itinerary for tomorrow. Please let me know if you have any questions. Don't worry about the details, I have you covered.

A: What time does my plane leave tomorrow morning?

B: Your flight information is here, I've already called to confirm, the plane is on schedule. Don't forget your itinerary. It will keep you on track.

A: Yes, thank you Sarah.

B: I've already booked your room for tomorrow night, but how many days should I book your hotel for? Will you require any additional accommodation?

A: I only need the days of the conference.

B: In that case, your arrangements have already been made. I've booked a standard non-smoking room at the Marriot hotel. Will that arrangement be acceptable?

A: Yes, thank you.

B: How long do you anticipate your Monday meeting with the stockholders will be?

A: It should be finished before lunch.

B: Excellent. You will have plenty of time to make your way to the airport for your return flight. Is there anything else you would like me to put on your schedule for Tuesday?

A: No. That will be all.

A：Sarah，你安排好我參加研討會的行程了嗎？

B：安排好了，Jacobs先生。這是您明天的行程安排。如果還有什麼疑問，儘管問我。不用擔心細節問題，我都為您安排好了。

A：我明天早上幾點的飛機？

B：您的航班資料在這兒，我已經打電話確認過了，飛行計畫正常。別忘了您的行程安排，它會保證您的一切井然有序。

A：好的，謝謝你Sarah。

B：我已經為您預定了明晚的房間，只是我需要訂幾天的？您要多住幾天嗎？

A：研討會期間就可以了。

B：如果是這樣的話，您的安排都已經做好了。我在萬豪飯店為您訂了一間禁菸的標準房，這樣安排可以嗎？

A：好的，謝謝你。

B：您預計週一和股東的會議要多長時間？

A：應該在午餐前結束。

B：好極了，在您前往機場搭乘回程航班之前，您會有很充足的時間。還有什麼事情要我安排到您週二的日程上的嗎？

A：沒有，就這些了。

實境對話 2

A: Edward, could you please come here for a minute. I need you to put together my itinerary for my trip to New York.

B: Certainly. When you would like to leave? What return dates are you looking at?

A: My meeting is Wednesday morning.

B: Your schedule for Tuesday is already full, so I suggest either flying the red-eye Tuesday night, or trying for an early flight Wednesday morning. Which would you prefer?

A: I would rather get a good-night's sleep so I can be fresh for the meeting. Can you book an early flight? I will have to be at the meeting by 10am.

B: I will call the airlines and see what I can do. Will you require accommodations Wednesday night?

A: Yes, the whole day will be packed with meetings, so I will stay in New York overnight and return the following morning.

B: The Hilton is a five minute drive from the airport. If I can book you the earliest flight, you should arrive at the hotel in plenty of time for your first meeting.

A: Excellent.

A：Edward，你能來這裡一會兒嗎？我需要你安排一下我去紐約的行程。

B：好的。您希望什麼時候出發？回程時間您看哪天合適？

A：我是週三早晨的會議。

B：您週二的行程已經滿了，所以我建議可以搭乘週二晚上紅眼航班，或選擇週三早晨的航班。您覺得哪個合適？

A：我傾向睡個安穩覺，頭腦清晰地參加會議。你能幫我訂早班機嗎？我上午10點得參加會議。

B：我會打電話給航空公司看能怎麼辦。您需要週三晚上的飯店住宿嗎？

A：是的，開一整天的會，所以我晚上會在紐約過夜，第二天早上回來。

B：希爾頓飯店距機場只有5分鐘的車程。如果我能夠幫您預定到最早的航班，
您就可以在第一場會議之前抵達飯店，時間比較寬裕。

A：好極了。

訂購辦公用品 Ordering Office Supplies

有鑑於辦公用品的損耗總是比我們想像得快，訂購辦公用品就成為秘書或助理必
要的功課。從商業角度來看，大量購買是最實惠（cost-effective）最有效的方式。

訂購前，先要統計缺什麼，什麼型號，數量多少。

⊙Are we out of staples again?
我們的訂書針又用完了嗎？

⊙I've checked the supply cabinet, I think it's time to make another order.
我剛檢查了文具櫃，我想該訂購了。

⊙There should be at least four reams of paper left before we need to call
the vendor again.
在我們再次打電話叫供應商之前，我們至少應該還有4令紙。

⊙What size of envelopes do you prefer?
您要什麼規格的信封？

⊙I need standard A4 size.
我要A4大小的。

⊙Let me know if I can help you with anything.
如果有什麼我能幫忙的，就儘管告訴我。

組織

專人專項定期檢查辦公用品的庫存（periodic inventories）情況，根據各項用品的損耗快慢，定期訂購。這樣既可避免重複訂購，又可以保證及時供應。

⊙ What's our inventory look like?
　我們的庫存情況怎麼樣？

⊙ Please prepare an inventory of our office supplies and have it on my desk by Monday.
　請準備一份我們辦公用品的清單，並在週一放到我的辦公桌上。

⊙ Ordering office supplies is the responsibility of the secretarial staff.
　訂購辦公用品是秘書人員的職責。

⊙ If you run out of office supplies or find our current supply lacking, please contact Jean Smith for requests and reorders.
　如果你辦公用品用完了，或者發現供應短缺，請向Jean Smith反映，要求重新訂購。

訂購方式

訂購辦公用品（placing orders）通常有兩種途徑：電話訂購或線上訂購。電話訂購的優點是有相關聯絡人（personal contact）負責，比較熟悉情況，熟悉訂購的種類。網路訂購的好處是可以根據公司網頁（company website）選擇產品種類，及時了解庫存情況，掌握送貨進度。

⊙ I'd like to make an order for supplies. We need 50 reams of paper, 10 boxes of legal sized self-adhesive envelopes, 10 boxes of ball-point pens, and 5 boxes of paperclips.
　我想訂購辦公用品。我們需要50令紙，10盒標準尺寸的背膠信封，10盒圓珠筆和5盒迴紋針。

⊙How soon will we receive our shipment?

多久我們能收到貨？

⊙Can you offer us any discounts?

你們能給我們打折嗎？

⊙We need both A4 paper and new ribbon for the printers.

我們需要A4紙和新的印表機色帶。

標準

為了保證辦公用品的有效利用和管理，有必要對辦公用品的採購實行標準化和制度化管理。例如，專人專項負責辦公用品供給保養（to maintain office supplies），根據實際使用情況提出一定時期內的購買預算。一定時期內（月、季或年）購買次數和總額要有限定。和供應商簽訂供應合約（contracted office supply vendor）以取得最實惠的價格。同時，固定的供應商也能了解公司辦公用品的損耗情況，可定期提供服務。

⊙Your monthly supply budget should not exceed $500. Please submit all receipts for office supply purchases to the Finance department for reimbursement.

你們的月供應預算不應當超過500美元。請把所有的辦公損耗發票交給財務部門報銷。

⊙Company policy says we can not exceed 3 orders of business supplies per month.

公司的政策是一個月內不能訂購辦公用品3次以上。

⊙The maintenance on our copy machine is under contract, so please contact our vendor for another toner cartridge.

我們影印機的保養還在合約的有效期內，請聯繫廠商為我們提供另外一個炭粉匣。

總結

為了避免突如其來的「彈盡糧絕」，或者沒有必要的浪費和無效利用，對於辦公用品的需求應當做到早調查、早預算、早安排；與固定的供應商簽訂合約，定期檢查、定期訂購。

單字表

ball-point pen 圓珠筆	copy machine 影印機
copy paper 影印紙	correction fluid 修正液
correction tape 修正膠帶	double-sided tape 雙面膠帶
dry-erase pens 可擦寫白板筆	duct tape 膠帶
envelope 信封	eraser 橡皮擦
fax machine 傳真機	fax paper 傳真紙
felt-tip pen 簽字筆	file cabinet 文件櫃
hanging file folder 懸掛式資料夾	highlighter pen 螢光筆
invisible tape 透明膠帶	legal pad 記事本
writing pad 信紙	marker 標籤
masking tape 封口膠帶	memo pad 便條簿
notebook 筆記本	paper clips 迴紋針
pencil 鉛筆	post-it flag 標籤貼
post-it note 便條紙	printer cartridge 印表機墨水匣
printer 印表機	ring binder 活頁夾
scissor 剪刀	staple 釘書針
stapler 釘書機	toner cartridge 碳粉匣

片語表 ··

be in a state 在……情況之下   be out of stock 沒有存貨

get on the ball 機靈些；機敏些 give (sb.) a deal 給（某人）待遇

實境對話 1

A: Are we out of staples again?

B: I've checked the supply cabinet. I think it's time to make another order.

A: We can't make another order so soon... Company policy says we can not exceed 3 orders of business supplies per month. Plus, there should be at least four reams of paper left before we need to call the vendor again. How many are there now?

B: Just two, I think.

A: Well, that's no good. What's the rest of the inventory look like?

B: I don't know, but we need both A4 paper and new ribbon for the printers. And the copy machine is out of toner again.

A: The maintenance on our copy machine is under contract, so that means we have to contact our vendor for another toner cartridge.

B: So our copier doesn't work, we're out of paper for the fax machine, and we're almost out of copy paper. Didn't anyone make any orders?

A: Ordering office supplies is the responsibility of the secretarial staff. Maybe we should ask them.

B: Good idea. They'd better get on the ball and make a call to our office supplier. In the state we're in, it's a wonder that anyone is getting any work done around here!

A：我們的訂書針又用完了嗎？

B：我剛檢查了文具櫃，我想該再次訂購了。

A：我們不能這麼快又訂購……公司的政策是一個月內不能訂購辦公用品3次以上。此外，在我們再次打電話叫供應商之前，我們至少應該還有4令紙。我們現在還有多少？

B：我想只有2令。

A：那可不太妙。剩下的庫存情況怎麼樣？

B：我不知道，但是我們需要A4紙和新的印表機色帶。而且影印機的碳粉又用完了。

A：我們影印機的保養合約還在有效期內，那意味著我們得聯繫我們的銷售商為我們再提供一個碳粉匣。

B：影印機故障，傳真紙用完了，而且影印紙也快用完了。就沒有人去訂購嗎？

A：訂購辦公用品是秘書人員的職責，也許我們應當找他們。

B：好主意。他們最好快點打電話給供應商。照目前情況來看，誰要是能把工作做完才真的是奇蹟呢！

實境對話 2

A: I'd like to make an order for supplies. We need 50 reams of paper, 10 boxes of legal sized self-adhesive envelopes, 10 boxes of ball-point pens, and a 5 boxes of paperclips.

B: You wanted legal sized self-adhesive envelopes? And what size of paper do you prefer?

A: Yes, that's correct. I need standard A4 size.

B: I'm sorry. The self-adhesive envelopes are currently out of stock. I have regular legal sized envelopes, will that be okay?

A: I suppose. How soon will we receive our shipment?

B: It should arrive within five to ten business days.

A: Can you offer us any discounts?

B: We are having a discount on fax machine paper. Normally they run five dollars per roll, I can give you a deal for three dollars.

A: Okay, we'll take 5 rolls of fax paper while we're at it.

B: Okay, I've got your order.

A：我想訂購辦公用品。我們需要50令紙，10盒標準尺寸的背膠信封，10盒圓珠筆和5盒迴紋針。

B：您想要的是標準尺寸背膠信封嗎？還有您要多大尺寸的紙？

A：對，沒錯。我要標準的A4紙。

B：對不起，標準尺寸背膠信封目前沒有存貨了。我有普通標準信封，可以嗎？

A：我想可以。多久我們能收到貨？

B：應該在5到10個工作日內。

A：你們能給我們打折嗎？

B：在傳真紙上我們可以給折扣。通常是5美元1卷，我給您3美元1卷。

A：好的，按照這個折扣我們要5卷。

B：好的，我已經確認您的訂單。

討論辦公設備 Discussing Office Equipment

辦公設備是你工作的忠誠夥伴。熟悉掌握不同辦公用品的名稱和使用方法，對於提高工作效率有著直接的影響。讓我們一起來認識一下這些與你的工作息息相關的工具吧！

辦公室格局

好的辦公室格局能使得辦公者精力集中（concentrate）。辦公桌上的用品一應俱全。電話（telephone）和傳真（fax machine）在辦公桌的右邊，電腦

在桌的中央，螢幕（monitor）正對著工作者，辦公座椅舒適（comfortable office chair）。一個櫃子抽屜（cabinet drawers）裡面有許多稿紙，另外一個抽屜裡有釘書機和訂書針、迴紋針、螢光筆、筆和橡皮擦（staples and a stapler, paper clips, highlighters, pens and erasers）等。房間內有舒適的沙發和扶手椅（armchair），在沙發的前面可以擺放一個沙發桌，放些企業雜誌（industry magazines）或飲品。

⊙This is my personal office. It's got a great view.
這是我的個人辦公室，視野很開闊。

⊙Which cubicle is yours?
哪個房間是您的？

⊙Can I put in for a new office chair? Mine isn't very comfortable.
我能換張新的辦公椅嗎？我的這張不怎麼舒服。

⊙We all need new office furniture.
我們都需要新的辦公傢俱。

⊙Office policy limits the display of personal artifacts on your desk to one photo or memento.
辦公室規定：辦公桌上的私人展示品僅限一張照片或一個紀念品。

⊙The coffee maker is on the fritz. We should have somebody look at it.
咖啡機有問題，我們應該叫人來看一下。

⊙We've got three potted plants that need to be watered daily.
我們每天要幫三盆植物澆水。

⊙Please be careful not to spill coffee on my sofa.
請當心別把咖啡濺到我的沙發上。

⊙The company gives all employees an office furniture allowance of $200.
公司給每個員工200美元的辦公傢俱津貼。

與電腦連接的設備

電腦連接印表機（printer）。印表機有不同的類別，大部分辦公室選用的是噴墨式印表機（ink jet printer）或者雷射印表機（laser printer）。電腦也可以和掃描器（scanner）相連，掃描器可以將文字檔和圖像轉化為數位資料（digital data）。大部分辦公室電腦都連接網際網路（Internet）。你的電腦可以連接網路線，或者透過外接數據機（external modem）和整合式服務數位網路卡（ISDN card）來連接網際網路。在比較大的辦公室，各個電腦可以通過電腦網路（computer network）相互連接。

⊙Can you help me hook up my new desktop?
　您能幫我接一下我的新桌上型電腦嗎？

⊙I think there's a glitch in the operating system.
　我覺得作業系統可能有故障。

⊙What is the name of your computer on the network?
　您的電腦在網路上的名字是什麼？

⊙Can you save the file in a sharing folder?
　能否把檔案存到共享資料夾嗎？

⊙The server is down at the moment, but the IT guys are working on it.
　現在伺服器已經關閉，IT人員正在修理呢。

⊙Would you mind scanning in the forms for me?
　你介意幫我掃描這些表格嗎？

總結

「工欲善其事，必先利其器。」現代辦公設備琳琅滿目、種類繁多，但都是快節奏的辦公所需要的。在商場如戰場的緊張工作中，能對所有的辦公設備都得心應手，那一定會提高效率，避免貽誤商機。

單字表

armchair 扶手椅

computer screen 電腦螢幕

cubical 立方；辦公隔間/工作間

drawer 抽屜

ISDN (integrated services digital)

network 綜合服務數位網路

modem 解調器；數據機

office equipment 辦公設備

operating system 作業系統

paper cutter 切紙機；切紙刀

paperclip 迴紋針

stapler 釘書機

telephone 電話

cabinet 櫃子；櫥

copy 影印

desktop 桌面；桌上型電腦

ink jet printer 噴墨印表機

laptop 手提電腦

laser printer 雷射印表機

monitor 顯示器

office furniture 辦公傢俱

overhead projector 高架投影儀

paper shredder 碎紙機

scanner 掃描器

swivel chair 轉椅

windows 窗戶；視窗

片語表

covert text and images into digital data 將文字檔和圖像轉為數位資料

potted plant 盆栽植物

office flora 辦公室植物

on the fritz 有故障

start the computer 開啟電腦

實境對話 1

A: Welcome to our team. Let me show you around the office.

B: Thanks. Which cubicle is yours?

A: This one over here. Your cubicle is right across the way. See, here we are.

B: Wow, it's pretty cozy. Can you help me hook up my new desktop?

A: Sure… Here we are. Wait a second. I think there's a glitch in the operating system. I'll try to fix it by going through the network to my computer.

B: What is the name of your computer on the network?

A: Oh, it's just listed under my name. "Bob's Computer". Easy to find. Nope, it looks like I can't even get into windows… Looks like your computer has some serious problems.

C: No, I don't think it's his computer. The server is down at the moment, but the IT guys are working on it.

A: Well, while we're waiting, why don't you take your office chair for a test drive?

B: (Sits down) Gee… Can I put in for a new office chair? Mine isn't very comfortable.

A: Haha. We all need new office furniture. See if you can get the boss to shell out the money.

B: Do you think I can put some of these desk references on my desk?

A: Books shouldn't be a problem. But office policy limits the display of personal artifacts on your desk to one photo or memento.

A：歡迎你加入我們的團隊。我帶你參觀一下辦公室吧。

B：謝謝。哪個辦公隔間是您的？

A：這邊這個就是。你的隔間走過去就是。看，就是這裡了。

B：哇，很舒服啊。您能幫我連接一下我的新桌上型電腦嗎？

A：當然……好了。等一下，我覺得作業系統可能有故障。我會透過網路從我的電腦那裡來修理一下。

B：您的電腦在網路上的名字是什麼？

A：哦，我把我的名字列在下面。「Bob的電腦」，很容易找。不會吧，好像連視窗都打不開……看來你的電腦問題比較嚴重。

C：不是的，我想不是電腦的問題。現在伺服器已經關閉了，但是IT人員正在修理呢。

A：那，你為什麼不趁我們等候的時間，試試你的辦公椅呢？

B：（坐下）哎呀……我能換張新的辦公椅嗎？我的這張不怎麼舒服。

A：哈哈，我們都需要新的辦公傢俱。就得看你能不能讓老闆掏腰包了。

B：我能放些參考書在我的辦公桌上嗎？

A：書應該沒有問題。但是辦公室規定，辦公桌上的私人展示品僅限一張照片或一個紀念品。

實境對話 2

A: Jane, could you follow me down to my office quickly? There's something I need your help with.

B: Sure. What can I do for you? Wow, is this your office? It's really nice.

A: Thanks. This is my personal office.

B: It's got a great view! And I love your sofa!

A: The company gives all employees an office furniture allowance of $200. I decided to buy a sofa and a coffee maker with some of the money. Would you care for coffee? Help yourself!

B: Thanks!

A: Oh, careful, please! Please be careful not to spill coffee on my sofa.

B: Sorry! It looks like your coffee maker is on the fritz. You should have somebody look at it. I love your flowers! How do you take care of them?

A: Sure takes care of the office flora. I've got three potted plants that need to be watered daily.

B: So what was it that you wanted me to help you with?

A: Oh yes, would you mind scanning in these forms for me? Can you save the files in a sharing folder?

A：Jane，你能跟我馬上去趟我的辦公室嗎？那裡有些事情需要你幫忙。

B：可以。我能為你做什麼？哇，這是你的辦公室嗎？真棒！

A：謝謝，這是我個人的辦公室。

B：視野真開闊！而且我實在太喜歡你的沙發了！

A：公司給了每個員工200美元的辦公傢俱津貼，所以我決定用一部分錢買了沙發和咖啡機。要喝咖啡嗎？自己來，別客氣！

B：謝謝！

A：哦，請小心！別把咖啡濺到我的沙發上。

B：對不起！好像你的咖啡機有問題，你應該叫人來看一下。我真喜歡你的花！你是怎麼照顧它們的？

A：辦公室植物當然得照顧。我每天還要幫三盆植物澆水。

B：那你要我幫你做什麼？

A：哦，對了，你介意幫我掃描這些表格嗎？能否把這些文檔存到一個共享資料夾裡？

填寫表格 Filling out Forms

填寫表格是國外旅行和國際貿易當中必備的技能。在你得到服務和產品（services and products）時，或者辦理各種手續時，通常都要求填寫表格。大部分表格都非常簡單。只要稍加練習，填寫什麼樣的表格都會易如反掌（second nature）。

無論如何，在你下筆之前，一定要先弄清楚表格要求填寫的內容。

⊙Please fill out this form in triplicate.
　請填寫該表格一式三份。

⊙Please answer the following questions for each person in your household.
　請每一位您的家庭成員回答如下問題。

⊙This question must be answered for all persons.

所有人員均需回答該問題。

⊙Please complete the form with black ink.

請使用黑色筆填寫此表格。

稱呼

幾乎所有的表格都會問你名字：

surname, last name 姓   given name, first name 名

middle name 中間名   middle initial 中間名簡寫

first initial 姓簡寫

稱呼：先生Mr. 夫人Mrs. 女士Ms. 小姐Miss 博士/醫生Dr.

⊙List surname first, followed by your given name.

先寫您的姓，再寫您的名。

⊙Use this space to write your middle initial.

在此空格填您的中間名。

⊙Please initial here.

請從此處開始。

⊙Write your full name, starting with your first name, middle name or

names, and last name. Do not use abbreviations.

寫您的全名，應先寫名，再寫中間名，最後寫姓。請不要簡寫。

出生資訊

出生資訊也經常見於表格，包括出生日期、出生地點、父母姓名、身分證字號、
護照號、社會安全碼。

⊙List your date of birth. Please use Month, Day, Year format (MM-DD-YY).

填寫您的出生日期。請按照月、日、年的格式（MM-DD-YY）。

⊙Write your birthday here, beginning with the year.

此處寫您的出生日期，以年作為開始。

⊙Put your social security number in this line.

在此行填寫您的社會安全碼。

⊙Print your mother's maiden name in these boxes.

在方框中填寫您母親的婚前姓。

常見資訊

還有一些常見資訊如：

國籍、民族或種族、性別（nationality, racial or ethnic origin, gender）

職業、教育背景、婚姻狀況、子女、聯絡資訊（occupation, educational background, martial status, children, contact information）

地址：通訊位址、永久位址、帳單地址（mailing address, permanent address, billing address）

電話號碼：夜間電話號碼、白天電話號碼、手機號碼（evening phone number, daytime phone number, mobile number)

⊙Please indicate your Nationality on this line.

請在此行填寫您的國籍。

⊙Check the appropriate box for race or ethnicity.

在合適的方框中選擇民族或種族。

⊙Complete your address, including mailing address if different from the address above.

填寫出您的地址，如果郵寄地址與上述地址不同，也請提供。

⊙Please provide a daytime phone number.

請提供您的白天（聯繫）電話號碼。

總結

無論是搭乘國際航班，還是銀行開戶；無論交個人所得稅，還是水電費，都要求填寫一張沒有半個小時就無法完成的表格。還好萬變不離其宗，寫過四五次，也會做到胸有成竹。

單字表

abbreviation 縮寫；簡稱

contact information 聯絡資訊；聯絡方式

daytime phone number 白天聯絡電話號碼

evening phone number 夜間聯絡電話號碼

gender 性別

given name 名字；起的名字

initial 初始的

maiden name 曾用名；婚前姓

marital status 婚姻狀況

middle name 中間名

nationality 國籍

passport number 護照號碼

place of birth 出生地點

social security number 社會安全碼

billings address 帳單地址

cramp 抽筋；痙攣

date of birth 出生日期

educational background 教育背景

ethnic origin 民族；種族

first initial 姓氏（首字母大寫）

first name 名字（歐美人姓名的第一個字）

identification 鑒定；身分

last name 姓

mailing address 通信地址；郵寄地址

middle initial 中間名

mobile number 手機號碼

occupation 職業

permanente address 永久地址

racial origin 種族來源

surname 姓

片語表 ···

How hard could it be? 它會有多難？　 wade through 艱難通過

take a look 看一下；瞧一瞧

實境對話 1

A: Yeesh! Have you seen these income tax forms? I have barely been able to wade my way through the first page! It's so complicated!

B: It can't be that bad. What information are they asking for?

A: Here, take a look.

B: "List surname first, followed by your given name. Use this space to write your middle initial." Well, that's not so bad at all. How hard can that be?

A: Keep reading...

B: "List your date of birth. Please use Month, Day, Year format (MM-DD-YY). Put your social security number in this line. Print your mother's maiden name in these boxes." I don't know what you're complaining about. This is all very basic stuff...

A: Well, except for my mother's maiden name. It's a little odd to ask for that.

B: "Complete your address, including mailing address if different from the address above."

A: Look at the next line.

B: "Please fill out this form in triplicate. This form must be filled out separately for each person in your household. Please complete the form with black ink." Wow, that's a lot of writing. Might get a cramp in your hand...

A：哎呦！您有沒有看過那些所得稅表？我剛硬生生把第一頁費力地讀完。太複雜了！

B：不會那麼糟糕吧。他們都要填寫什麼資料？

A：在這兒。看看吧。

B：「先填姓，接著填您的名。在此空填您的中間名」。根本就沒什麼。怎麼會那麼難呢？

A：繼續讀……

B：「填寫您的出生日期。請按照月、日、年的格式(MM-DD-YY)。在此行填寫您的社會保障號。在方框中填寫您母親的婚前姓」。我真搞不清楚你在埋怨什麼。這都是最基本的資料……

A：對，但是母親的「婚前姓」例外。問那個有點怪……

B：「填寫您的地址，如果郵寄地址與上述地址不同，也請提供。」

A：看下面一行。

B：「請填寫此表格一式三份。每位家庭成員必須分別填寫。請使用黑色筆填寫此表格。」哇！有好多要寫。手八成都要寫抽筋了……

實境對話 2

A: Excuse me. Do you think you could help me fill out this form? I am not sure how to do it.

B: Sure, no problem. Let me take a look. Okay, in this line write your full name, starting with your first name, middle name or names, and last name. It says not to use abbreviations.

A: Okay...

B: Put your passport number in this line.

A: Is that this line here?

B: Yes. Here they want you to check the appropriate box for race or ethnicity. You probably want to check the one that says Chinese.

A: Okay.

B: And you need to write the address of where you are staying here. Do you have a hotel?

A: No, not yet.

B: Well, I think they basically want a contact number or idea of where to reach you. Do you have any contact here in the USA?

A: Yes. My brother is picking us up at the airport. He lives here.

B: Well, write his information then. Do you have his phone number and address？

A: Yes, I do.

A：打擾您一下，我不知道您能否幫我填寫這個表格？我不確定該怎麼填。

B：當然，沒有問題。讓我看看。好的，在這條線上寫您的全名，先寫名，再寫中間名，最後寫姓。上面説不要用簡寫。

A：好的。

B：這條線上寫您的護照號碼。

A：是這條線嗎？

B：對。這兒他們希望透過適當的方框來確認您的民族或種族。您可能需要選擇「中國」的那個框。

A：好的。

B：您還需要填寫您在此地的停留住址。有飯店嗎？

A：沒，還沒有。

B：我想他們基本上是想要一個可以聯絡您的聯繫電話。您在美國有什麼聯絡方式嗎？

A：有的，我哥哥會在機場接我。他住在這裡。

B：好的，那就填他的資料。您有他的電話號碼和地址嗎？

A：是的，我有。

正式會議程序 Formal Meeting Procedure

會議的類型五花八門。但是，正式的會議（formal meeting）是在主席（chairman）主持下進行的。主持引導正式會議的大部分用詞都是公式化的（stylized），也就是說，一樣的話被用在所有的情景之中。當然，也分正式（formality）的程度。

會議開始

正式：

⊙Ladies and Gentlemen, I declare this meeting to be open.

　女士們先生們，我宣布本次會議開始。

非正式：

⊙Shall we start?

　我們開始嗎？

⊙Let's get started with our business for today, shall we？

　讓我們開始我們今天的議程，好嗎？

審查紀錄（Reviewing the Minutes）

正式：

⊙Could we get someone to move that the minutes of the last meeting be accepted?

　我們中有人願意提議接受上次會議的紀錄嗎？

⊙I so move we accept the minutes.

　我提議我們接受紀錄。

141

⊙Will we take the minutes as read?

　我們要讀一下紀錄嗎？

非正式：

⊙Has everyone seen the minutes?

　每個人都看過紀錄了嗎？

⊙May I read the minutes?

　我是否可以讀一下紀錄？

對照議程（Reviewing the Agenda）

⊙Could we add an item to the agenda?

　我們能否增加一項到議程中？

⊙I would like to delete item 3 from the agenda. Do we have a motion?

　我覺得應該將第三項從議程中刪除。大家有異議嗎？

⊙The first item on the agenda today is...

　我們今天議程的第一項是……

宣布會議的目的（Announcing the meeting's Purpose）

⊙The purpose of today's meeting is...

　今天會議的主要目的是……

⊙What we should consider first is...

　我們首先應當考慮的是……

給出發言權（Giving the floor）

會議主持人同意某會議出席人員發言。

正式：

⊙I would like to give the floor to Mr. Williams.

　我想將發言機會讓給Williams先生。

⊙David has the floor.

　請David發言。

非正式：

⊙What have you got to say about this Mary?

　Mary，對此您有什麼要説的嗎？

⊙Let's listen to what Jackson has to say.

　讓我們聽一下Jackson有什麼要説的。

要求發言（Taking the Floor）

正式：

⊙Excuse me, Mr. Chairman, may I say something please?

　對不起，主席先生，我能説點什麼嗎？

⊙With the Chair's permission, I would like to take up the point about...

　如果主席允許的話，我想接著關於……的話題。

非正式：

⊙I would like to say something here, please.

　請讓我就此説兩句。

⊙Can I make a point about...?

　我能否就……談談想法嗎？

結束一個主題（Finishing a Point）......................................

正式：

⊙Has anything further they wish to add before we move on the next item on the agenda?

在我們進入議程的下個題目之前，還有誰要補充的？

非正式：

⊙Anything else?

還有什麼嗎？

引導（Directing）...

當討論偏離主題的時候，以下語句可以用來引導與會者回到正題。

⊙Let's not loose sight of our main point.

我們別離題了。

⊙Let's get back to the issue under discussion.

讓我們回到討論的議題上吧。

⊙Are we getting sidetracked here?

我們是不是離題了？

通過議案（Passing a motion）.......................................

當某人有意推動形成某決定或制定某措施時，必須透過與會者對其議案進行表決。

⊙I move that...

我提議……

⊙I second the motion.

　　我支持該議案。

表決（**Vote**）

當與會者對某議案表決時，他們可以給出的回答有三種：是（Aye）、否（Nay）、棄權（undecided）。

⊙All in favor, say aye.

　　表示同意的，請説「是」。

⊙Any opposed?

　　有反對意見嗎？

維持秩序（**Keeping Order**）

正式：

⊙Mr. Laurence, you are out of order.

　　Laurence先生，現在不是您的發言時間。

⊙I shall have to call you to order, Mr. Michell.

　　我得提醒您注意秩序，Michell先生。

⊙Mr. Howard, would you please address your remarks to the Chair.

　　Howard先生，您是否可以向主席陳述您的評論。

非正式：

⊙We can't all speak at once. Ms. Peterson, would you like to speak first?

　　我們沒辦法同時都講。Peterson女士，您是否願意先説？

⊙Mr. Howard, you're talking out of turn.

　　Howard先生，現在不是您的發言時間。

總結

無論是正式的還是非正式的會議，都能夠按照固定程序有條不紊地進行，這樣就能最短的時間達成最多的成果。

單字表 ···

accept 接受

audit 審計；審核

dues 會費；稅款

inflation 通貨膨脹

minutes 會議紀錄

move (a movement) 提出；提議

oppose 反對

reflect 反射；反映

second (a movement) 支持；贊成

agenda 議程；議事日程

declare 聲明；宣布

extensively 廣闊的；廣泛的

membership 會員資格；成員

motion 運動；提議

nay 不；反對

rate 比率；費用

review 審核；複審

片語表 ···

be out of order 發生故障；秩序紊亂

financial reports 財務報告

hike up a rate 比例上升

open a meeting 會議開幕；會議開始

say aye 表示贊成

take up a point 接續話題

up for discussion 提出討論

worth our time 值得我們花時間

duly noted 充分注意到

fiscal year 會計年度；財政年度

in favor 贊成；支持

quite reasonable 相當合理；蠻划算的

strike from an agenda 從議程中刪除

talk out of turn 說話輕率；講話不合宜

vote nay 投反對票

實境對話 1

A: Ladies and Gentlemen, I declare this meeting to be open. Let's get down to business, shall we? Would someone please move that the minutes of the last meeting be accepted?

B: I so move that the minutes from the last meeting be accepted.

A: Any seconds?

C: I second the motion.

A: Great. Has everyone received a copy of the agenda? The first item up for discussion is to review the financial reports. The purpose of today's meeting is to complete the necessary preparations for the company audit. The first problem we should look at is our approved budget for the fiscal year.

B: Excuse me, Madam Chairman, may I say something please?

A: Mr. Williams, you have the floor.

B: Thank you. The approved budget for this fiscal year has already been extensively reviewed by all members of the financial department and has also received approval from our executive board. In my opinion, it is not necessary to spend much time reviewing them again in this meeting.

A: Your comments are duly noted. Does anyone else have anything further to add?

C: I move that the budget review item be struck from the agenda.

A: Mr. Carlson moves the agenda be revised, any second?

E: I'll second the motion.

A: All in favor say aye.

(Collective "aye")

A: Any opposed?

F: Nay.

A: Mr. Simmons, you vote nay?

F: Yes I do, Ms. Chairman. I believe it is still worth our time to review the budgets, even though they have already been reviewed.

A：女士們先生們，我宣布本次會議開始。讓我們進入正題，好嗎？我們中有沒有人願意提議接受上次會議的紀錄？

B：那我提議接受上次會議的紀錄。

A：有支持的嗎？

C：我支持。

A：好極了。每個人都拿到議程的影本了吧？要討論的第一項是審核財政報告。今天會議的主要目的是為公司的審計，完成必要的準備工作。第一個問題是我們要看會計年度已經通過了的預算。

B：對不起，主席女士。我能否說兩句？

A：Williams先生，請講。

B：謝謝。被批准的會計年度預算應當已經通過財務部成員的廣泛審核，而且得到了董事會的認可。在我看來，這次會議上就沒有必要再花那麼多的時間來複審了。

A：您的意見我們已經知道了。其他人還有什麼要補充的嗎？

C：我贊成「預算複審議」項從議程中刪除。

A：Carlson先生主張修改議程，有支持的嗎？

D：我贊成提議。

A：表示贊同的請表示（說是）。

（集體「贊成」）

A：有反對意見嗎？

E：反對。

A：Simmons先生，您投反對票？

E：是的，主席女士。即便他們審核過了，我覺得我們仍然有必要花時間再複審。

實境對話 2

A: With the Chair's permission, I'd like to take up the point about the increase of membership dues.

B: Ms. Learner, you have the floor.

A: I think the increase in membership dues is unreasonable. What increase of services do we receive for the increase in payment? Nothing!

C: That's not exactly true, Susan.

B: Mr. Howard, you're talking out of turn.

C: Sorry, but I just wanted to say, the increase is quite reasonable.

B: Let Ms. Learner finish.

A: Thank you, Mr. Chairman. As I was saying, the increase in cost does not reflect an increase in services, and so I move that we deny the increase.

B: Mr. Howard, would you like to say something?

C: The increase in fees is due to an increase in inflation. Members have been paying the same rate since for over twenty years now!

A: Exactly! So when you hike the rate up now, everyone will be upset!

B: Ms. Learner, you're out of order.

A：如果主席允許的話，我願意接著談增加會費的問題。

B：Learner小姐，您現在有發言權。

A：我覺得增加會費沒有任何道理。掏錢換來的增加服務表現在哪裡？什麼都沒有！

C：Susan，那不完全是真的。

B：Howard先生，還沒有輪到您發言。

C：對不起，我就是想說增加會費是合情合理的。

B：我們讓Learner小姐把話講完。

A：謝謝主席先生，正如我剛才所說，費用的增加沒有反映出任何服務的增加，所以我提議我們否定（會費）增加。

B：Howard先生，您有什麼要説的？

C：增加會費是因為考慮到通貨膨脹。同樣的費率會員們到現在已經付了20年了。

A：沒錯，那現在你大幅提高的話，大家都會失望。

B：Learner小姐，現在不是您的發言時間。

和同事建立良好關係
Building Relationships with Coworkers

和睦的同事關係（workplace relationships）可以讓你上班時間心情愉快；糟糕的同事關係可能讓你無法專心，甚至把一些差強人意（so-so）的工作搞得一塌糊塗、夢魇一般（nightmare）。一些交流的技巧可以幫助你和同事建立良好的關係。

首先，要友好，留心同事們的需要，樂於提供幫助和接受建議。

⊙How's it going?

怎麼樣了？

⊙How are you doing on (project)? Anything I can do to help?

在（專案）上做得怎麼樣？有什麼我能幫忙的嗎？

⊙How long have you worked here?

你在這裡工作多久了？

⊙What's your plan for lunch? Care to join me?

你午餐怎麼吃？願意和我一起去嗎？

⊙I brought in some doughnuts for our coffee break. Would you like one?

我帶了些甜圈圈，可以在喝咖啡時間吃，你想來一個嗎？

⊙Let me know if I can help you with anything.

如果有什麼我能幫忙的，就儘管告訴我。

尊重你的同事

互相尊重是友好關係的基礎（foundation）。儘量避免冒犯（avoid offending）你的同事。當然，如果碰上了容易得罪（easily offended）的人，那只能敬而遠之了。

⊙Please let me know if I've said or done anything to offend you. I can assure you, it was completely unintended.

如果我說了什麼冒犯你的話或者做了得罪你的事情，請一定要告訴我。我保證那絕對是無意的。

⊙I appreciate your work on (project). I feel like I can learn a lot from you.

我非常欣賞你在（某專案）上的工作。我覺得從你身上可以學到很多。

⊙Would you mind lending me a hand with...

您是否願意幫我……

⊙Don't worry about Anna, she's like that to everyone. Don't take it personally.

別擔心Anna，她對誰都那樣兒，別在意。

⊙Maybe he's having a bad day. We should give him some space.

可能他今天心情欠佳，我們應該多給他些空間。

⊙Don't hesitate to tell me if you don't feel comfortable with... I'll be happy to make special arrangements for you.

如果你對……感覺不舒服，儘管告訴我。我會很願意為你做一些特別的安排。

別討論讓你的同事感覺不舒服的話題

個人隱私、健康問題、政治、對工作或者個人生活的埋怨，都屬於應該盡量避免的話題（fall under the heading）。因為大部分人都會覺得這些話題是個人的隱私，不應該在辦公場合談論。如果有人和你聊起這些話題，你可以想辦法讓他知道你感覺不愉快，或者設法改變話題（change the subject）。

A : I had to go to the doctor yesterday to check up on my heart. You know, I've had this pain in my arm for the last few months. And I just got over the flu. So I still have a little cough. Well, I was worried about the cough being related to my diabetes, so I...

B: Wow, it sounds like you've had a lot of trouble with your health. I hope you feel better soon. So what were you saying about the marketing report?

A：我昨天不得不去找醫生檢查我的心臟。你知道，最近幾個月我手臂這塊一直痛。而且我流感剛好，所以還有點輕微的咳嗽。我一直都擔心咳嗽會不會影響到我的糖尿病，所以我……

B：哇，聽起來你最近身體欠佳。希望你能儘快好起來。我是想問一下你對行銷報告有什麼看法？

別道聽塗說，散布流言（Don't spread malicious gossip）

辦公室的流言蜚語（gossip）無非兩種。一種是小道消息（office grapevine），即使透過非正常管道獲得並在公司內部流傳的消息；另外一種是虛假資訊，或者即便是真的，也關係到個人隱私。無論哪種都應避免。

A: Did you hear? Barbara, who works as a secretary for Bob Jones, just got divorced from her husband. And I heard from Sally in finance that the reason might have to do with something going on between Barbara and Bob. Can you believe that?

B: Uh... It's probably not any of our business anyway. We'd probably better focus on our work rather than on talking about rumors which may or may not be true.

A：你聽説了嗎？Barbara，就是Bob Jones的秘書，剛和她老公離婚了。而且我還聽財務的Sally説，好像跟Barbara和Bob的事有關。你信嗎？

B：嗯……這可能不關我們的事。我們最好還是少説些是非不清的閒話，把注意力放在工作上。

總結

「關係」這個詞無論對哪種文化都有著特殊的意義，尤其是抬頭不見低頭見的同事關係。相敬如賓、樂於助人、真誠待人；對於那些性格怪癖的人物敬而遠之；對於流言蜚語做到濁者自濁、清者自清。相信我，這樣，你的同事就沒有不喜歡你的理由。

單字表

brief 簡介；短暫

complete 完成

doughnuts 甜甜圈

helpful 有幫助的

marketing 市場行銷

offer 提供

plan 計畫

rumor 謠言

standoffish 冷淡的；不友好的

coffee break 咖啡時間

diabetes 糖尿病

fault 錯誤

hesitate 猶豫

mention 提起；談起

orders 訂單；訂購

rough draft 草圖

several 幾個

swamped 淹沒

片語表 ··

care to (do sth.) 在意/願意（做某事）

do something to offend (sb.) 做某事冒犯/得罪某人

give (sb.) some space 給（某人）些空間

How are you doing on (a project)...? 在做……方面進展如何？

let (sb.) know 讓（某人）得知

now that you mention it 既然你提到了

be supposed to (do sth.) 應該（做某事）

take (sth.) personally 介意

check up on 檢查；校對

Do you think I could = Can I 我能否

figure it out 弄明白；搞清楚

have a bad / good day 有壞的/好的一天

have a minute 有空；有一分鐘（空閒）

just have to 只需要

lend a hand 幫個忙；伸援手

none of our business 不關我們的事

be related to 有關；和……有關係

trouble with (sth.) （某事上）遇到問題/麻煩

實境對話 1

A: Hi Jamie, how's it going? How are you doing on the office orders? Anything I can do to help?

B: I'm doing okay, thanks. The office orders are almost completed. In fact...there... I'm done. Thanks for offering to help. What's your plan for lunch? Care to join me?

A: I'm not hungry, actually. I brought in some doughnuts for our coffee break. I've eaten several of them already! Would you like one?

B: Uh, maybe later. You know, I was going to ask you about the work you did on the Martin account. Do you think I could get a copy of the brief? I think it would be helpful to me.

A: Oh, sure. I can give you a copy of it. Just let me know if I can help you with anything else.

B: Now that you mention it, would you mind lending me a hand with the marketing report. I am supposed to give the rough draft to Anna, but...

A: Don't worry about Anna. She's like that to everyone. Don't take it personally.

B: How did you know what I was going to say? I worried whether or not I said something to offend her because she has always been so standoffish to me.

A: How long have you worked here? If you haven't realized by now, you'll just have to figure it out. She just has good days and bad days. Maybe today she's having a bad day. We should give her some space.

A：你好，Jamie，還好嗎？辦公訂單做得怎麼樣？有什麼要我幫忙的嗎？

B：做得還算順利的，謝謝。辦公訂單差不多都完成了。事實上……就差……我做完了。謝謝你願意幫我。你午餐怎麼吃？願意和我一起吃嗎？

A：其實，我不餓。我為我們的咖啡時間帶了些甜甜圈，我已經吃了一些了，你要來一個嗎？

B：嗯，一會再説吧。你知道，我來是想問一下你做的有關Martin帳戶方面的事情。能給我一份概要的影本嗎？我想對我可能有幫助。

A：哦，當然。我可以給你一份影本。如果有什麼我能幫忙的，就儘管告訴我。

B：既然説到這兒了，能幫我看一下市場報告嗎？我得給Anna一份草稿，但是……

A：別擔心 Anna，她對誰都那樣。不用在意。

B：你怎麼知道我要説什麼？我還擔心是不是我説了什麼冒犯她的話，她總是對我愛理不理的。

A：你在這裡工作多久了？如果到現在你還沒有意識到的話，那你就真該弄明白。她時好時壞，也許今天她又心情欠佳。我們應該多給她些空間。

實境對話 2

A: Hi, Anna... Do you have a minute? I wanted to discuss something with you.

B: Well, I'm very busy. I have been so swamped. You know, I had to go to the doctor yesterday to check up on my heart. You know, I've had this pain in my arm for the last few months. And I just got over the flu. So I still have a little cough. Well, I was worried about the cough being related to my diabetes, so I...

A: Wow, it sounds like you've had a lot of trouble with your health. I hope you feel better soon. Anyway, what I want to ask you about is the marketing report. Have you finished looking it over yet?

B: Well, if that's all you wanted to know. I can't say whether I have or not. You know, it's not my fault that the secretary puts things in the wrong places!

A: So you're saying you haven't had a chance to look at the report yet?

B: Nope.

A: Anna, I sense that our communication hasn't been so effective. Please let me know if I've said or done anything to offend you. I can assure you, it was completely unintended. Don't hesitate to tell me if you don't feel comfortable with reviewing the reports. I'll be happy to ask someone else to do it.

B: Who else were you going to get to do it?

A: Barbara could do it.

B: Barbara? Bob Jones' secretary? Did you hear? Barbara just got divorced from her husband. And I heard from Sally in finance that the reason might have to do with something going on between Barbara and Bob. Can you believe that?

A: Uh... It's probably not any of our business anyway. We'd probably better focus on our work rather than on talking about rumors which may or may not be true.

A：嗨，Anna……有空嗎？我想和你聊聊。

B：那，我挺忙的，都有些應接不暇了。你知道，我昨天不得不去找醫生檢查我的心臟。你知道，最近幾個月我手臂這塊一直痛。而且我流感剛好，多少有些輕微的咳嗽。我一直都擔心咳嗽會不會影響到我的糖尿病，所以我……

A：哇，聽起來你最近身體欠佳。希望你能儘快好起來。不過，我就是想問一下你有關行銷報告的事。你已經看完了嗎？

B：哦，如果那就是你想知道的。我不能說我完成了沒有，你知道秘書把東西放錯地方了，這可不是我的錯！

A：你的意思是說你還沒來得及看報告？

B：還沒呢。

A：Anna，我感覺你我之間的溝通一直都不順暢。如果我說了什麼冒犯你的話或者做了得罪你的事，請一定要告訴我。我可以保證，那完全不是故意的。如果審核報告讓你感覺不舒服，請無需顧忌什麼，直接告訴我。我會很樂意換別的人來做。

B：你打算叫誰來做？

A：Barbara 能做。

B：Barbara？Bob Jones的秘書？你聽說了嗎？Barbara剛和她老公離婚了。而且我還聽財務的Sally說，好像跟Barbara和Bob的事有關。你信嗎？

A：嗯……這可能不關我們的事。我們最好還是少說些是非不清的閒話，把注意力放在工作上。

和主管討論問題
Discussing Concerns with Superiors

在工作中遇到問題在所難免。作何反應直接決定衝突是否能迅速有效（quickly and effectively）地解決。如果在辦公室處理時壓力重重（stressful），那去找老闆當面討論，可以作為一個不錯的選擇（take the initiative）。

走到主管面前時,首先要問他此刻是否有時間和你談話,開門見山地説明談話主題。

⊙I was wondering if you had a moment to discuss a concern I've been having with...
我想知道您是否有時間,跟我討論一件讓我很擔憂的事情。

⊙Can I talk to you for a minute? I'd like to bring up some issues that I need help to resolve.
我能和您聊一分鐘嗎?有一些事情我需要您的幫忙。

⊙I was wondering, is there anything we can do about...?
我就是想知道,關於……有什麼事情是我們可以做的?

⊙I have been working with a few challenges lately that I would appreciate your perspective on.
最近我工作上遇到了些挑戰,希望能夠得到您的指點。

⊙Can you give me some advice about what to do about...?
對於……該如何做,您能給我些建議嗎?

⊙Let me know if I can help you with anything.
如果有什麼我能幫的,就儘管告訴我。

評估事態

準確把握問題的嚴重程度(severity),確保(warrant)和老闆商談的必要性。商討前準備解決方案(potential resolutions),這足以表明你有能力分析事態並拿出解決之道。

⊙I was thinking, it might be possible to...
我在想,也許能夠……

⊙Maybe this problem could be solved by... What do you suggest?

也許這個問題可以透過……來解決。您的意思呢？

⊙Perhaps... could help resolve the issue. Do you think that is a good way to deal with it?

也許……有助於解決這個問題。您覺得那是處理這個問題的好辦法嗎？

⊙The way I see it, we could do X or Y. The benefits of X are..., but I also see drawbacks.

依我看，我們可以做X或者Y。X的好處在於……，但也有一些缺點。

⊙Can you give me some direction on this?

在這個方面您能給我什麼指示嗎？

誠實待己

大家都不喜歡犯錯，但勇於承認（acknowledge）錯誤有益於解決問題。把錯誤看作是學習和提高自己能力（job skills）的機會。

⊙I realize I might have contributed to this problem by... But I want to help solve the problem now.

我意識到可能是由於我……才造成這個問題。但是我現在想幫忙解決這個問題。

⊙Perhaps if I hadn't..., things might not have developed thus far. I didn't intend to make things worse, but now I want to make it better.

如果當時我沒有……，事態也許也不會發展到那步田地。我不是有意讓事態更加嚴重的，但是現在我希望能夠有所改善。

準備談話

選擇和老闆談話的合適時機，或請他安排一個適合（convenient）的時間。可以事先記錄下（jot down）要談的內容，收集相關資料作為實例。遵守會談邏

159

輯格式（logical meeting format），清晰地解釋問題，承認問題產生的原因，並請求建議。

A: What was the issue you wanted to talk about?

B: Our team is having problems meeting the deadline for our financial reports. I realize I might have contributed to the problem by being late in submitting our budget review. However, I think if we were able to delay some of the other projects and put them on the backburner while we move this project to the forefront, we should still be able to finish on time. Do you have any suggestions about how we can do that?

A：你有什麼問題想要談？

B：財務報告按時完工對我們組來說有困難。我意識到可能是由於我提出的預算審核晚了才造成這樣的問題。然而，我想如果別的專案能緩一緩，把它們挪後一點再把這個專案提前的話，我們是可以按時完成的。我們能這樣做嗎？對此，您有什麼建議嗎？

總結

當你遇到問題時，向主管請教他的見解是個不錯的選擇。為了避免被訓斥而歸，事先要做好準備工作，比如預備的解決方案、對產生問題的原因的分析等，並以充分的實例加以說明，最後問他「對此您怎麼看？」

單字表 ⋯⋯⋯⋯⋯⋯⋯⋯⋯⋯⋯⋯⋯⋯⋯⋯⋯⋯⋯⋯⋯⋯⋯⋯⋯⋯⋯⋯⋯⋯⋯

appreciate 感激；欣賞　　　　　　certainly 當然；確信無疑

challenges 挑戰　　　　　　　　　contribute 貢獻

deadline 時限；期限　　　　　　　flexible 靈活的；多變的

forefront 最前線；最前方

perhaps 或許；也許

realize 意識到

submit 提交

unproductive 無出產的；不毛的

grab 抓；抓取

perspective 透視

standoffish 冷淡的；不友好的

suggestion 建議

片語表

anything we can do 任何我們能做的

deal with 處理

have problems (doing sth.) （做某事）有困難

on time 準時

refuse to (do sth.) 拒絕做某事

resolve an issue 解決問題

this far 這麼久

Why don't you (do sth.) 你為什麼不（做某事）

crunch numbers 處理數據

give direction (on sth.) 在（某事上）給予指示

make things worse 使事情更糟

put (sth.) on the back burner 將（某物）保留；作為不重要的

the most I can do 我最多能做的

throw (sth.) out the window 某物扔出窗外

move back a deadline 往後調整最後期限

實境對話 1

A: Mr. Jones, I was wondering if you had a moment to discuss a concern I've been having with the financial reports. Can you give me some advice about what to do about our deadline?

B: Yes, I have a few minutes to spare now. Why don't you come down to my office with me and we can talk about it.

A: Great! Thanks! Let me grab my notes.

B: (In office) Now what was the issue you wanted to talk about?

A: I have been working with a few challenges lately that I would appreciate your perspective on. I was wondering, is there anything we can do about the deadline for the financial reports. Our team is having problems meeting the deadline. I realize I might have contributed to the problem by being late in submitting our budget review. However, I think if we were able to delay some of the other projects and put them on the backburner while we move this project to the forefront, we should still be able to finish on time. Do you have any suggestions about how we can do that?

B: Certainly we can't throw everything else out the window while you crunch numbers for the financial reports. I don't see your suggestion as feasible.

A: Maybe this problem could be solved by moving back the deadline. What do you suggest? Can you give me some direction on this?

B: The deadline is not very flexible. The most I can do is give you a couple extra days...

A: That just might be enough.

A：Jones先生，我想知道您是否有時間跟我討論關於財務報告的事？關於最後期限的問題，您能給我些建議嗎？

B：好的，我有幾分鐘的時間。你為什麼不來我的辦公室，我們可以聊聊。

A：好極了，謝謝！我拿上筆記本就去。

B：（辦公室裡）現在你有什麼問題要談？

A：最近我在工作中遇到了些挑戰，希望能夠得到您的指點。我就是想知道關於財務報告的最後期限，我們還有別的什麼可以做的嗎？按時完工對我們組來說有困難。我意識到可能是由於我提出的預算審核晚了才造成這樣的問題。然而，我想如果別的專案能緩一緩，把它們挪後一點再把這個專案提前的話，我們是可以按時完成的。我們能這樣做？對此，您有什麼建議嗎？

B：我們當然不能為了處理財務報告的數據而把別的都扔到一邊。我覺得這個建議不可行。

A：也許這個問題可以從放寬最後期限來解決。您的意思呢？在這件事情上能否給我們一些指示？

B：最後期限是定好的。我最多能給你幾天時間……

A：那應該就夠了。

實境對話 2

A: Do you have a minute? Can you give me some direction on something?

B: Sure. Come on in.

A: I was wondering, is there anything we can do about an unproductive employee? We've been having some communication problems between some of the members in our department. Several of the people in my department have been having trouble with Anna Smith. Since I work with her the most, I end up having most of the difficulties. She is now refusing to work with us.

B: Have you talked to Anna?

A: I was thinking it might be possible to solve this problem by talking to her directly, so yesterday I tried. Perhaps if I hadn't offended her yesterday when I asked her to finish the budget reviews, things might not have developed this far. I didn't intend to make things worse by talking to her, but now I want to make it better. Maybe this problem could be solved by transferring Anna to a different department. What do you suggest?

B: I will have to talk to Anna and also perhaps to some of the other members of the department to find out more about the situation.

A: Perhaps the Human Resources department could help resolve the issue. Do you think that is a good way to deal with it?

A：您有空嗎？您能否就一些事情給點建議？

B：當然。進來吧。

A：我想知道，對一個消極怠惰的員工，我們該怎麼辦？我們和部門內一些員工的溝通有問題。我們部門的幾個人都和Anna Smith有過節。在工作上，我和她接觸的機會最多，麻煩也最多。她現在拒絕和我們一起工作。

B：你和Anna談過了嗎？

A：我想過也許可以透過當面談來解決這個問題，所以昨天我試了一下。如果昨天我讓她完成預算審核時沒有冒犯她的話，事態也許不會發展到這步田地。我本無意把情況搞得更糟，現在我希望能夠有所好轉。也許把Anna調到別的部門可以解決這個問題。對此，您有什麼建議嗎？

B：我會和Anna還有部門其他同事談談，來了解更多的情況。

A：也許人力資源部可以解決這個問題，您覺得這是解決這個問題的好辦法嗎？

十項全能之六

高效組織會議

Meetings and Interviews

設計議程表 Designing an Agenda

會議議程表有助於與會者理解會議的目的（purpose）和內容，方便準備工作。議程表的內容應當簡明扼要、清晰易懂（understandable）。在會議召開的數日前，議程表就應該發出，讓與會人員有充足的時間（sufficient time）來準備。

如何才能將日程表準備得簡明扼要、清晰易懂呢？

⊙What is the purpose of our meeting today?
　今天會議的目的是什麼？

⊙Everybody, let's stay on track. Take a look at the agenda.
　各位，讓我們進入正題。來看一下議程表。

⊙I'm glad everyone could make it. Shall we start? First item on our agenda is...
　我很高興每個人都能來。我們可以開始了嗎？我們議程表的第一項是……

⊙Did you get a copy of the agenda for our meeting tomorrow? I sent it to your E-mail.
　你收到我們明天會議時間表的影本了嗎？我寄到您的電子郵件信箱了。

⊙There's a lot to talk about at the meeting on Tuesday. I hope the agenda makes matters clear.
　週二的會議要談很多內容。我希望議程表能夠讓人看得一清二楚。

⊙I didn't get a copy of the agenda yet. Could you resend it to me?
　我還沒有收到議程表的影本。您能再寄一次給我嗎？

會議時間

準備會議議程表的首要工作是選擇合適（appropriate）的會議時間。必須要確保所有的與會者都能準時出席；應當避免（avoid）在午餐後舉行會議，因為那個時候不太容易集中精神（hard to concentrate）；也應當避免在下班前開會，因為不能準時下班（on time），這不免讓人有些坐立不安。

⊙Can everyone come to the staff meeting on Thursday? It's scheduled for 11:00. If you can't make it, be sure to let me know ahead of time.

　每個人都能來參加週四的員工大會嗎？時間訂在11點。如果您不能出席，請提前通知我。

⊙How about setting our meeting for Friday at 2pm? Does that work for everyone?

　把我們的會議安排在週五下午2點如何？大家都能接受嗎？

⊙Let's begin our meeting around 3pm. That will give us plenty of time to finish our discussion before 5.

　我們下午3點左右開會。這樣，5點前我們就有足夠的時間來完成討論。

⊙Clear your schedules everyone. The boss has called a meeting for Monday morning, first thing.

　各位，請調整你們的議程表。老闆要求優先安排週一早晨的會議。

⊙I'm afraid if we hold the meeting at 1:30, everyone is going to be sleepy. Can we try for before lunch instead?

　我擔心如果我們1：30開會的話，大家都會想打瞌睡。我們能否調整到午餐前。

確認會議主旨

準備會議議程的第二步是確認會議主旨。應當在議程表中的醒目位置上用一句話來凸顯（highlight）會議的主旨，例如「主旨」（mission statement）一般列在議程的正上方。議程應當包含日期、時間、會議地點等重要的細節資訊。

⊙This meeting should accomplish working through all the financial issues for the merger project.

本次會議應完成合併專案的所有財務問題。

⊙Our game plan for the meeting on Wednesday, July 17th at 2:00pm is to...

我們對週三，7月17日下午2點的會議安排是……

⊙Our main objective for Monday's meeting is to... The meeting begins at 2:00 and will be held in conference room #405.

週一會議的主題是……會議訂在2點在405會議室召開。

⊙The purpose of this meeting is to examine marketing reports, budget reviews, and customer service evaluations. Please be prompt. Monday, September 27th, 10:00am, room 7B.

我們這次會議的目的是審查行銷報告、審核預算和評估客戶服務。請在9月27日，星期一的早上10點，到7B房間準時開會。

⊙By the end of the meeting on December 3rd at 9:00am in Marsha Smith's office, we should have a working budget put together.

12月3日早上9點到Marsha Smith辦公室召開會議前，我們要先彙整預算工作。

列出所有的議題

議程準備的第三項內容是列出所有的內容（items for discussion）。可以在每個議題前標明序號。應當將最主要的議題安排（arrange）在議程的最前面。

在會議一開始，可以透過安排所有的相關議題的統計資料和圖示，來協助與會者解決問題（tackle the problem）。

⊙Item 1, Staff Reports; Item 2, Budget Review; Item 3, Marketing Report.
　內容一，員工報告；內容二，預算審核；內容三，行銷報告。

⊙We need to talk about Sales, Marketing, Finance, and our upcoming conference.
　我們需要談論的包括銷售、行銷和財務，以及即將召開的座談會事宜。

⊙Most important is talking about our financial auditing. Let's do that one first.
　最重要的是討論我們的財務審核，讓我們先從那個開始。

為每項議程分配時間

準備會議議程的第四步是為每項議程分配時間（allocate time）。對於一些需要討論和腦力激盪（brainstorming）的內容可以多分配些時間，比方說該項的平均分配時間是10分鐘，你可以多給5分鐘。但整體而言，早半個小時結束比延後半個小時要好得多。

A: How long should it take us to go over the budget?
B: Not more than about 15 minutes. The budget report should be pretty straight forward with no troubleshooting or problem areas.
A：審核預算大概要多長時間？
B：不超過15分鐘。預算報告應該直接了當，不會涉及疑難排除或問題。

總結

議程是一個會議的中心思想。一個會議是否會漫天神遊、毫無建樹，只要看會議議程就知道了。只有議程做到清晰扼要、簡明易懂（short and simple），與會人員才會朝一個共同的方向來準備。一般情況下，會議議程不超過一頁。此外，一旦議程在手，那就得徹底執行（stick to）。

單字表 ....

attendance 出席;到場

budget 預算

customer relations 客戶關係

disciplinary action 紀律處分

evaluation 評估;評價

examine 考核;檢查

item 項目;條款

mandatory 強制的;義務的

marketing 行銷

minutes 會議紀錄;備忘錄

prompt 提示

report 報告

resend 重寄

secretary 秘書

staff 全體職員

troubleshooting 疑難排除;故障排除

片語表 ....

Are you sure? 你確定嗎?

customer service 客戶服務

game plan 行動計畫;策略

go over 複查;複習

haggle over 討價還價

hold a meeting 召開會議

I guess 我猜

It says here 這裡說的

last long 持續很長

make matters clear 釐清

yep 是(俚)

no kidding 不開玩笑

no problem 沒問題

pretty 非常的

problem areas 問題領域

spending all our time 付出我們所有的

take a look 看一下;瞧一瞧

時間

up for discussion 來討論

實境對話 1

A: There's a lot to talk about at the meeting on Tuesday. I hope the agenda makes matters clear. Did you get a copy of the agenda? I sent it to your E-mail.

B: I didn't get a copy of the agenda yet. Could you resend it to me?

A: Sure, no problem.

B: Oh wait, here it is. I have a hard copy on my desk. Let me take a look. "The purpose of this meeting is to examine marketing reports, budget reviews, and customer service evaluations." Seems like a lot to talk about in one meeting.

C: No kidding. When is the meeting supposed to be held again?

B: It says here on the agenda, "Monday, September 27th, 10:00am, room 7B. Please be prompt."

C: I guess they don't want us to be late. What are the items up for discussion?

B: Item 1, Staff Reports; Item 2, Budget Review; Item 3, Marketing Reports... I hope we don't end up spending all our time haggling over the budget. That's what happened last time.

C: Nah, I don't think it will be a problem this time. Hey Bill, How long should it take us to go over the budget?

A: Not more than about 15 minutes. The budget report should be pretty straightforward with no troubleshooting or problem areas.

A：週二的會議要談很多的內容。我希望議程表能夠清清楚楚。你收到議程的影本了嗎？我寄了電子郵件給你。

B：我還沒有收到。你能重寄一次給我嗎？

A：當然，沒問題。

B：哎，等一下，在這兒。我的桌上有個影印本。讓我看一下。「會議的目的是審查行銷報告、審核預算和評估客戶服務。」看來在這次會議上有不少要討論的。

C：別開玩笑了。會議什麼時候開啊？

B：議程上的時間是「9月27日，週一早上10點，在7B房間，請準時。」

C：我想他們不希望我們遲到。要討論哪些內容呢？

B：內容一，員工報告；內容二，預算審核；內容三，行銷報告……希望我們別把所有時間都花在預算的討價還價上。上次就是這樣。

C：不會吧，我想這次不會這樣了吧。嗨，比爾，審核預算大概要多久？

A：不超過15分鐘。預算報告應該直接了當，不涉及疑難排除和問題。

實境對話 2

A: Are you going to the meeting tomorrow morning?

B: Yeah, of course. Isn't it mandatory attendance? Anyway, it shouldn't last too long.

A: Are you sure? Have you seen the agenda?

B: Yep, here it is...

Staff Meeting, Monday, April 16th

Our main objective for Monday's meeting is to review staff evaluation reports. The meeting begins at 2:00 and will be held in conference room #405.

Welcome – Bob Johnson, HR

Minutes from last meeting –Joyce Campbell, Secretary

Reports
- Marketing Department
- Sales Department
- Financial Department
- Secretary

Schedules

●Managerial Meetings

●Staff Meetings

●Vacations

Special Needs

●Health absences

●Employee disciplinary action

●Other

Other Business

A: Looks pretty straightforward to me.

A：你參加明天的會議嗎？

B：是的，當然。不是説必須參加嗎？不管怎麼樣，應該不會開很久吧！

A：你確定嗎？你看過議程了嗎？

B：是的，在這裡……

員工大會，週一，4月16日

週一會議的主題是審核員工評估報告。會議定在2：00，在#405會議室召開。

歡迎詞——Bob Johnson，人力資源部

上次會議紀錄——Joyce Campbell，秘書處

報告

●行銷部

●銷售部

●財務部

●秘書處

附表

●管理會議

●工作會議

●假日

特別要求

●除非病假，不得缺席

●員工紀律

●其他

其他事項

A：看起來真是一目了然。

有效地開場 Starting a Meeting Effectively

開會首先要準時（on time）。一開始就確定會議的方向非常重要，以免有人借此機會閒話家常或打聽隱私。

要用友好而有力的語氣對與會者表示歡迎（a warm welcome）。假如與會人員（participants）之前從未謀面，就要安排些許時間讓他們相互介紹。另外，要記得介紹特別來賓（special guests）或者是第一次與會的人員。

⊙Hello everyone! Welcome and let's get started!

　大家好！歡迎與會，我們開始吧！

⊙Can everyone find a seat? Let's get down to business.

　大家都就座了嗎？言歸正傳，我們開始工作吧。

⊙I'm glad everyone could make it. Shall we start?

　真高興大家都能來。我們開始吧？

⊙Before we start, let's just take a minute to have everyone briefly introduce themselves. Can we start with you?

　在會議開始之前，我們先花幾分鐘的時間，大家簡單自我介紹。從你開始可以嗎？

⊙I'd like everyone's attention please. Today we'd like to especially welcome (name) who is visiting with us from (afflilation).

請大家注意了。今天我們要特別歡迎來自（某機構）的（某人的姓名）來參加我們的會議。

⊙Everyone, this is (name), he's new. Please make him feel welcome!

大家好，這是新來的（某人姓名）。大家歡迎他！

簡明地介紹議程

一開始就應明確會議目的（purpose），包括預期結果（desired outcomes）。會議開始前將議程（agendas）分發給與會人員，同時手邊要多備幾份影本（copies），有必要時逐一介紹每項議程。

⊙Remember, what we want to accomplish today is to iron out the financial issues for the merger project.

請記住，我們今天會議目標是要解決合併專案的財務問題。

⊙Let's review what's on our game plan today.

讓我們回顧一下今天的會議計畫。

⊙To start with, let's go over our objectives for this meeting.

首先，讓我們看一下今天會議的目標。

⊙On our to-do list today, we've got marketing reports, budget reviews, and customer service evaluations.

今天，我們的計畫表上面有市場銷售報告、預算審查以及客戶服務評價。

⊙We should have a working budget put together by the end of this meeting.

會議結束時，我們應該能有一份完整的工作預算。

⊙As a result of this meeting, I hope to see some more feasible projections from our design department.

我希望看到的會議成果是：我們的設計部門得拿出幾個更加確實可行的計畫。

⊙We need something we can show to the corporate offices by the end of today.

今天結束之前，我們要有能夠向總部展示的東西。

防止離題

會議中有可能出現偏離既定議程（prescribed agenda），牽扯到無關議題上的情況（unrelated tangents）。與會人員的一些行為也會干擾會議，比如滔滔不絕、一言不發、武斷批評、竊竊私語、遲到或者準備不足。對於這些干擾因素，主持人可以巧妙地提示離題者（offenders），儘快將討論導回正軌（back on track）。

⊙Are we getting off track here?

我們現在是不是有點離題了？

⊙Can we all live with that?

我們都能忍受那樣嗎？

⊙So what your saying is...

所以你的意思是……

⊙What have we decided?

那麼我們的決定是什麼？

借此機會促進團隊合作

在會議中，團隊成員（team members）有機會更了解別人的業務能力（professional capacities）。要知道，讓所有人離開日常工作安排（normal work schedule）參加會議，對公司來說就是在投資時間和金錢！有效地（effectively）利用會議時間提高團隊合作品質，不要浪費這項投資！

⊙This meeting is a chance for us to get to know each other a little better; a personal goal for me is to build teamwork.

這次會議可以讓我們相互更深入了解，對我個人而言則是建立團隊合作。

⊙Our problem is obvious to everyone, so let's work together to solve it.

我們的問題顯然也是每個人的問題，所以讓我們一起來解決它。

⊙We'll be working together for the next several months, so I hope we can build a fluid and dynamic team.

接下來的幾個月裡我們將一起工作，所以我希望我們能成為一個靈活高效能的團隊。

及時消除不團結因素

有時候，討論會開得非常激烈（get quite heated）。為了有效管理，防止傷害感情，迅速化解任何潛在的有害情況（damaging situations），對於主持人來說這是非常重要的。

A: So far everything the design department has come up with is completely useless. Don't they have any originality? Who thinks up this crap anyway?

B: Whoa, John. Take it easy. I can see you have strong feelings about this issue, but let's be fair.

A：到目前為止，設計部想出來的都是些無用的東西。他們有什麼創造性？到底誰想出來的這些廢物？

B：噢，John。不要這樣說。我知道你在這個問題上有不同的想法，但我們還是客觀公平點吧。

總結

事先想清楚並且分發詳盡的會議議程，將為你的會議打下良好的基礎。一旦開始會議，議程能幫你一步一步達到會議目標。不僅如此，還能推動團隊成長，控制潛在衝突將使你的會議錦上添花。一份完整的會議議程，能幫你成功地開始會議，進而有效地完成會議。

單字表

agenda 議程	briefly 簡短地
crap 廢物	especially 尤其是
feasible 可行的	finance 財務
folk 傢伙	introduce 介紹
issue 事務	marketing 市場行銷
merger 合併	objective 目標
originality 創造性	ought 應該
prompt 立即	review 回顧

片語表

as a result 作為結果	come up with 想出
customer relations 客戶關係	game plan 行動計畫
you all's 大家	iron out (problems, issues) 消除（問題）
make (sb.) feel welcome 歡迎某人	on their way... 在……的路上
pass (sth.) down 傳遞	put (sth.) together 歸總
sore spot 痛處	take a minute (to do sth.) 花一點時間
(to be able to) make it 做到	（做某事）
visit with (sb.) 訪問（某人）	waste (sb's) time 浪費（某人的）時間
working budget 工作預算	

實境對話 1

A: Hello everyone! I am glad everyone could make it this morning. Shall we start?

B: Uh... The folks from the design department aren't here yet. Do you think we ought to wait for them to get here before we start?

A: I'm sure they'll be along in just a few minutes. Tina, would you mind running down to their offices to make sure they're on the way? Thanks! I'd rather be prompt as to not waste you all's time here, so let's get right down to business. Before we start, let's just take a minute to have everyone briefly introduce themselves. Can we start with you Tom?

B: I'm Tom, I'm in Marketing.

C: Lisa here. I'm the number lady, I mean, I work in the finance department.

D: Joe, also from the Marketing department.

E: I'm Wen Yu, I am in customer relations.

...

A: Thanks every one, I see the design team is here now, please try to be more prompt next time. Before we take a look at our agenda items, I'd like everyone's attention. Today we'd like to especially welcome Mr. Laiwei Zhou who is visiting with us from Moxiford Industries.

F: Thank you, it's nice to be here today.

A: Now, does everyone have an agenda? Marcie, can you pass these extra copies down to the finance people? Okay. Let's review what's on our game plan for today... Remember, what we want to accomplish is to iron out the financial issues for the merger project. We should have a working budget put together by the end of this meeting.

A：大家好！真高興大家今天早上都能到。我們開始吧？

B：嗯……設計部的人都沒到啊，你們覺得我們要等他們到了再開始嗎？

179

A：我想他們馬上就來了。Tina，可不可以麻煩你下樓到他們辦公室跑一趟，看看他們是不是來了？謝謝！我想立刻開始，以免浪費大家的時間。現在開始做正事吧。在會議開始之前，我們先花幾分鐘的時間來簡要單地介紹一下自己。從你開始可以嗎，Tom？

B：我是Tom，行銷部的。

C：我是Lisa，是管帳小姐，我是說，我在財務部工作。

D：Joe，也是行銷部的。

E：我是溫玉，我在客戶公關部工作。

　　……

A：謝謝大家。設計部的人都來了，希望大家下次準時開會。在我們開始會議日程之前，請大家注意了，今天我們要特別歡迎來自莫克斯福特實業的周萊維先生來參加我們的會議。

F：謝謝，非常高興今天能來這裡。

A：現在，每個人都有會議議程了嗎？Marcie，能不能把這些多的影本傳給財務部的同事？好，讓我們回顧一下我們今天的會議計畫……請記住，我們的會議目標是解決合併計畫的財務問題。會議結束時，我們應該有一個整體工作預算出爐。

實境對話 2

A: Can everyone find a seat please? Let's get started.

B: Can I have a copy of our agenda? For some reason I couldn't print it off my computer this morning...

A: Sure, no problem. Here you go. Now, since you all know each other already, I won't waste time with introductions. I just want to introduce one of our new team members. Everyone, this is Ted, he's new. Please make him feel welcome.

C: Hi everyone.

A: To start with, let's go over our objectives for this meeting. As a result of this meeting I hope to see some more feasible projections from our design department. We need something we can show to the corporate offices by the end of today. Also, a personal goal for me is to build teamwork. We'll be working together for the next several months, so I hope we can build a fluid and dynamic team.

B: We're going to talk about the designs? Great! So far everything the Design department has come up with is completely useless. Don't they have any originality? Who thinks up this crap anyway?

A: Whoa, John. Take it easy. I can see you have strong feelings about this issue, but let's be fair.

B: Sorry, but I think we all know it's been a sore spot in our company for awhile...

A: Yes, the problem is obvious to us all. Let's work together to solve it.

A：大家都就座了嗎？我們開始吧。

B：能給我一份會議議程嗎？今天早上不知道怎麼搞的，我的電腦無法列印了。

A：當然沒問題。給你。現在，既然大家都相互認識了，我就不再浪費時間介紹了。我只想介紹我們團隊的一位新成員。各位，這是新來的Ted。大家歡迎他！

C：嗨，大家好。

A：首先，讓我們看一下今天會議的目標。我希望看到會議的成果，是我們的設計部門能拿出幾個更加確實可行的計畫，讓我們今天有能夠向總部展示的東西。另外，對我個人而言是要建立團隊合作。接下來的幾個月裡我們將在一起工作，所以我希望我們能成為一個靈活高效能的團隊。

B：我們要討論那些設計嗎？太好了！到目前為止，設計部想出來的東西都毫無用處。他們有什麼創造性？到底是誰想出來的這些廢物？

A：噢，John。別這麼說。我知道你在這個問題上有不同的想法，但我們還是客觀公平些吧。

B：對不起，但我想大家都清楚，這個困擾我們公司已經有一段時間了……

A：是的，很明顯這個問題關係到我們所有人。讓我們一起來解決它吧。

腦力激盪 Team Brainstorming

腦力激盪能催生大量未經雕琢（unedited）的想法。這個過程追求的是創造力。在尋求創造性解決方案和創新意識（innovate）的過程中，可以把完美主義的態度暫放一邊。討論在先，組織完善（organize and perfect）在後。

會議開始，主持人應鼓勵大家發言。

⊙Let's talk about how to solve our problem.
　我們來討論該怎麼解決我們的問題。

⊙Anyone have any good ideas about how to address this issue?
　誰有什麼好的辦法來解決這個問題？

⊙Let's take a minute to brainstorm this issue.
　讓我們花些時間在這個問題上腦力激盪。

⊙I want everyone to put their two-cents in.
　我希望每個人都能表達自己的觀點。

⊙Let's get creative, people!
　各位！讓我們來點創意吧！

⊙What do you think we should do about...?
　對於……你們有什麼想法？

如何開始

選出（delegate）一人或多人來負責在掛圖或白板上做記錄。鼓勵組員或隊員無論從何處講起（start anywhere）都可以。鼓勵他們積極思考、自由發言。

⊙Jamie and Terry, can I get you two to act as scribes for today's brainstorming session? Here, take a dry-erase pen.

　Jamie和Terry，是否能麻煩二位在我們的討論會期間扮演紀錄的角色？來，拿一枝白板筆。

⊙Larry's taking the notes, everyone speak up so he can hear you.

　Larry負責記錄，每個人發言都要聲音大點，讓他能聽清楚。

⊙Any possible answer is good. Let us know what you're thinking.

　任何有可能性的答案都是好的。讓我們了解你們是怎麼想的。

⊙Let's get started. Who has the first idea? Let's keep'em coming, guys!

　我們開始吧。誰先發言？各位，讓我們積極踴躍點！

⊙Thanks, Lucy. Great idea. What else we got?

　謝謝，Lucy。好主意。誰還有其他意見？

⊙Don't worry about feasibility. Just tell us your ideas.

　不用擔心可行性。告訴我們你的想法就行。

謝絕批評

批評，即便是出自善意也會將創造思維扼殺在搖籃中（Criticism, even well-meant, kills creativity）。在腦力激盪討論（brainstorming session）期間，一定不能允許有任何形式的批評存在，「後續加工」的過程可以放在會後。無論什麼想法，即便是有些怪異（weird），都應該「來者不拒」。不必在意任何的拼寫、發音或語法的錯誤。「那是個很蠢的主意」這種話千萬不能說。會後找時機再討論這些想法的價值。

A: What if we solved this problem by offering employee incentives?

B: I don't think that would work. It'd be too difficult to administer.

C: Wait a second, Bill. Save the criticism for later. Jill, keep those ideas coming. Employee incentives sound great.

A：透過發獎金給員工的辦法來解決這個問題怎麼樣？

B：我覺得那行不通。管理起來太困難了。

C：稍等，Bill。先別急著批評。Jill，請繼續闡述你的想法。員工獎金聽起來不錯。

數量VS品質（Quantity vs. Quality）

記錄下的想法越多越好。腦力激盪討論的目的，在於在有限的時間內生成（generate）儘可能多的主意。為了提高記錄的完整性，可以使用一些縮寫（abbreviations）。總之，要積極促成思想的自由跳躍。

⊙Good idea, Taylor! What else can you come up with?

　好主意，Taylor！還有什麼好主意嗎？

⊙Thanks for your contribution, Peggy. Can anyone else think of something along those lines?

　Peggy，非常感謝你的建議。還有誰對此有別的想法？

⊙I like what Barbara just said, let's keep that idea going.

　我喜歡Barbara剛才所說的。讓我們繼續討論這個想法。

⊙John just mentioned letting Human Resources handle things. Who else has a different idea?

　John剛才提到說由人力資源部來處理這些事。誰有不同的意見？

組織

創意階段之後緊跟著組織階段。讓參與人員將類似的內容（belong together）歸類。可以讓他們把腦力激盪所得到的想法分成3~7類。對每一類（categories）

進行命名。分類結束後，請他們總結展示成果，並對他們的辛苦工作表示感謝和祝賀（congratulate them）。

⊙Thanks everyone for your contributions. Let's take a look to see how they all fit together.

感謝大家的貢獻。我們來將他們組合一下。

⊙Mary, Tom, Larry... Can you spearhead putting the ideas on the board onto three different lists. Try to organize them a bit.

Mary、Tom、Larry……你們是否能帶頭把這些所有的想法分成三組寫在板上。試著把他們組織一下。

⊙Thanks everyone for putting your ideas forward! Let's take a look and see what we've got.

感謝各位能夠各抒己見。讓我們看看有哪些收穫。

總結

所謂腦力激盪就是要暢所欲言，出謀劃策。「仁者見仁，智者見智。」重在創新，提出的主意可以不專業，可以不夠完美，但絕不可以妄加評判，尤其是在會議上。只有這樣大家才能踴躍發言、自由暢談。所有想法都應當記錄下來，認真分類，之後加以逐項討論。

單字表 ···

administer 管理
demand 要求；需求
expect 期待；盼望
increase 增長
morale 士氣；民心

authorize 授權；批准
excuse 藉口
incentive 獎勵；激勵
issue 問題；議題
offer 提供；報價

overtime 超時；加班　　　　　　prompt 提示

socialize 社交；交際　　　　　　sponsor 贊助商

tardiness 拖延；遲到　　　　　　unfair 不公平

Phrases
片語表 ··

act as scribe 擔任紀錄　　　　　address an issue 應付/處理這個問題

agree with (sb.) 同意（某人）　　come up with 想出

compensate for (sth.) 補償（某事）　deal with 處理

dry-erase pen 白板筆　　　　　　have problems with 在（某方面）有問題

keep (sth.) coming 繼續提出　　　keep the midnight oil burning 熬夜；

lunch break 午休　　　　　　　　開夜車

let (sb.) handle (things) 讓（某人）　put (something) forward 假設（某事）；

掌握（某事）　　　　　　　　　假想（某事）

work from home 在家工作　　　　put in long hours 花費很長時間

put in your two-cents 表達你的想法　spearhead 先鋒

take notes 記筆記　　　　　　　　take work home (with you)（你）把

work overtime 加班　　　　　　　工作帶回家

實境對話 1

A: One issue we have to discuss today is how to deal with a something we've had increasing problems with here in the office. That is increasing tardiness among the staff. I realize that many of you put in long hours of overtime and sometimes keep the midnight oil burning all the way until the wee hours of the morning some days. But I feel it's become an excuse. We have to come up with a way to keep our office staff prompt. Let's talk about how to solve our problem. Anyone have any good ideas about how to address this issue?

186

B: I think it's unfair to expect someone to work overtime until 2 or 3am, and then demand they show up promptly at 9am the next morning.

A: I am sure many people agree with you. Let's take a minute to brainstorm this issue. I want everyone to put their two-cents in. Jamie and Terry, can I get you two to act as scribes for today's brainstorming session? Here, take a dry-erase pen. Let's get started. Who has the first idea?

C: What if we offered a longer lunch break to compensate for the late night hours.

A: Good idea Taylor, what else can you come up with? Let's get creative, people!

D: Could the company authorize some people to work from home, if they have a project that will make them work so late at night?

E: What if we solved this problem by offering employee incentives?

F: I don't think that would work. It'd be too difficult to administer.

A: Wait a second, Bill. Save the criticism for later. Jill, keep those ideas coming. Employee incentives sound great. Any possible answer is good. Let us know what you're thinking.

A：我們今天要討論一個導致辦公室中諸多麻煩的現象，那就是員工中日益嚴重的遲到問題。我了解你們當中很多人都加班，有時候熬夜到凌晨好幾點。但是我覺得這已經變成遲到的藉口了。我們必須找出一個能保證辦公室同仁準時來上班的方法。我們來討論一下該怎麼解決這個問題，誰有什麼好辦法能解決這個問題？

B：我覺得要求某人工作到凌晨兩三點，第二天早上9點準時上班有些不公平。

A：我相信很多人都和你的意見一致。讓我們花些時間在此問題上腦力激盪，我希望每個人都能表達自己的觀點。Jamie和Terry，是否能麻煩二位在今天的討論會上扮演記錄的角色？來，拿一支白板筆。我們開始吧。誰先發言？

C：我們提供比較長的午休時間來補償晚上加班怎麼樣？

A：好主意，Taylor！還有什麼好主意嗎？各位！讓我們來點創意吧！

D：如果有些專案，大家不得不工作到那麼晚，那公司是否可以授權這些人在家工作？

E：透過發獎金給員工的辦法來解決這個問題怎麼樣？

F：我覺得那行不通，執行起來太困難了。

A：等一下，Bill。先別急著批評。Jill，請繼續闡述你的想法，員工獎金聽上去不錯，無論什麼回答都是好的。讓我們了解你是怎麼想的。

實境對話 2

A: Larry's taking the notes, everyone speak up so he can hear you. What do you think we should do about improving customer service? John just mentioned letting Human Resources handle things. Who else has a different idea?

B: We could pull in some outside customer service training. Or maybe get the department heads signed up for some customer service workshops.

A: Thanks for your contribution, Peggy. Can anyone else think of something along those lines?

C: Maybe it's just a matter of improving company morale. If the workers are happier, they will be nicer to the customers.

A: I like what Barbara just said, let's keep that idea going.

B: Well, if we wanted to improve company morale, one thing we could do is sponsor more outside events and activities for employees to socialize outside of work.

D: Yeah, like maybe a sport's team or an enrichment class or something.

E: That would be fun.

A: Thanks everyone for putting your ideas forward! Let's take a look and see what we've got. Mary, Tom, Larry... Can you spearhead putting the ideas on the board into three different lists. Try to organize them a bit.

A：Larry負責記錄，每個人發言都要聲音大點，以便他能聽清楚。對於我們提高客戶服務你們都有什麼想法？John剛才提到説由人力資源部來處理這些事，誰有不同意見？

B：我們可以請人來做客戶服務培訓，或許讓部門主管參加客戶服務培訓。

A：Peggy，非常感謝你的建議。還有誰對此有別的想法？

C：也許只需要提高公司的士氣。如果員工們都很開心，那他們對客戶也會更好。

A：我認同Barbara剛才説的。我們來繼續討論。

B：那如果我們要提高企業的士氣，有一件事情我們可以做，那就是舉辦更多的員工戶外活動來促進交流。

D：是的，比如組運動隊或者才藝的課程，或是其他的。

E：那會很有意思。

A：感謝各位能夠各抒己見。讓我們看看都有哪些收穫。Mary、Tom、Larry……你們是否能帶頭把這些想法分成不同的三組寫在白板上。試著把它們組織一下。

提出論點 Presenting an Argument

會議的類型五花八門。但是，一種特別（specific）的會議是在主席（chairman）主持下的正式會議（formal meeting）。主持引導這樣的正式會議的大部分用詞都是格式化的（stylized），也就是説一樣的話被用在所有的情境之中，當然也根據「正式」程度有不同畫分。

開門見山，點名議題

⊙I would like to begin by saying...
首先我想説的是……

⊙The most important points seem to me to be...

　　在我看來最重要的地方是……

⊙To begin with...

　　以……來開始

⊙First,... second,... third,... finally,...

　　首先，……其次，……再來，……最後，……

⊙First, let's consider...

　　首先，讓我們考慮……

⊙There are four points I would like to make...

　　有四點是我想表明的……

介紹新的議題，並且將會前準備好的有關議題的資訊加入其中。

⊙In addition...

　　此外……

⊙Not only do we have..., but also...

　　不僅僅要做我們手頭的……，而且還有……

⊙Furthermore,...

　　此外，……

⊙I would like to address another issue briefly, that of...

　　我想簡略地處理一個問題，那就是……

⊙Another problem I'd like to focus on is...

　　我想另外的一個值得關注的問題就是……

⊙Moreover,...

　　還有，……

舉例說明，對比表達。

⊙A case in point is...
　　一個典型的例子就是⋯⋯

⊙Let me give you an example...
　　讓我為你們舉個例子⋯⋯

⊙On one hand..., but on the other hand...
　　一方面⋯⋯，而另一方面⋯⋯

⊙In spite of..., we should still remember...
　　儘管⋯⋯，但我們仍然應該記得⋯⋯

歸納總結並表明個人傾向。

⊙On the whole...
　　大體上⋯⋯

⊙Overall...
　　總之⋯⋯

⊙All things considered...
　　從整體來看⋯⋯

⊙I'd rather see...
　　我傾向認為⋯⋯

⊙I'd like...
　　我想要⋯⋯

綜合論述。

⊙Let me conclude with...

讓我們以……來作為總結。

⊙Finally,...

最後，……

⊙Let me conclude by reiterating that...

讓我最後重申……

⊙To summarize, I'd like to say...

作為總結，我想說……

⊙Allow me to conclude by saying...

請允許我最後說……

總結

「提出論點」可以被理解為表明自己的觀點，無論是舉例還是對比，概括還是下結論，都在表明自己的觀點，都是要告訴別人你想聽到什麼或者你傾向什麼。

單字表 ⋯⋯⋯⋯⋯⋯⋯⋯⋯⋯⋯⋯⋯⋯⋯⋯⋯⋯⋯⋯⋯⋯⋯⋯

accommodate 容納；協調

accommodation 住宿

elaborate 詳細述說；詳細的

eliminate 消除；刪除

earmark 專用

fiscal 財政的；財務的

gain 贏取；賺取

generation 產生；生成

monies 款項；資金

oversight 監督；檢查

popular 受歡迎的

proper 合適的；適宜的

prudent 審慎的；謹慎的

reiterate 重申

resource 資源；財力

taxpayer 納稅人

spending 支出；經費

venue 地點

片語表

auditing action 審核行動

discuss an issue 討論事宜

governing body 主管機構

influx of (sth.) （某事物）湧入

operating fund 營運資金；周轉基金

pressing issue 緊迫問題

take a moment (to do sth.) 花一點
時間來做（某事）

vote on (sth.) 表決（某事）

check and balance 制衡

earmark for 預留的

historical tourist site 歷史旅遊景點

lighten a burden 減輕負擔

pave roads 鋪路

sheer number 大量；眾多

tax cut 減稅

tax increase 增稅

實境對話 1

A: Before we vote on it, let's take a moment to discuss the issue. George, I believe you know more about the new tax cuts than anyone else. Would you care to share with us?

B: I'd be happy to. I would like to begin by saying tax increases are never popular, and everyone is interested in cutting taxes. However, the most important points seem to me to be the generation of fiscal resources and the check and balance of prudent spending.

A: Very well...

B: To begin with, the only way that governmental bodies can gain their operating funds is to collect taxes or to impose use fees. First, we all agree that we'd like to lighten the burden on taxpayers, but are unsure if tax cuts are the best way to do it. Second, we also agree that we need to find ways to generate more funding. Third, supporters of the tax cut propose that more funding can be generated by shifting around the current budget. Finally, I'd like to suggest that it is impossible to shift around the current budget without proper oversight from an outside agency.

A: Could you elaborate?

B: Let me give you an example. If the council were to start shifting monies around without an outside overseer auditing their actions, perhaps funding specifically earmarked for the schools would end up being used to pave the roads. On one hand, we are solving pressing financial issues, on the other, we are robbing Peter to pay Paul.

A: Understood.

B: Allow me to conclude by saying, even though tax cuts seem like a good idea, they introduce problems into our budgeting system. We cannot keep a balanced budget by shifting funding. To reiterate, we must have some form of financial oversight.

A：在我們進行表決以前，讓我們先討論這個問題。George，我相信你比任何人都了解新的減稅計畫，你是否願意和我們分享一下？

B：我很樂意。首先我想說的是增稅從來就不受歡迎，而每個人都對減稅比較感興趣。但是，在我看來最重要的是新的財政資源生成和審慎開支的制衡。

A：太好了……

B：首先，政府機構是透過徵稅或強制收取使用費來獲取運轉資金的。第一，我們大家都同意要減輕納稅人負擔，但是不能肯定減稅是最好的途徑。第二，我們也同意要開闢途徑來獲取更多的運轉資金。第三，減稅的支持者建議透過調整預算來獲取更多的資金。最後，我想說如果沒有外部機構合理的監督，調整預算是不可能實現。

A：能詳細說明一下嗎？

B：讓我來給您舉個例子。如果地方議會在沒有對其進行審計監督的話，撥給學校的專款可能就被用於鋪路了。一方面我們正在解決財政壓力的問題，而另一方面我們要挖東牆補西牆。

A：明白。

B：請允許我總結說明，儘管減稅看起來是個好主意，但是會給我們的預算系統帶來麻煩，轉移資金很難確保預算的平衡。重申一下，我們必須得有某種形式的財政監督。

實境對話 2

A: Now to the next item on our agenda, discussing the venue for the international convention. Susan, did you have something to say about this item?

B: Yes, thank you. There are four points I would like to make. First, to begin with, attendees for this convention will be coming from all areas of Asia, so I believe the city we choose to hold our event in must be easily accessible from international origins. That would eliminate some of our choices. In addition, not only do we have people coming from outside of China, but we also have language issues to address. We'll have to be able to accommodate those people who may not speak local languages. That would mean choosing a venue that has available translation support.

A: That is very insightful...

B: Moreover, because we expect an influx of thousands of visitors to the conference, we've got to consider accommodations. Another problem I'd like to focus on is the fact that three out of five of our choices are small cities which may not be able to handle the sheer numbers.

A: So that would leave two cities, Shanghai and Beijing.

B: My fourth and final point, is that first-time visitors to China would also be most interested in an area that would have more historical tourist sites. To summarize, I'd like to say that I see our only viable option for this convention is Beijing.

A：現在我們進入議程的下一項，討論關於國際公約（簽署）場地事宜。Susan，關於這項您有什麼要說的嗎？

B：是的，謝謝。有四點我要說明。首先，該公約活動的參與者來自亞洲各地，所以我認為我們要選擇的城市須有地緣優勢。這樣說來我們的很多選項將被排除。此外，我們有來自中國以外的國家的人，因此我們還得解決語言問題，我們必須關照到這些有語言隔閡的人，那就表示要選擇一個有合適的語言翻譯的場地。

A：這倒是很有見地……

B：還有，因為我們預計會有大量的訪問者參加該大會，那我們就必須考慮住宿。我想另外一個值得關注的問題就是，我們手頭上五個可供選擇的城市有三個是小城鎮，這三個小城鎮無法應對那麼多的來訪者的。

A：這樣說來就剩兩個城市了：上海和北京。

B：我的第四點也就是最後一點，第一次來中國的訪問者會對歷史旅遊景點有極大的興趣。總之，我想說，在我看來我們這次簽約的唯一選擇是在北京。

讓你的建議被採納
Making Your Suggestion Heard

你有一個很好的想法，而且你也深信它會改進（improve）工作，甚至可以幫公司省錢（save money）。你的想法能否實現完全取決於（depends on）你能否讓別人採納你的建議。

提出想法並且得到採納需要一套詳細的計畫。首先要提醒別人注意，說出你的大致目的。

⊙I have some ideas that might make a difference in this area.

我有些想法可能會在這個方面有所作為。

⊙Can I set a meeting with you sometime to discuss ways we can save money and improve our service?

我能否當面與您討論一些既可以省錢又能提高我們服務的辦法？

⊙I'd like to take the opportunity to present a few new options.

我希望能有機會介紹一些新的選項。

⊙Do you have time? I'd like to share a couple ways we can do better.

您有時間嗎？我很願意和您分享幾個我們能夠做得更好的方案。

⊙This idea could revolutionize the way we do business.

這個想法能為我們的生意帶來革命性的變革。

⊙I guarantee you'll be interested in what I have to say about this issue.

我保證您會對我所說的感興趣。

列出事實（Get the facts straight）

做好背景調查以確保你想法的可行性。資料是最直接有效的說服工具。決策階層只有在精準的資料和事實（accurate facts）面前才會考慮做決定。

⊙The sales stats from our competitors confirm that this is a market we yet to effectively reach.

從我們競爭對手那裡的銷售統計來看，我們還沒有對市場進行很有效地覆蓋。

⊙I have the budget projections here. You can see that if we implement my suggested changes, we'd actually be saving money in the long run.

我這裡有份預算評估。你可以看到如果我們實施我所建議的變革，從長遠來看我們會省錢。

⊙I've done the research into this issue, and it has become very clear that we need to do something fast before we fall too far behind. I suggest...

我已經做了這方面的調查，我們必須盡快採取措施，不然就會落伍，這個情況越來越明顯了。我建議……

⊙If you look at the data, you'll see that we can make a few minor adjustments and approve our consumer ratings very easily.

如果你留意一下資料，你就會發現只需做小小的調整就能夠輕而易舉地提高我們的消費者評價。

⊙Marketing data suggests that we can make some simple changes and see increased success.

市場資料表示我們只要做簡單的改變就能看見成效。

證明

做一個包含投資收益分析的（cost-benefits analysis）商業計畫書（business plan），以此證明透過你的主意可以賺/省很多錢。

⊙Implementing these changes will cost us in the beginning. I've estimated that we will spend around $10,000 initially in overhead. However, our investment returns tenfold.

實施這些變革在初期是會花一些錢。我估算大約要投入大約1萬美元。但是我們的投資會有十倍的收益。

⊙According to our numbers, if we were to make these changes, we'd be seeing an increase of profit by 20 percent.

根據我們的資料顯示，如果做這些更改，我們的收益將增加20%。

⊙I've prepared a business plan. Here's a hard copy of the material. If it is more convenient to have a soft copy, I will send that to your E-mail later.

我已經準備好了一份商業計畫。這裡有資料的備份。如果你覺得用電子郵件更方便的話，我隨後寄到你的電子信箱。

⊙The cost-benefit analysis of my idea shows an increased profit within the third quarter of implementation.
我這個想法的投資收益分析顯示執行三季後利潤就會增加。

態度積極，解決問題

透過你的工作來改善狀況，而不是埋怨問題的存在。提出你的解決方案而不是一味指責（pointing fingers）或者怨天尤人（blaming others）。

⊙For whatever reason this hasn't worked in the past, I think that we can overcome the problems currently facing us, if we'd only...
無論出於什麼樣的原因，在過去都沒有成效。我認為我們能夠克服目前面臨的困難，只要我們……

⊙Here's an idea that might help...
這裡有個想法可以幫助……

⊙Even though we've struggled with this in the past, I think there is something we can do about it. If we just...
儘管我們曾經努力過，但我仍覺得有些事情是能夠做到的。如果我們僅僅只是……

使用投影片軟體來提出想法

這樣你會看起來非常專業（look like a pro），並且能夠挑起每個人的興趣。爭取某個專家來支持你（to back you up），他會從專業角度來驗證你列出來的事實並回答所有問題。

A: So as you can see from my fiscal projections, this has the potential to save us a lot of money.

B: I see...

A: But you don't just have to take my word for it, I've invited our head accountant, Bill Monroe, to explain exactly how this would work.

A：正如您在我的投影片上看到的一樣，它很有可能幫我們省一大筆錢。

B：明白了……

A：您也沒有必要只聽我個人的一面之詞，我邀請了我們會計部的主管Bill Monroe來詳細解釋這個問題。

總結

說服別人是周密準備、步步為營的心理攻防戰。列舉資料和事實，以縝密的計畫來證明你的信心不是空穴來風。無論是投影片簡報的外在條件，還是請專家表態支持的人力資源，但凡能增強說服力的方法，都可以大膽使用。別忘了說明自己的建議會給公司帶來的利潤，攻克聽眾的最後防線。

單字表 ⋯⋯⋯⋯⋯⋯⋯⋯⋯⋯⋯⋯⋯⋯⋯⋯⋯⋯⋯⋯⋯⋯⋯⋯⋯⋯⋯⋯⋯⋯⋯⋯⋯⋯

concern 關心；重視

demographic 人口；人口統計；人群

effectively 有效的；起作用的

guarantee 擔保；保證

initially 最初；起初

PPT presentation 投影片簡報

projection 投影；放映

revolutionize 徹底變革；革命化

summary 摘要；概要

couple 一對

development 發展；開發

figure 價格；金額；數據；圖形

implement 實施；實現；工具

overhead 日常開支

present 禮物

product line 生產線；產品線

quarter 季；四分之一

suggested 建議

片語表

consumer confidence 消費者信心

do business 做生意

fall behind 落後;跟不上

focus on 聚焦;集中

get (sth.) on my desk by (deadline) 在(某時間前)將(某物)送到我的辦公桌上

in the long run 從長遠來看

open a market 開拓;打開市場

sales stats 銷售統計

take an opportunity 藉此機會

do better 做得更好

do research into (an area) 對(某領域)研究

for whatever reason 不管什麼原因

Got time? 有空嗎?

hard copy 硬拷貝(影印文件)

have (sth.) to say 有(事)要講

make a difference 有影響;有所作為

reach a market 覆蓋市場

set a meeting 設置;召開會議

with regard to 關於;至於

實境對話 1

A: Harry, can you review the sales reports and get a summary on my desk by Friday?

B: No problem. Actually, with regard to our sales in this quarter, I have some ideas that might make a difference. Can I set a meeting with you sometime to discuss ways we can save money and improve our sales? I guarantee you'll be interested in what I have to say about this issue.

A: How much time do you need? You got time now?

B: Sure. Do you have time? I'd like to share a couple ways we can do better. It should only take about ten minutes to discuss with you. I have a PPT presentation I can show you. This idea could revolutionize the way we do business.

A: Is that right? Well, get your computer and meet me in my office in five minutes.

B: Great!

B: (5 minutes later) I'd like to take the opportunity to present a few new options. Here are our sales figures from last quarter. I've done the research into this issue, and it has become very clear that we need to do something fast before we fall too far behind. I suggest opening up a new market to a new demographic.

A: A new demographic?

B: The sales stats from our competitors confirm that this is a market we have yet to effectively reach. I know you may be concerned about the cost of opening a new market, but take a look. I have the budget projections here. You can see that if we implement my suggested changes, we'd actually be saving money in the long run.

A: Hmmm...

B: But you don't just have to take my word for it, I've invited our head accountant, Bill Monroe, to explain exactly how this would work.

A：Harry，你能審核一下銷售報告並且草擬一份概要，週五之前放到我的辦公桌上嗎？

B：沒問題。事實上，就本季我們的銷售業績來看，我有些想法可能會有些改變。您能否安排一下，我們來討論一下既可以省錢又能提高銷售業績的辦法？我保證您會對我說的感興趣。

A：你要多長時間？你現在有時間嗎？

B：當然，您有時間嗎？我很願意和您分享幾個我們能夠做得更好的方案。可能只需要10分鐘的討論時間。我可以給您看投影片簡報。這個想法可能為我們的生意方式帶來革命性的變革。

A：真的嗎？那好吧，帶著你的電腦5分鐘內到我的辦公室。

B：太好了！

B：（5分鐘後）我想藉這個機會為您介紹一下我們的新選擇。這是我們上一季的銷售資料。我已經做了這方面的研究，我們必須儘快採取措施，不然就

會落伍，這個情況越來越明顯了。我建議針對新的（消費）族群，開闢新的市場。

A：一個新的消費族群？

B：從我們對手的銷售統計資料來看，我們還沒有對市場進行很有效地覆蓋。我理解您對開闢一個新市場的擔憂，但是看一下，我這裡有份預算評估。您可以看到如果實現我建議的變革，從長遠的角度來看，我們事實上是省錢的。

A：嗯……

B：您也沒必要只聽我的一面之詞，我已經邀請了我們的財務主管Bill Monroe 來詳細解釋這個問題。

實境對話 2

A: Have you seen the consumer ratings for our new product line?

B: No, not yet. Are they bad?

A: Here's a copy of the report. Read'em and weep!

B: Oh jeez. Well, Even though we've struggled with consumer confidence in our products in the past, I think there is something we can do about it. For whatever reason our marketing strategies haven't worked in the past, I think we can overcome the problems currently facing us if we'd only focus more on product development.

A: Product development?

B: If you look at the data, you'll see that we can make a few minor adjustments and approve our consumer ratings very easily. Marketing data suggests that we can make some simple changes and see increased success.

A: Wouldn't it be costly?

B: Implementing these changes will cost us in the beginning. I've estimated that we will spend around $10,000 initially in overhead. However, our investment returns tenfold. The cost-benefit analysis of my idea shows an increased profit within the third quarter of implementation.

A: Do you have something more concrete?

B: I've prepared a business plan. Here's a hard copy of the material. If it is more convenient to have a soft copy, I will send that to your E-mail later.

A：你有沒有看過消費者對於我們新產品線的評價？

B：還沒。糟糕嗎？

A：這兒有一份報告的影本。看看，真是欲哭無淚啊！

B：哦，天哪。儘管我們曾經為贏取客戶對以往產品的信心而奮力，但是，有些事情我們還是能夠做到的。不管出於什麼原因，我們原先的行銷策略看來沒有成效。如果能夠集中更多的精力在我們的產品發展上的話，我們就能夠克服目前所面臨的困難。

A：產品發展？

B：如果留意一下數據，你就會發現，我們只需做小小的調整就能夠輕鬆地提高消費者的評價。市場數據說明我們只要做簡單地改變就能見成效。

A：會很貴嗎？

B：實施這些改革在初期對我們來說是要花些費用的。我估計開始時需要投入1萬美元。但是，我們的投資會帶來十倍的收益。我這個想法的投資效益分析表說明，在執行三季後利潤額就會增加。

A：有沒有更具體的？

B：我已經準備了一份商業計畫。這是這些資料的影本。如果你覺得郵件更方便的話，我隨後寄到你的電子信箱。

表達觀點 Giving Opinions

在英語中，表達觀點的方式有很多種。根據你所要表達的觀點的語氣強弱來選擇合適的表達方式。

提示別人你有話要說。

⊙In my opinion...
　　在我看來……

⊙Generally speaking, I think...
　　一般來說，我認為……

⊙Personally, I think...
　　我個人認為……

⊙The way I look at it...
　　就我看……

⊙I'd just like to say...
　　我只是想說……

⊙I'm quite convinced that...
　　我非常確信……

⊙To be quite honest / frank...
　　老實說/坦白說……

⊙If you ask me...
　　如果讓我說……

表達相對中立的觀點

既然不願與對方的觀點「相去甚遠」，就應當更多地照顧對方的立場，儘可能表現得柔和一些，儘可能展現是你「個人」的感覺。

205

⊙I think...

　我想……

⊙I feel that...

　我覺得……

⊙As far as I'm concerned...

　依我看……

⊙As I see it...

　在我看來……

⊙In my view...

　以我的觀點……

⊙I tend to think that...

　我傾向認為……

表達較強的觀點

除了強調「個人」的同時，可以加上「肯定、絕對、堅持、無疑」等副詞來增強你的肯定語氣。

⊙I'm absolutely convinced that...

　我堅決認為……

⊙I'm sure that...

　我確定……

⊙I positively maintain...

　我積極堅持……

⊙I strongly believe that...

　我堅信……

⊙I have no doubt that...

　對於……我毫無質疑。

詢問別人的觀點

如果總是用「What's your opinon?」多少有些乏味，可以試試下面的不同説法。

⊙What do you think?

　你怎麼認為？

⊙What's your view?

　你有什麼樣的觀點？

⊙How do you see the situation?

　你怎麼看這個情況？

⊙What's your take on it?

　你怎麼看？

總結

如果你只是想讓對方了解你的想法，在意的是討論的過程而非論斷誰贏誰輸，一個「我想」、「我認為」就行了。如果你想「得理不讓人」，一定要辯出個是非曲直，那就用一些副詞來增強語氣，例如「我堅信」、「我肯定」。

單字表

candid 直率的	catchy 引人矚目的；動人的
combine 結合；集合	compromise 妥協
consolidate 鞏固；合併	criticism 批評

eliminate 消除;淘汰
feedback 反饋;回饋
integrity 整體性
organization 組織;機構
payroll 薪資總額;發薪名單
position 位置;職務
rearrange 重新整理;重新安排
unrest 動盪;動亂

evaluation 評估;評價
impending 臨近;即將發生
optimistic 樂觀的
overhead 開銷
pessimistic 悲觀的
prefer 傾向;更喜歡
submit 提交

片語表

artistic department 藝術部
crazy (for doing sth.) 瘋狂（做某事）
(do sth.) on purpose （故意）做某事
flow freely 自由流動
get here 到這裡
have something to do with... 和……
有關係
ought to (do sth.) 應該（做某事）
tend to 傾向於
up for discussion 來討論

conserve funds 節約資金
cut back (cost) 削減成本
economic recession 經濟衰退
generally speaking 整體而言;一般來說
go ahead 繼續;來吧
in order to 為了;以便
be not too fond of 不太喜歡
pink slip 解雇通知書
to be related 有關係;和……相關

實境對話 1

A: Hello everyone! Let's start our meeting. The first item up for discussion is evaluation of our new logo design.

B: Uh... The artistic department isn't here yet. Personally, I think we ought to wait for them to get here before we start. Since it's their design, I feel that they should be here when we discuss their work.

A: In my opinion, it might be better if we discussed their design before they got here. I'm quite convinced that people will be more candid about their opinions of the design if the artists aren't sitting here listening. In fact, I put this discussion item first and asked the artistic department to come later on purpose. I have no doubt that honest criticism will flow more freely this way.

B: If you ask me, I still prefer that they were here to get feedback on the design. But if you think this is a better way... Let's go ahead.

A: Okay, If everyone can take a look at the overhead projection. Here are three different logo designs the artistic team submitted. Jim, what's your take on these logos?

C: To be quite honest, I'm not too fond of any of them. The way I look at it, we should have something a little catchier, something more modern, more colorful. I feel that all three of these designs are too boring.

A：大家好，我們開始開會吧。第一個討論的議題就是評估我們新的標誌設計。

B：嗯……藝術部的還沒有到。我個人認為我們應該等他們到了以後再開始。因為這是他們設計的，我覺得我們討論他們工作的時候，他們應該在場。

A：依我看，在他們來之前我們就討論他們的設計會更好些。我比較贊同當藝術家不在場時，人們討論他們的設計才會暢所欲言。事實上，我是有意先討論該項的，並且讓藝術部的人晚點來。我堅信只有這樣，誠實的批評才會更加自然地流露。

B：那如果讓我說，我還是傾向於他們在場，這樣他們能夠得到對設計的回饋。但是如果你覺得那樣更好……那我們就開始吧。

A：好的，請大家看投影片，這裡是藝術部提出的三個不同的標誌設計。Jim，你怎麼看這些標誌？

C：老實說，沒有一個是我非常中意的。在我看來，我覺得應該更易懂、更時尚、更鮮豔些，我覺得這三種都比較乏味。

實境對話 2

A: So what's your view on the new company organization? If you ask me, I think Human Resources was crazy to combine the Sales team and the Marketing team into one department.

B: Generally speaking, I think that most people would disagree with this arrangement. I'd just like to say I think it's a usual way to try to deal with employee unrest.

A: Unrest? I'm absolutely convinced that it wasn't unrest that caused the rearranging. I'm sure that it had something to do with payroll. I strongly believe that they wanted to cut back on the cost of employees, so they decided to consolidate the departments.

B: You think that they consolidated the departments in order to eliminate some positions and lay people off? With the economic recession, I have no doubt that they are trying to conserve funds, but I tend to think that they wouldn't compromise the integrity of the departments.

A: Are you sure? As I see it, the realignment and impending pink slips are definitely related. How do you see the situation?

B: I like to think a little more optimistically about things.

A：那你對新的公司組織結構有什麼想法？如果你問我，我認為人力資源部將業務部和行銷部合併成一個部門的做法實在是有些瘋狂。

B：一般說來，大部分人都會對這個安排持反對意見。我只是想說這是回應員工不安狀態的一般方式。

A：不安狀態？我堅決認為這並非是不安狀態造成這樣的重組。我肯定這和薪資管理有關係。我非常確定他們是想削減員工開支，所以才合併了部門。

B：你認為他們合併部門是在削減職位並且解雇員工？隨著經濟的衰退，我相信他們正在節約資金，但我還是傾向認為他們不會因此來違背部門的整體性。

A：你確定嗎？照我看，調整以後緊接著就是解雇通知書。你怎麼看？

B：我對這比較持肯定態度。

贊同、反對和妥協
Agreeing, Disagreeing and Compromising

在日常生活中，我們要各種類型的人，當然也包括要接觸那些（in contact）不同類型和想法不一樣的人。不贊同並不是要聲嘶力竭、怒髮衝冠。和一個與你的觀點背道而馳的人客氣（polite）地討論是需要技巧和練習的（skill and practice）。

表達贊同

贊同別人的觀點，除了可以說「I agree with you.」以外，還有其他很多種說法。你也可以用absolutely、exactly、no doubt等副詞或片、慣用語來增強肯定語氣。

⊙I agree with you 100 percent. That's so true.
　我百分之百地贊同，那是正確無誤的。

⊙I couldn't agree with you more.
　我完全贊同您。

⊙Tell me about it!
　還用你說嗎！

⊙No doubt about it. You're absolutely right.
　毋庸置疑，您完全正確。

⊙Absolutely. You have a point there.
　毫無疑問，您說得有道理。

⊙That's for sure. That's exactly how I feel.

　那當然。跟我想的完全一樣。

⊙Exactly. I was just going to say that.

　沒錯，我正想這麼說。

⊙I'm afraid I agree with James.

　我贊同James。

⊙I have to side with Daniel on this one.

　在這個問題上，我站在Daniel這邊。

⊙(agree with negative statement) Me neither.

　（同意某否定意見）我也不（同意）。

⊙(weak) I suppose so. / I guess so.

　（較弱）我想是的。/我猜沒錯。

表達不贊同

向別人表達觀點（speak his mind）的機會。傾聽會讓你把注意力集中（focus on）到對話的內容上。即便你根本不同意對方觀點，你也要積極關注（being attentive）來表達您的尊敬。

⊙No way. I totally disagree.

　不行，我完全反對。

⊙I'm not so sure about that. That's not always the case.

　我不是那麼確定。不會總是那樣的。

⊙I'm afraid I disagree. That's not always true.

　我恐怕難以苟同。並非總是如此。

⊙I totally disagree.

　我完全反對。

⊙I'd say the exact opposite.

我認為正好相反。

⊙I beg to differ.

恕我不敢苟同。

⊙Not necessarily.

未必。

打斷

平心靜氣地討論，不要指名道姓，惡語中傷。要溫和體貼（courteous and consideration），引導對方朝你的觀點靠攏，在提出自己的觀點時也要兼顧對方的感受。即使話題被打斷的時候仍要做到承上啟下，保持禮貌。

⊙Can I add something here?

我能補充兩句嗎？

⊙Is it okay if I jump in for a second?

我能插句話嗎？

⊙If I might add something...

我能否補充點……

⊙Can I throw my two cents in?

我能說兩句我的想法嗎？

⊙Sorry to interrupt, but...

很抱歉打斷你了，但是……

⊙(after accidentally interrupting someone) Sorry, go ahead. OR Sorry, you were saying...

（在不小心打斷某人後）對不起，請繼續。或者：對不起，您剛才說……

⊙(after being interrupted) You didn't let me finish.

（在被打斷之後）你剛才沒有讓我説完。

妥協或轉換話題

當討論毫無結果（leading nowhere）時就該轉換話題了。如果雙方都已掃興就沒有必要繼續下去了。禮貌地請求對方或者自己主動換一個有趣的話題，也可以直接説想休息一下。

⊙Let's just move on, shall we?

讓我們談點別的，行嗎？

⊙Let's drop it.

讓我們先到此為止吧。

⊙I think we're going to have to agree to disagree.

我想我們只好各持己見了。

⊙Whatever you say.

你説什麼就是什麼吧。

⊙If you say so.

就按你説的吧。

總結

「理不辯則不明」，無論你是否贊同對方的觀點，都應當是「君子之爭」。要別人心悦誠服，就得先當謙謙君子，以理服人。即便是不贊同別人的觀點，也要認真傾聽，理解其出發點。如果沒有談下去的必要，就要審時度勢，調整話題，畢竟「友誼第一」。

214

單字表

carpet 地毯	climate 氣候
economic 經濟的	memo 備忘錄
misread 錯讀；誤讀	open house 開放參觀
practical joke 惡作劇	presentable 體面的；漂亮的
promote 促進；升級	qualified 合格的
repaint 重畫；重新繪製	repair 修復
replace 替換；取代	resale 轉售；轉賣
selective 選擇性的	

片語表

fixer-upper 有待修繕的	fix-me-up 尚需修整的
head (a department) 領導（一個部門）	hot new thing 熱門新事物
I bet 我敢打賭；我肯定	jump in 跳躍
jump on (sth.) 馬上抓住機會做某事	move on 繼續前移
on this one 就此一（動詞）	outta luck 不走運；運氣差
pretty 非常的	show a house 展示房子
side with (person) 站在……一側	take place 發生
takes time 需要時間	That's crazy. 那真是瘋了。
the joke's on (person) 跟（某人）開玩笑的	turn-around profit 周轉利潤
You'll never guess. 你永遠猜不到。	What were they thinking? 他們當時在想什麼？

實境對話 1

A: Did you hear about who got promoted to head the sales department?

215

You'll never guess! Daniel Barnes, the old maintenance guy. I don't know what the management was thinking!

B: What? Daniel Barnes just cleans the office. How can he do sales? That's crazy!

A: That's for sure. That's exactly how I feel. They must have made this decision as a practical joke!

B: No doubt about it. You're absolutely right. I bet they will tell us all tomorrow morning that the joke's on us.

C: Is it okay if I jump in for a second? If I might add something, I think you might have misread the memo. The new head of sales is Barney Daniels, not Daniel Barnes. And Daniel Barnes has also been promoted to maintenance department head.

A: Oh, I didn't realize that.

B: Me neither.

C: And if you don't mind. Can I throw my two cents in? I think that if the management did ask Daniel Barnes to lead the sales department, he might do a better job than Barney Daniels!

A: I totally disagree. I know Barney pretty well. I think he's pretty qualified.

B: I'm afraid I agree with James. I have to side with Barney on this one.

A：你有沒有聽說是誰被提升為業務部主管了？你絕對猜不到！是Daniel Barnes，維護保養的那個老傢伙。真不知道經理是怎麼想的！

B：什麼？Daniel Barnes只會打掃辦公室，他怎麼會做業務？太瘋狂了吧！

A：那當然。跟我想的完全一樣。做這樣的決定一定是個惡作劇！

B：錯不了。你絕對是對的。我打賭明天一早他們就會告訴大家那是在和我們開的玩笑。

C：如果你們不介意的話，我能插句話嗎？如果要我加點什麼的話，我想一定是你誤讀了備忘錄。新的業務部總監是Barney Daniels，不是Daniel Barnes。而Daniel Barnes也被提升為維修部的主管了。

A：哦，我還真沒有注意到那個。

B：我也沒有。

C：如果你們不介意的話，我能否表達一下我的想法？我想如果經理部讓 Daniel Barnes來領導業務部的話，他可能會比Barney Daniels幹得好。

A：我完全不同意。我很了解Barney。我想他完全能勝任。

B：我也贊同James所説的。在這點上，我站在Barney的這邊。

實境對話 2

A: The open house needs to take place next week. We've got to jump on this right away, or we might loose the opportunity.

B: No way. I totally disagree. There is no way that we can get the property ready by next week. There are so many repairs that must be made; the carpeting needs to be replaced, and all the rooms need to be repainted. It takes time to make a house presentable to buyers. If we show the house before it's ready we'll loose opportunity.

A: I'm not so sure about that. It's not always the case that buyers want a finished product. Many investors are looking for a fix-me-up. The hot new thing is buying houses that need a little work and making a turn-around profit on the resale.

B: I'm afraid I disagree. Maybe in last year's real estate market you might be able to load off a fixer-upper. But that's not always true in today's economic climate. Nowadays people are more selective.

A: I'd say the exact opposite. The economic downturn is the perfect time for people to pick up foreclosed properties at a fraction of their actual value. Investment in real estate is hot right now. We've got to move on this property or we're gonna be outta luck.

B: Not necessarily. I still think we should wait.

A：展示屋必須在下週完工。我們必須得馬上著手這件事，否則我們將會失去這個機會。

B：行不通。我完全反對。我們無法做到在下週前就把房子準備就緒。有許多地方需要修補。地毯需要換，所有的房間都需要重新粉刷。要讓房子煥然一新地出現在買家面前是需要時間的。如果還沒有準備好就展示房子，我們肯定會失去這次機會的。

A：我不這麼認為。並不是所有的買家都想要成品。許多的投資者都是在找有待修補的半成品。一個新的熱門物件就是買一個還需要整修的房子，稍作修繕後再賣。

B：我恐怕無法苟同。在去年那樣的房地產大環境下，你或許能夠賣掉整修的房子，但在今年的經濟氣候下就不是這樣了。現在人們更挑剔了。

A：我會說事實正好相反。經濟下滑使人們鑒於財務能力受限而更傾向於選擇待整修的房子。現在投資房地產正是炙手可熱的時機。在這個房產上我們必須積極進行，否則我們就倒楣了。

B：未必。我仍然覺得我們應該等。

有效地結束會議 Ending a Meeting Effectively

結束一個會議至關重要（critical）。也許還有一個議題沒有討論；一些關鍵的內容（key issues）已經確定；一些相關人等已經被分配了任務（given assignments）。與會者此時就要對會議的效果進行評估，或者是否達到了預期的效果。

....

首先，提醒大家會議已經接近尾聲，下面要進行總結。

⊙Thank you everyone for your participation in today's meeting.
感謝各位今天能夠與會。

⊙I think we've been over most of the important items on the agenda.

我想議程上的大部分重要議題都已經討論過了。

⊙It's getting time for us to wrap things up, any last comments?

現在是我們收尾總結的時間了，還有什麼要說的嗎？

⊙I feel like we've been able to accomplish a lot with today's discussion.

我覺得今天討論的成效斐然。

⊙I appreciate your comments. Let's review quickly before we close.

非常感謝您的意見，讓我們在結束前迅速回顧一下。

⊙Everyone, let's review what we've decided today.

各位，讓我們回顧一下今天的決議。

總結會議

首先宣布閉會在即（at hand），然後總結主要決定和行動方案（summarize key decisions and action item），確定工作安排、時限（timeline）和負責人。

⊙Our time is running out. Let's go over a few of the main points we've discussed today.

我們的時間不多了。讓我們把今天討論過的幾個主要議題回顧一下。

⊙Let's review what our action items are...

讓我們回顧一下我們的行動方案是……

⊙We've decided to approve the marketing reports and customer service evaluations. Louis is responsible for forwarding our corrections on the budget reviews to everyone by Monday.

我們已經決定了透過行銷報告和客戶服務評估。Louis負責在週一前把更正好的預算審核轉寄給每個人。

⊙Our to-do list includes Jill forwarding budget projections to the finance department this afternoon, Martin completing the blueprints by Tuesday and forwarding them to the board, and Kelly will complete the account summaries before Wednesday. Anything else I missed?

我們的工作清單包括：今天下午，Jill將把預算交到財務部，Martin週二前完成藍圖並轉給董事會，Kelly會在週三前完成財務總結。我有遺漏什麼嗎？

⊙We've got to wrap things up. The most critical thing we've talked about is our working budget.

我們必須結束會議了。我們討論過的最重要的事情就是我們的工作預算。

⊙We're done with the agenda, so let's prepare to close the meeting. As a result of this meeting we should have new projections from our design department by next week.

議程的內容都已經完成了，那就準備閉會吧。今天會議的成果之一就是我們的設計部將在下週前拿出新的設計。

重新對照議程

指明哪些內容已經討論過，哪些仍是懸而未決的。這樣，把一些可行性的議程內容（possible agenda items）移到（carried over）下次會議。

⊙Let's review the agenda. We've heard the department reports, discussed the scheduling for this month, and reviewed project analysis. Let's continue with the project analysis in our next meeting, which will be Thursday at 2pm, same place. Are we clear?

讓我們再對照一下我們的議程。我們已經聽取了部門的報告，討論了這個月的活動安排，也對專案分析進行了審核。我們下次會議繼續討論專案分析，下次會議定在週四下午2點，地點不變，都清楚嗎？

⊙We've talked about all our agenda items, except the vacation scheduling. Let's tackle that at next week's meeting.

除了休假安排外，議程的所有內容我們都已經討論過了。可以把那個（內容）留到下週的會議處理。

⊙Our next meeting will be held on September 25ᵗʰ at 9am in the conference room. Can you all make it then?

下次會議定在9月25日上午9點，在會議室舉行，你們都能來嗎？

時間分配

做好時間分配（distribution）。同樣，如果時間允許的話，給每個人一個最後簡單評論或承諾的機會。這樣會提高集體參與的積極性，加強對集體決策的責任感。少數人的意見（minority views）也得以表達。每個人最後發表的時間最好限制在一分鐘之內（under a minute）。

⊙Sally, can you E-mail a copy of this meeting's minutes to everyone this afternoon?

Sally，你能在今天下午把本次會議紀錄的影本，用電子郵件寄給每一個人嗎？

⊙Now, as a close to this meeting, I'd like to ask everyone to share a few last words. Please keep your comments brief.

現在我希望每個人都能説幾句來總結一下我們的會議。請大家發表時簡明扼要。

⊙Any last words? I'd like to hear from everyone. What decisions did you like best? What actions are you going to take after the meeting？

還有什麼要説的嗎？我希望能聽到每個人的發言。對於哪些決定你覺得最喜歡？本次會議結束後你將採取哪些行動。

⊙Thanks for your comment Jim. Lucy, did you have anything to add?

感謝Jim的意見，Lucy，你還有什麼要補充的嗎？

畫上圓滿的句號

要為會議畫上圓滿的句號，就是要讓每個人離開會議室時滿懷激情和幹勁，而不是精疲力竭或者挫折感十足。對於與會者的表現要積極肯定，對於他們的工作和對會議所作的貢獻要表示感激。

⊙Thanks everyone for your contributions to this meeting. I appreciate your hard work.

感謝大家對這次會議所作的貢獻，對於你們努力的工作我深表感激。

⊙I want to take time to thank everyone for a great job in coming together on these issues. We couldn't do it without you!

我想用點時間對於各位積極參與這些事物的討論和出色的表現表示感謝。沒有你們，我們不可能完成！

⊙I appreciate all your fine comments today. Thank you for putting your ideas forward!

對於每個人的意見我深表感激。感謝你們積極的獻策。

總結

開會的整個過程可以形容為「龍頭、鳳尾、美人腰」，即便是閉會也可以成為點睛之筆。對於會議的內容穿針引線做個概述，以此來加深每個人對會議成果的認識，運用會議議程表來查核會議內容是否有遺漏，對於會議決定的行動任務要釐清責任確實執行，最好還能讓每個人最後說兩句，達到展現決心的作用。此外，如果最後還能對大家的努力表達謝意，那更能確保每個人熱血沸騰、幹勁十足了。

ords

單字表 ·······

appreciate 欣賞；感激
brief 簡介；簡短的
comment 評論；意見
correction 更正；糾正
decide 決定
evaluation 評估；評價
participation 參與
review 複審；回顧
summary 摘要；概要

blueprint 藍圖；計畫
close 關閉；停止
continuing 持續的；連續的
critical 關鍵的
due 預期的；到期的
finance 財務
projection 設計；規劃；投影
schedule 進程安排；調度

Phrases

片語表 ·······

as a result of 由於；由於……的結果
before we close 在我們結束之前
customer relation 客戶關係
customer service 客戶服務
get through (an agenda) 貫徹（一個議程）
wrap things up 圓滿完成；順利結束
I feel like 我感覺；我覺得想要
keep (sb.) brief 保持簡明扼要
lose sleep over (sth.) 對……擔憂；擔心……而徹夜難眠
share comments 分享評論；分享意見
the board 董事會

go over 過（內容）
come together (on an issue) （因為某事上而）聚集到一起
forward to (sb.) 轉寄給（某人）
good idea 好主意
hear from (sb.) 收到（某人）來信；得到（某人）消息
in regards to 關於
last word 定論；最後說一句
be responsible for (doing sth.) 對（做某事）負責
take action 採取行動
to-do list 待辦事項；擬清單

實境對話 1

A: Thank you everyone for your participation in today's meeting. I think we've been over most of the important items on the agenda. It's getting time for us to wrap things up, any last comments?

B: I feel like we've been able to accomplish a lot with today's discussion. Especially in regards to the company finances. Thanks everyone for coming together on that.

A: I appreciate your comments. Let's review quickly before we close. Laura, can you help us review what we've decided today?

C: Sure. We've decided to approve the marketing reports and customer service evaluations. Louis is responsible for forwarding our corrections on the budget reviews to everyone by Monday.

D: Is it Monday or Tuesday that the budget reviews are due?

C: Oh, yes, that's right. Tuesday. Continuing, our to-do list includes Jill forwarding budget projections to the finance department this afternoon, Martin completing the blueprints by Tuesday and forwarding them to the board, and Kelly will complete the account summaries before Wednesday. Anything else I missed?

A: I think that's about it. Now, as a close to this meeting, I'd like to ask everyone to share a few last words. Please keep your comments brief. I'd like to hear from everyone. What decisions did you like best? What actions are you going to take after the meeting?

A：感謝各位參與今天的會議。我想議程上的大部分重要議題我們都已經討論過了。現在是我們圓滿結束的時候了。還有什麼要說的嗎？

B：我覺得今天的討論成效斐然。尤其是在公司的財務問題上，感謝大家積極地獻策。

A：非常感謝您的意見。讓我們在結束之前迅速地回顧一下。Laura，你能幫我們回顧一下今天的決定嗎？

C：好的。我們已經決定通過行銷報告和客戶服務評估。Louis在週一前將更正後的預算審核轉寄給各位。

D：預算審核預是週一還是週二？

C：哦，是週二。我繼續，我們的工作清單包括：今天下午Jill把預算案交到財務部；Martin週二前完成藍圖並轉給董事會；Kelly會在週三前完成財務總結。有什麼遺漏的嗎？

A：我想就是這些了。現在我希望每個人都能說幾句來結束我們的會議。請大家發表時簡明扼要。我希望每個人都能踴躍發言。你最喜歡的是哪幾項決議？此次會議結束後你將採取怎樣的行動？

實境對話 2

A: We've got to wrap things up. We're almost done with the agenda, so let's prepare to close the meeting. As a result of this meeting we should have new projections from our design department by next week. The most critical thing we've talked about is our working budget.

B: Before we close, let's review the agenda one more time.

A: Good idea. Can you help us with that Melanie?

C: Sure. We've heard the department reports, discussed the scheduling for this month, and reviewed project analysis. Then the last item was vacation scheduling.

A: Let's continue with the project analysis in our next meeting, which will be Thursday at 2pm, same place. Are we clear?

D: We haven't gotten completely through the agenda. Should we keep working on it?

A: We've talked about all our agenda items, except the vacation scheduling. Let's tackle that at next week's meeting. Sally, can you E-mail a copy of this meeting's minutes to everyone this afternoon?

D: No problem.

A: Okay, Any last words?

B: Thanks everyone for working so hard on the budget. I know that we've all lost a lot of sleep over it.

A: Thanks for your comment Jim. Lucy, did you have anything to add?

A：我們已經圓滿結束了。議程內容基本上都完成了，那我們就準備閉會吧。今天會議的成果之一就是我們的設計部將在下週前拿出新的設計。我們討論過最重要的事情就是我們的工作預算。

B：在結束之前，讓我們再回顧一遍議程吧。

A：好主意。Melanie您能幫忙嗎？

C：好的。我們聽取了部門的報告，討論了這個月的工作安排，也對專案分析進行了審核。最後一項是休假安排。

A：我們下次會議繼續討論專案分析，下次會議定在週四下午2點，地點不變。都清楚了嗎？

D：議程還沒有完全討論完。我們還要繼續嗎？

A：除了休假安排以外，議程的所有內容我們都已經討論過了。那項內容我們移到下週的會議上。Sally，今天下午是否能把這次會議紀錄的影本用電子郵件寄給每個人？

D：沒問題。

A：好的。還有什麼要補充的嗎？

B：感謝各位在預算工作上的辛苦努力，我知道大家在這個問題上費了不少心思。

A：感謝Jim的評論。Lucy，你還有什麼要補充的嗎？

十 項 全 能 之 七

拉近客戶關係
Client Reception

首次和客戶會晤
Meeting a Client for the First Time

第一次見面就要針對某專案和具體細節（nitty gritty）展開討論，這聽起來有些讓人望而卻步（daunting）。當你感到緊張的時候，不妨看看以下建議。這些內容可以幫助你把握一些可預測的基本狀況（predictable bases）。

首先，一定要牢記客人的基本資料：名字、職位和所在部門等。尤其在客人以群體形式出現的情況時，千萬不要稱呼錯了。見面時，主人要先做自我介紹以示禮貌，然後客人再做自我介紹。

⊙Mr. Jones? Hi! I'm Jiao Qiu. Thanks for taking the time to meet with me today!
是Jones先生嗎？您好，我叫焦秋。感謝您今天抽空與我見面！

⊙We're glad you could make it today, Mrs. Hatch. I'm Thomas Chen.
感謝您今天能來，Hatch女士。我是Thomas陳。

⊙I'll be showing you around today.
我今天先向您介紹環境。

⊙Please let me know if you have any questions.
如果您有什麼問題請告訴我。

⊙Welcome to our offices, did you find it okay?
歡迎來我們的辦公室，還好找嗎？

⊙I'd like to introduce you to our office manager, Nelvin Guo.
我想介紹您認識我們的辦公室經理，Nelvin郭。

滿懷信心
對你準備好的內容和要做的事情要滿懷信心（confidence）。掌握話語主動

權（get them to the table）。要消除緊張情緒，並把所有的疑慮都拋到腦後（back of your mind）。

A: Mr. Jones, welcome to our offices. I hope you found your way with no difficulty.

B: Yes, it was easy to find.

A: Shall we start right into our meeting? I am really looking forward to discussing our products with you.

A：Jones先生，歡迎您來到我們的辦公室。還好找吧。

B：是的，很容易找到。

A：我們現在可以開始會議了嗎？我很期待和您討論我們的產品。

挑選會晤地點

挑選會晤地點是不可忽視的細節之一。有時候最好在公共場所（public place），例如咖啡廳或餐廳。有時候你也可以邀請你的客人去你的辦公室或工作場所（place of work）。場所是否有網路也很重要，當然最重要的是你和客戶都感覺自在舒適（at ease）。

⊙Shall we meet at Starbucks?

　我們是否可以在星巴克碰面？

⊙If you'll follow me, I'll show you to the conference room. We can hold our meeting in there.

　請您跟我來，我帶您看一下會議室。我們可以在那裡開會。

⊙The office is a little stuffy. Let's make our way to the coffee bar across the street. They have wireless internet, so we can discuss our project there.

　這間辦公室有點悶，我們一起到對街的咖啡廳去吧。他們有無限網路，我們可以在那裡討論我們的計畫。

態度積極

考慮穿著和形象，給客戶一個好印象（good impression）。穿著要專業、整潔（well-groomed），並且準時，積極傾聽且適時發問。這樣才能展現你對他們所講的內容有興趣。問些有實際意義的問題（open ended questions）和有延續性的問題（follow-up questions）以確保談話不會冷場。

⊙What do you think about...?

　對於……你是怎麼想的？

⊙Tell me more about...

　能否告訴我更多有關……

⊙So you mean that...?

　那你的意思是……

⊙Let me see if I am understanding correctly. You mean...?

　讓我確認一下我的理解是否正確。你的意思是……

⊙Would you rather...?

　您願意……？

明確目標

對各自目的都要有所了解。透過有效的溝通（effective communication）達到會晤目的，同時別忘了花點時間來和客戶建立良好的關係（build a relationship）。確認你了解客戶的要求（requirements），以確保提供的服務正是客戶所需要的。實現上述目標的最好辦法就是以清單記錄的形式來總結。

⊙So tell me what I can do for you?

　請告訴我有什麼可以幫您的？

⊙What specific products and services are you interested in?

　您對哪些產品和服務有興趣？

⊙Can I answer any questions for you?

　有什麼問題我可以為您解答嗎？

⊙What we'd like to accomplish today is...

　我們希望今天能夠完成……

⊙We're looking to...

　我們期待……

⊙We hope that by the end of our time together today, we can...

　我們希望可以用今天的時間，我們可以……

總結

把自己擺對位置，弄清楚我是誰、他是誰就可以輕鬆應對；明白我要什麼、他要什麼，就能舉重若輕；權責分明、充分準備、周到考慮，就能信手拈來，有備無患。即便是第一次與客戶會晤，就算涉及很多細節，也不會緊張。

單字表

coffee bar 咖啡廳	corporate 合作
deadline 截止日	department head 部門經理
fabric 面料；布料	laptop 筆記型電腦
line 線	requirement 要求
stuffy 乏味的；悶的	swatch 色板；顏色板
textile 紡織品	via 經過；經由

片語表 ···

across the street 橫過馬路；對街

find one's way 找到自己的路

get busy 開始忙碌

if you like 如果您願意

looking forward to 展望；期望

make our way (to place) 讓我們去
（某處）

show sb to (place) 給某人展示（某處）

take the time (to do sth.) 花時間做
（某事）

burn the midnight oil 開夜車；挑燈夜戰

wireless Internet 無線網路

hold a meeting 召開；舉行會議

let us know 讓我們知道

make it 達到目的；獲得成功

office manager 業務經理；辦公室經理

products and services 產品和服務

start right in 啟動權

wireless card 無線網卡

實境對話 1

A: Mr. Jones? Hi! I'm Jiao Qiu. Thanks for taking the time to meet with me today! I'd like to introduce you to our office manager, Nelvin Guo. The office is a little stuffy. Let's make our way to the coffee bar across the street. They have wireless internet, so we can discuss our project there.

B: Oh, okay. My computer doesn't have a wireless card though...

A: Oh, well that's no problem. We could also hold our meeting here if you like. We can give you an Ethernet cable for your laptop. If you'll follow me, I'll show you to the conference room. We can hold our meeting in there.

B: Great.

A: So tell me more about your requirements for this project. What kind of deadline are we talking about?

B: Our corporate deadline is in two weeks, but the department head has given us a deadline of next Tuesday.

A: So you mean that we've got to really get busy! You want to get all the reports written and reviewed before next Thursday.

B: No, not before next Thursday. Before next Tuesday.

A: Wow, we've got to burn the midnight oil on this one!

A：是Jones先生嗎？您好，我是焦秋。感謝您今天抽空與我見面！我想介紹您認識我們的辦公室經理，Nelvin郭。辦公室有點悶，我們到對街的咖啡廳吧。他們有無線網路，我們可以在那裡討論我們的計畫。

B：哦，好的。但是我的電腦沒有無線網卡……

A：哦，那沒問題。如果您願意的話，我們也可以在這裡開會。我們可以提供您的手提電腦網路線。如果您願意跟我來的話，我帶您看一下會議室。我們可以在那裡開會。

B：好極了。

A：那請您再告訴我一些關於你們對這個專案的要求。我們現在談的截止日是什麼時間？

B：我們公司的截止日是兩週內，但是部門主管給我們的截止日是下週二。

A：那您意思是說從現在起我們就得忙起來了！您希望在下週四前拿到所有寫好並審核通過的報告。

B：不，不是在下週四前，而是下週二前。

A：哇，看來這次我們要挑燈夜戰了！

實境對話 2

A: I'm glad you could make it today, Mrs. Hatch. I'm Thomas Chen. I'll be showing you around today. This is Martin Shen, our production manager. Please let us know if you have any questions.

B: Welcome to our offices, Mrs. Hatch. I hope you found your way with no difficulty.

C: Yes, it was easy to find, thank you.

B: Before Thomas gives you a tour of the office, shall we start right into our meeting? I am really looking forward to discussing our products with you.

C: Oh, okay.

B: What specific products and services are you interested in?

C: From looking at the materials you sent me via E-mail, I think we are more interested in your textile line.

B: Can I answer any questions for you about the items you are interested in?

C: Actually I have several questions. We're looking to make an order of several hundred containers. What we'd like to accomplish today is to review the types and qualities of fabric we have to choose from.

B: Certainly! Thomas, would you please go get the catalog of fabric swatches for Mrs. Hatch to review?

A: I'd be happy to!

B: We hope that by the end of our time together today, we can help answer all of your questions and make a production order.

A：我們很高興您能來，Hatch女士。我是Thomas陳。我今天帶您認識環境。這位是Martin沈，我們的生產經理。有什麼問題就請告訴我們。

B：歡迎來到我們的辦公室，Hatch女士。還好找吧？

C：是的，很容易找到，謝謝。

B：在Thomas帶您參觀我們辦公室之前，我們能否先開始我們的會議？我很期待和您探討我們的產品。

C：哦，好的。

B：您對什麼產品和服務感興趣？

C：從看您用電子郵件寄給我的資料，我想我們對你們的紡織品更感興趣。

B：針對您感興趣的專案，有什麼問題嗎？

C：事實上，我有幾個問題要問。我們想要訂購幾百個貨櫃。我們希望今天能夠確認我們要挑選的布料類型和品質。

B：當然！Thomas，您能否拿布樣給Hatch女士看看？

A：好的！

B：我們希望可以用今天的時間，回答您所有的問題，並且能夠確認生產訂單。

交換名片 Exchanging Business Cards

名片是讓別人記住你的最直接（concrete tool）、最有效的方式。透過名片，別人可以知道你的基本資料，比如：你是誰、從哪裡來、怎麼聯絡等。一張別致的名片，一個適時的呈遞，會給人留下難以磨滅（tremendous）的印象。

你應該知道什麼時候積極主動（take the initiative）地遞上名片，或者當別人主動遞上時，你該如何優雅的互換名片。

⊙Do you have a card?

　您有名片嗎？

⊙How can I reach you?

　我該如何聯絡你？

⊙Here's my card.

　這是我的名片。

⊙Can I have your contact information?

　能否告訴我您的聯絡方式？

⊙How can I contact you in the future?

　以後我該如何和您聯絡呢？

⊙Did you have a card I could have?

　您是否可以給我一張名片？

接名片

當某人遞上名片的時候，你可以握住名片的邊緣對其道謝，並認真讀名片內容。如果只是抓過名片並塞進口袋，那你無意中（inadvertently）轉達給對方的印象可能是你並不那麼尊重他。注意卡片上的內容不僅表示你有興趣，也同樣給你一個機會來了解你面對的這個人或公司是否對你的生意有幫助，是否有必要把你們的萍水相逢轉換（transition）為一個有意義（meaningful）的談話。

⊙I see from your card that you also have offices in Sydney? Do you do much business in Australia?

我從您的名片上得知，你們在雪梨也有辦公室？你們在澳洲有很多生意嗎？

⊙So you're the Marketing Director? What areas will your company focus on marketing in the future?

所以您是行銷總監？你們公司未來將專注於哪些行銷領域？

⊙You're based in Chicago? We make several trips to Chicago for trade shows every year.

你們總部在芝加哥？我們每年因為貿易展的關係都會往返芝加哥好幾次。

⊙I noticed from your card that your company is a subsidiary of the Delport Corporation. What exactly does your company do?

我留意到您的名片上說您的公司是Delport的分公司。貴公司究竟是做什麼的？

給名片

最好發名片的辦法就是向別人索取名片。無論您是在和一個路人（passers-by）還是一個實力雄厚的新客戶談話，只要是對你的產品和服務有興趣的人，都不妨問句「能否惠賜一張您的名片？」這時，一定要記得遞上一張你的名片作為回應「這是我的名片」。過程很簡單，但是一定要真心誠意（be genuine）。交談之後別忘了換名片和握握手。索取名片時儘可能表現出風度翩翩（personable），這樣才能確保給對方留下良好的印象，為進一步地往來奠定基礎。

⊙Let me give you my card. You can reach me by E-mail, or this is our office phone number. You can also call me there.

我給您一張我的名片。您可以用電子郵件和我聯絡，或者這裡有我的辦公室電話號碼。您也可以打這個電話找我。

⊙Would you mind sharing a business card? I'd like to follow up with you about some of the things we have talked about. Oh, here's my card.

您介意惠賜一張您的名片嗎？我想就我們談到的一些事情進一步和您探討。對了，這是我的名片。

⊙I've got a card I can give you. This is my contact information if you have any other questions.

我給您一張名片。如果您還有別的什麼問題，這是我的聯絡方式。

該做的和不該做的

●確保名片上的資訊是最新的。

●交換名片時要溫文爾雅。

●一定要準備到位。

●接受名片時要表現出恭敬。

●破損的或資料有誤的名片切勿遞出。

●別把名片塞給那些根本沒有向你索要的人。

●別把名片放入個人的或有情感意義的信件中。

●對於一個新聯絡人別給兩次名片。

●別把名片放在皮包、口袋或錢包裡面。

總結

與其說是遞上一張小小的名片，不如說是開啟一扇往來的大門。能否做到讓別人有一天拿起你的名片時會想起你，全要看你當時給出名片時是否彬彬有禮，是否充滿誠意。一張名片就是一個機會，就看你怎麼把握了。

單字表

Asia 亞洲
correct 正確的
focus 焦點；論題
holding 股份
products 產品
trade show 貿易展

bulk 大批
domestic 國內
headquarter 總部
marketing 市場行銷
subsidiary 子公司

片語表

as a matter of fact 事實上
by E-mail 透過電子郵件
do business (in a place)（在某處）做生意
What exactly... 究竟……
hear more about 聽到更多關於
It's been great 看起來很棒
multi-national corporation 多國公司
set up shop 建立店面
We'll be in touch. 我們將保持聯繫。

based in 總部位於
contact information 聯絡方式；聯繫資訊
expand (in a specific market) 拓展
（在特定市場）
interested in 對……有興趣
marketing director 行銷總監
reach (someone) 聯絡到（某人）
State-side 美國的（用於在境外時指美
國）

實境對話 1

A: It's been great talking to you. I am interested in hearing more about your
   products. How can I contact you in the future? Do you have a card?
B: Yes! Here's my card. You can reach me by E-mail. Or this is our office
   phone number. You can also call me there. Would you mind sharing a

business card? I'd like to follow up with you about some of the things we have talked about.

A: Sure. Let me give you my card, too. So you're the Marketing Director? What areas will your company focus on marketing in the future?

B: Like I said, we are working on expanding in the Asian markets. We hope to set up a shop in Shanghai by the end of the year. I see from your card that you also have offices in Sydney? Do you do much business in Australia?

A: Yes, as a matter of fact, over a third of our holdings are based in Australia.

B: But your card says you're based in Chicago?

A: Yes, that's correct. We are headquartered there.

B: We make several trips to Chicago for trade shows every year.

A：很高興能夠和您談話。我想聽到更多有關你們產品的情況。以後，我該怎麼和您聯繫呢？您有名片嗎？

B：是的，這是我的名片。透過電子郵件您就可以聯絡到我。或者這裡有我的辦公室電話號碼，您也可以打這個電話找到我。您是否願意惠賜一張名片？我想就我們談到的一些事情下次繼續和您探討。

A：當然，我也給您一張我的名片。您是行銷總監？你們公司未來行銷將專注於哪些領域？

B：正如我所說的，我們正在致力開拓亞洲市場。我們希望在年底之前能在上海開一家店。我從您的名卡上得知，你們在雪梨也有辦事處？你們在澳洲的生意多嗎？

A：是的，我們控股公司的三分之一都在澳洲。

B：但是您的名片上顯示你們總部在芝加哥？

A：是的。我們的總部在那裡。

B：每年因為貿易展的原因，我們都會往返芝加哥多次。

實境對話 2

A: What's your contact information? How can I reach you in the future?

B: Let me give you one of my cards. Here.

A: Thanks! (takes time to study card) I notice from your card that your company is a subsidiary of the Delport Corporation. What exactly does your company do?

B: That's right, we are a part of Delport. We handle the bulk of the domestic market. Delport is a multi-national corporation. They have their hands full. We're only the state-side portion.

A: Oh, interesting...

B: Did you have a card I could have?

A: Oh yeah, of course. Let me find one for you, just a second.

B: No problem.

A: Here you go.

B: Thanks! We'll be in touch.

A：您的聯絡方式是什麼？以後我該如何和您聯繫呢？

B：給您一張我的名片。

A：謝謝。（仔細研究名片內容）我留意到您的名片上顯示您的公司是Delport 公司的子公司。貴公司是做什麼的？

B：是的，我們是Delport公司的一部分，我們負責大部分國內市場。Delport 是一個跨國公司，他們遍及各地，而我們只負責美國國內部分。

A：哦，很有意思⋯⋯

B：您能否給我一張您的名片？

A：哦，當然。我找一張給您，稍等。

B：沒問題。

A：給您。

B：謝謝，我們保持聯絡。

交換禮物　Exchanging Gifts

對於西方人來説，送禮不像東方人想得那樣複雜（complex），要注意的規矩很少。禮物的大小、樣式和種類與生意大小沒有直接的關係。無論是買方和賣方，還是合作夥伴之間，禮物都代表著彼此間的欣賞和喜愛（show appreciation）。

語氣輕鬆自然

拿出禮物前，大方地表示你帶了禮物。語氣一定要輕鬆自然，用「something」、「a little something」、「a small gift」這類自謙的説法代表「禮物」。

⊙I brought something for you, I hope you like it!
　　我帶了點東西給您，希望您能夠喜歡！

⊙Here's a little something just to show our appreciation for your friendship.
　　這裡有一點小東西來表達對您的情誼的感謝。

⊙Please accept this as a token of our appreciation.
　　請接受這個作為我們感激之情的小小表示。

⊙We wanted to bring you something special.
　　我們希望能給您帶點特別的東西。

⊙We've prepared a small gift for you.
　　我們為您準備了一個小禮物。

⊙How thoughtful of you! Thank you very much!
　　您考慮得真是太周到了！非常感謝！

了解禮物的贈予對象

禮物不在於形式（presentation）。最大的並不代表是最好的。中國人在接受禮物時可能會去衡量禮物的大小和價格，而西方人比較在意禮物被賦予的個別性（the individuality）和隱含的意義。禮物的好壞不在於貴重而在於是否合適。親手挑選（hand select）的禮物最有意義。對於你的明星客戶（star customers）或者你很想結交的客戶，考慮購買一些能夠滿足他們興趣的禮物。

⊙Since we know your interest in music, we hope you enjoy these recordings of Beijing Opera that we've put together as a gift for you.

知道您喜愛音樂，所以希望您能夠喜歡這些我們送您的北京京劇唱片。

⊙Because this is your first time to China, we wanted to give you a gift you'd remember. Here are some traditional Chinese...

因為您是第一次來中國，我們想送您禮物留作紀念。這是些中國傳統的……

⊙We know you're a golfing pro, so we'd like to present you with some special golf balls. If you look carefully, you can see an image of the Great Wall has been printed on each ball.

我們知道您是個專業的高爾夫球員，所以我們想送給您一些特殊的高爾夫球。如果您仔細看的話，會發現每個球上都有長城的圖案。

⊙We know you enjoy the arts, so we'd like to present you with these traditional Chinese watercolor paintings. The scenery depicted is the local area where you visited this time in China.

我們知道您喜愛藝術，所以我們想送給您這些傳統的中國水墨畫。上面描繪的地方都是您這次在中國參觀過的地方。

⊙You mentioned your favorite color is green. We hope you will enjoy this cashmere sweater from Inner Mongolia. We made sure to get your favorite color!

您提過說您最喜愛綠色。我們希望您能喜歡這件來自內蒙古的喀什米爾毛衣。我們特別挑了您最喜歡的綠色！

禮物贈一人？還是送多人？

要讓對方「很受用」，他（他們）的性別、興趣、職位等等是你選購禮物時要考慮的因素。一些禮物是你為某個人準備的，另一些是給某群人準備的。如果受贈方是一個公司的決策者（decision-maker），那可以送辦公桌面紀念物、獨特的植物，或者與其喜好相關的東西（hobby-related items）。如果你要送的是某一個辦公室的人，讓每一個人都喜歡的禮物最好還是吃的，有特色的咖啡、茶，或者比薩店的禮券。

⊙Here's a little something for the folks back at the office.

這裡有一些小東西帶回去給辦公室同事。

⊙I hope everyone likes...

我希望大家都喜歡……

⊙I hope you can take these back to share with your co-workers. Give them a taste of China, too!

我希望您能夠把這些帶回去和同事們分享，也讓他們體驗一下中國特色！

當面打開

美國人通常希望禮物一送出去就被當面（the moment）打開。看到別人收到禮物時的表情（expression on the face）對他們來說是件非常快樂的事。因此，一般情況下（common practice）禮物都是當面打開、當面讚賞。當你還不能確認贈送者是否願意當面打開的時候，你可以禮貌地問：「我可以現在打開嗎？或者是先留著？」

A: We've prepared a small gift for you. It's just a little something just to show our appreciation for your friendship.

B: How thoughtful of you! Thank you very much!

A: There you are. (gives the package)

B: That's very nice of you. Shall I open it now or save it for later?

A：我們為您準備了一個小禮物。這個小東西表達我們對您的情誼的感激之情。

B：您考慮得真是太周到了。非常感謝。

A：給您。（遞上包裹）

B：您真是太好了，我可以現在打開嗎？或是是先留著？

總結

我們中國人常說「禮尚往來」。一個小小的付出，也許可以收到意想不到的效果。禮物可以小，但「說法」卻一點也不能少。禮物可以反映你對一個人個性的了解，也可以反映你對你們交往的希望。細節雖小，卻大有文章。

單字表··

accept 接受

arts 藝術

considerate 體貼的；考慮周到的

during 在⋯⋯期間

folk 夥計；年輕人

host 主人

prepare 準備

token 標記；象徵

appreciation 欣賞

cashmere 喀什米爾羊毛

depict 描繪

enjoy 欣賞；享受

gorgeous 燦爛的；輝煌的

mention 提及

scenery 風景

watercolor 水彩；水彩畫

片語表 ·····

a gift to remember 一份禮物作紀念

back home 回到家

come to a close 即將結束

folks back at (home / the office) 帶給

（家裡的/辦公室的）夥計；同事

make sure to 請務必

show (sb.) around 帶（某人）到處參觀

take back with you 給你帶回去

體驗一下風味（某東西或某處）

as a token of appreciation 作為答謝

by the way 順便

favorite color 最喜歡的顏色

It's nothing, really. 這沒什麼，真的。

local area 區域

save for later 下次購買；留給下次

show appreciation 表示讚賞

have a taste (of sth. or some place)

too kind 太客氣；太好了

實境對話 1

A: Because this is your first time to China, we wanted to give you a gift you'd remember...

B: Oh, thanks! That's really nice of you guys!

A: You mentioned your favorite color is green. We hope you will enjoy this cashmere sweater from Inner Mongolia. We made sure to get your favorite color!

B: Wow, that's very considerate. Thank you so much!

A: It's nothing, really. Please accept this as a token of our appreciation. Oh, and we also prepared a small gift you can take back with you to the folks back at the office. I hope you can take these traditional Chinese candies back to share with your co-workers. Give them a taste of China, too!

B: The people back home will really appreciate these! You're too kind!

A: It's nothing at all. We're so happy to have had the chance to host you during your time here.

A：因為這是您第一次來中國，我們想送您禮物留作紀念。

B：哦，謝謝！你們真是太客氣了！

A：您提過説您最喜歡綠色。我們希望您能喜歡這件來自內蒙古的喀什米爾毛衣。我們特別挑了件您喜歡的綠色！

B：哇！你們想得真是太周到了。非常感謝！

A：真的沒什麼。我們的一點心意還請笑納。哦，我們還準備了一些小禮物給您辦公室的同事們。我們希望您能把這些中國傳統的糖果帶回去與您的同事們分享，讓他們也體驗一下中國特色！

B：家裡的人一定會非常喜歡的。你們真是太好了！

A：沒什麼的，我們很高興能有個這機會在這兒招待您。

實境對話 2

A: It's been great visiting with you these last few days. Thank you so much for showing me around China.

B: It has certainly been our pleasure, Mr. Jones. As our time together is coming to a close, we've prepared a small gift for you. We hope you like it!

A: You're too kind!

B: We know you enjoy the arts, so we'd like to present you with these traditional Chinese watercolor paintings. The scenery depicted is the local area where you visited this time in China.

A: Wow, they're gorgeous! That is so considerate. Thank you very much. I really like them.

B: We're glad you like them.

A: Oh, by the way, I brought something for you, too. It's just a little something to show our appreciation for your friendship.

B: How thoughtful of you! Thank you very much!

A: There you are. (gives the package)

B: That's very nice of you. Shall I open it now or save it for later?

A：最近這幾天能夠和您一起參觀真的好極了。感謝您帶我遊覽中國。

B：榮幸之極，Jones先生。我們在一起的時間即將結束，我們為您準備了一份小禮物。我們希望您能夠喜歡！

A：你們真是太好了！

B：我們知道您喜愛藝術，所以我們想送您這些中國傳統的水墨畫。畫中描繪的這些地方都是您在中國這段時間參觀過的。

A：哇，簡直是絢麗多彩！你們真的是太體貼了。非常感謝，我非常喜歡。

B：我們很高興您能喜歡。

A：對了，順便說一句，我也帶了些東西給您。這個小東西表達了我們對您的情誼的感激之情。

B：您考慮得真是太周到了！非常感謝！

A：給您。（遞上包裹）

B：您真是太好了，我可以現在打開嗎？或是先留著？

寒暄　Making Small Talk

寒暄是在友好的情況下閒聊、發展友誼的同時有意識地建立業務關係、開拓商機。為了給對方留下好印象，你的儀表要整潔、態度要隨和（easygoing）、談吐要得體。

如果雙方事先不認識，要先做自我介紹。寒暄的話題不宜過於沉重，也無需刻意表現，自然（be yourself）輕鬆就好。

⊙Hi there. My name is Whitney Johnson. What's your name?

你好，我叫Whitney Johnson，怎麼稱呼您？

⊙Let me introduce myself. I'm Han JinBo. Looks like we both came a long way today.

我來自我介紹一下。我叫韓金波。今天我們倆好像都是遠道而來的。

⊙How do you like...?

你認為……怎麼樣？

⊙Don't you think...?

你不覺得……嗎？

⊙I love your dress. It's such a nice color.

我喜歡你的衣服，顏色很好看。

⊙Don't you just love this weather?

你不覺得今天天氣不錯嗎？

寒暄是相互的

注意什麼時候該停頓，給別人講話的機會。這樣也可以繼續深入話題，有利於尋找共同點。

⊙So what brings you to this meeting?

那您是抱著什麼目的來參加這個會的？

⊙What do you do for a living?

您從事的是什麼工作？

⊙What do you think of...?

您怎麼看……？

⊙Where are you from?

你來自什麼地方？

⊙Is this your first time to...?

這是您第一次來……嗎？

⊙How many kids do you have?

你有幾個孩子？

⊙Have you ever been to (place)?

您有沒有去過……（地方）？

⊙Have you been here for a long time?

您來這裡很久了嗎？

⊙How do you know (host)?

您是怎麼認識（主人）的？

⊙How long was your flight?

飛機飛了多長時間？

避免冷場，玩笑適宜

幽默和玩笑是拉進人與人之間距離的法寶，但是要有適當的分寸，不要讓對方認為是嘲笑。講述某故事也不宜過長，可以跨過背景細節（background details），凸顯精彩的部分。

⊙Looks like you've got your hands full there. You need some help? I'll go ask someone for you.

看起來你好像應接不暇。你需要幫忙嗎？我可以請人來幫你。

⊙I went to California once. Loved it! We visited lots of different places. I think the kids liked Disneyland the best.

我去過一次加州，太喜歡了。我們去了好多不同的地方。我想孩子們還是最喜歡迪士尼樂園。

⊙I remember a time when meetings wouldn't last more than ten minutes. Seems like it takes ten minutes just for everyone to sit down these days.

我記得以前的會議最多10分鐘。現在好像每個人都需要10分鐘才能入座。

且聽且問

傾聽並且提問表明你對對方所講的內容有興趣，也可以更多了解對方的背景，同時避免冷場的尷尬。

A: So what do you do for a living?

B: I'm a doctor. A cardiac surgeon, actually.

A: Wow, that's a very demanding job. What do you think is the most challenging aspect of what you do?

A：您是做什麼工作的？

B：我是個醫生。確切地說是心臟外科醫生。

A：哇，那可是要求很高的工作啊。您覺得您所從事的工作中最具挑戰性的是哪個部分？

A: How do you know Bob?

B: He's my old college roommate. We both went to Harvard.

A: Is that right? What do you think about Harvard's business school?

A：你是怎麼認識Bob的？

B：他是我大學的室友。我們兩個都念過哈佛。

A：是嗎？那你覺得哈佛的商學院怎麼樣？

話題穩定

別太快轉換話題，談話儘量深入，但如果真的無話可說了，那就換個話題。

A: What do you think about this conference?

B: Oh, it's interesting, I guess.

A: Which parts did you find the most interesting?

B: Oh, I don't know. I guess the financial workshops weren't too bad.

A: Yeah, I think I learned a little about finance... So where did you say you were from again?

A：你覺得這個論壇怎麼樣？

B：我想會很有意思的。

A：你覺得最有意思的是哪個部分？

B：哦，我不知道，我覺得金融研討會還不錯。

A：是的，我也學到一些有關金融的……對了，您說您是從哪裡來的？

總結

寒暄絕對不是無聊的搭訕或者簡單的噓寒問暖，要和一個人或一群人聊在一起、打成一片，不僅需要勇氣，還需要技巧。出門在外靠朋友，也許聊著聊著就聊出了商機。但也不能目的性太強，閒談還是要以發展友誼為主，不然別人會以為碰上了推銷員。

單字表

actually 事實上

cardiac 心臟的

challenging 挑戰性的

demanding 要求過高的

aspect 方面

chairman 主席

committee 委員會

wow 哇

east coast 東海岸
quite 相當；十分
training 訓練；培訓

feasible 可行的
surgeon 外科醫生
workshop 廠房；工作室

片語表 ···

Don't you just love (thing)? 難道你不
喜歡（某物）？
Is that right? 是嗎？那樣對嗎？
off to college 上大學
quite a few 不少；相當多的
Sure do! 當然！
take part in 參加；參與
these days 當今

for a living 為生；謀生
I (did sth.) once. 我就（做過某事）一次。
Not too bad. 還可以。（不算太壞。）
over the last few years 在過去的幾年裡
seems like 感覺像；好像是
take a minute (to do sth.) 花一分鐘時
間（來做某事）
You mean... 你的意思是⋯⋯

實境對話 1

A: I love your dress. It's such a nice color.

B: Oh, thanks!

A: My name is Whitney Johnson. What's your name?

B: I'm Linda Stevens. Don't you just love this weather?

A: It's a little too cold for me. I'm from California. We don't do winter in California.

B: I went to California once. Loved it! We visited lots of different places. I think the kids liked Disneyland the best.

A: How many kids do you have?

B: Two, a boy and a girl. But they're grown and off to college by now. So have you been here for a long time?

A: Here in New York you mean? I just arrived last week.

B: Is this your first time to come to the city?

A: No, I've come to New York city quite a few times over the last years on business.

B: What do you do for a living?

A: I'm a doctor. A cardiac surgeon, actually. I come to New York to take part in medical trainings.

A: Wow, that's a very demanding job. What do you think is the most challenging aspect of what you do?

A：我很喜歡您的衣服，顏色真好看。

B：哦，謝謝！

A：我叫Whitney Johnson。您叫什麼？

B：我叫Linda Stevens。您不覺得天氣不錯嗎？

A：對我來說有點冷。我來自加州，我們那裡沒有冬天。

B：我去過加州一次，很喜歡。我們去過很多不同的地方。我想孩子們最喜歡的還是迪士尼樂園。

A：您有幾個孩子？

B：兩個，一個男孩和一個女孩。他們都已經長大成人，現在都上大學了。那您來這裡很久了嗎？

A：您是説紐約嗎？我上週才來。

B：您是第一次來這個城市嗎？

A：不，最近這幾年因為工作關係，我來了好多次了。

B：您從事的是什麼工作？

A：我是個醫生。確切地説是心臟外科醫生。我來紐約是參加一個醫療培訓的。

B：哇，那可是要求很高的工作啊。您覺得您所從事的工作中最具挑戰性的是哪個部分？

實境對話 2

A: Let me introduce myself. I'm Han JinBo. Looks like we both came a long way today.

B: You are coming from China? That is a long way. How long was your flight?

A: About 15 hours. Not too bad.

B: Not too bad? Seems like a lot. I only flew from the East coast. About 5 and a half hours.

A: Where do you live on the East coast?

B: Actually I don't live there. I was just in Washington DC for meetings.

A: So now you're at another meeting. I wonder when they will get started?

B: I remember a time when meetings wouldn't last more than ten minutes. Seems like it takes ten minutes just for everyone to sit down these days.

A: You know the committee chairman, Bob Evans?

B: Sure do!

A: How do you know Bob?

B: He's my old college roommate. We both went to Harvard.

A: Is that right? What do you think about Harvard's business school?

A：我來自我介紹一下。我叫韓金波。看起來我們倆今天好像都是遠道而來的。

B：您來自中國？那可真遠。要飛多長時間啊？

A：還好，大概15個小時。

B：還好？還是很遠的。我只是從東海岸飛過來，大概5個半小時。

A：您住在東海岸什麼地方？

B：事實上我不住那裡。我去華盛頓參加一個會議。

A：那您現在又參加另外一個會議。我想知道他們什麼時候開始？

B：我記得以前的會議最多持續10分鐘。現在好像每個人都需要10分鐘才能入座。

A：您認識委員會主席Bob Evans嗎？

B：當然！

A：您是怎麼認識Bob的？

B：他是我大學的室友。我們兩個都念過哈佛。

A：是嗎？那您覺得哈佛的商學院怎麼樣？

工作午餐 The Working Lunch

商業午餐是一個在非正式的環境中和客戶互相了解（get to know each other）的過程，雙方聊生意、拉進感情，建立更深入的關係（build a relationship）。

提出邀請

雖然是非正式的午餐，事先還是要向客人提出邀請，問客人愛吃什麼，什麼時間方便就用餐。

⊙Let's do lunch。

　我們一起吃午餐吧。

⊙What's your favorite food?

　您最喜歡吃什麼？

⊙Are you a vegetarian?

　您吃素嗎？

⊙What about (cuisine), would that be alright for lunch?

　午餐吃（菜系名）好嗎？

⊙Can I meet you for lunch this afternoon?

　午後我能和您共進午餐嗎？

⊙Let's go over things at lunch.

　吃午餐的時候，我們再談。

⊙We can talk more about it over lunch.

　我們吃午飯的時候再聊。

氣氛

用餐時要關閉手機。你需要做的事情就是傾聽，但也不能只聽不答，共同點或相異之處都是可以是深入話題的契機。可以用一些比較私人的問題活絡氣氛（ice-breaking），例如：「您是在哪裡長大的？」

⊙Where did you grow up?

　您是在哪裡長大的？

⊙What do you think of...?

　對於……您覺得呢？

⊙Tell me more about...

　再告訴我一些有關……

⊙Have you always...?

　您總是……嗎？

⊙I wanted to ask your opinion about...

　我想知道您對……的想法。

點菜（cater）

點菜時要詢問客人的喜好和禁忌，避免點那些容易噴濺的食物（messy foods）。不要以為所有的外賓都喜歡西餐，如果能介紹一些他們不熟悉的美味也是很好的選擇，不過要事先告訴他們菜的內容，如果他們面露難色，就不要勉強。點菜時不能猶豫。此外，應當避免喝太多酒（excessive drinking）。因為無論如何，午餐還是在談生意的過程中。

⊙Shall we order the fish? I love lobster, but I'm afraid it might be too messy.
我們可以點魚嗎？我很喜歡龍蝦，但是我擔心會濺汁。

⊙The Peking Duck here is excellent. Should we give it a try?
這裡的北京烤鴨非常棒。我們要嚐嚐嗎？

⊙Let me suggest the pasta primavera. It's delicious.
我推薦素菜麵。很好吃。

⊙Do you like eggplant? We could order stir-fried vegetables.
你喜歡茄子嗎？我們可以點些炒素菜。

⊙Would you like a knife and fork? Or would you rather use chopsticks?
你想要刀叉還是筷子？

⊙I was thinking of trying the new Thai restaurant. Does that sound appealing?
我本來想著試一下新開的泰國餐館。你有興趣嗎？

⊙Would you rather have Chinese or Western food?
你喜歡吃中餐還是西餐？

買單

你要堅持為午餐買單（pay for lunch）。也有例外情況，女士付錢（pick up a tab）會讓一些男士感覺不舒服，有一些公司禁止員工接受請客（being treated for meals）。無論如何，都不應在付帳時爭來爭去。

A: Here's the check...
B: Oh, I'll get it. After all I can put it on the company expense account.
A: No, I insist. Today is my treat.

A：錢在這裡……
B：我來吧。我可以把它歸入公帳。
A：別這樣，我堅持。今天是我請你。

A: Well, before we go, I'd like to show you a copy of our sales report. Can we take a look together?

B: Sure, let's have a look.

A：嗯，臨走前我給您看一下我們公司的銷售報告影本。要看嗎？

B：當然，我們一起看。

總結

在觥籌交錯之間，人與人之間容易拉近距離。吃什麼餐是次要的，談什麼才是主要的。不僅要讓客人吃好喝好，更重要的是加強彼此的信任。

單字表

adventurous 冒險	appealing 吸引人的
aspect 方面	eggplant 茄子
excellent 棒極了	involvement 參與
Italian 義大利的	liability 責任義務
pasta 義大利麵食	Peking duck 北京烤鴨
rather 寧願	review 複審；評估
sales report 銷售報告	stir-fried 炒的
suggest 建議	vegetarian 素食主義者

片語表

a little more familiar 更熟悉一點	around the corner 轉彎處
thinking (of doing sth.) 考慮做某事	catch (sb.) 碰上（某人）；趕上（某人）
do lunch 共進午餐	down the street 沿著街

from a... standpoint 從……觀點來看

go-ahead 請吧

move forward 往前挪；移動

pizza place 比薩店

sound appealing 聽起來有吸引力

go into (a field) 從事（領域）

It's a date. 就這麼決定了。

not a big (sth.) fan 對……迷戀

pose a liability 構成法律責任

實境對話 1

A: Joan, I was hoping to catch you this afternoon. Let's do lunch. Do you have time? I was hoping to review our sales report.

B: Today? Yeah, I guess I have time.

A: Great! What's your favorite food? I was thinking of trying the new Thai restaurant around the corner. Does that sound appealing?

B: Thai? Well, I might not be that adventurous. Also, I'm not a big meat fan.

A: Are you a vegetarian? I didn't realize that. Well, we can try something a little more familiar. Would you rather have Chinese or Western food?

B: What about Italian, would that be alright for lunch? There's a pizza place just down the street.

A: Sounds great. I'll meet you there in about an hour?

B: It's a date.

A：Joan，我原本打算今天下午去找你。我們共進午餐吧，你有時間嗎？我一直希望能夠評估一下我們的銷售報告。

B：今天？好的，我想我有時間。

A：太好了！你喜歡吃什麼？我想去試一下轉角那家新開的泰國餐廳。你有興趣嗎？

B：泰國菜？嗯，我不是那麼有冒險精神。當然，對肉食我也不那麼迷戀。

A：你吃素嗎？我都不知道。那我們就去熟悉的地方吧。你喜歡吃中餐還是西餐？

B：午餐吃義式好嗎？這條街就有一家比薩店。

A：聽起來不錯。我一個小時後在那裡等你？

B：就這麼決定了。

實境對話 2

A: Let me suggest the pasta primavera. It's delicious.

B: Thank you. I actually prefer Chinese food, though.

A: Well, the Peking Duck here is excellent. Should we give it a try?

B: Sounds good. Do you like eggplant? We could order stir-fried vegetables.

A: Good. Let's get that too.

B: So tell me more about the Martin account. What are the current developments now?

A: We have already received the go-ahead to move forward. Actually, I wanted to ask your opinion about the legal aspects.

B: Shoot.

A: Well, do you think that our involvement poses a liability for the company?

B: From a legal standpoint, no.

A: Have you always wanted to go into law? What do you think about the place law plays in today's business world?

A：我向您推薦蔬菜義大利麵，非常好吃。

B：謝謝。但我還是比較喜歡中餐。

A：好的，這裡的北京烤鴨非常棒。我們要嚐嚐嗎？

B：聽上去不錯。你喜歡吃茄子嗎？我們可以點些炒蔬菜。

A：好的，我們也點那個。

B：告訴我一些關於Martin帳戶的情況吧。現在有什麼新的進展嗎？

A：我們已經得到可以進一步發展的許可。事實上，我想問一下你在法律方面的想法。

B：説吧。

A：好的，你覺得我們的介入會不會構成公司的法律責任？

B：從法律的角度來説，不會。

A：你一直都從事法律行業嗎？你覺得法律在當今的生意圈裡扮演怎樣的角色？

觀光 Sightseeing

做國際貿易的好處（perks）之一就是商務旅行（travel on business），可以藉此機會順便旅遊。

在接待外國客人時，你可以帶他們四處觀光，去遊覽些名勝景點，盡地主之誼。

⊙Is this your first time to visit China?
　　這是您第一次來中國嗎？

⊙What would you like to see while you are here?
　　您在本地期間想看什麼？

⊙I can be your translator and tour guide.
　　我很願意做您的翻譯和嚮導。

⊙I hope to have time to visit the Eifel tower while I am here.
　　我希望在此期間能有機會參觀艾菲爾鐵塔。

⊙Can we make arrangements to see the Statue of Liberty?
　　我們能安排去看自由女神像嗎？

⊙Would you like to see Tiananmen square?

您想去參觀天安門廣場嗎？

⊙Did you have anything in mind that you wanted to see?

您想去哪裡看看嗎？

了解旅行資訊

如果你要去國外旅行，一定別忘了要事先研究（do your homework），對你的目的地要有個整體概念，包括博物館、當地名勝、酒吧、餐館等，這對你適應環境很有幫助（fit in）。

⊙Can you tell me how to get to the train station?

您能告訴我怎麼到火車站嗎？

⊙What time does the bus come?

公車幾點來？

⊙Will this shuttle take me to the airport?

這班車能帶我去機場嗎？

⊙How can I get to the Empire State Building?

我怎麼才能到帝國大廈呢？

獨自旅行

跟團去觀光能省點麻煩，但你別忘了獨自旅行也是很特別的體驗（adventure）。去一些旅行指南（guidebook）上找不到的地方會非常有意思。一般遊客對主要景點趨之若鶩，但聰明的旅行者會選擇一些大部分人不會留意，但也引人入勝（totally fantastic）的地方。而且，在這些地方總會撿到一些便宜貨。

A: Do you want to go with me to the Metropolitan Museum?

B: Sure. Let's take the bus instead of a taxi. We'll see a little more of the city that way.

A: Okay. Look, they have a bus line that goes there directly.

A：你想不想和我一起去看大都會博物館？

B：當然，我們搭公車去吧，不要搭計程車了。這樣我們可以更貼近欣賞這個城市。

A：好的，你看，他們有去那裡的直達車。

A: Shall we visit Ellis Island with the tour group tomorrow?

B: Actually, I was thinking of walking down to Central Park and doing a little sightseeing on my own. Want to come with me?

A：明天我們要跟團一起去遊覽艾力斯島嗎？

B：其實，我打算走路去中央公園，自己走走看看。想和我一起嗎？

國際客戶

當你接待外籍客戶（international guests）時，你可以教他們些簡單的當地語言，比如說，您好、謝謝、是/否和再見等。這樣，他們就可以與當地人有更多地互動，也可以更加豐富（enrich）他們的文化體驗（cultural experience）。

A: Let me teach you a few useful phrases. Try this. "Ni Hao" That means Hello.

B: "Nee How."

A: Good job!

A：我來教您幾句日常用語吧，「Ni Hao」的意思是説「你好」，試試。

B：「Nee How。」

A：真棒！

飲食和文化特色

當你要為客戶介紹當地主要名勝（tourist attractions）時，別忘了介紹當地的飲食和文化特色。同時，要看的景點總是比時間允許得還多，所以，千萬別搞成讓人精疲力竭的旋風（whirlwind）式觀光。要先對客戶的體力有大致地評估，一般情況下時差（jet lag）對他們多少有些困擾。要確保每個客人都能跟上大家的步伐（pace）。

⊙Would you like to try using chopsticks? I can teach you how.

您想試著用筷子嗎？我來教你怎麼用。

⊙Try the Peking duck. It's a specialty food from this area. It's very famous, and delicious, too!

嘗一下北京烤鴨，這可是當地的風味。很有名也很好吃！

⊙How are you feeling? Do you feel up to going to the Temple of Heaven this afternoon?

您感覺怎麼樣？今天下午還能去天壇嗎？

⊙How about we take a rest this afternoon at the hotel before we continue our tour.

今天下午我們先在旅館休息，然後再繼續我們的遊覽行程。

總結

「有朋自遠方來，不亦樂乎？」更何況是來做生意，為你提供賺錢的機會。本著讓客人「高興而來，滿意而歸」的宗旨，在公事之外的活動上多花些心思，他們會永遠記著你的人情。同樣，為了生意和生活兼顧，在到國外出差之前你就要多打聽、多學習。如果有機會欣賞到一般遊客沒有注意到的風景，那才是真的高人一籌。

單字表

central park 中央公園
Eifel Tower 艾菲爾鐵塔
Empire State Building 帝國大廈
Forbidden City 紫禁城；故宮
Metropolitan Museum 大都會博物館
Summer Palace 頤和園
the Big Apple 紐約（別名）
tour guide 導遊

east coast 東海岸
Ellis Island 艾力斯島
feasable 可行
Great Wall 長城
Statue of Liberty 自由女神像
Temple of Heaven 天壇
Tiananmen Square 天安門廣場
translator 翻譯

片語表

a short drive from 短短的車程
feel up to (doing sth.) 感受最多（做某事）
I was thinking of (doing sth.) 我原本想著（做某事）
jet lag 時差
make time (to do sth.) 抽時間（做某事）
so far 迄今；到目前為止
take a rest 休息一下

as a matter of fact 事實上
for sure 確定無疑的；毫無疑問的
if time would allow 如果時間允許
in mind 銘記；記住
make arrangements 安排；籌辦
no worries 無需擔憂
take (sth.) into consideration 考慮（某事）
to be honest 老實說

實境對話 1

A: Is this your first time to visit China?

B: As a matter of fact, it is. I have really enjoyed my trip so far. It's so different than Germany, however.

A: For sure! What would you like to see while you are here? I can help you make arrangements for some sightseeing. I can be your translator and tour guide.

B: That's very thoughtful. Thank you very much. I hope to have time to visit the Great Wall while I am here. Can we make arrangements to see the Forbidden City as well?

A: I'm sure that can be arranged. The Great Wall is a short drive from the city. Would you like to see the Summer Palace?

B: Well, certainly, if time would allow...

A: How are you feeling? Do you have jet lag? Do you feel up to going to the Temple of Heaven this afternoon?

B: To be honest, I am feeling rather exhausted from the trip...

A: No worries. How about we take a rest this afternoon at the hotel before we continue our tour?

B: That would be wonderful.

A：這是您第一次來中國嗎？

B：其實是的。我過得非常愉快。和德國太不一樣。

A：當然！這段期間您想去看些什麼？我可以幫您安排觀光，我很願意做您的導遊和翻譯。

B：那真是太體貼了，非常感謝您。我希望在此期間能有機會去爬長城。我們能安排去參觀一下故宮嗎？

A：我確定都是可以安排的。長城離城市的車程不遠。您想去參觀頤和園嗎？

B：那當然。如果時間允許的話……

A：您感覺怎麼樣？還有時差嗎？今天下午還能去天壇嗎？

B：老實說，旅途讓我有些筋疲力盡……

A：別擔心，要不然下午我們先在旅館休息，晚點再繼續我們的遊覽行程？

B：那太好了。

實境對話 2

A: How exciting! We're actually in the Big Apple! I have always wanted to visit New York City, and now, because of our international training meeting, we're actually here. I hope we can make time to see some of the sights while we are here.

B: I'm sure they've taken sightseeing into consideration when putting our schedule together. In fact, we are totally free this afternoon. Did you have anything in mind that you wanted to see?

A: Do you want to go with me to the Metropolitan Museum?

B: Sure. Let's take the bus instead of a taxi. We'll see a little more of the city that way.

A: Okay. Look, they have a bus line that goes there directly. I wonder when the bus comes.

B: We can ask that guy. Excuse me, what time does the bus come?

C: Uh. It should be here every twenty minutes or so. There's a bus schedule on the wall over there.

A: Thanks!

B: Shall we visit Elis Island with the tour group tomorrow?

A: Actually, I was thinking of walking down to Central Park and doing a little sightseeing on my own. Want to come with me?

B: Maybe. I wanted to visit the Statue of Liberty, though. Also, I want to see the Empire State Building.

A: Maybe this bus will take us there, too. Let's ask the driver. Excuse me, how can I get to the Empire State Building?

A：太興奮了！我們現在在紐約了！我一直都非常想來紐約遊覽的，因為我們的國際培訓會議，現在我們竟然真的在這兒了。我希望我們在此期間能抽空去看一些景點。

B：我相信，他們已經將觀光規劃進時間表中了。其實，我們今天下午有空，你想去哪裡看看嗎？

A：你想不想和我一起去參觀大都會博物館？

B：當然。我們搭公車去吧，不坐計程車了。這樣我們可以更貼近欣賞這個城市。

A：好的。你看，他們有去那裡的直達車。不知道車幾點來。

B：我們可以問一下那個人。打擾一下，公車幾點來啊？

C：嗯。應該是差不多每20分鐘一班。那邊牆上有公車的時刻表。

A：謝謝！

B：明天我們跟團去遊覽艾力斯島嗎？

A：其實，我打算步行去中央公園，自己走走看看。你和我一起去嗎？

B：也許吧。我本想著去參觀自由女神像。而且我也想去看看帝國大廈。

A：也許這輛公車可以帶我們去那裡，我來問問司機。對不起，我們怎麼才能到帝國大廈呢？

考察工廠　Factory Tours

要讓客戶對你的產品和服務都有所認識（learn about），最有效的方式就是請他參觀你的工廠。工廠考察是發展長期合作夥伴關係（lasting business partnerships）的重要因素。透過現場考察，賣家對你的產品品質和技術都可放心（assured of）。

考察通常從會議室或辦公區的歡迎致辭開始。這個部分應占總體參觀時間的2分鐘。

⊙Welcome to our factory site. It's a pleasure to have you visit this morning.
歡迎您來到我們的工廠。今早您能大駕光臨讓我們備感榮幸。

⊙Let me be the first to welcome you to Milton Manufacturing. We hope you enjoy your tour today.

首先請允許我對您到訪Milton製造表示熱烈歡迎。我們希望您今天的考察能夠愉快。

⊙Since it's your first time to visit our factory, I want to be sure to answer any questions you might have.

這是您第一次來我們工廠，我很願意解答您的任何問題。

⊙Please feel free to ask questions at any time during our presentation.

在我們介紹期間，您有什麼問題請隨時提問。

⊙We'll start our tour by introducing a little more about our company organization.

我們將透過對我們公司和機構的進一步介紹來開始我們的考察。

⊙We'd be delighted to conduct a tour for you when you are in the area.

我們非常樂意帶您在該地參觀。

⊙Please make yourselves at home.

一切自便，不用客氣。

全面概述

對公司的產品、服務和專案做一個全面概述（broad overview），同時對重要環節做詳細介紹。這部分的介紹也應該在會議室，大約5分鐘。

⊙We'll be able to see each step in the production process, from initial designing to finished product.

我們將看到從最初設計到成品的每一步生產過程。

⊙During our tour, you will see the precision craftsmanship coming together at every step in production.

在您參觀期間，您將看到每一個生產環節的精湛工藝。

⊙Ningbo Toy Manufacturing has been in the toy business for over thirty years.

寧波玩具製造從事玩具生意已經有30多年的時間了。

⊙We export our products to over 60 nations and territories.

我們的產品出口到60多個國家和地區。

⊙Our quality control processing has been awarded national recognition for three years consecutively.

我們的品質控制處理技術已經連續三年得到國家的認證。

⊙You'll see that in our factory, safety first is our motto.

在我們的工廠中您將看到，安全第一是我們的座右銘。

⊙You will meet the dedicated team that makes up the Ningbo Toy Manufacturing family.

您將認識構成「寧波玩具製造」大家庭的精英團隊。

⊙We engineer and build quality products that will give consumers many years of enjoyment.

我們設計和生產的高品質產品使我們的客戶受益多年。

參觀貫穿整個廠區

每個環節大約3~5分鐘。每個環節上介紹內容應包含：

●這裡是哪一道流程？

●有什麼用途？

●此流程的結果是什麼樣的？

●工藝和品質監控以及別的相關資訊（pertinent information）。

⊙Here's where...

這裡是……

⊙You can see...

你可以看到……

⊙I'd like to draw your attention to...

我希望您能留意到……

⊙If you look carefully, you'll notice...

如果您仔細看的話，您會發現……

⊙Let me introduce...

讓我來介紹一下……

總結（wrap-up）和問答階段：做一個綜合敘述並給提問時間，大致5分鐘。

⊙That's about it. Does anyone have any questions?

大致就這些了，有哪位有問題嗎？

⊙Now we come to the end of the tour. Any questions?

現在我們的參觀進入了尾聲，有什麼問題嗎？

⊙If you have any further questions or want to know more, simply send us
a note through the Customer Relations or call us.

如果您還有別的什麼問題或想了解更多，您可以透過客戶關係部留言給我們
或者打電話給我們。

總結

客戶如果不是為了眼見為實、追根究柢，一般不會千里迢迢來考察一個工廠。
為了使客戶不虛此行，在參觀過程中你可以把公司的服務精神、品質信心、負
責態度貫穿其中。這樣客人在下訂單的時候才不會有太多的顧慮和擔憂。

單字表

craftsmanship 工藝
enjoy 欣賞；享受
motto 座右銘；格言
precision 精密
production 生產
team 組；隊
welcome 歡迎

dedicated 專用的；傑出的
export 出口
overall 全部的；全面的
presentation 介紹
spend 花（時間）
territory 地區；區域

片語表

any (thing) you might have 您有任何
需求
draw attention to... 對……表示注意
feel free 無需拘束；不用客氣
initial design 初步設計；原設計
make up 化妝；補償
production process 生產流程
quality control 品質監控
raw materials 原材料
the (name of organization) family
（某機構）的大家庭

come together 走到一起；集合
wrap up 完工；結束
factory site 廠址
finished product 成品
Let me be the first to welcome you.
請允許我先對您表示歡迎。
quality assurance 品質保證
question and answer 問答
safety first 安全第一
be in business 從事貿易；做生意

實境對話 1

A: Welcome to our factory site. It's a pleasure to have you visit this morning.
Let me be the first to welcome you to Ningbo Toy Manufacturing. We

hope you enjoy your tour today. Since it's your first time to visit our factory, I want to be sure to answer any questions you might have. Also, Please feel free to ask questions at any time during our presentation.

B: I have a question. How long will the tour last?

A: We'll spend about 5 minutes in orientation, 20 minutes on the factory floor, and about 5-10 minutes wrapping up with question and answer at the end. Overall, the tour should last no more than half an hour. During our tour, you will see the precision craftsmanship coming together at every step in production. We'll be able to see each step in the production process, from initial design to finished product. You'll also meet the dedicated team that makes up the NingBo Toy Manufacturing family.

B: How long has Ningbo Toy Manufacturing been in business?

A: Ningbo Toy Manufacturing has been in the toy business for over thirty years. We export our products to over 60 nations and territories.

A：歡迎您來到我們工廠。今早您能大駕光臨讓我們備感榮幸。首先請允許我對您光臨寧波玩具製造表示熱烈歡迎。希望您考察愉快。由於這是您第一次訪問我們工廠，我很願意解答您的問題。當然，在我們介紹期間，您隨時可以提問題。

B：我有個問題，我們的考察將會持續多久？

A：我們將花5分鐘做介紹，20分鐘參觀工廠車間，最後還有5至10分鐘的問答。整個參觀加起來不會超過半小時。在參觀的過程中，您將看到每一個生產環節的精湛工藝。我們將看到從最初設計到成品的每一步生產過程。您也將見到組成寧波玩具製造大家庭的精英團隊。

B：寧波玩具製造成立多久了？

A：寧波玩具製造從事玩具生意已經有30多年了。我們的產品出口到60多個國家和地區。

實境對話 2

A: I'd like to draw your attention to this machine over here. This machine controls the temperature of the raw materials before they are poured into the metal molds. You can see, the machine is equipped with several internal temperature gauges. If you look carefully, you'll notice that the gauges are connected to our overhead computer system. We monitor the temperature within a tenth of a degree Celsius.

B: Is that really necessary?

A: For safety reasons and for quality assurance, we make sure the temperature is not too hot. You see, in our factory, safety first is our motto.

B: You said the temperature monitoring is also for quality assurance?

A: Yes, it is. Our quality control processing has been awarded national recognition for three years consecutively. Let me introduce Mary Lin, one of our quality control managers. Mary, can you share with our visitors more about what we do to make sure the quality of our products is second to none?

C: Certainly!

A：您請注意看這邊的這台設備。這台設備控制著原材料在澆灌到金屬模具之前的溫度。您可以看到這個機器配備好幾個內置計量表。如果您仔細看，您會發現計量表是和我們頭頂的電腦系統相連的。我們將溫度控制在十分之一攝氏度以內。

B：有必要嗎？

A：出於安全和品質的關係，我們確保溫度不能太高。您看到了，在我們工廠，「安全第一」是我們的座右銘。

B：您剛說到的溫控也是出於品質保證的考慮嗎？

A：是的。我們的品質控制技術已經連續三年獲得國家的認證。為您介紹一下

我們的品質控制主管之一Mary Lin。Mary，你能否為我們的客人介紹一下我們在確保品質方面所做的工作？

C：好的！

告別和道謝　Farewells and Thank Yous

一封感謝短信的重要性常常被忽略。但事實上人們總是對最後的接觸（last interaction）印象深刻。一封表達感謝的短信正好能擔此重任。

一般在會議、訪談和面試之後都可以適時發出一封短信，感謝對方所給予的時間和關注。

⊙Thank you for spending the afternoon with us。

　感謝您和我們共度這個下午。

⊙Let me leave you with my card.

　給您我的名片。

⊙Thanks again for all your help.

　再次感謝您的幫助。

⊙Let's be sure to keep in touch!

　我們一定要保持聯絡哦！

⊙I am glad you had a chance to take a factory tour. Can I answer any last questions?

　我很高興您能有機會參觀工廠。還有什麼問題要為您回答嗎？

⊙Thanks for making all the arrangements for us and for seeing us off at the airport.

　感謝您為我們所作的所有安排，還來機場為我們送行。

⊙Thanks for everything!

　感謝您所作的一切！

⊙We wish you the best!

　我們祝您一切順利！

⊙Take care!

　保重！

方式

一般致謝信通常是在事後24~48小時之內寄出。手寫的感謝信總是更能展現情真意切。公司信紙（business's stationary）或卡片也是可以考慮的。正確的格式是問候在左上方（upper left），簽字在右下方，時間在右下方。正式的商務感謝應當是列印出來，記得請語法通順、用詞得當、書面整潔（neatness）。

⊙I appreciate everything you did to make our visit a success.

　感謝您為我們的訪問成功所作的一切。

⊙It was a great pleasure for us to have the opportunity to...

　我們為能夠有機會……感到非常榮幸。

⊙How grateful we are for your contributions to our success!

　我們非常感激您為了我們的成功所作的貢獻！

⊙We wish you the best in all your future endeavors.

　我們祝您萬事如意，馬到成功。

⊙May you see future success.

　祝您一切順利。

⊙I send my warmest wishes and my deepest appreciation.

　送上我最誠摯的問候和最深切的感激。

其他形式

透過電子郵件來表達謝意在時間上佔有優勢，所以也是可考慮的方式之一。電子郵件與書面感謝信的格式一樣。電話感謝也是可以考慮，電話無法接通時可以透過語音信箱留言（leave a voicemail）。面試後的感謝信是非常必要的，如果面試同時有好幾個人，那就把信寄給那個有決定權的人。在問候時要使用正確的稱謂，對於女性最好用「女士」（Mrs.），顯得更正式些。

⊙Mr. Johnson, thank you for taking the time to meet with me last Thursday.
  Johnson 先生，非常感謝您上週二抽空見我。

⊙I appreciate you making time out of your busy schedule to discuss...
  我非常感激您從百忙中抽空來討論……

⊙If there is anything else I can help you with or any other questions you
  may have, please don't hesitate to contact me.
  如果有什麼我可以幫忙的或者您有什麼問題，請儘管和我聯繫。

⊙I look forward to the next opportunity we have to visit again.
  我期待我們能有機會再次訪問。

⊙I look forward to hearing from you again soon.
  我期望能儘快聽到您的音訊。

⊙Please let me know if there is anything more I can assist you with.
  如果還有別的什麼事情我能夠協助的，請一定要通知我。

如果是面對面的告別，你還應當：
●對於對方的努力和貢獻表示感激。
●積極評價。
●指出一到兩項如此感激的原因。
●透過一個小禮物或紀念品表達祝福。

A: I've really enjoyed the time we've spent together Bob. I know you've made a great contribution to the development of our current business proposal while you've been here. We all appreciate you as a brilliant resource.

B: Now, now... I probably just got in your hair!

A: Seriously, we appreciate your visit.

A：Bob，在與你一起度過的時間裡，我感覺非常愉快。我知道你在此期間為我們的商業發展計畫有很大的貢獻，我們很賞識您的足智多謀。

B：過獎，過獎⋯⋯我可能給你添了不少的麻煩！

A：說真的，我們對您的訪問深表感激。

A: Next time, please remember to bring your fishing pole! On our off time, you can show us those fishing skills we heard so much about this week!

B: Ha ha, yeah right.

A: Seriously, if you have any more questions about our project after you get back to your office, be sure to give us a call.

A：下次可別忘了帶你的釣竿！休假的時候你可以向我們秀一下你的釣魚技巧，這個星期我們已經聽您說很多！

B：哈哈，好的。

A：話說回來，你回到辦公室後，對於我們的計畫如果還有什麼別的問題，一定要打電話告訴我們。

總結

我們常說「禮多人不怪」。一封感謝信不但不會讓人「責怪」，反而會給對方留下你辦事細心周到的印象。告別時一兩句感謝的話、一個小小的禮物，都會使彼此的關係提升，為友誼奠定基礎。

單字表　⋯⋯⋯⋯⋯⋯⋯⋯⋯⋯⋯⋯⋯⋯⋯⋯⋯⋯⋯⋯⋯⋯⋯⋯⋯⋯⋯

appreciate 感激；讚賞

benefit 利益；效益

contribution 貢獻；付出

handwritten 手寫的

partnership 合夥關係

resource 資源

arrange 安排

brilliant 巧妙的；令人印象深刻的

development 發展；進步

opportunity 機會

viewpoint 觀點；看法；見解

thoughtful 周到的；深思的；體貼的

片語表　⋯⋯⋯⋯⋯⋯⋯⋯⋯⋯⋯⋯⋯⋯⋯⋯⋯⋯⋯⋯⋯⋯⋯⋯⋯⋯⋯

a nice touch 印象深刻；感覺良好

be sure to 一定要

deepest appreciation 最深切的感激

in person 親自；本人

keep in touch 保持聯絡

look forward to (sth.) 期待（某事）

open (sth.) up 打開（某物）

take a look 看一下

take care 照顧；保重

wonder (what / who)... 想知道（什麼/誰）

arrange a visit 安排訪問

business proposal 商業建議

get in (sb's) hair 打擾某人

It's been my pleasure. 這是我的榮幸。

leave (sb.) a card 給（某人）一張名片

make a contribution 作出貢獻

please don't hesitate to (do sth.) 儘管/無需猶豫（做某事）

take time out of a schedule 抽空

warmest wishes 最誠摯的祝福

實境對話 1

A: I've really enjoyed the time we've spent together Bob. I know you've made a great contribution to the development of our current business proposal while you've been here. We all appreciate you as a brilliant resource.

B: Now, now... I probably just got in your hair!

A: Seriously, we appreciate your visit.

B: Well, I'm sure I've benefited as well. Thanks for letting me spend the afternoon with you. I really appreciate your viewpoint on our business models.

A: Oh, it's been my pleasure.

B：Here, let me leave you with my card. If there is anything else I can help you with or any other questions you may have, please don't hesitate to contact me.

A: Thanks! Thanks again for all your help!

B: I look forward to the next opportunity we have to visit again.

A: Yes, I look forward to hearing from you again soon. Let's be sure to keep in touch!

B: Take care!

A：Bob，在與您一起度過的日子裡，我感到非常愉快。我知道您在此期間為我們的商業發展計畫有很大的貢獻。我們很賞識您的足智多謀。

B：過獎，過獎……我可能給您添了不少的麻煩！

A：說真的，我們對您的訪問深表感激。

B：我也是受益匪淺。感謝您和我共度這個下午。我非常欣賞您關於我們商業模式的見解。

A：哦，那是我的榮幸。

B：給您一張我的名片。如果有什麼我可以幫助的或者您還有什麼問題，請儘管和我聯繫。

A：謝謝！再次感謝您的幫助！

B：我期待著我們能有機會再次見面。

A：是的，我希望能儘快聽到您的音訊。我們一定要保持聯絡哦！

B：保重！

實境對話 2

A: You've got a note in the mail. Looks like it's postmarked from Beijing. Wonder who that could be from...

B: Beijing? Really? Well, let's open it up and take a look. Oh, it's a thank you card from Mr. Zhang. That's nice.

A: Mr. Zhang? Who's that?

B: Mr. Zhang is an Chinese engineer who came last week for a meeting. He's written a very thoughtful thank you note. Here, listen:

A: Yeah...

B: "Dear Mr. Johnson. Thank you for taking the time to meet with me last Thursday. I appreciate everything you did to arrange my visit, and I especially appreciate you taking time out of your busy schedule to discuss the contributions our company can make to your current projects. It was a great pleasure for us to have the opportunity to meet in person and build a stronger partnership. We wish you the best in all your future endeavors and send our warmest wishes and deepest appreciation."

A: Is the note handwritten? That's a nice touch!

A：信箱裡有你一封信。看郵戳是從北京來的。不知道是誰寄的⋯⋯

B：北京？真的嗎？好，我們打開看看。哦，是來自張先生的一封感謝卡。真是太好了。

A：張先生？是誰啊？

B：張先生是上週來開會的一個中國工程師。他寫了一封感謝信。來，你聽：

A：嗯⋯⋯

B：「親愛的Johnson先生：非常感謝您上週四抽空與我們見面。我很感激您為我的訪問所做的所有安排，而且我要特別感謝您從百忙中抽空，討論關於我們公司參與您目前規劃的事宜。能夠與您當面會晤並建立密切往來，

我們深感榮幸。我們祝您在未來的工作中萬事如意，並送上我們最熱情的祝福和最誠摯的感激。」

A：是手寫的嗎？感覺還真不錯！

十項全能之八

介紹自己和公司
You and Your Company

自我介紹 Introducing Yourself

與某人的初識對以後彼此關係的發展有著決定性的作用。由於這個原因,相互介紹就顯得非常重要了。你的所言和所行一定要再三斟酌。一舉一動(every move you make)都會給別人留下印象,成為別人對你的定位,從而決定是否有必要和你更深的接觸。

如果你想結識某人,不妨主動上前自我介紹,選擇一個雙方的共同點引起對方注意。

⊙Hi, I noticed your presenter's badge. My name is Charles Mckay, I am a presenter, too. What are you going to be talking about today?

嗨,我留意到您的講師名牌。我叫Charles McKay,也是位講師。今天您將談些什麼?

⊙My name is Malcom Johnson, I'm with Medicom Entertainment. It's nice to meet you.

我叫Malcom Johnson,我來自Medicom娛樂。很高興認識你。

⊙Let me introduce myself. I'm Xiaoping Zhang. I'm the CEO of Megatron Electronics.

我來自我介紹。我叫張小平。我是Megatron電子的董事長。

⊙Hi, I'm Zhang. I'll be working with your team for the next few days.

嗨,我是張。在未來的幾天裡,我將和您的小組一起共事。

久仰大名
告訴對方你對他是久仰大名,會容易讓對方對你產生親近感。這個時候,自我介紹會給對方留下深刻的印象(nice touch)。

⊙Mr. Samuels, It's great to have a chance to finally meet you. I've heard so much about you from my coworkers.

Samuels先生，終於有機會認識您了，真是太好了。我常聽到我的同事們談起您。

⊙It's Mark, right? I'm glad to have a chance to know you. I'm Jill Madison.

是Mark嗎？很高興能有機會認識您。我叫Jill Madison。

⊙Ms. Mitchell, It's such a pleasure to meet you. My name is Noelle Stevens.

Mitchell 小姐，認識您真是榮幸之極。我叫Noelle Stevens。

⊙How is everything going, John? Let me introduce myself, I'm Nancy.

John，都還好嗎？自我介紹一下，我叫Nancy。

設一個情節

共識（mutual acquaintance）或者相似的背景（background）是開啟對話的鑰匙。這樣能夠讓對方知道你不是無緣無故地在浪費他的時間（waste their time）。

⊙Mary at Autonamics gave me your name. She said you're the perfect person to ask about marketing strategies.

Autonamics的Mary給了我您的名字。她告訴我說您是諮詢行銷策略的最佳人選。

⊙I believe you've probably been contacted by Bob in our finance department about some accounting advice. I wanted to follow up with you about your suggestions for us.

我相信您已經和財務部門的Bob在帳目方面接觸過了，接下來我想聽聽您對我們有哪些建議。

提問

問對方他們做什麼工作、喜歡做什麼，以及他們的經歷。人們總是喜歡談及自己。所以你要讓對方儘量說，但是絕不可以接二連三的審問（rapid-fire interrogation）。

⊙So how long have you worked for Microblast? Have you always worked in accounting?

那您在Microblast工作多久了？您一直都在作會計方面的工作嗎？

⊙What brought you here to this meeting? Is it your first time to visit Bangkok?

您出於什麼原因來參加這個會議？這是您第一次到曼谷嗎？

⊙Have you worked with broadcasting before? What are the major projects your department has been working on this year?

您曾經在廣播方面工作過嗎？您所在的部門今年主要致力於哪些專案的工作？

自信傾聽，積極回應

對方會透過你專注的眼神讀到更多的尊重；及時地回饋會讓對方知道你對他表達的內容有很充分的理解，而且有興趣。透過對方的故事容易發現更多的共同之處，從而深入對話，加深彼此的了解。

A: Our marketing team really came together for this presentation. I am pleased with the way it has turned out.

B: That's great, congratulations. You said Bob was the marketing head, right? Did he come along for the presentation?

A：我們的行銷小組通常都是一起來展示的，我對於這種方式的成效很滿意。

B：那太好了，恭喜。您剛說Bob是行銷主管，對嗎？他也來參加講座了嗎？

A: It's been difficult to get used to the California market.

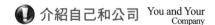

B: That's right, you said you're originally from New York. So tell me, what are the newest trends in the industry on the East Coast?

A：適應加州的市場很難。

B：是的。您說過您來自紐約，那告訴我，在東海岸行業的最新趨勢是什麼？

回答

回答提問是介紹自己和公司的好機會。可以穿插一些市場訊息（marketing message），但介紹不宜過長，否則就很可能成為獨角戲了（dominate the conversation）。

A: Which company did you say you're with?

B: I work for Charlon Computers. I am in charge of new product development. We're currently looking to expand our laptop offerings, and we are also investing in the development of AI.

A：您説您是來自什麼公司？

B：我在Charlon電腦公司上班。我負責的是新產品的研發。最近我們正在拓展我們的手提電腦產品，而且在人工智慧方面我們也有所投資。

A: So is it your first time visiting China?

B: Yes, it is. I've really enjoyed my stay so far. Our trip this time will focus on developing partnerships for our exportation business. We work mostly with small farm equipment manufacturers. We'd like to move into a new market, we're looking into heavy construction equipment。

A：那這是您第一次來中國？

B：是的。這段時間我都過得很開心。我們這次來主要是為發展我們的出口生意夥伴關係。我們的生意主要是小型農機設備，我們有意轉向新的市場領

287

域，我們正在了解重型建築設備。

總結

勇於結識新朋友、建立新聯絡的人，總是比羞答答故步自封的人有更多機遇。
自我介紹是第一步，也是別人將你在腦海中定位的關鍵，隻言片語之間就能反
映你的涵養和信心。交朋友不一定都是為了做生意，但人們都願意把生意交給
熟悉的或印象深的朋友。

單字表

AI 人工智慧
broadcasting 廣播；播放
construction 建築
farm equipment 農機設備
industry 工業
partnership 合夥關係
trend 動向；趨勢

badge 證章；標牌
CEO 首席執行官；總裁
exportation 出口
finally 最終；終於
manufacturer 生產商；製造者
presenter 主持；講解

片語表

as a matter of fact 事實上
be pleased with... 對……滿意
complete education 完成學業
have a chance 有機會
heavy equipment 重型設備
marketing strategies 行銷策略
Nice to meet you. 很高興認識你。
programming director 程式設計主管

as well 也
come together 一起來
expand offerings 擴展產品
hear so much about (sb.) 久聞（某人）
marketing head 行銷主管
move into a new market 轉入新的市場
product development 產品研發
represent (a company) 代表（一公司）

right person to talk to 談的合適人選
tech support 技術支援
turn out 結果

talk about 談及
to be with (a company) 來自⋯⋯公司
work on 致力於

實境對話 1

A: Hi, I noticed your presenter's badge. My name is Charles McKay. I am presenting this morning as well. What are you going to be talking about?

B: Mr. McKay, it's nice to meet you. I'm actually not presenting until tomorrow afternoon. My name is David Samuels. I am the head programming director at Microblast computers. I will be talking about our new AI projects. What company are you representing?

A: Mr. Samuels, It's great to have a chance to finally meet you. I've heard so much about you from my coworkers. I work for Charlon Computers. I am in charge of new product development. We're currently looking to expand our laptop offerings, and we are also investing in the development of AI. What kind of new AI projects is Mircoblast working on now?

B: Well, I'll certainly be talking more about that in my presentation. We've got some new and very exciting developments. I hope you can attend my presentation. Our marketing head, Bob Johnson, is the right person to talk to for more information if Charlon Computers is interested in partnership on AI.

A: Great, I actually know Bob quite well. He's mentioned many of your projects. Didn't they have their presentation yesterday?

B: Yes, as a matter of fact, they did. Our marketing team really came together for the presentation. I am pleased with the way it turned out.

A: That's great, congratulations. You said Bob was the marketing head, right? Did he come along for the presentation?

A：嗨，我留意到您的講師的名牌。我叫Charles McKay，我也是今天早上開講座。您要介紹什麼內容？

B：McKay先生，很高興認識您。事實上明天下午才是我的講解時間。我叫David Samuels。我是Microblast電腦的首席程式設計主管。我會談到我們的人工智慧產品。您代表哪個公司？

A：Samuels先生，終於有機會認識您了，真是太高興了。我從同事那裡聽過許多關於您的事。我在Charlon電腦公司上班。我負責新產品的研發。最近我們正在開發手提電腦產品，同時在人工智慧方面也有所發展。Microblast目前正研發的是什麼人工智慧專案呢？

B：我將在我的介紹中著重談那方面，我們已經有了一些令人振奮的進展。我希望您能來我的講座。如果Charlon電腦對人工智慧項目的合作有興趣的話，那得和我們的行銷主管Bob Johnson先生多談一些。

A：好的，事實上我和Bob也很熟。他提過很多您的專案。他們昨天不是也有講座嗎？

B：是的，事實上他們已經辦過了。我們的行銷小組通常都是一起來作展示的。我對這種方式的成效很滿意。

A：那太好了，恭喜。您剛才說Bob是行銷主管，對嗎？他也來參加講座了嗎？

實境對話 2

A: It's Mr. Zhang, right? I'm glad to have a chance to know you. I'm Jill Madison.

B: Ms. Madison, it's a pleasure. Let me introduce myself. I'm Xiaoping Zhang. I'm the CEO of Megatron Electronics.

A: Please, call me Jill. Yes, Mr. Zhang, I know you are with Megatron. Mary at Autonamics gave me your name. She said you're the perfect person to ask about marketing strategies.

B: Is that right? Well, Mary is a good friend of mine. Who did you say you were with?

A: Oh, forgive me. I forgot to introduce myself properly. I am the media consultant for Siemend Imports.

A: So is it your first time visiting China?

B: Yes, it is. I've really enjoyed my stay so far. Our trip this time will focus on developing partnerships for our exportation business. We work mostly with small farm equipment manufacturers. We'd like to move into a new market, we're looking into heavy construction equipment.

B: Farming and construction equipment are very different from what we do. However, I am very aware of the condition of the Chinese market these days, so I would be happy to answer any specific questions you might have.

A: Thank you, thanks very much!

A：是張先生嗎？很高興有機會認識您。我叫Jill Madison。

B：Madison女士，很榮幸認識您。請允許我自我介紹一下。我叫張小平，是 egatron 電子的董事長。

A：請叫我Jill。我知道您是Megatron公司的。Autonamics公司的Mary告訴了 我您的名字。她告訴我說您是諮詢有關行銷策略的最佳人選。

B：是嗎？ 哦，Mary是我的一個好朋友，您說您是來自？

A：哦！請原諒，我忘了介紹了。我是Siemend進口的媒體顧問。

B：那麼說這是您首次來中國？

A：是的。這段時間我過得很開心。我們這次訪問主要是為我們的出口生意找 合作夥伴。我們的生意主要是小型農機設備，我們有意轉向新的市場領 域，我們正在了解重型建築設備。

B：農用和建築設備和我們的生意大相徑庭。但是，我對近期的中國市場條件 有所了解。如果您有任何具體問題，我都願意解答。

A：謝謝您，真的是非常感謝！

介紹上司、同事和訪客
Introducing Your Boss, Coworkers and Visitors

介紹老闆、同事和訪客要遵循和自我介紹大致相同的規則（follow the same rules）。此外，還有一些禮節（etiquette）也需留意。

介紹雙方時，姓和名都要說清楚。

⊙Alison, I'd like you to meet Jordan Weber. Jordan, this is Alison Snow.

Alison，我來介紹你認識一下JordanWeber。Jordan，這位是Alison Snow。

⊙Let me introduce Micheal Lumbard, Joan Summers, This is Michael.

讓我來介紹一下Micheal Lumbard。 Joan Summers，這位是Michael。

⊙Hello everyone, meet Jin Hongwei, He's our new marketing executive. Jin, this is Martin Michell, Harry Miller, and Jean Smith.

大家好，認識一下金宏偉，我們新來的行銷部主管。Jim，這是Martin Michell，Harry Miller，還有Jean Smith。

⊙Dr. Potter, do you have a minute? Let me present Lina Chin. Lina, this is Dr. Harold Potter.

Potter博士，您有空嗎？讓我來介紹一下Lina Chin。Lina，這位是Harold Potter 博士。

頭銜

如果你要介紹的人有頭銜，一定要記得附加在姓名之後。頭銜往往表明教育水準（如：教授、博士）、專業（如：法官、老師）、軍銜（少校、上校、將軍）或者政治地位（大使、主席、議員）。

⊙John, this is Dr. Sally Ford. Dr. Ford is the head physician at Saint Mary's hospital. Dr. Ford, please meet John Flynn.

John，這位是Sally Ford醫生。Sally Ford醫生是聖瑪麗醫院的主任醫師。Ford醫生，請您來認識一下John Flynn。

⊙Professor Smith, let me introduce to you Gertrude Childs. Gertrude, this is professor Jack Smith.

Smith教授，讓我來為您介紹一下Gertrude Childs。Gertrude，這位是Jack Smith教授。

⊙Dr. Zeng, may I take a moment to introduce Margaret Xia? Margarget, this is Dr. Jindong Zeng, he is the head of the Physic's department.

曾博士，能允許我介紹一下Margaret Xia嗎？Margarget，這位是物理系主任曾金東博士。

⊙Judge Cole, this is Jessica Liu. Jessica, this is Judge Thomas Cole.

Judge Cole，這位是Jessica Liu。Jessica，這位是Jude Thomas Cole。

順序

出於禮貌應主動將較年輕的（less prominent）介紹給年齡稍大的（more prominent）；先介紹女士、後介紹先生，先介紹和自己關係較遠的、後介紹和自己親密的（如：先介紹訪客、後介紹老闆）。

⊙Arthur Reed, I'd like you to meet Professor Georgia Harris.

Arthur Reed，我想讓你認識一下Georgia Harris教授。

⊙Captain Smith, let me present Colin Ricks. Colin is a recent recruit, but he shows a lot of promise. Colin Ricks, this is Captain Albert Smith.

Smith上尉，讓我來為您介紹一下Colin Ricks，他是位新兵，但前途無量。Colin Ricks，這位是Albert Smith上尉。

特殊關係

如果你介紹的人和你有特殊關係（specific relationship），介紹時一定要將此
關係表明清楚，加上類似「我的老闆」、「我的同事」或「我的秘書」等説明。

A: Dr. Zeng, may I take a moment to introduce my coworker Margaret
   Xia? Margaret, this is Dr. Jindong Zeng, he is the head of the Physic's
   department.
B: Ms. Xia, nice to meet you.
A: Margaret is the administrative assistant for Mr. Jones.

A：曾博士，耽誤您一點時間，介紹您認識我的同事Margaret Xia。
B：夏小姐，很高興認識您。
A：Margaret是Jones先生的行政助理。

A: Professor Smith, let me introduce to you my boss Gertrude Childs.
   Gertrude, this is Professor Jack Smith.
B: Hello Ms. Childs. It's a pleasure to meet you.

A：Smith教授，讓我為您介紹一下我的老闆Gertrude Childs。Gertruede，這
   位是Jack Smith教授。
B：你好，Childs小姐，很高興認識您。

介紹一個人給一群人的時候，先介紹團體成員，再介紹個人，無論級別或地位
（social position）如何。

A: Dr. Villaba, I'd like you to meet the members of our department. Kurt Xu,
   Miyonghee Kim, and Sean Martin. Everyone, this is Dr. Jorge Villaba.
B: Hello everyone! I look forward to getting to know you better.

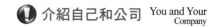

A：Villaba博士，我想讓您認識一下我們部門的成員。Kurt Xu、Miyonghee Kim還有Sean Martin。各位，這位是Jorge Villaba博士。

B：大家好，希望我們能更多了解彼此。

A: Steve, let me introduce our finance team. This is Merlin Lewis, he's the department head. Joan Andrews, our account supervisor, and Jacky Ding, our financial Secretary. Everyone, this is Steve Simmons, head of auditing from the corporate offices.

B: Welcome, Steve! Let us know if you have any questions.

A：Steve，讓我來介紹一下我們的財務團隊。這位是Merlin Lewis，他是部門主管、Joan Andrews，我們的會計主任，還有Jacky Ding，財務秘書。各位，這位是Stevens Simmons，來自我們總公司的審計主管。

B：歡迎，Steve！有任何問題就請告訴我們。

遺忘名字

把名字介紹錯了是非常不禮貌（impolite）的。如果忘記了名字或不清楚，可以道歉並承認自己沒有記清楚（name escaped you）。

⊙Would you mind refreshing my memory about your title? I remember you are working for an airline company, is that right?

您能否再告訴我一次您的頭銜？我記得您在航空公司上班，對嗎？

⊙Hi, I'm Charles Stevens. Mr. Jack Jones is our company CEO. I am in charge of the marketing department. How do you know Jack?

你好，我叫Charles Stevens。Jack Jones是我們公司的CEO。我負責行銷部。您是怎麼認識Jack的？

總結

別人在聽你介紹老闆、同事或訪客時，感興趣的不僅是被介紹者的名字，還有大致的背景。姓名之後附加頭銜，或者介紹先後順序都展現這些資訊。

單字表··

add 添加；融入	appreciate 感謝；感激
auditing 審計；查核	certainly 無疑
considerate 體貼；周到	consultant 顧問
doctorate program 博士專題	experience 經驗
forensic 法醫的；法庭的	willingness 積極；樂意
memory 記憶	observe 觀察；了解
present 主持	project 計畫
refresh 使恢復	researcher 研究員
team 組	

片語表··

focus on 集中注意力在	follow me 跟著我
get settled 安頓	get to know better 深入了解
I'd like you to meet... 我想介紹您認識……	If you would please... 如果您願意……
	in action 行動
look forward to 希望	make arrangements 安排；組織
personal assistant 私人助理	start right away 馬上開始
be a pleasure 很榮幸	start with 開始
work one's way up 晉級	working space 辦公室
work together 共事	

實境對話 1

A: Welcome to our office, Dr. Villaba. I hope you were able to find our office with no difficulty.

B: Oh, yes, thank you. It was actually not too difficult to find. I am very familiar with this part of Shanghai. Thank you for inviting me to come.

A: Of course! It's a real pleasure to have you working together with us on this project. Well, to start with, I'd like to introduce you to our team. If you would, please follow me.

B: Certainly.

A: Here we are at our working space. Dr. Villaba, I'd like you to meet the members of our department. Kurt Xu, Miyonghee Kim, and Sean Martin. Everyone, this is Dr. Jorge Villaba.

B: Hello everyone! I look forward to getting to know you better.

A: Dr. Villaba will be consulting us on the Martin case. As you are all aware, Dr. Villaba is an expert in Forensic medicine. We all really appreciate his willingness to add his knowledge and experience to our work.

B: It's my pleasure.

A: Shall I show you to your office? We've made arrangements for you to have your own working space here while you are with us.

B: Well, that's very considerate. Thank you very much.

A：歡迎您來我們辦公室，Villaba博士。希望我們辦公室不是很難找。

B：哦，謝謝。事實上並不難找。我對上海的這個地區很熟悉。感謝您邀請我來。

A：當然！在這個專案上您能和我們共事真的讓人很高興。好的，那我們切入正題吧，我想向您介紹我們的小組。如果您不介意的話，請跟我來。

B：當然。

A：這兒是我們工作的地方。Villaba博士，我來介紹您認識一下我們部門的成員：Kurt徐、Miyonghee Kim和Sean Martin。各位，這是Jorge Villaba博士。

B：大家好！我希望我們能有更多機會彼此了解。

A：Villaba博士將是我們在Martin事務上的顧問，正如大家所知道的，Villaba博士是Forensic製藥的專家。我們對他用自己的知識和經驗指導我們工作表示誠摯的謝意。

B：這是我的榮幸。

A：我帶您看一下您的辦公室好嗎？在您與我們共事期間，我們為您準備了一間您自己的辦公空間。

B：您考慮得太周到了。謝謝您。

實境對話 2

A: Professor Smith, let me introduce to you my boss Gertrude Childs. Gertrude, this is professor Jack Smith.

B: Hello Ms. Childs. It's a pleasure to meet you.

A: I'm sure that Gertrude can help you get settled here at our company.

B: Thank you, I really appreciate the opportunity to observe your company in action.

C: Professor, if you have any questions, please be sure to ask me, I am very happy to make your time with us more comfortable. Oh, and this is my personal assistant Alison Snow. Alison, I'd like you to meet Professor Jack Smith.

D: Professor, welcome.

B: Thank you.

A: Why don't I take you down to the research department. I think you'd like to meet our team of researchers.

B: That would be great, thank you.

A: Here we are. Everyone, this is Professor Jack Smith. He'll be joining us for a few months as he does research for some of his doctorate programs. Professor, these are our lead researchers. Let me present Lenny Marcus, Jordan Weber, Martin O'Hara, and Penny Han.

A：Smith教授，讓我來為您介紹一下我的老闆Gertrude Childs。Gertrude，這位是Jack Smith教授。

B：您好，Childs女士，很榮幸認識您。

A：我相信有Gertrude的幫助，您在我們公司裡會感覺很安心的。

B：謝謝您。我能有機會在活動中了解您的公司，我非常感激。

C：教授，如果您有任何問題，請一定要告訴我。我很樂意讓我們在一起的時間能更自在些。哦，還有這位是我的私人助理Alison Snow。Alison，我很想讓您認識Jack Smith教授。

D：教授，歡迎您。

B：謝謝您。

A：我想帶您到下面看看我們的研發部門？我想您一定願意認識一下我們的研發小組。

B：那太好了，謝謝您。

A：這裡。各位，這位是Jack Smith教授，在做博士專題研究的這幾個月裡他將會和我們在一起。教授，他們都是我們的研究主管，我來介紹一下，Lenny Marcus、Jordan Weber、Martin O'Hara還有Penny韓。

介紹公司各部門
Introducing Company Departments

每個公司都有獨特的（unique）組織結構，但是在每一個行業內都有類似的部門處理著內外日常工作。如下的內容將對公司部門的介紹有幫助。

概括介紹

首先以一兩句話概括介紹公司的總體架構，或某個部門的主要職責。

⊙Our company is divided into three major sections: Marketing, Finance and Account Management.

我們的公司主要分成的三個部分：行銷、財務和帳戶管理。

⊙Let's take a look at the breakdown. Here's Service, Sales and Tech support.

讓我們來看一下解析圖。這裡是服務、業務和技術支援。

⊙Most of our workload is handled by the accounting department, but they are supported by finance and sales departments.

大部分的工作都由會計部門完成，但是財務和業務部門也對他們提供支援。

⊙We also have a great HR department that keeps the rest of us running smoothly.

我們同樣有一個非常出色的人力資源部，來確保我們其餘的人可以有條不紊地工作。

⊙We are an integrated team, with members from our designing department, our implementation department, R&D department and sales.

我們是一個密切聯結的團隊，成員分別來自設計部、執行部、研發部和業務部。

組織結構

考慮到訪客可能對公司的結構和分工（work division）不是很熟悉（be familiar with），有些時候就需要解釋每個部門具體負責（responsible for）的任務。

⊙This is our artistic department. We have over 50 graphic designers who do most of the creative development of our products. They also support our sales team in internal projects.

這是我們的藝術部，我們有50多名繪圖設計師來負責我們的產品創作。他們也支援業務團隊的內部專案。

⊙The finance department consists of four accountants, one auditor, and one financial secretary. They manage all of the financial issues, including keeping track of all incoming and outgoing funds, expenditures and profits.

我們的財務部包括四名會計人員，一名查帳員和一名財務秘書。他們負責所有的財務事宜，包括了解所有的資金流入和支出，花費和收益。

⊙Welcome to the sales department. Our sales team manages all existing accounts, evelops new markets and manages current projects.

歡迎您來到我們的業務部。我們的業務團隊負責現有客戶、發展新市場、執行現有計畫。

⊙This is our managerial team. They keep an eye on the crew and keep things running smoothly.

這是我們的管理團隊，他們統管全部並且保證萬事有條不紊地進行。

⊙Human Resources is very important for keeping our company functioning at top-notch. They're also responsible for staff hiring and employee discipline.

在保證公司高效運轉方面，人力資源部就非常的重要。同時他們也負責招聘和員工培訓。

代表介紹

也可以透過介紹部門的主管（department head）或部門的專家（specialists），
來達到全面介紹公司各個部門的目的。

⊙This is Mary Miller, our Marketing director. She's in charge of the marketing
department, and overseas the development of new markets.
這位是我們的行銷主任Mary Miller。她負責行銷部以及海外新市場的拓展。

⊙I'd like you to meet Paul Smith, he's our Sales team head. The Sales
department has more than 50 employees, and they all answer to Paul.
我來引薦一下我們業務團隊的主管Paul Smith。我們的業務部有50多名人員，
他們都向Paul報告。

⊙Say hello to our designers that make up our artistic development
department. This is Joan Stevens, Miller Jones, Liu Yang, and Linda Ma.
跟我們藝術發展部的設計師們打個招呼吧。這是Joan Stevens、Miller Jones、
Liu Yang和Linda Ma。

總結

掌握到訪者對公司各個部門了解程度的需求，從不同程度和角度來介紹。可以
從部門名稱和關係的介紹來表現相互協助、各盡其職的特點；也可從介紹各個
部門的負責人和專家，讓到訪者經由人事的角度深入了解公司的各個部門。

單字表

bookkeeping 記帳	breakdown 分解
enjoyable 令人愉快的	function 運轉
HR (human resources) 人力資源	impressive 令人讚歎的；令人驚歎的

integrated 密切聯繫；完整統一

internal 內部的

likewise 同樣

major 主要的

managerial 管理的

section 部分；塊

team 團隊

tour 遊覽；參觀

trend 動向；趨勢

workload 工作量；工作負擔

片語表

answer to (sb.) 對某人負責；回應

as a matter of fact 事實上

as needed basis 在有需要的基礎上

be swamped 不堪承受；應接不暇

employee discipline 員工培訓

graphic design 繪圖設計

handle accounts 處理帳目

if you would 如果你願意

in total 總共

keep an eye on (sb. or sth.) 留意/注意

offer support 提供支援

（某人或某事）

run smoothly 順利運轉

say hello to 打招呼

step in (to help) 授之以手；主動幫助

tech support 技術支援

thrown in the mix 編入；混入

be at work 在工作中

be with (a company) 為（某公司）效力

top notch 最出色的

turn out 證實；結果是

實境對話 1

A: Welcome to Harris Publishing group. Before your meeting today with our company president, Mr. Martin, he has asked me to take you on a short tour of our company. I hope you'd find that enjoyable?

B: Sure, that would be great. I'd like to see what goes on around here.

A: Wonderful. Well, should we get started then? Please, if you would follow me.

B: Okay!

A: Our company is divided into three major sections: Design, Editing, and Finance. We are an integrated team. We also have a great HR department that keeps the rest of us running smoothly.

B: How many employees in total do you have?

A: We have over 200 employees total. Most of the employees are in design and editing, however. This is our artistic department. We have over 20 graphic designers who do most of the creative development of our products. They also support our sales team in internal projects.

B: Wow, that's pretty impressive.

A: Here are some designers at work now. Say hello to our lead designers. This is Joan Stevens, Miller Jones, Liu Yang, and Linda Ma.

B: Nice to meet you all!

C: Likewise!

A: Here is the HR department. Human Resources is very important for keeping our company functioning at top-notch. They're also responsible for staff hiring and employee discipline.

B: Interesting.

A: Oh, here comes someone I'd like you to meet. This is Paul Smith, he's our Sales team head. The Sales department has more than 50 employees, and they all answer to Paul.

A：歡迎您來到Harris出版集團。在與我們公司的總裁Martin先生會面之前，他讓我先帶您參觀一下我們公司。您有興趣嗎？

B：當然，好極了。我很願意看看這裡的環境。

A：好極了！那我們現在就開始？請跟我來。

B：好的！

A：我們公司由三個主要部分構成：設計、編輯和財務。我們是一個密不可分的團隊。我們也有人力資源部來確保其餘的員工有條不紊地工作。

B：你們一共有多少員工？

A：我們一共有200多人。大部分人都負責設計和編輯。這是我們的藝術部。我們有20多個繪圖設計師來創作我們的作品，他們也支援我們業務團隊的內部專案。

B：哇，真令人讚歎啊。

A：這裡有一些設計人員在工作。跟我們的首席設計師們打個招呼吧。這是Joan Stevens、Miller Jones、Liu Yang和Linda Ma。

B：很高興能認識各位！

C：彼此彼此！

A：這裡是人力資源部，在保持公司可以正常營運方面，人力資源部就非常重要的重要。同時他們也負責招聘和員工培訓。

B：有意思。

A：哦，我來引薦一下業務部主管Paul Smith。業務部有50多名員工，他們都向Paul報告。

實境對話 2

A: So let me explain a little more about how our company works. Let's take a look at the breakdown. Here's Service, Sales, and Marketing.

B: Which department handles financial bookkeeping?

A: Well, we've also got an accounting department thrown into the mix. Most of our workload is handled by the accounting department, but they are supported by the sales department.

B: So you mean the Sales department does more than just manage accounts? They handle financial matters too?

A: Yep. But only on an as-needed basis. The accounting department consists of four accountants, one auditor, and one financial secretary. They manage all of the financial issues, including keeping track of all incoming and outgoing funds, expenditures and profits. It's only in the even that they're swamped do the Sales employees step in to offer support.

B: Who makes the call of when they need to help out?

A: Oh, our managerial team makes those kinds of decisions. This is our managerial team. They keep an eye on the crew and keep things running smoothly.

B: I see.

A: Here's someone I'd like you to meet. This is Mary Miller, our Marketing director. She's in charge of the marketing department and oversees the development of new markets.

A：我再介紹一下我們公司是如何營運的。我們來看一下這個解析圖。這兒是服務、業務和行銷。

B：哪個部門負責財務簿記？

A：我們有一個會計部門被混編在內。大部分的工作都是由會計部門來完成，但是也支援業務部。

B：那你的意思是説業務部除了管理帳目以外還要負責別的？業務部也處理財務？

A：是的，但是有必要的前提。我們的財務部門包含四名會計人員，一名查帳員和一名財務秘書。他們負責所有的財務事宜，包含了解所有的資金流入和支出，花費和收益。只有在他們應接不暇的時候，業務部的員工才會介入提供支援。

B：他們需要幫忙的時候由誰來安排？

A：哦，我們的管理團隊來做這方面的決策。這是我們的管理團隊。他們統管全部並保證各項業務有條不紊地進行。

B：我明白了。

A：我想給您引薦個人，這位是我們的行銷主管Mary Miller，她負責行銷部以及海外新市場的拓展。

介紹你的公司 Describing Your Company

介紹公司就是要讓聽者對公司形象有清楚的認識，所以要對公司的組織、產品和服務（organization, products and services）做全面的介紹。要面面俱到是不可能的，但至少要簡短且凸顯重點。

介紹過程中客戶可能問到的問題。

⊙Tell me a little bit about the products you offer.

再告訴我一些有關你們所提供的產品。

⊙What services are available?

提供哪些服務？

⊙What are the payment options?

付款的選擇有哪些？

⊙How can your company help me?

你們公司可以怎麼幫助我？

⊙Who makes the decisions in your company? Who are the department heads and what do they do?

你們公司是誰說了算？部門主管都有誰？他們都做些什麼？

⊙What can I do to learn more?

我怎麼才能有更多的了解？

了解資訊

首先你要做到對公司的服務和產品瞭若指掌。產品包括性能、用途、價格和有效期限等細節。服務包括種類、費用、付款方式、品質保證和聯絡方式等。可以主動介紹，也可以根據對方的問題來應答。

⊙We are China's leading manufacture of electronic components. We supply computer parts for many international brands, including Dell, IBM, Haier and Lenovo.

我們是中國電子零件生產的主要企業。我們為許多的國際品牌,諸如戴爾、IBM、海爾和聯想提供電腦零件。

⊙Our customers can expect a full-service solution. We not only help you evaluate your company needs, but we also help you design a custom-built improvement plan.

我們的客戶可以得到全面的服務。我們不僅幫助您評估您的企業所需,而且也可以幫您量身定做完善規劃。

⊙We can help you in the development of your products, and the implementation of your services.

我們可以幫助您發展您的產品,完善您的服務。

⊙Here is our current company catalog. You'll find we offer more than three thousand different product specifications.

這是我們公司的產品目錄,您會發現我們可以提供超過三千種的產品規格。

有針對性

如果人們著眼產品壽命(longevity),你就多介紹一些產品的可靠性和持久性(consistency and durability);如果你的服務特點是便利,那就多介紹些經濟實惠、維修簡單等特點(minimal upkeep);如果你的產品特點是時尚,那就應該多鼓吹迎合潮流、與時共進。總之,要根據對方的需要來介紹。

⊙The strength of our products is their economy. The quality is very high, while the cost remains low. We offer the best value on the market.

我們產品的優勢主要表現在它的物美價廉上。我們的價格是市場上最具競爭力的。

⊙Our services are very flexible, we can customize for your particular situation.
我們的服務非常地靈活，我們可以根據您的特殊需求來訂做。

注意保護智慧財產權和商業秘密（**trade secrets**）

當涉及產品的尖端技術時，應該考慮到安全因素，尤其是對一些涉及智慧財產權（IP——Intellectual Property）的產品。這不僅有利於避免競爭，也有利於對企業利益的保護。一般情況下，對於客戶的探詢婉言謝絕即可。如果客戶執意要求，則需要簽署《保密協定》（NDA——Non-Disclosure Agreement）。

A: Our technology is cutting edge. This particular model has a patented design.
B: Can you tell me more about how the mechanism actually works?
A: I can't go into too much detail, but I can let you know that you won't find a comparable product with any of our competitors。

A：我們的技術是最頂尖的。這種特別的樣式是專利設計的。
B：您能否再多說些這個零件運轉的道理？
A：我無法涉及更多的細節，但是我可以告訴您，在我們的任何競爭對手那裡都找不到類似的產品。

⊙Before I detail more about this particular product line, I wonder if you would mind signing a confidentiality agreement.
在我詳細說明這條特別的生產線之前，我想知道您是否介意先簽署一份保密協定。

⊙Please review the nondisclosure agreement carefully before signing it. I am looking forward to sharing more about what our company does.
在簽署保密協定之前請先認真閱讀。我很樂意和您分享更多有關我們公司的業務。

總結

在客戶眼裡你就是公司的代表，就是公司的廣告。無論介紹產品還是服務，只有在深入學習了解的基礎上才能對答如流、面面俱到。此外，還要「投其所好」根據聽者的需要來介紹。不要誇大其詞，吹噓的結果只會讓對方對你失去信任。

單字表

affordable 能夠接受的

brief 簡潔的；簡報

consultation 諮詢；商討

economy 經濟

introduction 介紹

patented 獲得專利的

reliable 可信賴的；可依靠的

websites 網址

basic 基本要素；基礎設施

component 成分；零件

costing 成本計算

flexible 靈活的；可變動的

mission 使命

products 產品

support 支持

片語表

at all 根本

best value 最好價值

comparable product 類似的產品

custom design 按照客戶要求設計；定做

I'd love to. 我願意。

no problem 沒有問題

product specifications 產品規格

best possible 最大努力

Can you tell me about...? 你能告訴些關於……嗎？

full-service 全面的服務

marketing plan 行銷計畫

no uncertain terms 明確有力的

specialize in 專門研究（或從事）

tell me more 告訴我更多
to be honest 老實說

be familiar with 通曉；熟悉
You won't find... 你無法找到……

實境對話 1

A: Can you tell me more about what your company does?

B: Certainly! I'd love to share with you a brief introduction to our products and services. How familiar are you with Martin Managing?

A: To be honest, I don't know much about your company at all.

B: No problem, I'll just start with the basics. We are a full-service marketing consulting agency that specializes in creating marketing plans for small to medium sized companies. Our mission, in no uncertain terms, is to help small businesses everywhere get bigger.

A: What ways do you do that?

B: We provide companies with the best possible marketing plans. We don't focus on the cheapest designs or direct mailings and websites. But what we do is focus on the absolute best way to grow a small business. We create a reliable, affordable, easy to understand, and effective way to successfully develop business ideas.

A: I see. What specific support could you offer my organization?

B: If you're interested, I can schedule you a free consultation with one of our marketing experts. They can help design a custom marketing plan specifically designed for your organization.

A: Great!

A：您能再告訴我一些關於你們公司所從事的業務嗎？

B：當然！我很願意給您簡介我們的產品和服務。您對Martin Managing了解有多少？

A：老實說，我對你們公司知之甚少。

B：沒問題，我從一些基礎的開始。我們是一家專門從事為中小企業制定行銷發展計畫的全方位諮詢代理機構。我們的目標很明確，就是幫助那些小企業逐步變大。

A：透過什麼樣的途徑來實現呢？

B：我們向那些企業提供最好的行銷計畫。我們並不把注意力集中到最廉價的設計或者直接的郵寄廣告和網頁，而是想辦法如何使小生意真正地成長。我們創造一個可靠的、實惠的、易於理解並且有效的方式，來成功發展商業理念。

A：我明白了，對於我們的企業您能提供哪些具體的協助呢？

B：如果您感興趣的話，我可以為您安排一個向我們的行銷專家們免費諮詢的時間。他們可以幫助您設計一個針對您企業的行銷計畫。

A：太好了！

實境對話 2

A: What kind of products does your company offer?

B: We are China's leading manufacturer of electronic components. We supply computer parts for many international brands, including Dell, IBM, Haier, and Lenovo. Here is our current company catalog. You'll find we offer more than three thousand different product specifications.

A: Do you offer custom design as well?

B: That's no problem. We do offer support for custom design, although the product specifications must be developed by your team and you must fill an order of over 10,000 units. Our manufacturing is very flexible, we can customize for your particular situation.

A: Great. What about costing?

B: The strength of our products is their economy. The quality is very high while the cost remains low. We offer the best value on the market.

A: What about this model here?

B: Our technology is cutting edge. This particular model has a patented design.

A: Can you tell me more about how the mechanism actually works?

B: I can't go into too much detail, but I can let you know that you won't find a comparable product with any of our competitors.

A：你們公司都提供哪些產品？

B：我們是中國電子零件生產的主要企業。我們為許多的國際品牌，如戴爾、IBM、海爾和聯想等提供電腦零件。這裡有我們最新的產品目錄。您會發現我們可以提供3000多種規格的產品。

A：你們是否也接受客戶設計訂單？

B：沒有問題。對於客戶設計我們完全可以支援，但是產品規格的設計必須出自您的團隊之手，而且訂單的量不少於10,000件。我們的製造非常地靈活，我們可以根據您的特殊需求來定做。

A：那太好了，費用如何？

B：我們產品的優勢主要表現在它的物美價廉上。我們的價格是市場上最具競爭力的。

A：這個樣式怎麼樣？

B：我們的技術是最尖端的。這種特殊的樣式是專利設計的。

A：你能否告訴我更多些關於零件如何工作的原理？

B：我無法告訴您太多的細節，但是我可以告訴您，在任何一個我們的競爭對手那裡，您都找不到類似的產品。

介紹新產品 Introducing a New Product

如果你的新產品對消費者來說是聞所未聞的（unheard）新鮮事物，那應當詳細介紹產品的成分、功效、維護保養、使用注意事項（notes）等。總之，儘可能全面；如果某種產品是對舊產品的改良，則需重點突出進步之處，如更實惠、更方便、更耐用等。

介紹產品時切忌空洞，透過比較（comparison）和舉例，讓客戶感覺到「看得見摸得著」的好處。

⊙Our newest model is economical and practical. It costs 20% less than the previous model, and is much more durable.

我們新款既經濟又實用。比舊款的花費少了20%，而且更加持久耐用。

⊙We now have improved longevity. This product is not only reliable, but also boasts consistency and durability.

我們現在提高了產品壽命。這個產品不僅值得信賴，而且在持久耐用上也值得稱許。

⊙If you do a price comparison with our products and the leading competitors, you will clearly see the advantage of our products is their affordability.

如果你將我們的產品和那些主要的競爭對手相比較，顯而易見，我們產品的優勢表現在它的實惠上。

⊙With our new patented design, we can blow the competition away.

用我們最新的專利設計，我們可以將對手一舉擊潰。

對不同客戶採用不同的介紹方式

明確界定潛在客戶群（potential customer），從而決定介紹產品的方式。如果是高科技或者工業產品，面對面介紹是個不錯的選擇；如果目標客戶群是時

尚意識較強的年輕人（young），則可以考慮網路上圖文並茂的介紹；如果希望引起批發商（distributor）或代理商（agent）的興趣，可以選擇郵寄樣品和目錄，透過電話解答疑問或者請其到公司召開介紹會。

⊙Our new product appeals to a younger audience. We need to market heavily on the Internet and other teen-friendly media.
我們的新產品主要是迎合那些年輕的人群。我們需要將重點放在網路和年輕人喜歡的媒體上。

⊙What's our demographic? Should we focus on direct mailing?
我們的目標客群是什麼人？我們是否應該將精力集中到直接郵寄上？

⊙Our target audience will most likely find our products online. We don't need to worry so much about retail issues.
我們的消費族群將多半透過網路了解我們的產品。我們不需要太擔心零售的事。

⊙What's our profit margin? Can we afford more aggressive marketing?
我們的利潤呢？我們是否還有能力來負擔更積極主動的行銷呢？

知己知彼

人們喜歡貨比三家，你就應當對競爭對手（competitors）的同類產品（similar products）認真研究和調查，彙整新產品在價格、品質等諸多方面的優勢。在介紹中，用比較的方式向聽者說明你們產品更勝一籌的理由。

⊙What is our competition doing to boost their sales in this market?
我們的競爭對手將會如何提高他們的市場銷售呢？

⊙Have you got the marketing reports back yet? We need to know what it is they are doing so that we can get our product off the ground!
你拿到市場報告了嗎？我們必須對他們現在的行動瞭若指掌，才能使我們產品的銷售順利進行！

問與答

有效的產品介紹不是大段背誦準備好的演講稿，而是在與聽眾的互動中針對聽者提問回答，因為聽者的問題關係到他們的切身利益。此外，可以將產品初期投入市場的反應作為介紹的參考內容，調整行銷策略。

A: What's the feedback on our product launch?

B: According to the numbers, we're not doing so well with the traditional target audience. I think we need to go back to square one.

A: What we ought to do is to pursue non-traditional market arenas?

A：我們的產品上市後反應怎麼樣？

B：從數字來看，我們在傳統目標客群中做得還不夠好。我想我們需要重頭再來。

A：在非傳統市場領域的推廣我們應該如何著手呢？

A: We've lost money already? I thought the product launch campaign was going pretty well... Maybe I was mistaken!

B: No, you weren't mistaken. The product launch was very successful. Primary research indicates a positive reception by our target audience. The only problem is, it will take a little time to show up in the numbers. We just need to be more patient.

A: It's hard to be patient when there's pressure on the pocketbook!

A：我們已經賠錢了嗎？我還以為我們的市場反應調查顯示一切順利……也許我搞錯了！

B：不，你沒有搞錯。我們的市場反應非常成功，只不過在數字的顯現上可能需要點時間。我們只是需要更加耐心一些就好了。

A：囊中羞澀的時候是很難讓人有耐心的！

總結

「酒香不怕巷子深」雖然有理，但是與其坐等客戶聞到酒味上門，還不如主動出擊。介紹一個新產品需要將專業技能、調查研究、客戶心理相結合。鋪天蓋地的吹捧不一定能讓聽者買帳。抓住產品的特點，介紹最吸引客戶的部分，在互動中做到有效地宣傳。

單字表 ·····

aggressive 積極主動的
demographics 人口；人群
economical 經濟的；實惠的
launch 上市；發行
number crunching 數字運算
practical 實際的；客觀的
retail 零售

anyway 無論如何
durable 耐用的；結實的
feedback 回饋的
longevity 持久的
online 線上
reception 接受；歡迎

片語表 ·····

blow (sb.) away 橫掃/打敗（某人）
direct mailing 直接郵寄
get (sth.) off the ground 開始/起始
（某事）
in the black 有盈餘；順差
market arena 市場領域
not so fast 不要太快
There's pressure on the pocketbook.
囊中羞澀。

boost sales 促進銷售；增加銷售額
focus on... 集中精力在……
go on 進展；正在進行
research (a market) 研究（市場）
in the red 赤字；虧損
marketing campaign 行銷/促銷活動
patented design 專利設計
target audience 目標族群
show up in the numbers 數字顯示/表明

play for (a market) 經營/致力於（某
市場）

profit margin 利潤額

sell itself 銷路很好；暢銷

實境對話 1

A: So how are we going to market this new product anyway? I don't even know how to get started!

B: It's not too difficult. I believe in the strengths of this product, so I think it might even sell itself! To start with, let's make a list of the advantages...

A: Well, as I see it, our newest model is economical and practical. It costs 20% less than the previous model, and is much more durable. If you do a price comparison with our products and the leading competitors, you will clearly see the advantage of our products is their affordability.

B: Not only that, but we also have improved longevity. This product is not only reliable, but also boasts consistency and durability.

A: With our new patented design, we can blow the competition away.

B: Not so fast. We did some research into this market, and it might be more difficult than we think to get our share of the market.

A: What is our competition doing to boost their sales in this market?

B: They've got a really aggressive marketing campaign going on. We have to figure out if we share the same demographics, or if there is a nitch market we can play for. Bob is working on the report now, I think.

A: Have you got the marketing reports back yet? We need to know what it is they are doing so that we can get our product off the ground!

A：那我們到底該如何將這種新產品投入市場呢？我都不知道該從哪裡入手！

B：並不是很難的。我對這種產品的實力滿懷信心，我覺得它一定會很暢銷。讓我們先把優勢列出來……

A：正如我所看到的，我們的最新款式既經濟又實用，比上一款節省了20%的費用，而且更加持久耐用。如果你將我們的產品和我們主要競爭對手的相比較，很顯然，我們產品的優勢在於它的實惠。

B：不僅僅是那樣，我們現在提高了它的壽命。這個產品不僅值得信賴，而且持久耐用也值得稱許。

A：用我們最新的專利設計，我們可以將競爭對手一舉擊潰。

B：沒有那麼快。我們也做過一些市場調查，增加市場的佔有也許沒有我們想象得那麼簡單。

A：我們的競爭對手正在採取哪些措施來提高市場銷售呢？

B：他們開展了一個很有成效的行銷活動。我們要明確的是，要和他們分食同一客群還是另闢蹊徑。我想，Bob正在做相關的報告。

A：你拿到市場報告了嗎？我們必須對他們現在的行動瞭若指掌，才能使我們產品的銷售順利進行！

實境對話 2

A: What's the feedback on our product launch?

B: According to the numbers, we're not doing so well with the traditional target audience. I think we need to go back to square one.

A: What we ought to do is to pursue non-traditional market arenas.

B: What's our demographic? Should we focus on direct mailing?

A: I'm not so sure direct mailing would be effective. Our new product appeals to a younger audience. We need to market heavily on the Internet and other teen-friendly media.

B: There are practical benefits to a younger target audience. Because they will most likely find our products online, we don't need to worry so much about retail issues.

A: That's true. But I still feel we ought to be more aggressive. What's our profit margin? Can we afford more aggressive marketing?

B: Like I said, we're not operating in the black.

A: We've lost money already? I thought the product launch campaign was going pretty well... Maybe I was mistaken!

B: No, you weren't mistaken. The product launch was very successful, primary research indicates a positive reception by our target audience. The only problem is, it will take a little time to show up in the numbers. We just need to be more patient.

A: It's hard to be patient when there's pressure on the pocketbook!

A：我們的產品上市後反應怎麼樣？

B：從數字來看，我們在傳統目標客群中做得還不夠好。我想我們需要重頭再來。

A：在非傳統市場領域的推廣我們應該如何著手呢？

B：我們的目標客群是什麼人？我們是否應該將精力集中到直接郵寄上呢？

A：直接郵寄的方式是否有效不敢肯定。我們的新產品主要是吸引那些較年輕的族群。我們需要將重點放在網路上和年輕人喜愛的媒體上。

B：在年輕的目標族群中存在很大的實際利益。因為他們大多數可能透過網路了解我們的產品，我們無需過多擔心零售的問題。

A：那倒是真的，但是我還是覺得我們應該更加主動。我們的利潤呢？我們是否還有能力來負擔積更極主動的行銷呢？

B：正如我所說的，我們沒有獲利。

A：我們已經賠錢了嗎？我還以為我們的產品上市顯示一切順利⋯⋯也許我搞錯了！

B：不，你沒有搞錯。我們的市場反應非常成功，只不過在數字的顯現上可能要花點時間。我們只是需要更多一點耐心就好了。

A：囊中羞澀的時候是很難讓人有耐心的！

介紹你的服務 Describing Your Service

在介紹你所服務的機構時，與其大肆宣傳公司的光榮歷史和輝煌業績，不如細緻介紹一下公司能為客戶提供的服務，這才是與客戶的需求息息相關的部分。

如果能夠成功地解答「我們都做些什麼？」就代表著對公司服務的介紹已基本到位，之後再透過一些例子說明我們怎麼做、做什麼。

⊙Let me give you an overview of our services.

讓我來大致介紹一下我們的服務。

⊙This is what we can do for you.

這就是我們能夠為您做的。

⊙Let's go over a few of our service options.

讓我們大致了解一下我們的服務專案。

⊙I'd like to introduce a few of our services.

我很願意介紹一下我們的部分服務。

⊙Here's a list of our current services.

這裡有一張我們最新的服務清單。

⊙We can help you find the best solution for your situation. Let's take a look!

這是我們能夠為您的情況找到最好的解決方案，請過目！

時間對比

在詳述（detailing）目前服務的同時，可以提供一些實例來說明以前是怎麼做的。這樣，客戶就可以了解你們的服務經驗。

⊙Here's a list of our past clients. As you can see, we have provided solutions for many internationally known corporations.

這裡有一張我們以往客戶的名單。正如您所看到的，我們曾向許多著名的國際知名企業提供解決方案。

⊙We've provided comprehensive marketing consulting in over sixty major industries since first opening our doors in 2001.

從2001年開業起，我們相繼對60多個較大的企業提供全面的市場諮詢。

⊙We were partners for the Beijing 2008 Olympic games.

我們是北京2008年奧運會的贊助商。

⊙In the past four years, we have expanded our services to include not only traditional markets, but also non-traditional and international arenas.

在過去的4年裡，我們將我們的服務從傳統型市場擴展到非傳統型市場和國際領域。

⊙Today we offer a full range of services for public and private companies of any size.

我們現在提供全方位的、不同層次的公眾和個人服務。

⊙We offer both commercial and corporate services.

我們既提供商業服務也提供企業服務。

⊙There is no client too large, and no client too small. We can help you find customized solutions for every problem.

我們沒有太大不能做的客戶，也沒有太小不願做的客戶。我們可以幫助您在任何問題上找到解決方案。

有針對性

在介紹服務的同時，可以從提問或回答問題觀察聽眾的興趣點，並做詳細講解。

⊙Tell us about your needs and let us recommend the best services solution for your business.

告訴我們您的需要，讓我們為您的生意提供最好的服務方案。

⊙Let's start with the basics. I can help you find out everything you need to know about our services, including how they work and what you need to get started.

那讓我們從基礎講起。我可以幫您查到任何有關您想了解我們的服務內容，包含如何運作和您需要如何開始。

⊙Can you tell me more about your specifications? I want to find a solution that will work best for you.

您能否再告訴我一些您的細節要求？看我能否為您找到最適合的方案。

⊙Tell me your type of business, I can help compare the service solution best suited for your industry.

告訴我您業務的類型，我能幫您找到與您的行業最匹配的服務方案。

服務宗旨

介紹服務宗旨的目的在於表現服務的專業化，增強客戶對你們的信心，並對所提供的服務有大致的把握。

⊙Our mission is to help clients achieve their most ambitious marketing goals and strategic communications objectives. We do this by providing strategic counsel, creative solutions, and responsive services.

我們的使命是幫助客戶實現其最充滿熱情的行銷目標和策略傳播目標。我們實現的途徑是提供策略諮詢、創造性的解決方案、敏捷迅速的服務。

⊙Our firm's mission is to provide a high quality, creative, and result-oriented legal team to individuals and businesses. Our services allow us to be a primary resource and partner for our client's growth and development.

我們公司的使命是為個人和企業提供一個高品質、創新、注重成效的法律小組。我們的服務使我們成為客戶成長和發展的首要資源和合作夥伴。

有效回答

準確並積極地回答客戶提問能展現服務的專業化。當客戶根據自己的實際需要提出問題的時候,應當詳細解釋讓客戶滿意。

A: What exactly is included in your service package?

B: There are several options for our services, depending on your needs. We offer a full-service option, as well as custom designed, depending on what works best for you .

A:你們的全套服務到底包括哪些?

B:我們的服務有不同的類型,這要取決於您的需求。我們提供全方位服務選擇,也包括客戶量身定做,要看哪種對您最有利。

A: How long will our service contract last?

B: Depending on the needs of your company, we can make arrangements for the contract to last from 6 months all the way up to 5 years.

A:你們的服務合約簽多長時間?

B:這要看您公司的要求,我們可以調整的合約有效期為6個月到5年。

總結

說清楚我們的服務項目不難,但要讓介紹正好落在客戶的心坎上則沒那麼簡單。從服務的宗旨到服務專案,再到服務的效果,以及服務的實例,總之要想

客戶之所想，讓他們感覺錢花得有價值。介紹中，要熱情體貼、不急不躁、耐心周到，讓客戶切實感覺到你們的良好服務。

單字表

arena 領域；區域
basics 基礎要素
client 客人
consulting 諮詢的
industry 行業；工業
offer 提供
recommend 提議；勸告
switch 開關；轉變

asset 資產；財產
brochure 小冊子
comprehensive 全面的；廣泛的
corporate 法人的；公司的
IT 資訊科技
option 選擇
solution 解決方法；方案

片語表

aim to (do sth.) 做……的目標
company literature 企業資料
feel free 輕鬆隨便；無所拘束
in particular 特別；尤其
include in (package) 包含
non-traditional 非傳統的
over the phone 透過電話
service contract 服務合約
be in good hands 可靠的；放心的
troubleshooting 疑難排解

all the way up to 一直到
customized solutions 量身定做的方案
go over (sth.) 將……過一遍；講解
in the market (for sth.) 尋求……
make arrangements 做安排
on site service 現場服務
personal banking 個人銀行業務
service package 服務組合；套裝服務
start with 首先；以……起始

實境對話 1

A: Hello, welcome to Happy Valley Bank. Can I help you?

B: Uh... Yes. Actually, I was hoping to find out more about what kind of services your bank offers. We are considering switching banks. Can you tell me more about what options I have with Happy Valley?

A: Certainly! I'd be happy to go over some of our services with you. Let's start with the basics. I can help you find out everything you need to know about our services, including how they work and what you need to get started. Is there anything in particular you are interested in?

B: Yeah. Actually, we were hoping for some financial consulting.

A: We've provided comprehensive financial consulting for over sixty major industries since first opening our doors in 2001. In the past four years, we have expanded our services to include not only traditional markets, but also non-traditional and international arenas. We offer both commercial and corporate banking services.

B: Well what about personal banking?

A: Yes, of course, we also have individual banking. There is no client too large, and no client too small. We can help you find customized solutions for every problem. Tell us about your needs and let us recommend the best services solution for you.

A：您好，歡迎光臨Happy Valley銀行。有什麼可以為您效勞的？

B：嗯⋯⋯是這樣的，我一直都想對貴行提供哪些服務有更多地了解。我們正在考慮換家銀行。您能否詳細地講解一下在Happy Valley我可以有哪些選擇？

A：當然，我很樂意把我們的一些服務給您講一遍。那我們從基礎的講起吧。我可以幫您查到任何您想了解的有關我們服務的內容，包含如何運作和您需要如何開始。看有沒有您特別感興趣的？

B：是的，事實上，我們希望能夠得到些財務方面的諮詢。

A：從2001年開業起，我們相繼為60多家大型企業提供了全面的財務諮詢。在過去的4年中，我們將我們的服務從傳統型市場拓展到非傳統型市場和國際領域。我們不僅提供商業服務，也提供企業銀行服務。

B：那個人銀行業務呢？

A：是的，當然我們也有個人銀行業務。我們沒有太大不能做的客戶，也沒有太小不願做的客戶。我們可以幫助您為任何問題找到解決方案。告訴我們您所需要的，我們可以為您推薦最好的服務方案。

實境對話 2

A: Our mission is simple. We want to help you make technology an asset for your business, not a problem. Our services are aimed to do that. We can help you evaluate your needs and build a custom service arrangement.

B: That sounds great! We are currently in the market for a new IT support team. Can you tell me more?

A: Sure. Well, to start with, here's a list of our past clients. As you can see, we have provided solutions for many internationally known corporations. You're in good hands when you put your IT concerns with us.

B: What exactly is included in your service package?

A: There are several options for our services, depending on your needs. We offer a full-service option, as well as custom designed, depending on what works best for you. We offer on-site service as well as over-the-phone troubleshooting.

B: How long will our service contract last?

A: Depending on the needs of your company, we can make arrangements for the contract to last from 6 months all the way up to 5 years.

B: Do you have any company literature I can take with me?

A: Yes, of course. Here's our brochure. Feel free to take a look and ask any questions you might have. Can you tell me more about your specifications? I want to find a solution that will work best for you.

A：我們的任務很簡單，就是要幫助您將技術轉變為價值，這不是問題。這就是我們的服務宗旨。我們會幫助您對您的所需進行評估，然後建立客戶服務安排方案。

B：聽起來不錯！我們正在尋找一個IT支援小組，您能否說得更詳細些？

A：當然，我們先看一下這裡的一張我們以往客戶的名單。正如您看到的，我們為許多國際知名的企業提供方案。把您對IT的擔憂交給我們，您就可以高枕無憂了。

B：你們的全套服務到底包括哪些？

A：我們的服務有不同的類型，這要取決於您的需求。我們提供全方位服務項目，也包括為客戶量身定做，要看哪種對您最有利。我們提供現場服務也提供電話指導排除障礙。

B：你們的服務合約簽多長時間？

A：這要看您公司的要求，我們的合約有效期可以調整，從6個月到5年不等。

B：貴公司有能帶走的介紹嗎？

A：當然有，這是我們的手冊。您可以了解一下，有什麼問題就儘管問我。您能否再告訴我一些您的細節要求？看我能否為您提供最合適的方案。

十項全能之九

成為談判高手
Negotiation

對事不對人
Separating the People from the Problem

做生意要和不同類型（personality types）、不同背景（backgrounds）的人打交道。談判中也難免遇到讓你頭昏腦脹的人。這個時候，管理自己的情緒，把人和事情分開來對待（dealing with）就非常關鍵。

⋯⋯⋯⋯⋯⋯⋯⋯⋯⋯⋯⋯⋯⋯⋯⋯⋯⋯⋯⋯⋯

無論如何你要保持清醒的頭腦，掌握話語的主動權。僵持不下時要分析問題的癥結所在，引導對方保持理性。必要時可以提議休息片刻。

⊙Let's get back to the issue on hand.
　讓我們回到手頭的問題。

⊙We've been over this before, but I still feel we haven't reached a good solution.
　這個以前我們反覆研究過，但是我覺得我們仍然還沒有找到好的解決方案。

⊙I feel frustrated with the problems we are encountering. Let's take a little break before we go back to this area.
　對於我們現在遇到的問題，我感到有些煩躁，讓我們休息一下再回來。

⊙I can see that we have some conflict here.
　我知道我們在這兒有些衝突。

⊙I know that we haven't seen eye to eye on all these issues, but let's try to iron out the problems.
　我知道我們並不是在所有的事情上都意見一致，但是，讓我們一起嘗試著逐一解決這些問題。

⊙I can feel you are frustrated about some of the terms of our agreement, is that right？
　我感覺您對於我們協議中的一些條款有些苦惱，對嗎？

⊙Let's focus on what we can do to solve our problem.

讓我們把注意力集中在如何解決我們的問題上。

⊙Let's take a look and see what areas are workable.

讓我們來看看哪些領域是可行的。

避免敵意

避免談判參與方感覺自己被批評或被攻擊（criticized or attacked）。如果對方感到敵意或不滿而處處防衛（on the defensive），則意味著要說服他接受你的建議是相當的困難。為了避免不必要的誤會，可以做解釋，釋放善意。

⊙I understand that you have a different opinion. I understand why you feel that way. Let me explain the reasons why I see another option.

我明白你有不同的觀點，我也明白您為什麼那樣想。讓我解釋一下為什麼我有另外的想法。

⊙We know we aren't seeing eye to eye. But let's work to solve the problem together.

我知道我們的意見無法一致，但是讓我們一起來解決問題。

⊙You're right on about that aspect, but I wonder if you have considered...

在這個方面來說您是對的，但是我想知道您是否考慮過⋯⋯

⊙I know you don't agree with my idea, but maybe you can explain another way to meet my needs.

我知道您不同意我的觀點，但是也許您能用另外的方式來滿足我的要求。

著眼全局

將注意力集中在解決問題的方式上，而不因對方的隻言片語就捕風捉影。主動體諒對方（put yourself in their shoes），不要總覺得對方不懷好意（malignant）。總之，要管理自己的心思意念，顧全大局。

331

⊙The errors with the shipment were nobody's fault. We need to work out our miscommunications so there are no future errors.

船運的錯誤不是誰的過錯。我們得消除不良溝通才能避免未來的錯誤。

⊙I understand you can't meet my shipment deadline. However, we need to come up with some options that will get my delivery there faster. Let's brainstorm.

我理解你無法滿足我們的貨運時間底限。但是，我們得拿出一些選項來使得我的交貨更快些。讓我們來腦力激盪。

自我調適

即便是衝突出現的時候，也要互相體諒，給對方些許時間來「消消氣」（let off steam）。發現自己的情緒有些激動的時候，就提議休息片刻（take a break），調整情緒。動怒不會有任何的幫助，反而會「火上澆油」。

A: I can't believe you are being so unreasonable. You have to guarantee a shipment date of two weeks, or we will just have to call off the whole deal. You won't even budge on this one. I can't stand it!

B: Okay, I can see we have some conflict here. I know that we haven't seen eye to eye on all these issues, but I am sure we can work together to iron out the problems. I can see that we are both frustrated. Maybe we should take a little break before we continue talking about this area.

A：我真不敢相信你這樣不講理。你必須保證2週的貨運時間，否則我們將取消整個交易。你連這點都不讓步，我真受不了！

B：好的，我們在這裡是有些衝突了。我知道我們無法在這些事情上有一致的觀點，但是我相信我們一起努力就能解決問題。我明白我們兩個都有點煩躁了。也許我們應該在繼續談這個問題之前稍作休息。

總結

一團和氣的談判太少見了，矛盾的衝突反而是平常的。如果不能從大局著眼，就事論事，雙方只會爭鋒相對、相持不下。總之，要積極引導、自我調整、互相理解、取得雙贏。總不能因為不喜歡對方的個性就放棄機會，那不是在和錢作對嗎？

單字表

error 錯誤

investment 投資

negotiation 談判

quotation 報價

shipping 船運

term 條件

frustrate 沮喪；受挫

miscommunication 誤解；溝通不利

production 生產

satisfy 滿足；滿意

supplier 供應商；供應商

workable 可行的；行得通的

片語表

be over (go over) sth. 反覆研究；仔細琢磨

issue on hand 手頭的問題

make an investment 投資

more power to you 加油

price tag 價格標籤；價格牌

see eye to eye 看法一致

shipping method 運送方式/貨運方式

the whole problem 整個問題

focus on 聚焦；集中於

free to (do sth.) 無需拘束的去做（某事）

just yet 但只要；恰好這時

meet needs 滿足需求

no kidding 不開玩笑

reach a solution 找到方法/解決方案

settle for 滿足於；勉強接受

solve a problem 解決問題

You'd better (do sth.) 你最好（做某事）

實境對話 1

A: Let's get back to the issue on hand. We need to agree on the price and the delivery times. I know we've been over this before, but I still feel we haven't reached a good solution.

B: We've be over this so many times! If you are not satisfied with our quotation, you're free to look elsewhere. You really won't find anyone much lower than us. And if you do, more power to you.

A: No, Mr. Lin, we are not interested in looking for a new supplier just yet. We have already made an investment of time in this negotiation. So let's focus on what we can do to solve our problem.

B: We cannot offer you any more of a discount unless you are willing to settle for a later delivery date.

A: Let's take a look and see what areas are workable. You say the discount you originally offered is related to the production date, so if we want a sooner production date, we have a higher cost. Is that right?

B: Yes. That's the whole problem. We need time for production.

A: You're right on about that aspect, but I wonder if you have considered different options for shipping. If we choose a different shipping method, perhaps we could still keep a later production date but receive our products sooner.

B: That won't work because the faster shipping also comes with a higher price tag. If you want a lower price, you'd better think of something else.

A: I know you don't agree with my idea, but maybe you can explain another way to meet my needs.

A：讓我們回到手頭的問題。我們得決定價格和交貨時間。我知道這個問題以前我們反覆研究過了，但是我覺得我們仍然沒有找到一個很好的解決方案。

B：這個問題我們已經談過很多次了！如果您對我們的報價不滿意，您可以到別處看看。您找不到比我們價格更低的了。如果您願意（找），那就儘管找吧！

A：不是的，林先生，我們這個時候沒有興趣再找一個新的供應商。在這筆生意上我們已經投入了很多時間。所以我們還是將精力集中在如何解決問題上吧。

B：如果您無法接受稍晚的交貨時間，我們沒有辦法再給您任何折扣了。

A：我們來看看在哪個環節還能調整。您說之前提供的折扣跟生產日期有關，所以，如果我們要更早的生產時間，我們就要付更高的費用，對嗎？

B：是的，所有的問題都在於時間。我們生產是需要時間的。

A：從這點上來講您是對的，但是我想知道您是否考慮不同的運送方式，如果我們選一個別的貨運方式，也許我們可以延後生產時間卻可以提前到貨。

B：那行不通，因為更快的貨運同樣伴隨著更高的費用。如果您想要更低的價格，您得考慮別的方面。

A：我知道您不贊同我的觀點，但是也許您可以找別的方式來滿足我的要求。

實境對話 2

A: I can't believe you are being so unreasonable. You have to guarantee a shipment date of two weeks, or we will just have to call off the whole deal. You won't even budge on this one. I can't stand it!

B: Okay, I can see we have some conflict here. I know that we haven't seen eye to eye on all these issues, but I am sure we can work together to iron out the problems. I can see that we are both frustrated. Maybe we should take a little break before we continue talking about this area.

A: No, that's okay. Sorry, I just need you to understand how important the timing is on this shipment. The last shipment we got was a month late, and the result was that we ended-up losing a ton of money on that deal.

B: The errors with that shipment were nobody's fault. We need to workout our miscommunications so that there are no future errors.

A: No kidding!

B: I can feel you are frustrated about some of the terms of our agreement, is that right?

A: Yes. The whole problem is the timing. We aren't seeing eye to eye, but let's work to solve the problem together.

B: We can't meet your shipment deadline now because there is not enough time to make application to customs.

A: I understand you can't meet my shipment deadline. However, we need to come up with some options that will get my delivery there faster. Let's brainstorm.

A：我真不敢相信你這麼不講理。你必須保證2週的貨運時間，否則我們將取消整個交易。你連這點都不讓步，我真受不了！

B：好的，我們在這裡是有些衝突了。我知道我們無法在這些事情上觀點一致，但是我肯定我們一起努力就能解決問題。我知道我們兩個都有點兒煩躁了。也許我們應該在繼續談這個問題前先稍作休息。

A：不，沒事。對不起，我就是想讓您知道貨運的時間是多麼的重要。上一次的貨運晚了一個月，導致那筆交易我們賠了很多錢。

B：上次的船運不是誰的錯。我們得消除不良溝通才能避免未來的錯誤。

A：別開玩笑了！

B：我感覺您對我們協議中的一些條款有些苦惱，對嗎？

A：是的，所有的問題都在於時間。我們的看法無法一致，但是我們一起努力就能解決問題。

B：我們現在無法滿足您的貨運時間底限，因為我們沒有足夠的時間來向海關申請。

A：我理解你無法滿足我們的貨運時間底限。但是，我們得拿出一些選項來使得我的交貨更快些。讓我們來腦力激盪。

注意立場背後的利益
Focusing on the Interests Behind the Positions

洞察對方觀點背後的利益和需求（interests behind the positions），可以避免走很多冤枉路。如果在談判中混淆立場（你說你想要的）和利益（你實際需要的），雙方就很可能糾纏不清，難以達成共識。

變換不同的提問方式，從各個面向了解對方的利益所在。

⊙Can you tell me why it is that (position) is so important to you?
  您能否告訴我為什麼那（立場）對您那麼重要？

⊙What is it about (position) that is so vital to your business?
  為什麼（立場）對你的生意那麼重要？

⊙I sense you are very concerned about (position), can you tell me why?
  我感覺您對（立場）非常擔憂，能告訴我是為什麼嗎？

⊙What's your reasoning about (position)?
  您堅持（立場）是出於什麼原因？

⊙Help me understand more about (position) and why it's important to you.
  能否讓我更多地了解您的（立場），能告訴我為什麼它對您如此的重要。

⊙What can I do to make (position) work for both of us?
  我怎麼才能夠讓（立場）對你我都行得通？

337

避免衝突

在談判中產生一些摩擦（conflicts arise）很有可能源於雙方截然相反的觀點（direct opposition）。只要找到立場背後的利益，這些不必要的分歧是完全可以避免的，相反的還能發現一些創造性的解決方案（creative solutions）。

⊙I understand that you have a different opinion. Help me understand why you feel that way. Let's see if we can make this work.
  我理解您有不同的想法。讓我了解一下你為什麼那麼想。讓我們看看可以怎麼處理。

⊙Is there a way to make this work for both of us?
  有沒有對你我都能行得通的辦法？

⊙I can see that we have a conflict here. Maybe we can find a way around it.
  我能明白我們的癥結所在，也許我們圍繞著它能找到一條路。

⊙What if we attacked the problem by...?
  如果我們透過……來解決問題怎麼樣？

避免偏激

當談判者專注於自己的立場時，原本已定義的條件將變成孤注一擲（all-or-nothing terms），把自己的立場和要求作為解決分歧的唯一標準（conform），而完全不考慮對方的觀點。

A: Either you accept the price we have offered or we will have to abandon this deal. We can't give you any more of a discount. That's the best we can do!

B: Can you tell me why is its that you can't offer a lower price? I know you say there isn't any room to negotiation on the price, but what is the reason?

A：要不就接受我們提的這個價格，要不就我們就放棄這筆交易。我們無法再給出任何的折扣了。我們最多能做到這個地步！

B：能否告訴我為什麼您不能給出更低的價格了？我知道您說沒有任何討價還價的餘地了，但是為什麼？

A: The payment must be received in 60 days. It's mandatory! We really can't go for less. You either accept that, or the deal is off.

B: Can you tell me why it is that you can't extend a longer payment grace period? What concerns do you have about a 90 day grace period?

A：必須在60天內付款，不能商量！我們真的不能再少了。如果您不接受的話，這筆交易就取消。

B：您能告訴我為什麼不可以延長付款時間呢？對於90天的付款寬限時間您的擔憂是什麼？

化干戈為玉帛

切勿被一度空間的立場所誘惑（one-dimensional positions）（通常表現為「我就是要這個」或者「我就不要那樣！」）而是要和談判夥伴共同努力澄清「為什麼」。當態度背後的利益被明朗化後，往往發現其實雙方的利益是可以並立（compatible）的。

A: I want an increase of our profit share by 20%. I don't want to have to cover the insurance fees, and we must have our delivery by March 15th.

B: Well, it is clear where you stand. But let's explore some options that might work best for us both. Can you tell me why it is you have to have your order so soon? What is it about the insurance fees that are so important to you? What is your reasoning for an increase in the profit share?

A：我想把我們的利潤占比增加20%。我不想承擔保險費用，而且必須在3月15日前到貨。

B：嗯，您的立場非常明確了。但是讓我們試著找一些對彼此都合適的選擇。您能否告訴我為什麼您那麼著急要貨？保險的費用為什麼對您那樣重要？又是什麼原因您要增加您的利潤占比呢？

總結

如果談判者一意孤行地堅持自己在談判桌上的方案，談判一開始就註定失敗了。談判其實大部分都是從討論中找到折中的方案，讓雙方的利益都得到最大限度的滿足。遇到單向思考的談判夥伴時，就應當多問一句「為什麼？」，待雙方都說明情況表明「苦衷」之後，就一定可以找到「魚和熊掌兼得」的解決方案了。

單字表

accept 接受	authority 權威；當局
buffer 緩衝	discount 折扣
economical 經濟的；節約的	exemption 免除
extend 延長	grace period 寬限期；額外時間
increase 增加	insurance 保險
mandatory 強制的；命令的	policy 政策
possible 可能的	reasoning 推理；推論

片語表

at this time 此時；此刻	cover (fees) 負擔（費）
explore options 探索可能性	extend a deadline 延長時限

figure cost into your / our end 將費用算入你們/我們帳上

worth a try 值得一試

have to (do sth.) 必須做（某事）

my hands are tied 束手無策；無能為力

set in stone 一成不變的；無法更改的

where (sb.) stands 立場；觀點

find a way around (a problem) 圍繞（某問題）找到一個方法

have in mind 在腦海裡；想到的

just in case 以防萬一

profit share 利潤占比

be important (to sb.) （對某人）很重要

實境對話 1

A: I want an increase of our profit share by 20%. I don't want to have to cover the insurance fees, and we must have our delivery by March 15th.

B: Well, it is clear where you stand. But let's explore some options that might work best for us both. Can you tell me why it is you have to have your order so soon? What is it about the insurance fees that are so important to you? What is your reasoning for an increase in the profit share?

A: The delivery date of March 15th is set in stone. We can't accept anything later.

B: What is it about receiving your shipment by March 15th that is so vital to your business?

A: We are due to give the product to our distributors by March 20th. We need a few extra days buffer just in case.

B: Okay. Well, what concerns do you have about covering the insurance fees? Certainly, if we give you a deeper discount, this shouldn't be an issue...

A: Actually it is an issue because our company has a policy regarding insurance coverage. It is not economical to do it from our end.

B: Unfortunately, we cannot offer insurance at this time. We just don't have the service. Let's see if we can make this work. What if we attacked the problem by contacting a third-party insurance company and figuring the insurance cost into your end?

A: That might be possible.

A：我想把我們的利潤占比增加20%。我不想承擔保險費用，而且必須在3月15日前到貨。

B：嗯，您的立場非常明確了。但是讓我們試著找尋一些對彼此都合適的選擇。您能否告訴我為什麼您那麼著急要貨？保險的費用為什麼對您那樣重要？又是什麼原因您要增加您的利潤占比呢？

A：3月15日到貨是非常確定的事了。我們無法接受再晚的時間了。

B：3月15日到貨對您的生意那樣的至關重要嗎？

A：我們得在3月20日前把貨交到批發商手裡，我們得有一些緩衝時間以防萬一。

B：好的。那您為什麼那麼擔憂由您來負擔保險的費用呢？當然，如果再給您一些優惠，那這個就不是問題了……

A：實際上還是有個問題，因為我們公司對負擔保險有相應的政策。由我們來做的話就不划算了。

B：不好意思，這次我們不能承擔保險費用，我們沒有這個服務。我們看看怎麼解決這個問題。那如果我們聯絡協力廠商保險公司然後把保險費用再算到你們的帳上呢？

A：那倒可能行得通。

實境對話 2

A: The payment must be received in 60 days. It's mandatory! We really can't go for less. You either accept that, or the deal is off.

B: Can you tell me why it is that you can't extend a longer payment grace period? What concerns do you have about a 90 day grace period?

A: It's company policy. I am not authorized to offer anything more than 60 days. I sense you are concerned about not having 90 days. Can you tell me why?

B: For one thing, it takes 30 days for the wire transfers to be completed from all of our distributing agents. We can't make the payment before we have received the funds in our own accounts. I worry if there is any delay, if would affect our credit.

B: Hmm... I can understand your concern. However, there isn't much I can do. My hands are tied.

A: I can see that we have a conflict here. Maybe we can find a way around it.

B: What did you have in mind?

A: You mentioned you don't have the authority to extend a longer deadline. Would your supervisor perhaps have the executive ability to make a special exception to company policy?

B: Maybe. It's worth a try anyway.

A：必須在60天內付款，沒得商量！我們真的不能再少了。如果您不接受的話，這筆交易就取消吧。

B：您能告訴我為什麼不可以延長付款時間？對於90天的付款寬限時間您的擔憂是什麼？

A：這是公司的政策。我沒有權利超過60天。我感覺你對少於90天付款表現出很擔心，能告訴我為什麼嗎？

B：只因為一件事情，我們的經銷商要30天才能完全把錢匯入，在匯款到我們的帳戶之前，我沒有辦法支付。我擔心如果有什麼延誤，會有損我們的信譽。

B：嗯……我能理解您的擔憂，但是，我不能再讓步了。我無能為力。

A：我明白我們的癥結所在了。也許我們可以圍繞著它想想辦法。

B：您有什麼想法？

A：您說您沒有權限來延長時限。也許您的主管有能力來爭取公司政策上的特例？

B：也許。無論如何，值得一試。

創造雙贏的選擇
Inventing Options for Mutual Gain

有成效的談判源於對各種技巧的運用，找出新的選擇從而使雙方的利益得到最大限度的滿足。談判專家總是勇於創新、善於摸索，提出既能實現自身利益又能兼顧夥伴利益的方案。

從詢問中充分了解對方的立場和訴求，探索雙方都能接受的利益點。

⊙What do you think if we were to...

你認為假如我們要……怎麼樣？

⊙What if we solved this problem by...?

如果我們透過……來解決問題怎麼樣？

⊙If we... then we could make it work for both of us.

如果我們……的話，那就對你我都行得通了。

⊙I know you want..., and I want..., so what can we do to get them both?

我知道你想要……，而我想要……，那我們看看是否能夠雙贏？

⊙Would it work if we...

如果我們……能行得通嗎？

⊙How about doing it this way?

　如果這樣做的話怎麼樣？

⊙Look at it like this, we can try...

　看看這樣子，我們可以試著……

腦力激盪，慎重選擇

卓越的談判者會通過營造一個氛圍來鼓舞（encouraged）大家整合成一個整體，腦力激盪（Brainstorming）共同探索有潛力的解決方法。只有符合雙方利益（mutual interests）的選擇才是可取的，而此過程並非都是順利的。

⊙Let's brainstorm to see if we can come up with a solution for both of us.

　讓我們腦力激盪看我們能否找到對你我都適用的方案。

⊙If we... then it would accomplish your objective, but what about...

　如果我們……的話，就可以實現你的目標，那如果……會怎麼樣？

⊙Both of us are looking to... so we might as well...

　我們雙方都試圖……所以我們也可以……

⊙That idea is a good start, but what about adding...

　那個主意是個好的開始，但是如果再加上……會怎麼樣？

定位與思考

正確的態度是將談判夥伴視為同盟者（allies）而不是對手（adversaries）。不要陷入對立觀點的糾纏之中，而是要洞察根本利益。無需擔憂彼此間部分利益的差異，而是要尋找實現利益互補的方式。

⊙What you're interested in is... , is that right? Well, I would like to see...

　because...

　你感興趣的是……，對嗎？那我想看……因為……

⊙That dovetails nicely into my requirements, if we... then both our requirements will be satisfied.

那與我的要求正好吻合,如果我們……那我們雙方的要求就都可以滿足了。

綜合完善

當雙方基本上認可的共同利益形成時,必須將主旨更明確。總之,要把初步的意見具體化、正式化(formalized),讓雙方都能夠一目了然。

A: Okay, let's review our terms once more. You are interested in a lower overall budget because your current available resources are limited. I can only offer a lower price if we limit our on-site support. We can't afford to give a lower discount if our employees are working overtime and getting paid overtime. So I think if you agree to supply your own on-site workers, we should be able to give you the discount you need.

B: Sounds like it should work for both of us!

A:好的,讓我們再審視一下我們的條件。由於你們最近的可用資源有限,所以您所感興趣的是一個較低的總預算。如果在現場支援上降低要求,那我可以給出一個更低的價格。如果讓我們的員工加班工作還要額外支付加班費的話,那我沒有辦法再便宜了。所以我想如果你們提供自己的現場員工的話,我們可以給出您所要求的折扣。

B:聽上去對我們雙方都適用!

總結

通常人們將談判視為唇槍舌劍的對抗性活動,或者理解為談判雙方在利益面前勢不兩立。事實上,談判是不動干戈地創造雙贏機會、共同努力的過程,需要尋找共同利益、相互取捨,最終達成共識、握手言歡。

Words
單字表

accept 接受

aspect 方面

dovetail 接榫；吻合

insurance 保險

on-site 現場

practical 實用的；實際的

regulation 規例；條例

specifications 規格；性能規範

workmanship 工藝

anyway 無論如何；不管怎樣

discount 折扣

economical 划算的；節約的

materials 材料

overall 全部的

redesign 再設計

retailer 延誤

workable 可行的

Phrases
片語表

clear customs 通關

cut a budget 削減預算

have connections (with sb.) 與……有往來

look to (do sth.) 試圖……

move up a date 時間提前

on-hand 現成的；手頭有的

be worth (doing) 值得……

turn around time 周轉時間

cover (fees) 負擔（費用）

cut corners 偷工減料

limited resources 有限資源

look into (doing sth.) 研究（做某事）

might as well 倒不如；也可以

No can do. 不可行。

be more likely (to do sth.) 更有可能做某事

實境對話 1

A: It's going to be difficult to accept the price you've given us in the quotation. Is there any way you can give a better discount?

B: I know you want a lower discount, and I want to make this project economical for our company, too. So what can we do to get both?

A: Both of us are looking to save money, so we might as well look at some different options. Could you give us a better discount if we changed some of the terms?

B: Maybe. What do you think if we were to let your side cover the insurance fees?

A: No can do. It's just not practical. Your company already has the connections with the insurance companies and you can get a better rate anyway. What if we solved this problem by redesigning the project to use less expensive materials? We could cut corners by using lower quality on the less important aspects.

B: That might be worth looking into. However, we do have building regulations to adhere to. What you're interested in is cutting your budget just a little, is that right? Well, I would like to see a way we could cut costs without affecting the workmanship because the products we deliver are quality.

A: Well... What about the on-site employees?

B: Now, that sounds workable! You are interested in a lower overall budget because your current available resources are limited. I can only offer a lower price if we limit our on-site support. We can't afford to give a lower discount if our employees are working overtime and getting paid overtime. So I think if you agree to supply your own on-site workers, we should be able to give you the discount you need.

A: Sounds like it should work for both of us!

A：我們很難接受您報價裡的價格，您有什麼辦法能給我們更大的折扣嗎？

B：我知道您想要的是一個較低的折扣，但我也想為我們公司做一個經濟實惠的計畫。怎麼才能兩全其美呢？

A：我們兩個都想省錢，那我們不妨看看一些不同的選擇。如果我們改變一些條件的話，您能否給我們一個更大的折扣？

B：也許吧，如果讓您這邊來負責保險費，您覺得怎麼樣？

A：不行，那不實際。你們的公司已經和保險公司有往來而且可以得到一個特別的費率。那如果我們修改計畫並使用一種沒有那麼昂貴的材料怎麼樣？我們可以試圖降低一些次要部分的品質。

B：那倒是值得研究一下。但是我們有建設的法規要遵守。您所感興趣的是削減一部分預算，是這樣嗎？好，我倒願意找到一個減少費用但是不影響成品的方法，因為我們所完成的產品都是有品質的。

A：那……現場員工呢？

B：現在聽上去倒是可行！你所感興趣的是一個較低的總預算，由於你們最近的可用資源有限。如果在現場支援上降低要求，那我可以給出一個更低的價格。如果讓我們的員工加班工作還要額外支付加班費的話，我沒有辦法給更低的折扣了。所以我想如果你們提供自己的現場員工的話，我們可以給出您所要求的折扣。

A：聽上去對我們雙方都適用！

實境對話 2

A: Would it work if we moved up the production date by two weeks? I just got notice from the shipping company that our order will take 15 days to clear customs. In order to meet our deadline with retailers, we have to figure a way to get the product here sooner.

B: Uh... Moving up the deadline for production shouldn't be a terribly big issue, If we received a finalized specifications order, then it would accomplish your objective, but what about confirming the specifications? Can you do it on short notice?

A: Hmm... That might be a problem. The artistic department has to come up with the design and then it has to be approved by the executive committee. That takes about a month. It wouldn't give you enough time for production. Let's brainstorm to see if we can come up with a solution for both of us.

B: How about doing it this way. We can give you a catalog of the standard product molds we already have on hand. You can show that to your executive people, and have them make a decision. That would bypass the designers and save us some valuable time.

A: That idea is a good start, but how about adding more than just your standard molds. I think if they were offered more choices, they might be more likely to find something they like.

B: Look at it like this, we can try with the standard catalog first, then if they aren't satisfied, they can give us a holler, we'll get our own designing team to throw something together. Their turn around time is only about a day or so...

A: That dovetails nicely into my time requirements, if we use your standard catalog items, then have your designers make the minor adjustments we need then both our requirements will be satisfied.

A：我們可以把生產時間提前兩個星期嗎？我剛從船運公司得到消息說，我們的訂貨可能將在15天內通關。為了使這些零售商趕得上我們的時間底限，我們得儘快把貨物運到這兒來。

B：嗯……如果我們能夠收到訂單生產規格的話，提前生產的時間底限也不是什麼大不了的事情，你也可以實現你的目標了。那關於確認的規格怎麼辦？你能在短時間內完成嗎？

A：嗯……那可能是個問題。藝術部必須拿出方案，然後必須要董事會通過。那需要一個月的時間。那你就沒有足夠的生產時間了。我們腦力激盪看看能不能找到對你我都通用的方案。

B：這樣行不行？我可以把我們手頭上有的標準產品類型的目錄給你，你可以

拿給主管看，然後他們做決定。這樣可以跨過設計人員而爭取更多寶貴的時間給我們。

A：這個想法倒是一個很好的開始，但是在裡面增加更多的標準規格會怎麼樣？我想他們的選擇越多，他們找到喜歡的東西的可能性就越大。

B：你看這樣子，我們先用標準目錄，到時候如果他們不滿意，發一些牢騷，我們就讓自己的設計團隊再調整，他們的調整時間只要一天或……

A：那正好和我的時間要求相吻合，如果我們用你的標準目錄，那設計者們就可以做最小範圍的修改，這樣我們的要求就都能滿足了。

使用獨立的標準 Using Independent Standards

要避免在談判中因為利益抵觸而導致的僵局（deadlock），一個靈丹妙藥就是堅持使用（insist on）公認的、獨立的標準。用普遍可接受的、公認的、客觀的標準來證明自己所要不是信口開河，對方的條件與「標準」有差距，從而促使對方調整。

談判前就要做足功課，了解市場行情，將相關資料記錄下來，談判時可以隨時查閱。

⊙Let's take a look at what's standard market value for these items.
讓我們看看這些貨的市場行情價。

⊙How much would we end up paying if we bought them from any other upplier?
如果我們從別的供應商那裡買貨，到底要付多少錢呢？

⊙The going-rate for... these days is...
目前……的一般價是……

⊙What's the blue book value?

藍皮書的價格是多少？

⊙I'm offering market value prices.

我給的是市場行情價。

⊙Take a look at comparable markets. You won't find a better deal.

看下同類別的市場，你找不到更好的了。

⊙I'm offering what's fair.

我給出的本身就是公平合理的。

買方的標準

作為買方，可以透過市場調查（marketing research）或者別的供應商報價來判斷賣方給的是否是合理價格（fair price）。

⊙The average listing on comparable properties within a 10 kilometer radius of the property you are offering is 20% lower than your asking price. Considering the market, don't you agree a discounted price would be more fair?

半徑10公里以內同類型的房地產價要比您的要價低平均20%，考慮到市場情況，您不覺得應該更便宜些才會更合理嗎？

⊙We've received quotations from several other suppliers for products similar to what you've offered. We'd rather work with you, so do you think you can match their prices and give us a fair deal?

我們也收到了一些與你們的產品相類似的供應商報價。我們比較傾向於和你們合作，所以你看你們能不能向他們的價格看齊，給我們一個公平的待遇。

⊙Similar quality items usually go for $20 per unit. Do you think you could reconsider your price quotation to reflect the current market?

同類型的產品價格一般是每個20美元，你不覺得應該重新考慮你的價格以符合市場行情嗎？

⊙I think $50 per unit is more than fair. According to *Consumer Reports*, the industry standard is between $30-$60, $60 being high-end.
我覺得每個50美元更合理，根據《消費者報告》，同行標準是在30美元到60美元之間，60美元就是高標了。

尋找準則

貫徹公正原則時需要找到雙方（both sides）都能認可的獨立標準。比如同行普遍通行的報價、知名企事業或政府機構的證明等。

⊙*Kelley Blue Book* reports the 2003 Mini Cooper to be worth $11,000 with private party sale. Since you're asking more than the Blue Book value, can you tell me why?
凱樂藍皮書（美國最受歡迎的新車和舊車資訊來源）報告說2003年迷你旋風從私人處購買的價格是11,000美元，你要的價格比藍皮書上的還貴，您說這是為什麼？

⊙The *Consumer Reports* published pricing is $800 per unit. I expect no less than what is fair.
公開出版的《消費者報告》標價是每個800美元，我要的是公平合理。

⊙According to the national standard, all units must be quipped with stainless steel appliances.
根據國內標準，所有的都必須配備不銹鋼家電。

理智

堅持標準時要求理智（rationale）而非情緒（emotion），因此自制必不可少。一些成功的談判者在整個談判過程中，都能保持耐心和平穩的情緒。

A: $35 per unit? That's absolutely outrageous! That's flat out robbery!

B: I understand you might feel my price is unreasonable, but let's take a look at what is standard for the industry right now. According to third-party marketing research, you can see the going rate for similar items is $40 per unit. I have given you a break on the price, but I simply can't offer you any more of a discount. I hope you can understand.

A：每件35美元？太荒謬了！那簡直就是明目張膽地搶劫！

B：我理解您可能覺得我的價格有些不合情理，但是讓我們看一下現在的同行標準。根據第三方市場調查，你會看到類似的項目費率是每件40美元。在價格上我已經讓步了，但是我無法再給任何更多的折扣了，我希望您能夠理解。

總結

談判到了雙方僵持不下時，可以設法找一個「說了算」的標準來參照。如果能夠找到一個獨立的、客觀且有說服力的標準來證明對方的出價不合理，就有可能打破僵局。迫使別人讓步需要耐心而非情緒。

單字表

appliances 家電

comparable 比擬；類似的

outrageous 豈有此理；不像話

several 幾個；若干

stainless steel 不銹鋼

third-party 第三方

upkeep 修理；保養

appraisal 評價；鑑定

expensive 昂貴的

refurbish 翻新

similar 類似；相似

standard 標準

unfortunately 不幸地；不巧地

vender 賣主；銷售者

Phrases

片語表

ask price 詢價；要價

find a deal 找出辦法

give (sb.) a (fair) deal 公平對待（某人）

go for (sth.) 贊成（某事）

market value 市場價格

match quality 品質配對；匹配品質

offer a price 報價；出價

take a dive 暴跌；突然降價

flat-out robbery 明目張膽地搶劫

these days 目前；現在

discounted price 折扣價

flat-out 坦白的；直率的

yield results 取得成功；取得成果

going rate 現行利率

match a price 匹配價格；價格調整到一致

be equipped with 配備

since you're (doing sth.) 既然你（做某事）

give a break (on a price)（在價格上）作出突破

實境對話 1

A: I received your quotation. Unfortunately, the price you offer seems much more expensive than we can go for right now. We've received quotations from several other suppliers for products similar to what you've offered. We'd rather work with you, so do you think you can match their prices and give us a fair deal?

B: I'm sorry, but I will have to stand by the numbers I sent you in the quotation. I'm offering market value prices. I'm offering what is fair.

A: Take a look at the information. You'll see that the price they offer is only $20 per unit. That's half of what you want!

B: Okay, well, I will offer you a deeper discount of $35 per unit. Take a look at comparable markets. You won't find a better deal. The level of quality you will get from other venders can't match ours.

A: $35 per unit? That's absolutely outrageous! That's flat-out robbery!

B: I understand you might feel my price is unreasonable, but let's take a look at what is standard for the industry right now. According to third-party marketing research, you can see the going rate for similar items is $40 per unit. I have given you a break on the price, but I simply can't offer you any more of a discount. I hope you can understand.

A：我收到了您的報價。不幸的是您出的價格與我們目前所能接受的相去甚遠。我們也收到了一些與你們的產品相類似的供應商報價。我們比較傾向於和你們合作，所以您看你們能不能向他們的價格看齊，給我們一個公平的交易？

B：不好意思，對於寄給您的報價中的數字我無法調整。我現在給的就是市場行情價。我給的本身就是公平的。

A：透過這些資訊，您就能看到他們的出價是每件僅20美元，是您要價的一半！

B：那好吧，我願意給一個更優惠的折扣，每件35美元。看一下類似的市場，您找不到更好的了。我們的品質水準是別的賣家無法匹敵的。

A：每件35美元？太荒謬了！這簡直就是明目張膽地搶劫！

B：我理解您可能覺得我的價格有些不合情理，但是讓我們看一下現在的同行標準。根據第三方市場調查，您會看到類似的項目費率是每件40美元。在價格上我已經作出突破了，我無法再給更多的折扣了，我希望你能夠理解。

實境對話2

A: To be honest, I am very interested in negotiating with you on this property. However, the asking price seems a little unreasonable. The average listing on comparable properties within a 10 kilometer radius of the property you are offering is 20% lower than your asking price. Considering the market, don't you agree a discounted price would be more fair?

B: The going-rate for properties such as this these days is $400,000. We had the place appraised. The listed price reflects the value assigned by the appraiser.

A: What was the timeline on the appraisal? It was over a year ago! Since the current market has just taken a nose-dive, I wonder if a more recent appraisal would yield similar results. Since you're asking more than the going rate, can you tell me why?

B: The property has excellent upkeep and has just be refurbished with all new stainless steel appliances. *Consumer Reports* published pricing on such units would indicate a higher value. Take a look at comparable properties. You won't find a better deal.

A: According to the national standard, all units must be quipped with stainless steel appliances. I still think we need to reach agreement on a lower price。

A：坦白説，我很願意和您就這戶房產進行談判。但是，出價有些不合情理。半徑10千米以內同類型的房地產價要比您的價格平均低20%。考慮到市場情況，您不覺得便宜些才會更合理嗎？

B：當前類似的不動產的費率是40萬美元。我們曾對這地方進行了評估，單子上的金額是經過評估師確認的價值。

A：是什麼時間的評估？是一年多以前的！最近市場行情暴跌，我想知道再一次評估的話是否會得出類似的結果。您所要的比市場行情高，您能否告訴我是為什麼嗎？

B：這戶房產保養極佳，翻新時配備的是全套的不銹鋼家電。剛出版的《消費者報告》上説是此類型應有更高的價值。您可以看一下同類型的房產，沒有比這更好的了。

A：根據國家標準，所有的都必須配備不銹鋼家電。我仍然覺得我們只有以更低的價格才能達成協議。

考慮最佳備案
Considering the Best Alternative

談判前就應該考慮到協定無望時的最佳備選方案。備用方案相當於經過深思熟慮後的應急計畫（contingency plan），類似於B計畫而有別於底線（bottom line）。因為底線意味著談判到了窮途末路時的無奈選擇，意味著最糟糕的結果（worst possible outcome）。

考慮備選方案前，一定要弄清楚對方的立場，確認第一方案是否真的無望了。

⊙I will have to take your offer into consideration.

　我一定會考慮您的出價。

⊙Is this the best you can do?

　這是您能給出的最優惠嗎？

⊙What's your final offer? Can you do any better than this?

　您最後的出價是多少？還能給出比那更好的嗎？

⊙I hope we can make this negotiation work. Can you offer me anything more attractive?

　我希望我們能夠談出個結果。你們還能給出什麼更具吸引力的嗎？

⊙I am very interested in working with you. However, with what you are currently able to offer, I may have to decline this time.

　我很有興趣和您一起共事。可是，根據您剛才提出的，我這次必須要謝絕了。

⊙I appreciate all you've done to make this deal work. Problem is, I may not be able to accept the terms you've offered.

　我很感激您為這筆交易所作的努力。問題是，我不能夠接受您剛給出的條件。

⊙I'd like to see this work. What is your last price? Can you give me a slightly better deal?

我得看一下這個方案，您最後的價格是多少？您還能再稍微優惠些嗎？

用途

對於最佳選擇方案（best alternate solution）要有一個清晰的概念，避免接受一些有利程度還不如（less favorable）無需談判就能擁有的選擇。

⊙I'm sorry, I can't accept a price of $30 per unit. I already have another offer with a different supplier for less.

對不起，我無法接受每件30美元的價格，別的供應商給我的價格比這個要低。

⊙I will have to decline. I have received several other offers.

我不得不謝絕了，我已經收到了一些別的出價。

⊙Your offer is tempting; however, I will have to consider my options.

您的提議很有吸引力，可是，我還必須考慮我的選擇。

⊙I would like to be able to help you out, but I can't afford to loose money on this deal.

我很樂意幫您，但我在這筆交易上可賠不起。

選擇時機

成功談判專家（successful negotiator）的必修課之一就是學會什麼時候拋出備案，不要輕易放棄探索可以有更好談判結果（negotiated settlement）的嘗試。

A: I know you were hoping for a lower price, but that might not be feasible. Like I said, considering all the extras we're throwing in, $200 per unit is a very reasonable price.

B: Well, perhaps. I appreciate all you've done to try and satisfy my requirements, but I don't think we can reach agreement with a final price of $200 per unit.

A：我知道您期待的是一個更低的價格，但那是行不通的。如我所說，考慮到所有我們額外奉送的，一件200美元是一個非常合理的價格了。

B：嗯，也許吧。我非常感謝您為了滿足我的要求所作出的努力，但是我覺得以每件200美元的價格無法達成協議。

B: Do you have any better offers from anyone else?

A: Perhaps. Can you offer better than what you've offered so far?

A: Our profit sharing on this partnership can't be less than 40/60. We're absorbing all of the overhead costs, we should be entitled to a higher percentage of the proceeds.

B: Is this the first joint venture project your company has dealt with? You should know that 40/60 is a very reasonable profit divide.

A: We have an offer from another entity which will give us 50/50.

A：您是否收到了別處給出的更好的出價？

B：或許吧，您還能給出比原先更好的出價嗎？

A：我們與合夥人利潤占比不能少於40/60。我們負擔了所有的營運開支，我們應該享有更高的百分比收益。

B：這是您的公司第一次做合夥交易嗎？您應該知道40/60是一個很好的利潤占比比例。

A：別處給了我們50/50的出價。

總結

談判就要在雙方的利益之間尋找平衡點，在取與捨之間拿捏。上述內容不是教你妥協，而是迂迴，把利益的損耗減到最少。談判前要想好所有替換性方案，找出最實際的退路。此外，還應當學會準確估計對方在進退兩難時會拋出什麼樣的備選方案，做到「知己知彼」。

單字表

additional 額外；附加

appreciate 感激；欣賞

consider 考慮

feasible 可行的

portion 部分；一部分

tempting 有吸引力的；誘人的

anticipate 預期

benefit 福利

extra 其他的

nope 不；不行；沒有

slightly 稍微

片語表

work out 制定；算出

benefits package 福利待遇；福利套餐

can't afford to (do sth.) 無法承擔做……

help (sb.) out 幫助（某人）做成……

loose money (on a deal) 在（某交易上）賠錢

Problem is... 問題在於……

salary range 薪資幅度

shipping partner 航運合作夥伴

take (sth.) into consideration 將考慮（某事）

accept a term 接受條件

best (sb.) can do （某人）最多可以

final price 最終價格

inclusive of 其中包括

May I ask...? 我是否可以問一下……？

number crunching 計算

relocation costs 搬遷費

satisfy requirements 滿足要求

stock options 認股權

throw in 額外奉送的

實境對話 1

A: I appreciate all you've done to make this deal work. Problem is, I may not be able to accept the terms you've offered. Is this the best you can do?

B: Well, I can't give you much more of a discount on the price. But what if I threw in an additional 10% discount on your next order of 10 thousand units ?

A: Your offer is tempting; however, I will have to consider my options. Is this the best you can do?

B: I would like to be able to help you out, but I can't afford to loose money on this deal. What if I talked to our shipping partner and got you insurance discounts on the shipping portion?

A: I will have to take your offer into consideration. If you offer us a discount on insurance, it will still figure into more than $15 per unit for shipping. Hold on, let me do some number crunching. Nope, still not working out for the price we'd like to get. I'd like to see this work. What is your last price? Can you give me a slightly better deal?

B: I know you were hoping for a lower price, but that might not be feasible. Like I said, considering all the extras we're throwing in, $200 per unit is a very reasonable price.

A: Well, perhaps. I appreciate all you've done to try and satisfy my requirements, but I don't think we can reach agreement with a final price of $200 per unit.

A：我很感激您為這筆交易所作的努力。問題是，對於您提到的條件我無法接受。難道這是您能給出的最好條件嗎？

B：嗯，在價格上我不能再給折扣了。不過，下一個一萬件的訂單我額外奉送10%的折扣，您覺得怎樣？

A：您的提議很有誘惑力，但是，我還必須考慮我的選擇。這是您能給出的最好條件嗎？

B：我很樂意幫您，但我在這筆買賣上賠不起錢。如果我和我們船運公司的合作夥伴談談，設法在貨運部分給您保險折扣，你覺得怎麼樣？

A：我會考慮您的提議。如果您在保險上給我們一個折扣，那每件還是得有15美元的運費。等一下，讓我算算。不會吧？還是比我們預期的價格要高。我要研究一下，這是您的最低價格了嗎？您還能略微再優惠些嗎？

B：我知道您預期的是更低的價格，但是未必可行。如我所説，考慮到所有這些我們額外給出的，200美元一件是非常合理的價格了。

A：嗯，也許吧。我非常感謝您為了滿足我的要求所做的所有努力，但是我覺得以每件200美元的價格無法達成協議。

實境對話 2

A: Congratulations. It's my pleasure to tell you Contra Communications would like to offer you a position with our company as director of media relations.

B: Thank you very much, I am very pleased with your offer. Of course, I will have to take time to think it over before I make my decision. May I ask, what is the salary range of the position you are offering.

A: We are prepared to offer you a salary of $40,000 including partial benefits.

B: Oh, I see. I must be honest with you, that is a bit lower than I anticipated. Depending on your benefits package, I may be able to consider a salary of $50,000 per year.

A: Our partial benefits package is inclusive of full medical and dental coverage. Full benefits also include 401K contributions and stock options. I may be able to offer $45,000 with partial benefits, or $40,000 will full benefits.

B: I hope we can make this negotiation work. Can you offer me anything more attractive?

A: I'm afraid our economic constraints limit us to a final offer of $45,000 plus full benefits.

B: I am very interested in working with you. However, with what you are currently able to offer, I may have to decline this time.

A: I may be able to throw in relocation costs as well.

B: I am sorry, I will have to decline. I have received several other offers.

A：恭喜您。我很高興地通知您，Contra Comunication願意為您提供一個媒體公關主任的職位。

B：非常感謝，對於您能提供這個機會我很高興。當然，在作決定之前，我還得再仔細考慮一下。我能否問一下，您提供給我的這個職位薪資幅度是怎樣的？

A：我們準備給您的薪水是4萬美元，包括一定的福利。

B：哦，知道了。老實說，這比我預期的要低。這取決於您的福利計畫內容，我可能會考慮5萬美元的年薪。

A：我們的部分福利計畫有全面的醫療，包含牙科。全額福利還包含401K提撥和認股權。我應該可以給您4萬5千美元包含部分福利，或者4萬美元含全部福利。

B：我希望我們能夠商量。您還能提供更具吸引力的條件嗎？

A：恐怕我們的經濟限制因素，沒法讓我們給出4萬5千美元且包含全部福利的出價。

B：我很有興趣和您一起共事。但是，如果按照您剛才的出價來看，這次我只得謝絕了。

A：我也許可以附加搬遷費。

B：對不起，我得謝絕了。因為我已經收到一些別的出價了。

十 項 全 能 之 十

瀟灑做簡報
Presentations

簡報當天 On the Day of Presentation

當眾講話（public speaking）對很多人來說是引發（called upon）壓力的來源。以下的一些提醒可以幫助你克服當眾講話的恐懼，說出一個讓人印象深刻的（memorable）的演說。

開場白

簡報開場，首先要問候聽眾，然後進入主題。

⊙Thank you for inviting me today.
感謝你們今天的邀請。

⊙It's great to be here with you today.
今天能在這裡和你們相聚真是太好了。

⊙Today I'd like to start things off by sharing a story...
今天我想用一個小故事來開始我們的討論……

說明細節

當你提出一些細節資訊，像名字、事實、實例、資料、故事或者類比（names, facts, examples, statistics, stories or analogies）的時候，要做到簡潔明確、點到為止，無需進行討論，否則會本末倒置，時間分配不均。這個環節要的是廣度而不是深度（breadth rather than depth）。聽眾通常對廣泛的實例和證據的會留下深刻的印象。

⊙Let me give you a few examples...
讓我給你們一些例子……

⊙We can see this is true from...
透過……我們能夠看到這是正確的。

⊙Here's a story to illustrate my point.

這個故事可以證明我的觀點。

熟能生巧（Practice makes perfect）

在車裡或在臥室裡，甚至在洗澡的時候可以預演一下，看看自己該如何簡報、展開問題、引導思路以及證明觀點。開始前先調好設備，確保在使用時運轉正常。投影機的故障會打亂所有的預先安排，使你無所適從。文字和心理（literally or mentally）的準備越充分，壓力就會越小。

⊙Can you show me the projector before we get started?

在我們開始之前，能讓我看一下投影機嗎？

⊙I'd like to have a few minutes alone before we start, if that's okay.

能否在我們開始之前，讓我單獨待幾分鐘。

⊙Let's try out the equipment before everyone gets here, is that alright?

在大家到這裡之前我們調好設備，好嗎？

預測在簡報中或過後可能被提出的問題

要熟悉各方面的主題，無論深度還是廣度都要事先調查研究，這樣才能胸有成竹，不再緊張。如果碰巧被問到了一個你不是很肯定的問題，千萬別瞎猜。猜測有損聽眾對你的信任（damage your credibility）。要明確地告知，如果你不知道這個特別問題的答案，但是會後（to follow-up）會去了解並解答給提問人。他們不指望你無所不知，你不必掩飾或主動打擊自己的信心，聽眾會理解的。你只需要將注意力放在下一個即將來臨的問題就好。

⊙I'm not totally 100% sure about the answer to your question. Let me find the answer and get back to you.

關於您的問題，我不是百分之百肯定，讓我找到答案後再回覆您。

⊙To be honest, I don't know the answer to your question. Can I find out and get back to you?

老實説,我不知道您問題的答案。我能否找到隨後再回答您?

有效運用投影片

別當著聽眾的面讀投影片上的內容。不僅僅是因為枯燥(boring),而且會把你固定在(fixed position)螢幕前,甚至讀完後會想不起來接下來該説什麼。除非是涉及到投影片上的一些非常細節的資料(specific data),否則都沒有必要。投影片或圖片的作用之一是提示你(cue you)需要講解的內容,用自己的話來介紹遠比讀投影片上的內容更有意義(entertaining)。

⊙Let's take a minute to talk about this area...

讓我們用一分鐘時間來講這個部分……

⊙As you can see from this photo...

正如諸位在圖片中看到的……

⊙This photo reminds me of...

這張照片讓我想起……

總結

簡報當天的緊張和壓力經常會讓人感到如履薄冰、魂不守舍。最好的鎮靜劑就是把注意力集中在內容的分析和細節上的準備。透過緩慢的呼吸來放鬆,假裝鎮靜不僅會瞞過聽眾,也會瞞過自己。講話過程中語速放慢,這樣不僅觀眾聽得清楚,也能給自己更多的時間來思考。不要受主席台和演講台空間的限制,可以走到聽眾中去,不僅能拉近聽眾的距離,更會放鬆自己。對自己準備的內容要有信心,只要不斷貫穿主線,就可以善始善終,即便是眾目睽睽,也能遊刃有餘。

單字表 ··

appealing 吸引人的

comparison 比較；對照

consumer 客戶

equipment 設備

labeling 標籤；標記

point 點

projector 投影機

share 分享；共用

workshop 研討會；車間；工廠

brand 品牌

consultation 諮詢；商量

device 設備

industrial psychology 工業心理學

logo 標誌

prior 在此之前；預先的

remarkable 非凡的；不平常的；顯著的

training 培訓

片語表 ··

as a result of 由於……的結果

call (people) in 讓（某人）進來

eye catching 引人注目的；惹眼

gather oneself 使振作；做好準備

get inside (sb's) head 了解（某人的）想法

if that's alright 如果合適；如果正常

look forward to 期待；盼望

outside opinion 外界輿論

sales figures 銷售指數；銷售數字

take a look 看一下；瞧一瞧

the point of (sth.) is （某事）的重點在於……

better business bureau 商業促進局

expert advice 專家意見；專家諮詢

feel free (to do sth.) 無需拘束；輕鬆自由地

get started 開始

hook up (equipment) 連接；插上

in the first place 首先；起初

move on 前進；繼續移動

put together 放在一起

start things off by... 以……作為開端

take a minute (to do sth.) 用/花點時間（做某事）

try out (equipment) 試用（設備）

實境對話 1

A: Thanks for coming today to share with us. I'm really looking forward to your presentation. Here's the room where you will be presenting.

B: Can you show me the projector before we get started? I'd like to try out the equipment before we start, if that's alright.

A: Of course. Here, let me get it hooked up for you. There...

B: Perfect. Thank you.

A: Is there anything else I can get you before I call everyone in?

B: I'd like to have a few minutes alone before we start, if that's okay. If you could just give me five minutes to gather myself, then call everyone. That would be wonderful.

A: No problem.

(5 minutes later, everyone is assembled.)

A: We'd like to welcome our speaker today. Mr. Rutherford Peterson is visiting us today from Shanghai Solutions. He has put together a great training workshop for us on brand development. Let's all welcome Mr. Peterson.

B: Thank you for inviting me today. It's great to be here. Today, Id like to start things off by sharing a story...

A：感謝您今天的到來。我真的非常期待您的簡報。這裡是您做簡報的房間。

B：在我們開始之前,能否讓我看一下投影機?如果沒什麼問題的話,我想在開始前試用設備。

A：當然,在這兒。我幫您接起來。好了……

B：太好了,謝謝您。

A：在叫大家進來之前,您還需要我為您做什麼?

B：在我們開始之前,如果可以的話,我想單獨待一會兒。如果您能給我5分鐘來調整一下,然後再叫大家進來,那就太好了。

A：沒問題。

（5分鐘以後，大家進來就座。）

A：我們歡迎今天的演講者。今天來訪的是來自上海諮詢方案的Rutherford Peterson先生。他將就品牌的發展為我們的研討會培訓帶來一場出色的分享。讓我們一起歡迎Peterson先生。

B：感謝各位的邀請。我很高興能來這裡。今天，我想用一個故事來開始我們的探討⋯⋯

實境對話 2

A: Feel free to ask questions at anytime during the presentation. Let' move on to our first point. (shows first slide) Let's talk about the importance of design to our marketing success. As you can see from this photo, color is one of the most important eye catching devices you can use in the design of your logo or product labeling. We can see this is true from the sales figure comparisons done between our products before the logo change and after the logo change. Let's take a look at the graph (shows second slide). It's quite remarkable, really, when you consider the only change made was to the label color.

B: Why did they decide to change the color in the first place?

A: The decision was made as a result of prior marketing research and a consultation with an industrial psychologist. Let's take a minute to talk about this area. The point of our marketing is to make our product available and appealing to more consumers. If we want to get inside the consumers' head, it's very helpful to get outside opinion and expert advice. Let me give you a few examples. In 2004, our department hired an independent consultant to evaluate the effectiveness of our marketing strategy...

C: Sorry to interrupt, but I was wondering who the consultant was?

A: I know it was a professional that was recommended by the Better Business Bureau, but to be honest, I am not certain of the name. Can I find out and get back to you?

A：在介紹期間都可以自由發問。讓我們進入第一點。（放第一張投影片）我們來談談設計對於市場行銷的重要性。正如各位在圖片中看到的一樣，在標誌和產品商標設計過程中，顏色是最吸引目光的工具之一。可以透過標誌轉變之前和轉變之後的銷售指數對比明顯地看到這一事實。我們來看圖表（放第二張投影片），考慮到唯一的改變只是標籤的顏色，效果還是很明顯的。

B：他們為什麼決定改變當初的顏色？

A：這個決定是諮詢市場研究和工業心理學專家後的結果。讓我們花一分鐘來談論這個。行銷的要點在於使產品變得實用、有吸引力從而迎合更多的消費者。如果想了解消費者的心理，外界評價和專家的建議是非常有用的。我來舉些例子。2004年的時候，我們部門雇了一位獨立顧問，以評估我們行銷策略的有效性……

C：對不起打斷一下，我想知道那位顧問是誰？

A：我知道是商業促進局推薦的專業人士，不過老實說，我不是很確定他的名字。我找到後再告訴您，好嗎？

滿懷信心的開場　Beginning with Confidence

當眾講話，緊張（nervous）是無可厚非的。即便心裡七上八下、忐忑不安（the butterflies flying around in your stomach），如果能牢記以下環節，你仍然可以讓自信滿滿。

問候聽眾

講話開始時先問候聽眾，然後自我介紹；聲音洪亮清晰，讓聽眾耳目一新（Greet your audience）。如果聽眾中有人對你還不是很了解，可以再簡單自我介紹一下。但如果有人已經介紹過你了，這個環節就可以省略。

⊙Hello, thank you for inviting me today. I'm Matthew Walberg.
　各位好，感謝你們今天的邀請。我叫Matthew Walberg。

⊙Hello. It's great to be here with you today.
　你們好，今天很高興能在這裡見到各位。

⊙Let me introduce myself. I'm Xiaoping Zhang. I'm happy to be here.
　我自我介紹一下。我叫張小平。很高興來到這裡。

⊙Hi, I'm Jordan Zhang. It's my pleasure to be presenting to you this morning.
　大家好，我是Jordan張，很榮幸今天早上和大家見面。

⊙Thank you for having me here today. It's great to be here.
　很感謝有這個機會能和各位再次聚首。能來這裡我很高興。

破題

點明你要講的大意或主題。別迷信「以笑話開端會引起聽眾興趣」的說法。幽默如果不能恰到好處，會讓人感覺有些不倫不類，尤其是在背景差異很大的人群中（mixed crowds）。直接破題（get down to business）還是比較保險。

⊙Today I will be addressing...
　今天我要講……

⊙My topic for discussion is...
　我今天討論的題目是……

⊙This afternoon, we'll be spending a good deal of time talking about...

今天下午，我們將用大量的時間來談論……

⊙What I'd like to share with you today is...

我今天要和各位分享的是……

增強說服力

你需要讓聽眾了解你有什麼資格（qualified）來談論這個題目。不要以大篇幅來介紹你的簡歷，更不要吹噓自己（brag about yourself），而是要提及在該題目研究上你的資歷憑證（credential you）和相關經歷，幾句話就行。如果某人在此之前已經介紹了你的背景，此環節可以省略。

⊙I was involved with the original development of this particular kind of software, and I have been a technological consultant for the central government.

我參與此類型軟體的最初開發，而且我一直擔任中央政府的技術顧問。

⊙I was trained at Harvard Business School, and *Fortune* magazine has named me as one of the leading business minds in China.

我受教於哈佛商學院，被《財富》雜誌評為中國商業頭腦之一。

強調好處

告訴聽眾從你的簡報中他們可以得到哪些好處（benefits they will gain）。這是一個有效講解的重要部分（crucial part），會使你的演講馬上脫穎而出，引起關注（relevant to their concerns）。給聽眾的好處通常表現在提高收益、減少花費上，或者是一些解決問題的良策、進步的機會等。當聽眾都聚精會神看著你的時候，你會發現做一個有理、有力、有效的解說會越來越容易。

374

⊙In this presentation are ideas that may save us $600,000 annually, and increase our bonuses.

此次介紹中的想法可以每年為我們節省60萬美元，而且能增加我們的獎金。

⊙This issue affects all of us in the following ways...

這個問題會從以下幾方面影響到我們……

⊙If you listen carefully and apply some of the suggestions I will give you today, you'll be able to...

如果諸位用心聽並採納一些我今天給的建議的話，您可以……

讓聽眾了解簡報大綱

預告（forecast）你簡報的大綱。無需涉及太多的細節，只要兩三句話列出主要內容。告訴聽眾你希望什麼時候提問和解答：任何時間？每個部分結束後？還是在整個解說結束後？

⊙First, I'd like to address training, then I'll talk about operational readiness, and I'll finish up by discussing effectiveness.

首先，我要講培訓，隨後是運作準備，最後是討論效益。

⊙We'll have a question and answer period at the end, so if you'll please hold your questions until then.

在結束期間我們會有問答時間，您可以把問題保留到那個時間。

⊙Feel free to ask questions at any time.

如果有問題可以隨時提問。

開始第一項內容的詳細介紹

直截了當地開始，進入第一項主題。

⊙Let's start with my first point, which is...

讓我們開始第一點，是……

⊙Now let's begin with the first item, which is...

現在讓我們開始第一項，是……

總結

一個有「高度」的「自我介紹」不僅僅能讓聽眾對你信心十足，也能增強自己的信心；告訴別人你演講之中輕鬆就能獲得的諸多好處，不是為了吊別人的胃口，而是吸引所有人的注意力。清楚的架構是為了條理清晰、輪廓分明。總之，如果「好的開始是成功的一半」，那麼一個充滿信心的開始便是成功講演的一大半。

單字表..

affect 影響；感動
background 背景
development 發展；開發
effect 效應；效果
expert 專家；能手
international relations 國際關係
market 市場
perspective 透視；觀點
Stanford 史丹佛大學
technology 技術；工藝
workshop 研討會；車間

annually 每年；年度
broadcasting 廣播；播音
diplomatic relations 外交關係
effectiveness 有效性；效果
Harvard 哈佛大學
issue 問題
mention 提及；説起
research 研究；調查
technological 技術的；工藝的
welcome 歡迎

Phrases
片語表

a little more of sth. 多一點的（某物）
be a part of 一部分；屬於
build relationships 建立關係
experience success 成功經驗
feel free to (do something) 不要拘束；隨心所欲
in the following ways... 如下方式……
line up 排隊
see results in (aspect) 見（某方面）的成果

address sb. 對（某人）演說/演講
break for lunch 午餐休息
come out for (a meeting) 聚集（開會）
guest speaker 演講嘉賓；特邀發言人
have an impact... 對於……有影響
in addition to... 除了……以外；另外
let me tell you (that)... 讓我告訴你……
put together 放在一起；加在一起
spend a good deal of time 花大量時間
world-renown 世界著名的

實境對話 1

A: Good morning everyone! We're happy you've all come out for our monthly business meeting. Today we have a great workshop put together for you. Let's welcome our guest speaker, Dr. Calvin Taylor. Dr. Taylor is a world-renown expert in the field of technological development. He's been involved in technological research and development for over twenty years, and has taught at Stanford University since 1990. Let's welcome Dr. Taylor!

B: Hello. It's great to be here with you today. Thank you for inviting me to be a part of your meeting. My topic for discussion is what impact new technologies will have on the development of international relations in a modern world. This afternoon, we'll be spending a good deal of time talking about how technology can help international diplomatic relations. Mr. Linden has already introduced my background, but let me also tell you that in addition to being a professor at Stanford, I am also a technological consultant for the United States government. I have seen first hand how technology can help diplomatic relations. This issue affects all of us in the following ways. With improved diplomatic relations between countries, we can experience a greater success in our businesses. If you can use technology to help build relationships, you can improve your economy and see results in your businesses. Today, the first thing I'd like to address is a historical perspective. Then I'll talk about what we're doing now. I'll finish up by discussing how these ideas can help us in the future. Feel free to ask questions at any time. Let's start with the first part of my presentation, which is a look at the history...

A：各位早安！我很高興各位都能來參加我們每月的商務例會。今天我們為各位的到來準備了一個極具吸引力的研討會。讓我們歡迎我們的演講嘉賓Calvin Taylor博士。Taylor博士在技術發展領域享譽世界。他從事技術研發有20餘年，從1990年起任教於史丹佛大學。讓我們熱烈歡迎Taylor博士。

B：大家好，今天很高興能在這裡見到各位。感謝邀請我來參加你們的會議。今天要討論的題目是「新技術對現代國際關係發展的影響」。今天下午，我們將花相當多的時間來討論科技如何幫助改善國際外交關係。Linden先生已經介紹了我的背景，但是我想告訴你們的是，我不僅是史丹佛大學的教師，還是美國政府的技術顧問。我親身體驗到科技是如何促進外交關係的。這個問題從以下幾個方面影響到了我們的生活：改善外交關係後國家之間可以取得商業上的成功。如果你借助科技來保持發展關係，你就能提高經濟水準，看到商業上的成果。今天，我要演講的第一個話題是從歷史的角度。此後我會談一些我們現在所做的事情。最後，我會討論這些想法如何在未來幫助我們。有什麼問題隨時可以提問。讓我們開始第一部分的介紹，就是從歷史的角度看……

實境對話 2

A: First, I'd like to welcome you all to our general training meeting. Our program today features a great line up of speakers I'm sure you will all enjoy. Our first speaker this morning will be Mr. Fang Guoliang from Beijing Business Consulting. Mr. Fang will address us, and then we'll break for lunch before the rest of the training sessions. Let's all welcome Mr. Fang.

B: Thank you very much, Mr. Chairman. Hello, everyone. As just mentioned, my name is Fang Guoliang, and I am the General Director of Beijing Business Consulting. Today I will be addressing *How to Expand Your Business in the Asian Market*. First, let me introduce a little more of my background. I was trained at Harvard Business School in the United States. My own company, Beijing Business Consulting, has been in operation for the last 5 years and has seen profit increases of over 20% per year. *Fortune* magazine has named me as one of the leading business minds in China. In this presentation are ideas that may save your business as much as $600,000 annually and increase your profit by at least 10%. First, I'd like to address business training, then I'll talk about operational readiness, and I'll finish up by discussing effectiveness. We'll have a question and answer period at the end, so if you'll please hold your questions until then. Now let's begin with the first item, which is business training...

A：我對各位今天出席培訓大會表示熱烈歡迎。我們今天安排好幾位演講者，我肯定所有人都會盡興。今天早上的第一位演講者是來自北京商務諮詢的方國良先生。在方先生的演講之後，是午餐休息時間，然後是其餘的培訓研習。讓我們歡迎方先生。

B：謝謝主席先生。大家好，正如剛才說的，我叫方國良，我是北京商務諮詢的總經理。今天我要演講的題目是「如何在亞洲市場拓展生意」。首先，

讓我再補充介紹一些我的背景。我受教於美國哈佛商學院。我的公司,北京商業諮詢創辦5年來每年的利潤增長超過了20%。我被《財富》雜誌評為中國的商業頭腦之一。此次演講中的理念將為您的生意每年節省大約60萬美元,並提高至少10%的利潤。首先,我要講「商業培訓」,隨後我會談「運作準備」,最後以討論「效益」來結尾。最後會有問答時間,如果您有什麼問題可以留到那個時候。現在我們進入第一項,商業培訓……

組織論點 Organizing Your Points

一個好的觀點論述的組織方法(in an organized fashion)可分為三步驟:提出一個論點,清楚表達;用證據或實例來支援論點;重申你的論點,並進到下一個論點。

提出論點
開門見山提出一個論點,可以借助投影片,讓聽眾有明確的認識。

⊙The next point I'd like to make is...
　下一個我要說的是……

⊙As you can see from this graph...
　如圖所示……

⊙Not only are... important, but we must also consider...
　不僅僅在……重要,而且我們必須也要考慮到……

⊙So, just to reiterate, we should remember...
　那,重申一下,我們應當牢記……

⊙This point is clearly illustrated by...
　透過……這個觀點將顯而易見……

觀點介紹

在闡述論點前，你需要用25個字之內（25 words or less）進行整體的概述，使聽眾了解以下要說哪些具體內容。使用一些具有指示性質的語句，以提示聽眾已經說明到哪裡了。

⊙My next point is...
　我的下一個論點是……

⊙Point 2 in my presentation is...
　我講解內容的第二點是……

⊙Another thing we have to talk about is...
　還有一個我必須要說是……

⊙Next to discuss today is...
　下一個今天要討論的是……

列證據、舉實例

列出用於證明你觀點的所有證據、實例、故事等清單，可以講故事、列統計資料表、舉例、講笑話等，這樣不僅可以活絡氣氛，而且讓論點更有說服力。例證和實例都必須簡潔並有說服力（quick and convincing）。

⊙Let me give you some examples.
　我來舉一些例子。

⊙Here are some statistics you might find helpful.
　這裡有些統計表可能對你們（理解）有幫助。

綜述

重申論點，這樣聽眾更會信服你的結論。用提示性（signpost）的語言做總結，告訴聽眾論點的論述已結束。

⊙To summarize this point...

　對該點進行總結……

⊙(At the very end of your talk) In conclusion...

　（在講話末了）總而言之……

⊙And so...

　那麼因此……

下一個論點的過渡

用過渡型的語言，將聽眾的注意力引到下一個論點。

⊙That leads me to the next point.

　那引伸出了我的下一個論點。

⊙Now, let's move on...

　現在，讓我們轉到……

總結

統整論點的過程與議論文的寫作有異曲同工之妙，無非都是「破題、論述、總結、過渡」；都需要論據（實例、資料、統計表等）來充實觀點。無論是讀者還是聽眾，必須準確引領他們的思路到達你的指定地方，信服你的觀點。

單字表

advanced 高級的；現代的	advertising 廣告
auditing 審計	budget 預算
clearly 顯然的；明顯的	communication 通訊；溝通
demographic 人口統計的；人口的	expenditure 支出；開支

market research 市場調查

polling 查詢；調查

schedule 時間表

summarize 綜述；概述

update 更新

modernize 現代化

product 產品

statistics 統計

test group 實驗組

片語表

...and the like 等等；以及諸如此類

as you can see (from...) 從……你可以看到

illustrate (a point) 證明（某論點）

invest in 投資；投資於

make a point 證明論點；闡述論點

potential customers 潛在客戶

reach (a customer) 發展（一個客戶）

take (sth.) into consideration 把……考慮其中

target audience 目標公眾；目標消費群

when it comes to... 當涉及到……

a large percentage 佔有較大比例

dominate (a market) 主導（市場）

give an example 舉個例子

Internet user 網路用戶

It's easy to see why 原因顯而易見

marketing strategy 行銷策略

product development 產品開發

spend more time and money (doing th.)（在做某事上）花更多的時間和更多錢

yet only 只有才

well-received by 廣為（某人）接受

實境對話 1

A: The next point I'd like to make is the importance of modernizing our communication. This point is clearly illustrated by taking into consideration the potential customers we could reach if we update our marketing strategies. As you can see from this graph, a large percentage of our demographic are Internet users. Yet only 2% of our marketing budget goes to Internet advertising. Here are some more statistics you might find helpful. Our competition spends 45% of their marketing budget on Internet and other high technology advertising. They have been able to dominate the market and it's easy to see why! To summarize this point, we need to think in more advanced ways when it comes to our communication and advertising.

B: I agree!

A: Thank you. Now, not only is changing the way we communicate with our customers important, but we must also consider the strength of our products. My next point is that we need to spend more time and money in developing products that will be better received by our target audience. Let me give you some examples. If we hope to reach a younger market, we should spend time understanding what kind of products teenagers are interested in. We can invest in polling and market research, test groups and the like.

C: But that costs money...

A: Very true. But that leads me to my next point. To make money, first we have to invest money...

A：我要講的下一點是通信現代化的重要性。如果我們更新我們的行銷策略，我們就會開發到潛在客戶，考慮到這個內容，這個觀點也就不言自明。如圖所示，網路用戶占我們人口總數的比重很大，但我們對於網路廣告的預算只有2%。這裡還有一些統計表將有助於你們了解這一點，我們的競爭對手將45%的行銷預算花在網路和別的高科技的廣告中。他們能夠領導市場的原因也就顯而易見了。最後我總結這一點，我認為在我們的通訊和廣告上，我們需要更先進的媒體方式。

B：我同意！

A：謝謝。現在不僅要改變我們和客戶間的溝通方式，也要考慮我們產品的優勢。我的下一個論點是我們需要投入更多的時間和資金，研發更為目標消費群所接受的產品。讓我舉一些例子。如果我們希望獲得年輕人的市場，

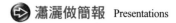

我們應當花時間理解什麼樣的產品才是青少年感興趣的。我們可以投資調查和市場研究，測試小組等。

C：但是那是要花錢的⋯⋯

A：沒錯。這正好引出了我的下一個觀點。要賺錢，首先我們必須要投資⋯⋯

實境對話 2

A: So, just to reiterate, we should remember the importance of planning. My next point is addressing how to schedule the auditing process. Here is the auditing schedule; you can see we will plan to evaluate the financial records one department at a time. I hope that all the department heads can pay attention to your department's scheduled date, and make all the financial data available to us at this time. Next to discuss today is what kind of data we will require...

B: Uh, I have a question.

A: Yes?

B: I see from your calendar that the production department is last on the list. Because we make most of the expenditures, shouldn't we be first?

A: It really doesn't matter which department is audited first, because we evaluate each department separately. Now, as I said, my next point is what information will be required by our auditing team. You must prepare financial accounting for all expenditures your department has made. If you have any specific questions about this issue, please contact any of the auditing team or myself. Now, let's move on. Another thing we have to talk about is when the management will approve the budgets for next year...

A：那再重申一下，我們應當牢記計畫的重要性。我要講的下一點是如何來安排查核時間。這裡有一份查核時間表，你們可以看到我們計畫一次一個部

門的審核財務記錄。我希望每個部門的主管都能注意到安排給你的部門的時間，並且確保在這個時間給我們財務資料。下一個要討論的是我們所需要的資料類型……

B：嗯，我有個問題。

A：什麼問題？

B：我看到議程中生產部門是最後一個。因為我們花費最多，我們是否應該是第一個？

A：哪個部門先接受查核沒有關係。因為我們分別審核每個部門。現在，就如我剛才所說的，接下來的重點是我們查帳小組需要什麼資訊。你們需要準備部門所有支出費用的財務核算。關於這環節的任何問題，你們可以和查帳小組的任何成員或我本人聯繫。現在，我們繼續。另外一個我們需要談的是管理部門對明年預算的審核批准……

用心回答問題 Handling Questions with Care

回答問題是演講成功的關鍵之一（major key），因為透過問答階段（Q&A session），聽眾就能夠發現你對主題的了解和應用程度。

說明提問時間

在演講之初就應該說明提問時間。演講過程中的插話會拖延時間、分散焦點（harder to keep focused），但如果善加利用，也可以使講演更有互動性、更有趣（interactive and more interesting）。

⊙We'll have a question and answer period at the end, so if you'll please hold your questions until then.

在接近尾聲的時候會有問答時間，您可以把您的問題保留到那個時候。

⊙Feel free to ask questions at any time.

有問題可以隨時提問。

⊙There will be time for questions at the end of every section, so please feel free to ask questions when we come to the end of each item.

每個段落結束的時候都會有提問時間,所以請在每一段結尾的時候儘管提問。

應對複雜問題

提前準備若干可能問及的問題,將複雜問題分解依次回答(tackle difficult questions one part at a time)。如果有人一次問了3個或者4個問題,別驚慌(panic)。回答問題的第一部分,然後再請他們重複第二個問題。一次回答一個(one at a time)問題就沒有那麼複雜,效果也會比較好。

⊙Now what was your second question?

現在您的第二個問題是什麼?

⊙I think that should cover your first question, what was the second part of your question?

我想應該答覆您的第一個問題,您問題的第二部分是什麼?

⊙Does that answer your question?

是否回答了您的問題?

注意傾聽問題

仔細傾聽提問者的問題,並且給足時間來完成提問表達。如果有必要,你可以請他重述問題(restate the question),確保理解他的問題內容,尤其是當問題比較複雜,或者所在會議室很大,不是所有的聽眾都能聽清問題的時候。

⊙So you're asking about..., is that correct?

所以您是想問……,對嗎?

⊙Do you mean...?

您的意思是說……?

⊙For those of you who didn't catch that, this gentleman just asked me...
對於沒有聽清楚的人（我解釋一下），這位先生剛才問我……

永遠支持發問

講演者在陳述問題時，可能在毫無意識的情況下說出有傷害意味的言論（unintentionally hurtful）。所以在某人發問後，當你說「好問題」的時候要多加小心，因為對一個人說過就得對其他人也這麼說，否則會被誤認為後面的問題沒有前面的好。

⊙Let me answer your question this way...
讓我這麼來回答您的問題……

⊙To answer your question...
要回答您的問題……

回答簡明了當，不必虛張聲勢

最好別給一個冗長的答覆（longwinded answers），越是簡短被記住的機會就會越多。同樣，如果你不知道怎樣回答，也不必虛張聲勢（don't bluff）。簡單說句「我不清楚」，無論如何都要給出答覆，並且越快越好（ASAP）。有時會後給出答案比當下解決問題要好，因為這樣可以和提問者建立積極的關係（build a positive relationship）。

⊙To be honest, I'm not really sure about the answer to your question.
老實說，對於您問題的答案，我不是很肯定。

⊙I don't know the answer to your question, but I can find out and get back to you about it.
我不知道您問題的答案是什麼，但是我會找出來並且回覆您。

⊙I'm not sure how to answer your question, could you elaborate?
我不確定該怎樣回答您的問題，您能否詳細說明？

總結

之所以要用心應對聽眾的提問，是因為問題是考驗講演者是否有真憑實學，也是考驗演講者是否有將演講的理論運用於處理實際問題的能力，更是讓聽眾心服口服的捷徑。有些問題是可以預先準備的，那會讓你當場得心應手許多。有些則需要認真傾聽，臨場應對。即便是遇到無法回答的問題，也應該如實相告，盡可能在互動中表現尊重和真誠。

單字表

clarify 澄清；弄清

consumer 消費者；顧客

correlation 相關

design 設計

effectiveness 有效性；效果

flexible 靈活的；多變的

interest 興趣

marketing 行銷

strategy 戰略；策略

technology 技術；科技

comment 評論

copyright 版權

danger 危險

direction 方向；方位

few 少數的；很少的

hesitancy 猶豫；躊躇

issue 問題

presentation 介紹；講解

survive 生存；倖存

trend 趨勢；時尚

片語表

be responsive to... 對……作出反應/回應

charges of 收費的

clear up (an issue / problem) 清除（問題/麻煩）

don't be shy 不要害羞；不用拘束

in reference to 關於；就……而言

catch (sth.) 聽清楚（某事）；趕上

clarify an issue 澄清問題

copyright infringement 侵犯版權

deal with (an issue / problem) 處理（問題/麻煩）

reverse a trend 扭轉趨勢

keep up with (a trend) 緊跟（趨勢/時尚）
where (sth.) is heading （某事）走向
product line 生產線
raise your hand 舉手
something to say 要說的話
to be pending 尚未了結的

open it up (for questions) 恭候提問；等待提問
incorporate (sth.) into (sth.) （某物）納入/融入（某物）
to be heading towards (sth.) （某事）朝什麼方向發展（前進）

實境對話 1

A: We've come to the end of my presentation. Now we have time for a few questions. We have about twenty minutes. Please don't be shy, if you have questions or something to say, please just raise your hand. I'm very interested to hear your comments. Yes?

B: Can you clarify what you said about the copyright issues?

A: Do you mean the copyright issues in reference to our new product line?

B: Yes...

A: For those of you who didn't catch that, this gentleman just asked by about the copyright issues on our new product line. The legal department has been dealing with charges of copyright infringement on our designs, but the whole issue is still pending. We aren't able to move forward on this line until the issue is cleared up.

C: What do you think about the future direction in marketing? Do you think we can keep up with future trends? Don't you see some danger with the way the economy is heading?

A: As far as the future direction in marketing, I think we're heading towards an increased use of technology. We need to be more flexible about incorporating new ideas into our marketing strategy. Now what was your second question?

C: What about the way the economy is heading? Do you think we should be worried?

A: Let me answer your question this way... in order to survive in a modern economy, we must be responsive to the changes in the market. As long as we can stay close to our customers, I feel very optimistic about the future.

A：到了我介紹的尾聲。現在的時間大家可以來提一些問題。我們大約有20分鐘的時間。不用拘束，你們有什麼問題或有什麼想說的，請舉手。我很有興趣來聽你們的意見，好嗎？

B：您能否詳細解釋一下您剛才談到的關於版權的事情？

A：您所説的是關於我們生產線的版權嗎？

B：是的……

A：對於沒有聽清楚的人，這位先生是想問有關我們新生產線版權的事情。法務部門正在處理我們的設計遭侵權的版權費，但是還沒有結果。如果這個問題不能弄清楚，我們就不能繼續向前。

C：您怎麼看未來行銷的方向？您覺得我們能夠趕上未來的趨勢嗎？您覺察到經濟走向的危險了嗎？

A：就未來的行銷而言，我認為我們正面對的是對技術運用的與日俱增。我們需要更靈活地在行銷策略中放入更多的新思維。現在您的第二個問題是什麼？

C：經濟走向怎麼樣？您覺得我們是否該為此擔憂？

A：讓我這樣來回答您的問題……要在現代經濟中生存，我們就必須對市場的變化有回應。我們越靠近客戶，就越能感受到對於未來的樂觀。

實境對話 2

A: ...And with that, I'd like to conclude my presentation. Now I'd like to open it up for questions. Yes, you in the back?

B: Thank you for your presentation. I do have a question, however. You mentioned trends in the market are tending towards hesitancy and consumer restraint. I was wondering what your take is on the reasons why we are seeing this...

A: To answer your question, I think there is a very direct correlation to the current state of the economy. When the economy is in recession, you start seeing these types of things.

C: So can you talk a little more about recovery?

A: I'm not sure how to answer your question, could you elaborate?

C: I mean, what kinds of actions should the government be taking to reverse these trends? Can we overcome the damage that has already been done? What can we do as individuals to help improve the situation.

A: Well the government is increasing spending and approving stimulus funding to get things back on track. I think that should cover your first questions. What was the second part of your question?

C: What is it we can do?

A: Well, yes, as individuals, we have to learn to live within our means and support small businesses. That will jump start the economy in a grassroots kind of way. Does that answer your question?

A：到這裡，我就結束了我的簡報。現在，開始回答問題。好，坐在後面的那位？

B：感謝您的簡報。然而，我有個問題。您提到說市場的趨勢是傾向保守和消費者的自制。我想知道您有什麼理由讓我們這樣認為……

A：就您的問題，我覺得是和目前的經濟狀況直接相關的。如果經濟衰退，您將會看到以上的情況。

C：那您能否再進一步談一下經濟復甦的問題？

A：我不是很確定您的問題，您能否詳加說明？

C：我的意思是，我們的政府應當採取哪些措施來扭轉這個趨勢？我們能否克服已經造成的損害？就個人來說，我們應當怎樣來幫助改善這種狀況？

A：我們的政府正在增加開支並且批准了刺激資金計畫來使事情回到正軌上。
我想這樣應該回答了您的第一個問題，您問題的第二部分是什麼？

C：我們能做什麼？

A：好的，就個人來説，我們應當量入為出，支持小型企業，這將會從根本上
推動經濟的發展。這算回答您的問題了嗎？

收尾有力　Concluding with Power

有效的收尾是一個集邏輯和情感（logical and emotional elements）於一
體，巧妙挑動聽眾情緒的過程。如果想要一個令人振奮、印象深刻的結尾，可
以嘗試以下步驟。

收尾信號

首先是收尾信號(stop sign)。收尾信號是提示聽眾接近尾聲的口頭暗示
（verbal signal）。表達時語氣要堅定，當聽眾聽到最後的詞語，精神會為之
一振（perk up）。

⊙In conclusion...

　　總而言之……

⊙In summary...

　　總之……

⊙To sum things up...

　　最為總結……

總結中心想法

回顧（Recap）你簡報中的主要觀點。一句帶過，點到為止。

393

⊙What we've talked about today is...
　今天我們所討論的是……

⊙So, we've discussed A, B and C.
　因此，我們討論過了A、B和C。

⊙I hope everyone now has a better understanding of A, B and C.
　我希望每個人對於A、B和C有了更深的認識。

激勵聽眾

明確告訴聽眾，簡報中的想法和主意執行起來並非易事（not to easy to implement），但同時也要盡可能地鼓勵他們，甚至可以透過行動來帶動大家面對挑戰。此外，還要表現出樂觀的態度（optimism），堅信未來將會成功。最後的話語要提高聲調、感染聽眾。

⊙I believe we can all make a difference on this issue.
　我相信我們都能夠在這個事情上有所作為。

⊙We can be successful, if we just...
　只要我們……我們就會能成功。

⊙I know I will work harder in this area, and if you are all willing to jump on
　board, we will see success in the future.
　我知道我在這個方面需要更加努力，如果你們願意與我同舟共濟，我們就能
　見到成功的曙光。

暫停並致謝

致謝表示已近尾聲（signals the finish），並且在聽眾鼓掌期間稍作暫停，向聽眾點頭致意。

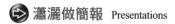

⊙So, let me say, thank you very much for your time.

因此，我想説，非常感謝各位的時間。

⊙Thank you. I appreciate your time and attention.

謝謝大家。我感激各位的時間和關注。

暫停

直到觀眾的掌聲漸弱，這時可以請求解答疑問（solicit and answer questions）。

⊙Are there any questions?

有什麼問題嗎？

⊙Does anyone have any questions they'd like to ask?

還有誰有什麼問題想問的嗎？

⊙Thank you. I'd like to open it up for questions now.

謝謝。我現在可以回答問題。

總結

收尾的好壞直接決定是「前功盡棄」還是「錦上添花」。釋放結尾的訊號、重點性的回顧，可帶動聽眾一起與你挑戰未來。如果最後能以激勵的格言來結束你的講演，那一定是一個擲地有聲的收尾。

單字表

appreciate 欣賞；感激　　　　aspect 方面
brand 品牌；品牌化　　　　　custom 風俗；習慣
customer 消費者；客戶　　　　edgy 銳利的；前衛的
element 元素；成分　　　　　fashion 時尚

increase 增加

particular 特別的；尤其的

profit 利潤；利益

relative 相對的；相關的

retention 保留；保持

success 成功

trendy 時尚的；流行的

willing 樂意的；願意的

lightweight 羽量級；輕型的

practicality 實用性；實效

relationship 關係

retain 保留；留存

stage 舞臺；階段

successful 成功的

visibility 能見度；可見性

片語表

back on track 回到正軌

be on top (of the competition) 勝出
（競爭）

customer service 客戶服務

heavy duty 重型的

implement technology 實施/運用科
技……

let me say... 讓我說……

(sth.) transfer to (sth.) （某物）轉變成
（某物）

what will make the difference 視情況
更改

be committed to... 致力於……

brand development 品牌發展

customer loyalty 客戶的忠誠度

grow a brand 品牌成長

I know 我知道；我很清楚

in conclusion 在結尾；最後

jump on board 上船；同舟共濟

make a difference 有影響；起作用

time and effort 時間和精力

to be vital to... 對……至關重要

with time 隨著時間推移；逐漸地

實境對話 1

A: In conclusion, we must spend more time and effort in customer retention. What we've talked about today is why customer relationships and customer loyalty is so important to developing our brand. I hope everyone now has a better understanding of brand development, customer service, and how to make customer loyalty transfer into profit increases. I know I will work harder in this area, and if you are all willing to jump on board, we will see success in the future. (Pause) So let me say, thank you very much for your time. (Applause) (Pauses until applause finishes) Does any one have any questions they'd like to ask?

B: I have a question. Do you think that customer loyalty is more important than brand visibility?

A: Do you mean importance in the development of the brand?

B: Yeah.

A: Actually, both customer loyalty and brand visibility are both vital to growing your brand, but the relative importance of each aspect changes depending on the particular stage your brand is in. In other words, in the very beginning, perhaps brand visibility is more important, but with time, customer loyalty is what will make the difference for your brand.

B: I see. Thank you.

A：綜合以上所述，我們必須在客戶維繫上投入更多的時間和精力。我們今天所談的是為什麼客戶關係和客戶的忠誠度對我們品牌的發展如此的重要。我希望每個人都對品牌發展、客戶服務，以及如何將客戶的忠誠轉化為收益有更深的了解。我知道我在這個方面需要更加努力，如果你們願意與我同舟共濟，我們就一定能見到成功的曙光。（掌聲）所以我想說，非常感謝各位的時間。（鼓掌）（停頓到掌聲漸弱）還有誰有什麼問題要問的嗎？

B：我有個問題，您是否認為客戶的忠誠度要比品牌的知名度更重要？

A：您是說品牌發展的重要性嗎？

B：是的。

A：事實上，客戶的忠誠度和品牌的知名度對於品牌的成長都至關重要，但是，隨著品牌發展所處的階段不同，各方面的相對重要性也隨之變化。換

句話說，在最開始的階段，品牌的知名度更重要些，但是隨著時間的推移，客戶的忠誠度將影響您的品牌。

B：我明白了，謝謝。

實境對話 2

A: In summary, the project design we have customly created for your company contains elements of practicality and fashion. At the same time we've implemented advanced technology and retained our edginess to keep you on top of your competitors. At Cosmetic Design, we are committed to helping our clients be successful and trendy. I believe this design can make a real difference for your company. (Pause) Thank you. I appreciate your time and attention. Are there any questions?

B: What materials are you using to construct the backdrop on our platform?

A: Let me show you the slide on that again. If you look carefully, you can see the backdrop is constructed out of a lightweight, heavy duty plastic material that will be easy to ship to the exposition site, but at the same time be durable to last.

A：總之，該專案的設計是為貴公司量身定做的，兼具實用性和潮流性。與此同時，我們運用了高科技，保證你們比你們的競爭對手略勝一籌。在外表設計上，我們努力證明客戶能完全展現成功和時尚。我相信這個設計在貴公司會大有作為。（掌聲）謝謝。感謝各位的時間和關注。還有什麼問題嗎？

B：您使用什麼樣的材料來建造平臺背景？

A：我再放一下投影片。如果您仔細看，您就會看到背景是用一種輕且耐用的塑膠製成，把它運輸到展覽地點，極其容易，並且持久耐用。

國家圖書館出版品預行編目資料

商務英語職場王 / Amanda Crandell Ju著；巨小衛譯
--初版--臺北市：瑞蘭國際, 2013.11
400面；17 x 23公分 --（繽紛外語系列；28）
ISBN：978-986-5953-52-2（平裝附光碟片）
1.商業英語 2.讀本

805.18   102021594

繽紛外語系列 28

商務英語職場王

作者｜Amanda Crandell Ju・翻譯｜巨小衛・責任編輯｜王彥萍
校對｜王彥萍、王愿琦

內文排版｜余佳憓・印務｜王彥萍

董事長｜張暖彗・社長兼總編輯｜王愿琦・副總編輯｜呂依臻
主編｜王彥萍・副主編｜葉仲芸・編輯｜周羽恩・美術編輯｜余佳憓
業務部主任｜楊米琪・業務部助理｜林湲洵

出版社｜瑞蘭國際有限公司・地址｜台北市大安區安和路一段104號7樓之1
電話｜(02)2700-4625・傳真｜(02)2700-4622・訂購專線｜(02)2700-4625
劃撥帳號｜19914152 瑞蘭國際有限公司・瑞蘭網路書城｜www.genki-japan.com.tw

總經銷｜聯合發行股份有限公司・電話｜(02)2917-8022、2917-8042
傳真｜(02)2915-6275、2915-7212・印刷｜宗祐印刷有限公司
出版日期｜2013年11月初版1刷・定價｜420元・ISBN｜978-986-5953-52-2

Original title: 商務英語職場王
By Amanda Crandell Ju 著
由中南博集天卷文化傳媒有限公司授權出版 All rights reserved